AN AGENT OF INFLUENCE

AN AGENT

── OF ──

INFLUENCE

RICHARD COX

Richard Cox.

Secker & Warburg
London

First published in Great Britain 1988 by
Martin Secker & Warburg Limited
Michelin House
81 Fulham Road
London SW3 6RB

Copyright © Richard Cox 1988

British Library Cataloguing in Publication Data

Cox, Richard, *1931*–
    An agent of influence
    I. Title
    823′.914[F]

    ISBN 0 436 10989 1

Printed and bound in Great Britain by
Richard Clay Ltd, Bungay, Suffolk

ACKNOWLEDGEMENTS

I owe thanks for encouragement over a long period of time from many people, including Steven Schneider, Peter Grose and Barley Alison; as well as to Sarah Fisher and my wife for typing the various drafts and revisions of this book.

Richard Cox
Alderney and Nairobi

CHAPTER ONE

Stainton's warning came too late. We were already watching the television news in the library – Mother followed the progress of the Falklands fighting with unselfconscious patriotism – when the phone shrilled discreetly. I took the call, turning down the TV sound.

'Can I speak to Lady Hartman?' The voice was peremptory and somehow familiar, though I didn't place it until he said who he was. This was a Saturday evening, after all, and Father was abroad. I handed the phone across to Mother, irritated by Stainton's tone. He was the director I trusted least. On the now silent screen, the shots of warships at sea ended. The newscaster appeared again, mouthing words I could not hear. She was well groomed and good-looking. I wondered what she was saying.

'But Frank!' I heard Mother suddenly protest, sitting upright, taut and anxious. 'What do you mean by "disappeared"?'

In that moment a photograph of Father appeared on the screen, the features unmistakable: the strong face crowned by a mane of greying hair, the protuberant nose which cartoonists delighted to exaggerate, the eyes hidden by dark glasses. His mouth was twisted and chin defiant as though he had been answering a hostile question. I pressed the sound control. The newscaster's voice became audible.

'Sir James, chief executive of the multinational Hartman Trust conglomerate, was on a flight across Africa but failed to arrive. It is feared his private jet may have crashed.'

The still photograph hovered on the television, taunting us. It must have been taken in Africa, because Father's glasses reflected back glaring sunlight and the lines on his forehead seemed more deeply etched than usual. The half scowl was uncharacteristic too. Much as he hated reporters he usually kept himself under tight control. The programme editor had probably sorted through

I

dozens of prints to choose the least flattering. That was the way they worked on newspapers too, at least on the ones we owned.

All Mother's attention was on the screen. She said something distractedly and put the phone down.

'Sir James had left Kenya for the Zaïre capital, Kinshasa, this morning,' the newscaster went on.

The photograph was abruptly replaced by a short clip of film showing Father striding across tarmac to a gleaming white jet which I recognized as the Gulfstream. Typically it bore no company insignia. He did not believe in advertising his presence when he was abroad. Nor did he need to. In Africa he was invariably welcomed by a senior government official or minister. Many ambassadors were treated with less respect.

'In London a Hartman Trust spokesman said Sir James was on routine business. He could not comment on reports that the financier was missing.'

The newscaster passed on to the next item. I switched the set off and turned to Mother. She was shaking her head in an angrily puzzled way. I sat beside her on the sofa and held her hand.

'He probably changed his mind and went somewhere else instead,' I said. 'It's a false alarm.'

That was a far more likely explanation than a crash. Father used planes the way ordinary businessmen use limousines. The Gulfstream was partly fitted up as an office, with desks that came out of the bulkheads and big armchairs. The rear of the cabin had a sofa that turned into a bed, while beyond were a small changing room cum washroom and, of course, a galley. I used to think it would have made a convenient bachelor apartment.

'Where was he going? Frank did say.'

Years of disciplining herself not to be worried by Father's incessant travels had made her deliberately uncurious about where precisely he was. She could always get in touch with him through the office. A prodigious flow of information pursued him round the globe – from stud farm training reports to trading figures from the hundred or so companies in the group. Mother's queries over dinner party guests joined the telexes and were always promptly answered by the secretary who flew with him.

'They said Kinshasa. It's on the west coast. He was flying practically the whole way across Africa.' I thought of Ibn Majid, the Arab map maker, patiently guiding Vasco da Gama on the long voyage around the Cape of Good Hope in 1498. As an Arabist at London University I knew the pendulous, swollen-topped outline of Africa well. Arabs had colonized the shores of the dark continent a thousand years ago. Today Father's plane would have crossed from one side to the other in a few hours. Or should have done.

As I spoke, reassuring her that Father often changed his destination after phone conversations en route, our own phone rang once more.

'It's probably Frank, again,' Mother said.

'Don't worry,' I cut in, taking the call.

I was quick in case this time it was a reporter. You only have to be pursued by the Press once to be instinctively cautious thereafter. Owning newspapers had no more kept the Press off our backs than it had given Father serious political influence.

However the person on the line was Frank Stainton, so I handed it over, listening myself on an extension.

'Is that you, Lady Hartman?' Stainton was invariably obsequious with her, though when he changed to Christian name terms, it sounded just as forced. In his early fifties – which meant he was a useful decade younger than Father – he was ambitious and devious. 'Anne, my dear,' he went on, calm, restrained and unconvincing, I'm desperately sorry that you should have heard this from the media before I could speak to you fully. We had an extremely rare breakdown in our communications . . .'

As he explained I guessed he had probably been at the races, and why not on a day like this? Through the library windows I could see across the lawns to the trees along the river bank beyond. Everything was lush with early summer and a warm haze lay over the countryside. I could imagine the tropical jungle which the Gulfstream had to cross on its way from east to west. Like parts of South America, central Africa held some of the few truly remote areas of the modern world. A plane could vanish there without trace.

'Surely they had a radio?' Mother's voice became higher pitched.

'Transmissions would not necessarily be picked up. That's why I'm optimistic.' If he was, Stainton didn't sound it. 'They could have made an emergency landing and been unable to contact anyone.'

'You must start a search at once.'

'We've already hired two planes in Nairobi. Unfortunately, it's night out there now.'

'You mean you can't do anything before tomorrow? You mean we just have to sit and wait?'

'Anne, believe me, we're doing everything we can. I shall personally be at the office all tomorrow, although it's Sunday.'

I wondered how he could be there other than personally. But Stainton was the kind who ended letters with the phrase 'kind personal regards'. He saw himself as heir apparent to the job of Chief Executive, though in truth there was no heir.

Then, after all this sententiousness, he blew it completely.

3

'If Jim's still missing on Monday,' he added, 'there'll be hell to pay on the stock market. The Consolidated takeover could go bad on us.'

'The wretched takeover can wait. I'm concerned about my husband. Can you understand that?' She sounded taut enough to break.

'I do indeed, Anne, I assure you I do. I merely intended to emphasize the urgency we will devote to the search.' He oiled on a little more, his hasty retraction made less and less convincing by every fresh remark. 'If there's anything you want, let me know at once.'

'Just find him, Frank. That's all I want.'

Stainton had been grotesquely tactless, but he was right. In the public mind Father *was* the Hartman Trust. The share price was certain to plummet and that wouldn't only affect the bid for Consolidated Diamond Concessions: it would lay the Trust itself open to what the City called a raid.

'Money!' Mother said bitterly. 'They're so wound up in their intrigues they can't think about people.' She looked at me keenly. 'Robert, darling. Would you go out there if I asked?'

'To Africa?'

'To find your father.' She hesitated. 'To make sure they really do their best. Would you?'

I knew why she was nervous. My feelings about him had been equivocal long before I walked out when I was twenty-one. Our subsequent reconciliation remained edgy and constrained. On the other hand, for her I would have gone anywhere.

The phone buzzed again, delivering me temporarily from having to give an answer.

This time it was a reporter, and I went through to the hall to be out of Mother's hearing. Why was Sir James in Africa, the man asked. Who was with him? Was it true the Trust was having problems with the takeover bid for Consolidated Diamond Concessions? When had he left? Was Lady Hartman available?

Parrying the questions, I realized there was only one query I could answer with certainty.

'No,' I said firmly, 'Lady Hartman cannot come to the telephone.'

'You mean I have to go on ringing until she does?' demanded the reporter nastily. 'Ask her if she knows about the lady friend in Nairobi. Maybe that'll change her mind.'

Shaking with anger, I hung up and immediately rang the supervisor at the exchange to ask for our calls to be intercepted.

'Are you the subscriber, Sir?'

The necessary explanations took several minutes.

For all I knew, Father might have a girlfriend. So long as she never discovered I didn't much care. The balance between them often seemed more like an armed truce than tranquillity: a truce in which my own refusal to follow in his business footsteps was an influential element.

To that extent this weekend had begun typically. Father had been away a great deal lately and on Friday Mother had indicated that she was tired of rattling around in the house by herself. My own three-year love affair with Camilla was in an 'off' phase so I had cheerfully forsaken my London flat and driven down to Surrey to keep her company. Not that she was alone in the strict sense of the word. Godstow was a big house and there were servants. However, I quite understood what she meant. She was not as self-sufficient as she appeared to outsiders, nor would she accept social invitations for the sake of having something to do.

Dinner on this Saturday ought to have been a relaxed, chatty occasion during which we caught up with what we had each been doing. She had made the traditional preparations for such an evening, telling Hooson, the butler, to leave the dishes on a hot-plate after he had served us so that we could talk undisturbed by his discreet attentions. Now she made a stab at asking normal questions, but after the phone had rung yet again and the operator asked if we would take a call from another newspaper, the façade cracked.

'There's not a lot we can do, Ma.' I held out my hand across the table. It was barely two hours since we had heard the news and already it threatened to overturn our lives. How would it feel tomorrow or in a week? I had unwelcome memories of a school friend whose father had vanished, leaving his mother powerless even to draw money from the bank, because he could not be proven dead. The worst thing is to have no word.

Mother squeezed my fingertips briefly and I felt the tension as palpable as electricity.

'Would you mind if I smoke?' she asked, making a visible effort to steady herself. None the less her hand shook as she held the cigarette out for me to light.

Normally she would never smoke during a meal. This tiny infraction of a code imposed by my grandfather, the General, told me how distressed she was. All too often one does not observe one's parents with any real perception: they are too familiar as figures of authority. But the premature death of a father changes everything. I would become head of the family, with huge decisions to make about the inheritance. By my grandfather's canon Mother would be merely a dowager running Godstow until I married. Even though I felt this was crazy, Father had intended founding a dynasty. Her feelings wouldn't be altered by that not having quite worked out. I understood. Muslims also have ruthless principles of succession. At bedrock most societies do. I looked at

5

her affectionately across the table, knowing that unless Father was found a whole series of conflicts would be unleashed before their time.

Mother was still a beautiful woman at fifty-one, her face scarcely lined, her skin clear, only the gold that her hair used to be subdued by growing older. There was a portrait of her in the drawing room, done by Annigoni when he was at a peak of his fame after the Queen had sat for him, and the only substantial difference between my mother then and now was that her natural good looks had matured into a more stylized elegance. It was painful to watch that self-assurance disintegrating.

'You know, darling,' her voice wavered huskily, 'we may have rows, but I don't know what I should do without your father. It may seem a funny thing to say but after all these years I'm still in love with him.'

I nodded silently, pressing her hand again. Their marriage had not been easy. Father was German born, a boyhood fugitive from Hitler's Germany. Citizens of a country that has never been terrorized, he used to insist, can never really understand the disorientation and despair of living in a dictatorship. Every refugee, young or old, knows what it is like for life to fall apart. My mother, English to her marrow, had been the antidote to his ingrained fear of the dawn knock on the door and the Gestapo. In turn she had recognized in him an elemental force that both attracted and overwhelmed her. Over the years he had brought her comfort and wealth. I was less sure that he had given her much happiness.

These thoughts all ran through my head during a long silence, at the end of which Mother extinguished her cigarette with an almost desperate finality by screwing it hard down into a small silver ashtray.

'Will you go, Bob?' she asked. 'If we don't hear anything tomorrow will you go and find out what's really happening? You could phone me from Africa, couldn't you?'

There could hardly have been a worse time. Today was May 22nd and in the coming week my final year undergraduate student at the University's School of Oriental and African Studies would start sitting examinations that ran through into mid-June, with all the agonies of last-minute revision and psychological trauma those involved. For them this was the climax of three years' work: four years if they'd added Arabic or Persian to the course. Furthermore, I was not merely a tutor. I was a Senior Lecturer in my particular part of the School, which was the Near and Middle East Section of the History Department. I could think of two students who were so tense about their Finals that they might not turn up at all if I didn't shepherd them through to the end: one of those was a potential suicide, at least I feared he was. If ever there was a time the staff needed to be on hand, this was it.

'Surely the School would understand?'

Mother read my thinking, though not as accurately as Camilla might have done. Camilla maintained that my ambitions in a relatively obscure academic field were a retreat from everything Father stood for. I maintained that late twentieth-century Europe had to learn more about Islam and the Arabs. Either way, Camilla knew better than Mother that I hadn't achieved the Senior Lectureship without plenty of calculated in-fighting. Promotions in a university are no less governed by internal politics than they are in any other profession, while the School's were made more significant by its small size and international reputation. Going away at this moment would look thoroughly bad.

'Please phone the Professor, darling. This evening, if you would.' Mother bit her lip. 'I don't often ask you for things, do I?'

The Professor responsible for my section was named Ali Muhsin. He would 'understand', because the Koran lays down strict filial obligations. But the more senior Englishman in charge of the History Department as a whole would definitely count absence against my qualifications for a Readership, which was the next step up. So why should I be so damned virtuous towards a father who had never shown me real consideration? 'Children, honour your parents,' my old housemaster used to remind us at the end of every term. Nothing about parents honouring their children. The fact was that Father had behaved like a bastard right up to the day I mutinied and walked out. Let the Trust organize the search for him. There was little I would be able to contribute anyway, except towards Mother's peace of mind.

'Ali Muhsin's away for the weekend,' I said, making the most of available truth. 'He'd have to ask the Head of the Department too.'

Mother gazed at me pleadingly, then looked up at the ornate, ormolu mounted clock on the mantelpiece. 'I suppose we ought to watch the television again.' She touched the bell for Hooson, eased her chair away from the table, not waiting for me to help her, and led the way back to the library. The Gulfstream had not landed at any of a string of African airports and Father remained missing. I felt a bastard myself for not being more responsive and prayed that tomorrow would bring positive news.

7

CHAPTER TWO

Our butler, Hooson, always laid the newspapers out on a side table in the breakfast room. On Sunday morning I went down early to see what they had said, anxious to know the worst.

Father's disappearance was widely covered. I poured myself coffee, took bacon and eggs and kidneys from the chafing dishes on the hot-plate and settled down to one of the 'quality Sundays'. The front page was almost entirely devoted to the Falklands landings, with only two short paragraphs on Father. But inside there was half a page on his career, written as though his death had been confirmed, centred on his typifying a generation of European émigrés who had made good in Britain and America after World War Two and making his rags-to-riches story sound half miracle and half conspiracy.

A few sentences will give the flavour:

> Like Czech-born Robert Maxwell, the publishing millionaire; like 'Tiny' Rowlands of Lonrho, James Hartman rose phoenix-like from the ashes of the World War II holocaust to become British, rich and famous.
>
> What was his secret?
>
> How did plain Hans Hardtmann, son of a Düsseldorf Nazi, become Sir James Hartman of Godstow Abbey, Surrey? How did this teenage Hitler Youth activist win our own Military Medal, marry into the aristocracy, found the multinational conglomerate which bears his name and end up one of the wealthiest men in Britain?
>
> By any standard his has been an extraordinary transformation.

My first instinct was to throw this garbage away before Mother could be upset by it. I might not be Father's greatest admirer, but this deliberate twisting of the truth infuriated me.

Father had never denied being in the Hitler Youth. As he

pointed out, every German schoolboy had to join. His class at the Düsseldorf *Gymnasium* was enrolled *en bloc*. As for my grandfather, he was the manager of a small sanitary appliance firm, an archetypal petit bourgeois, too frightened not to join the Party. Their portrayal as activists dated from the early 1970s, part of a smear campaign intended to disrupt a deal Father was doing in Israel. He had taken this remarkably calmly, issuing a formal denial, but otherwise shrugging it off. When a story gets into the library files of newspapers it's virtually impossible to correct. This near-libel had reappeared regularly since, sometimes incongruously rehashed along with his remarkable escape from Germany as a teenager early in 1937. He had then been given a scholarship by the sympathetic headmaster of a minor public school near Bristol.

Because the school gave him a good character he was allowed to join the army in 1942, and after the war that earned him a British passport. He married mother in 1951. Nor was she an aristocrat: just the daughter of a career officer who had risen to the rank of Major-General.

The article concluded with a broad hint that the deal which had taken Father to Africa had made him powerful enemies. The huge amount of money at stake in the Consolidated takeover was quoted, and Father's extraordinary rise to riches illustrated by a photograph taken on the day the Trust's new headquarters building was officially opened nine years ago.

The picture took me straight back to one of the most bitter days of my life, reminding me of forgotten details like the morning coats we wore and my mother's wide-brimmed hat. The topping out ceremony had been held on my twenty-first birthday. It was a gesture organized with Father's usual strong sense of purpose and I had been wary of the coincidence from the first. He was not noted for the finesse with which he pursued his aims.

Father was in an expansive, good-humoured mood that day, and with reason. The architect had produced precisely what he wanted. Hartman House was a clean, almost elegant example of modern architecture: the outside a huge expanse of smoky coloured glass which proudly reflected back the images of less distinguished neighbours, while the interior suggested a well-bred self-confidence. Overall it was the structural embodiment of the way Father saw himself: a merchant prince in dark glasses. He showed Arthur Watson, Mother and me round before the ceremony with delight.

'Space in the City of London may be the most expensive,' he told us, smiling in the controlled yet aggressive way he always did on public occasions, 'however our bankers and brokers will be able to get to us faster when we want them.'

That was typical. One of Father's favourite sayings was 'He who pays the piper calls the tune.' He often abbreviated it to the phrase 'He who pays . . .', assuming that English audiences would recognize the proverb, which of course wasn't always the case.

'Whether you're in the City or not,' Arthur Watson commented, 'you'd make a fortune on this development if you sold again.'

Watson was Father's tame government minister: a tall, untypically gaunt Yorkshireman whose silver hair and easy manner gave him the appearance of a diplomat, albeit a worried one. The strain of being in Heath's administration showed in the dark pouches under his eyes.

'We are not selling,' Father replied curtly. 'This is now our headquarters.'

'It's all very, very splendid, darling,' Mother chipped in hastily. 'Isn't it, Bob?'

I agreed quickly, surprised by Watson's naïveté. Even at twenty-one I was not so wet behind the ears as to imagine that erecting Hartman House within the square mile of the City had anything to do with being close to advisers. Father was an outsider, and he intended being seen to have stormed the citadel of British financial power. Indeed the Right Honourable Arthur Watson, Privy Counsellor and Member of Parliament, had only been asked to unveil the plaque because of his rank and connections. I suppose he thought he was being complimentary by pointing out that Father had made a killing. Anyway, Father reacted with the lack of constraint he displayed to anyone who served him.

'Come on, Bob,' he said, walking away. 'There's something I want you to help me with. We won't be long, Anne.' He didn't bother to excuse himself to Watson, simply left him standing.

I followed, embarrassed, as Father led me to his own magnificently panelled office on the fourteenth floor. There he picked up a framed photograph lying ready on the desk and proceeded to select a place to hang it.

'This is the ceremony which means Hartman House is in operation. Everything later will be a formality. Necessary for the Press and the shareholders only. Here, hold it up for me.' He thrust the picture into my hands while he stepped back to decide if the positioning was right.

Of course I knew about the significance of this fading sepia-toned photographic print. It showed Father and his most enduring business associate, Patrick Van Rensburg, standing outdoors in a dry African landscape. Both were much younger then, in their thirties. They wore bush shirts and baggy shorts. Although the sun beating down on their wide-brimmed hats cast their faces in shadow, they were visibly triumphant. Everything about them, the way they stood with their feet firmly apart, their hands on their hips, their heads held high, proclaimed confidence. On the frame an engraved silver plaque announced 'RUKANGA MINE, 25 March 1957'. Rukanga was shorthand for the foundation of the Trust.

'Miles and miles of bloody Africa and we got the concession with the rubies.' Father stepped forward with a pencil to mark the wall above the picture as I endeavoured to hold it still. 'You know something, Bob? Patrick had staked the exact ground the vein ran through. You could dig the stones out with your hands in places. The other prospectors lost their shirts. Or if they weren't going bankrupt we bought them out.'

I had tried before to imagine him camped in the bush, enduring heat and flies and dust. Father was tough. He had a war record to prove he was as rugged as the best. Yet I found it hard to visualize him as a pioneer.

'Fine.' He motioned me away, hammered a thin picture hook into the wood, hung the picture, then stepped back and nodded with pleasure.

'That picture can tell you the world is your oyster. You can have what you want if you get off your backside. People call me lucky. Balls. I just know what I want. If you know what you want you can do anything.' He stressed the word and repeated it. 'Anything. When you have doubts, think of Rukanga.'

Despite his seriousness I was not impressed. He had been spicing our private conversations with comments on his approach to life since I was fourteen or fifteen, and this was the eternal banality of father telling son what makes the world go round. I didn't like being lectured on my birthday either, especially since I was being forced to share part of the day with thirty assorted Hartman Trust executives and the Press. As always, when Father made a plan everyone else was expected to fall in with it. I was relieved when we rejoined the others. I hadn't yet appreciated how far this particular plan went.

At the lunch following the topping out ceremony I found myself prominently seated on Arthur Watson's left: a placing made more clear when Father rose and announced the happy coincidence of this also being my twenty-first birthday.

'I should like to propose a joint toast,' he said with slow clarity. Excellently as he spoke English, he always stayed with safe, well worn phrases on formal occasions. 'Long life, good health and prosperity to my son Robert: and the same to the Hartman Trust.'

Friendly laughter greeted this. Taken by surprise I could only stand up and selfconsciously stutter a few sentences in reply, which received absurdly generous applause. I was embarrassed by his publicly linking my future with that of the company. But although Father had not warned me, he had evidently alerted Frank Stainton, who replied on behalf of the Board and the shareholders with some well oiled and ingratiating remarks. Then, as we settled down to coffee and liqueurs, Watson leant confidentially towards me.

'You know, Robert, it might not do you any harm to start taking an interest in politics.'

'Should I?' The intrigue-ridden, toadying world of student politics had thoroughly put me off.

'We could find you a place on a local Council. Useful stepping stone to the House of Commons if you felt so inclined. You'll be living in London after you graduate?'

'To be honest, Sir, I'm not sure.' I began to bridle at these assumptions. 'I might take a postgraduate degree.'

'But you'll be joining the Trust in due time?' He made it sound more like a received truth than a question. 'Believe me, with a Parliamentary seat and the connections it brings, the other directors here would welcome you on the Board at thirty.' He indulged in a definite wink, directed sidelong at me, which hardly fitted his austere and dignified face. 'The trick in life, my boy, is to start at the top. No quicker route than through the House of Commons, believe me.'

I stumbled in thanking him, annoyed and curious to know if the offer had been made at Father's orders. That evening I discovered.

We dined at our London apartment in Vincent Square, a location chosen by Father because it was close enough to have a Division bell installed for the benefit of his political friends. If they could not be summoned back to the House to vote, they were effectively chained to the Palace of Westminster. At that time the government only had a majority of thirty and even as a minister Arthur Watson was on edge for the bell.

In theory this was my private birthday celebration. However Father had again made it less of a family affair than it ought to have been by inviting both Watson and Frank Stainton. It was as though he couldn't bear to relinquish the triumphs of the morning, and his guests played on this, encouraging him to relate how he had acquired a bomb site left over from the wartime blitz and constructed Hartman House on it. Those bomb sites had remained a feature of the City for twenty years after the war, ugly gaps in otherwise respectable streets where weeds grew out of the cracked concrete and car park operators made quick profits. Their utilization only began in earnest when the Church Commissioners rebuilt the devastated area around St Paul's Cathedral in the late 1960s. However, when Father acquired this site in 1969 the redevelopment was under way. So there was a degree of mystery in how he had pulled it off.

'There was an opportunity,' he agreed cautiously, 'and I recognized it before anyone else.'

'Come on, Jim,' Stainton urged. 'You're being too modest. It was a coup.' He spoke to me. 'Listen to this young man and you'll learn something.'

I stared back at him angrily. He was blatantly sucking up to Father. Lunch had already been a business occasion. Why should dinner be forced into the same mould? Then I looked at Father and saw that he was enjoying the flattery.

'Well,' I asked reluctantly, 'what was the secret? Why didn't the car park operator develop the site himself?'

Father grinned disarmingly and slipped into the kind of colloquialisms he had first picked up in the army and never really lost. It was odd how he had two such different ways of talking, the formal and the 'off-duty', though he kept his language more or less clean in front of Mother.

'The bloody fool couldn't be bothered. Ninety car owners paying him five quid a day each and all he had to do was man the barrier and collect the cash. He thought it was money for old rope. He told me so himself.'

'You knew him?' I was astonished. 'Surely the moment you made the offer he must have guessed what you were after?'

The fifteen storeys of our headquarters might overlook the slums of the East End on one side: none the less they stood firmly within the square mile. Shortly before today's ceremony Father had let three floors to an Arab bank and the rental per square foot had set a record. Instantly the building had become worth £30 million as against the £20 million it had cost.

'I told you, Bob.' Father was enjoying himself, teasing the solution out of me. 'His mind was on car parks.'

'How do you suppose we tackled him?' Stainton remarked. 'Try some lateral thinking, if they teach you that at Oxford.'

I was damned if I was going to be patronized by Father's sidekick. 'If you were all so clever,' I said, 'why not just tell me and I'll clap.'

There was a thunderous silence. I could not have created more effect if I'd thrown my wine in Stainton's face. He flushed and glanced at Father for support.

'For the record, Robert,' Father spoke with a gentleness I did not expect, 'we bought a car hire company and they acquired the site. That made sense to the owner. He bargained like hell and thought he'd scored when we gave him three years' earnings. Then we exercised his option to buy a long lease.'

'The rest is history,' Stainton added, ill-advisedly.

'The rest is on the bottom line,' Father snapped. 'History is bunk.' He softened this rebuke slightly by adding, 'The future is what counts.'

13

I sat silent, wondering if I had drunk too much and thinking that there was no need for Father to search the world for the philosopher's stone, as people did in the Middle Ages, because the ability to create wealth lay stored inside him when he was born. But I wished to God he didn't have to display it on my birthday.

I was beginning to realize that the champagne had gone to my head a little, when the butler entered to announce that the Division bell was ringing.

'Forgive me, Jim.' Watson immediately rose to his feet, wiping his mouth with his napkin as he did so. 'You all understand, I know. I'll be back in time for coffee, if there isn't a second vote.' He folded the white linen napkin, placed it rather oddly on his chair as if reserving his place, and left.

'What was his price for today's fun and games?' Stainton asked caustically. 'He knows we've made a killing.'

Father shrugged off the remark. 'I've invited him and his wife to the new hotel in St Lucia for a week. Nothing more. Arthur is a good friend.'

'Keeps his nose clean, you mean, now he's in office.'

'I mean nothing of the bloody sort.' Father glared at him and again I wondered how I fitted into this and why he was defending his relationship with Watson. Perhaps for the sake of my supposed illusions. 'You talk too much, Frank. You might do better in one of the overseas companies. Africans like talking all the time.'

The threat of being shunted aside was transparent and I swear Stainton's hands trembled. Certainly he moved them swiftly out of sight, down on his lap somewhere. He wasn't leaning confidently on the table any more. He was frightened of Father, and that was the moment when I first realized how easily fear can mature into hate.

'Please darling, must we talk shop? It is Robert's birthday.' Mother intervened, knowing that if Father was in a mood to put someone down he didn't care who was listening.

'Talking of your birthday, Bob,' Father relented and changed the subject. 'Our distinguished guest brought a present he may not have told you about.'

'You mean an entry to politics?'

On such a special occasion I felt confident enough to joke about the patronage surrounding Father's activities, though I was still relieved when it did provoke laughter.

'Typical Arthur. Always thinks of politics first. Suggesting you stood for Parliament was only an afterthought.'

As I speculated yet again on what was intended, Father smiled benevolently. When he switched on the charm it really was like illuminating a room. At this time, in 1973, he had just turned fifty-two. His thick hair was only brushed with grey. His strong features were creased enough to be interesting without suggesting age. Familiar as his face was, I could see exactly why others found him so compelling. He had star quality. Now he laughed with the comfortable assurance of a man who always got his own way.

'Old Arthur tends to get the cart before the horse. That's why they made him a minister. Politics can come later, if you're interested. What Arthur's found for you is a job with Consolidated Diamond Concessions.'

'But Dad . . .' I found myself afflicted with an inexplicable stutter.

'It's a generous offer, young man,' Stainton chipped in. 'One of the biggest independent mining groups in the world and they only take a handful of trainees a year.'

'But I want a university career.'

The protest merely produced a blink from Father, a tiny dent in the good nature with which he was letting his sidekicks perform his advocacy for him.

'They need Arabic speakers, I should think,' he observed.

'You'd learn a hell of a lot,' Stainton added, and noticing him glance at Father I guessed my own future might not be the only consideration. You couldn't grow up in a household like ours without instinctively watching out for unexpected angles to any proposition. 'Not just a girl's best friend' – Stainton was trying to sound light and witty – 'though the general public is reckoned to own several billion dollars' worth of diamond jewellery. There are industrial uses and the profit margins are huge. All firms like Consolidated have to do is dig the stones out of the ground, clean them and sell them.' He was still talking in a bantering, slightly high-pitched tone. 'What the smugglers don't get away with, that is. Last year De Beers' Central Selling Organization auctioned $529 million of stones and they'll double that in three years or I'm a Dutchman. Consolidated markets through the CSO.'

There was a catch in this. Instinct warned me. What had Father said earlier when he hung up the Rukanga photo? 'People call me lucky. Balls, I just know what I want.' Why would he wish to have me working for Consolidated, which was in some senses a rival?

'So they just dig the stones out of the ground,' I said to Stainton. 'How do they know where to look?'

'Geological studies. Traces of kimberlite. All very technical.'

'Also political,' Father observed. 'That was a good question, Bob. In certain countries some exploration concerns will become less welcome.'

'How would Mr Watson persuade Consolidated to accept me?' I asked.

'The chairman owes him a favour. Don't look a gift horse in the mouth, Bob. As Frank says, this is the opportunity of a lifetime.'

In every respect save one Father had the original poker face. His failing, of which I don't think he was aware, was that whenever there was a lot at stake he slipped into those conventional clichés of language that he had learnt so carefully when he first came to Britain as a refugee. It happened now because he wanted me inside Consolidated to get trained and act as a spy, both at once. Only he wouldn't say so straight out. The concept appalled me, and I must have been a trifle drunk to counter it with an attempt at sarcasm.

'So I get two birthday presents for the price of one. A job and an entry into politics. Why should Mr Watson be so concerned about my future?'

'I told you, Bob. He's a good friend of ours.' Father's patience was cracking. 'You couldn't ask for a better preparation for joining the Trust. When the day comes and I hand over the reins . . .'

'A long-distant day,' Stainton echoed.

I disregarded him. There are moments when the past comes back at you overwhelmingly. It may be triggered by a song or a smell or a phrase. 'A better preparation' had done it for me now. I was an eleven-year-old again, being transferred from a school I loved to one where Father thought they would prepare me better for winning a scholarship. My mid-term marks had been disappointing. He stormed down one summer's day and physically removed me while other boys gawped and the headmaster pleaded. I felt so ashamed that I had to stifle tears all the way home, huddled in the back of his white Mercedes. In fact I still associate the smell of leather upholstery with total misery. When the two schools played each other in a rugger match I deliberately cheered my old friends on the opposing side, earning sharp reprimands. Nothing went right. Eventually I failed to get the scholarship – not that Father was after the money, simply the distinction – and instead of admitting he had made a mistake he was furious. I wasn't going to let him press-gang me again.

'I'm not interested in working for Consolidated,' I said, aware of being flushed, 'I refuse to steal documents, or spy, or whatever else it is you want.'

'Bob darling.' Mother's tone betrayed her alarm. 'No one is . . .'

'He's drunk too much,' Father cut in savagely. 'Listen to me, Robert. You're going to accept his offer and learn how a rival multinational company operates. Have some mineral water and sober up.'

I wasn't actually tipsy. I knew that, even though we seemed to have been consuming champagne most of the day. Father was merely attacking a weak point, as he always did. Tomorrow he might adopt a different tactic, if I stayed around and let him. In any contest he constantly shifted his stance, like a boxer.

'Robert, old chap.' He reverted to the confident parental firmness that I knew so well. 'In due course you will inherit my control of the Trust. I want you to be equipped for that responsibility. Do you understand?'

There was silence. Stainton sat in a pose of sympathetic concern, his right arm resting on the table. I looked across at Mother. Her lips were parted.

'Darling,' she said gently, 'this has all been rather sudden for Bob. We really ought to let him sleep on the idea.'

'Sleep it off, you mean. This is his last term at Oxford and a time for decisions.' He turned to me. 'Arthur Watson is expecting you at ten tomorrow and we'll take things from there.'

There was no escape and he did not intend there to be. But I was an adult now, not a schoolboy who could be bundled around like a parcel. I swallowed some water to moisten my throat.

'I shan't be going to see Mr Watson,' I said. 'Tomorrow or any other time. I'll decide my own future.'

With that I got up and walked out, half expecting to be physically prevented. But although Father shifted his chair, he did nothing more. As I closed the door I heard him say:

'Bloody young fool. He'll be back.'

The photograph made that memorably unpleasant day alive again. In fact it was over four years before I did go back. A lot happened during that time. When my College elected me to a junior Fellowship it was announced in *The Times* and Mother wrote a warm and spontaneous letter of congratulation. A semi-clandestine and emotional meeting with her followed. Until then I had not attempted to contact either of them, unfair as it was to her. I wanted to be completely free. The eventual reconciliation with Father late in 1977 hinged on the settlement I was due at my twenty-fifth birthday. He had made some stupid threats, through solicitors. Luckily he withdrew them.

Those mid-years of the decade were proving the emptiness of legal power anyway. The miners' strike had toppled the government which Arthur Watson served and he retired with a peerage from the Labour administration which took over. A couple of years later the United States reached some kind of nadir with President Carter's fumbled handling of the Iranian hostage crisis. By then I was a Lecturer at London University and acquiring a slight reputation as a Middle Eastern expert. The oil price hikes of the late 1970s brought the bonus of a part-time consultancy, more valuable for its prestige and interest than the additional income. In 1979 I met Camilla. For many people the 1970s had been years of uncertainty. For me they ended on a pretty high note, with Father forced to accept that I had created a career on my own merits.

When Mother eventually came down, it was obvious from her eyes that she had endured a wretched night. None the less, she insisted on facing up to the muck in the papers, including a suggestion that Father might have been kidnapped. Then she phoned Stainton, but there was no news.

'Bob, darling,' she said, perhaps guessing what had been going through my mind, 'the past is the past. In this life we each only have one father. Please will you go out to Africa.'

'If you really want me to,' I conceded, trying not to sound as reluctant as I still was. I had no relish for dealings either with Stainton or with Lord Watson of Malton, whose appointment as Chairman of the Trust in 1979 had seemed like a bad lapse of judgement. I had little faith in either man doing much for Father in an emergency.

After lunch Stainton rang us, however, and I spoke to him.

'Tell Lady Hartman we are reasonably certain the aircraft did not come down in Kenya or Uganda and we will be extending the search over Zaïre tomorrow.' His voice assumed a more confidential tone. 'Frankly, old chap, what with that part of Africa being thick tropical forest, the pilots have one hell of a task.' He paused. 'Not that I want your mother to be worried by our problems. Just tell her we're doing everything we can.'

'She doesn't doubt that, Mr Stainton.' I guessed his underlying message was that he did not want interference from us. 'But naturally she is worried sick and she's asked me to fly out on her behalf.'

Silence greeted this, followed by a far less cordial: 'And what do you think you'll achieve that the company can't?'

'Possibly no more than telephone her every night, with a more personal version of what you would have told her anyway.'

'Exactly, wasting everyone's time.'

'She wants me there, Mr Stainton, and I'm going. At our own expense.'

'I appreciate your desire to help,' he conceded. Perhaps he realized that he had been too sharp, given the size of our shareholding in the Trust.

'Good,' I said firmly. 'Then I'll be at the office first thing in the morning and I'd appreciate a briefing on the purpose of Father's trip.'

'So would we.'

The caustic comment threw me.

'I'll expect you at midday,' Stainton said, scoring a minor victory of delay, and cutting short my intended mention of the kidnap theory. 'If you're determined to go.' He could be incisive when he wanted, despite the ingratiating façade. He wouldn't have survived on the Board otherwise.

'I'm going,' I repeated curtly, 'and I should like to be shown Father's itinerary.' Then I rang off. I had already decided that the only sensible approach was to find out what he had been doing before he left, and if possible why, and to work forward from there. For that I would need a collaborator in London while I was abroad.

With hindsight – I am writing this account much later – it might have done more for Mother's peace of mind to have left Father on the Missing Persons file and organized a memorial service.

CHAPTER THREE

'Why are you here Robert?' Camilla stood in the doorway of her flat, caught by surprise at my unannounced arrival. She was swathed in a blue kimono I'd brought back from Japan one time, her short hair unbrushed and her face without make-up. She had an elusive, elfin kind of beauty which the cropped hair emphasized, though I'd always liked it better long.

'I need your help.'

'Mine, or just anyone's?' She shook her head, keeping a firm hold on the door, blocking my entry. 'Please.' Her tone was unrelated to happy memories. 'We agreed. Don't try and bounce me.'

'Father's disappeared.'

'So? I always said you'd have to get involved in the end.'

I began to explain what was happening, while she eyed me coolly. I could hardly blame her. Our disagreements had all revolved around her belief that I could not keep him at arm's length for the rest of his life, nor retreat to the sanctuary of the University when I inherited his business interests. I had argued that this should not affect us, any more than it ought to stop me pursuing my own career, but it had been the rock on which our relationship capsized.

'If I'm going to search for him, I need someone I can trust to follow things up at this end,' I concluded. It sounded lame, especially standing in the corridor of a block of flats, like an importunate encyclopedia salesman. However it did the trick.

'Well, I suppose you'd better come in. But don't think we're starting all over again, Bob, because we're not. No hocus-pocus, okay?'

She led the way into the once familiar living room, the windows surveying the classical white façade of Pelham Crescent opposite. Apart from having this outlook the place was nothing special, a bleak 1930s apartment, only given life by her belongings: bead-work mementoes of a trip to Africa hung in a pattern on one wall, an engraved glass goblet some other boyfriend had given her, a large wooden bowl full of book matches from restaurants – despite her elfin looks Camilla had eaten her way through some good menus in her twenty-six years – and photographs and sketches everywhere.

The sketches were her own. She had a talent for caricaturing people as birds, getting their beaked likenesses down on paper with a few scratchily telling lines. I noticed that I was still there in the staring-eyed guise of a barn owl perched in an obscure stone niche, a black academic gown cloaking its wings, a minuscule student clutched in one talon. The fiercely defensive expression of the owl had always struck me as unjust. She had drawn Father too, but kept the result hidden, perhaps on account of my being too cruelly featured in it.

'Would you like a drink, Bob?' She tightened the belt on her kimono. 'I'm not going out until later.'

I asked for a whisky, feeling a surge of jealousy that was as stupid as it was inevitable. You can't just throw away three years of being together. I had proposed absurdly soon after we first met and she'd insisted we shouldn't rush our fences. Then a year later she was enthusiastic, by which time I was unsure. And so on. Last November I had decided this sleeping alternately at each other's places could not go on. We ought to get married. Far from agreeing, she had backed off completely. 'You're only saying that because you're afraid I'll walk out one day. It's not enough, dar-ling. You still haven't come to terms with your parents. You ought to sort that out before you start giving them grandchildren. In some ways, I love you very much. But I want a husband who knows where he's going. Yes, you have a career. But you're running away from reality just the same. You could do so much more if you wanted.'

After this speech and a memorably depressing dinner, she had walked out for good.

She brought the drinks, then sat on the carpet with her legs tucked under her, well away from me.

'Now,' she said, putting her finger on the main point like the trained researcher she was, 'you're going to Africa tomorrow for your mother's sake, is that right?'

'Basically. And because I don't trust Frank Stainton.'

'To look after your interests?'

Was she mocking me? I couldn't be sure. I did know I had captured her attention.

'Well,' she said drily, 'if you don't decide to look after them nobody else will. Or rather, someone will, but not for your benefit.

Are you sure this man Stainton's concern about the share price is hocus-pocus, not loyalty?'

The idea of Frank Stainton being faithful to anyone except himself made me laugh out loud.

'All right,' Camilla said, 'but what can I do about it?'

'You could keep track of what's going on while I'm away. Any public statements he makes, any Press releases the Trust puts out, what they say about the progress of the search.'

'Hardly a full-time job.'

'I'll pay the going rate.'

'Well,' she admitted, 'I suppose I haven't much else to do. The TV series I've been working for ends this week.'

She worked as a freelance and I knew television was a cut-throat business.

'You'd be free to look around for something else while you're doing this,' I suggested.

'Thank you, Bob. That's nice of you. I mean it.' She allowed me a quick nervous smile. 'Let me sleep on it, though. You see Stainton tomorrow morning and I'll meet you for lunch afterwards.'

'How about Rules? Add another trophy to your match collection.'

'My collection,' she said mischievously, sounding more like the Camilla I used to know, 'is piling up quite nicely as it is, thank you Mr Hartman.'

'I'll see you tomorrow just the same?'

She nodded, a little reluctantly I thought, then saw me to the door very properly. In the passage I heard the firm click of the lock turning, which left me wondering just what kind of debate was going on in her mind.

Camilla stayed pressed against the door, her forehead leaning on the wood, half tearful, half relieved. She was afraid he might come back and agonized because he didn't. All this was so typical of Bob: turning up unexpectedly, overwhelming her with the drama of the moment, using her as a sounding board in the perpetual mistrust between him and his father. If she hadn't seen the headlines she'd have suspected him of inventing this disappearance. Was he really taking the initiative this time, or merely placating Lady Hartman? She turned away from the door, upset in spite of herself. Why did he have this effect on her? If she'd let him stay they'd have ended up in bed again, and if she longed for that physically, intellectually she most definitely did not. She told herself to forget about him and go out.

As she was crossing the room her eye fell on the caricature, and she could not help reflecting that it had got Bob absolutely pinned down. She had drawn that soon after they met, and first impressions often were the right ones. He and Sir James were birds of prey, both of them: handsome and in different ways predatory. Bob was an owl rather than a hawk. His nose wasn't as protuberant as his father's, while his eyes were wider set and warier, occasionally blinking in confusion, just as they had done when she'd turned down that final, stupid, marriage offer. The caricature made full use of his almost straight eyebrows, which arched down to meet in the middle with a trail of black hairs. She'd always wanted to pluck those and he had resolutely refused to let her. It was funny how he shied off feminine interferences, even thoughtful ones.

'Why do I have a student in my claw?' he had protested. 'I mean they play hell with me for God's sake!'

But that was the point. He was simply a less confident version of Sir James. Defensive and vulnerable, as the owl's sheltering in a dark niche showed, yet also unscrupulous and able. If, like so many sons of successful men, Bob had been demonstrably of less calibre than his father she might not have cared where either he or the great fortune went. She'd have happily left him to the first alluring gold digger who chanced along. What had gradually eaten into her was the realization that he had the capacity to turn his inheritance into something vastly greater, whether through straight business or as a philanthropic Trust, or whatever, and that instead he was turning his back on it, fooling himself into believing he could have an equally distinguished future as an academic. She felt quite passionately that one had a duty, whether to oneself, to society or to God, to make the most of what one had been given.

Gazing at the drawing she asked herself if Sir James's vanishing would force him to do that. But even if it did, why should she again become embroiled in the drama? Why should she be the Girl Friday who did the dirty work? She caught sight of herself in the mirror, flushed and discomposed, and was furious at the answer the reflection handed back.

Monday morning brought only gloom. Thirty-six hours was a long while for a plane to be missing. 'Hopes fade for missing financier,' said one newspaper, echoing a general feeling, while its City editor commented: 'Hartman Trust's rumoured £270 million bid for Consolidated Diamond Concessions looks untenable without the master on hand, when Consolidated's assets in mineral resources are theoretically five times as much.'

The figures, if they were correct, showed that Father was up to his tricks and there was a lot at stake, as Stainton had said. But for the moment I was more concerned for Mother, and was glad for her sake that otherwise the story was eclipsed by events in the Falklands, where the commandos and paras were following up their landings at San Carlos Bay. Even so, I was afraid there would be photographers hanging around Hartman House, waiting on the off-chance of a picture.

Mercifully, when I arrived there were neither photographers nor reporters. One of the commissionaires took my Porsche off to the underground garage, while another greeted me with a mournful-faced variant of his usual welcome.

'Good morning, Mr Robert, Sir. We're all extremely distressed at the news, Sir.'

I stopped in the wide marble-floored entrance hall and chatted to the man for a moment. His sincerity was not in question. With few exceptions the non-executive staff at the Trust were inspired by a near-feudal loyalty, addressing me on my occasional visits in a manner more appropriate to a country estate. It was a nice para-dox that Father's own employees felt so secure, when he was notorious for imposing redundancies on companies he took over. 'Name any company that's ripe for a bid,' he used to declare. 'You'll find it has too many people.'

'We'll be keeping our fingers crossed, Sir,' the commissionaire promised as he escorted me to the lifts. 'Don't you worry. Sir James will be all right.'

I went straight up to the fourteenth floor, where the directors had a private reception area. 'The Fourteenth Floor' was referred to throughout the organization as if it were a personality in its own right. Up there I would find Frank Stainton and, more usefully, Christianne, Father's personal assistant, who had wormed her way into a position of considerable influence, not least because she was half French and the Trust did a lot of busi-ness in francophone Africa.

The Fourteenth Floor smelt of money and power. Not a good description, but I cannot think of a better one. You stepped out of the lift onto thick oyster-grey carpeting to find a wide rosewood reception desk a few yards ahead and deep, cream-coloured leather sofas to each side. There were huge vases of flowers standing on antique tables against the panelled walls, and french windows which gave on to an internal courtyard with a lawn and a fountain. When you registered the pictures more closely you saw one was a Matisse of a woman, another an early blue period Picasso of a boy with a horse, the third a Van Gogh landscape, with wheat waving in the wind and crows flying across a tortured blue sky. Mother had always coveted the Picasso for the dining room at Godstow, but had to be content with a Canaletto of the Thames at Blackfriars because Father insisted it was more appropriate to formal occasions: and of course it was a subtle and expensive reminder of his City connections.

24

'Mr Robert Hartman is here.' The carefully made-up girl behind the desk spoke into an intercom, then smiled. 'Do please sit down, Sir. Christianne will be out in a moment.'

I sat down. A copy of the *Financial Times* lay folded on a table. A headline rose out of the pale pink paper: 'Hartman Riddle'. I had read a little when Christianne Dessenon appeared and invited me to come through. She was tall and slim and dressed with a touch of vulgarity, while her ash blonde hair, coiled in a gleaming bun, was of a colour quite unknown to nature. Today, typically, she was wearing a tight red skirt and a sheer black blouse.

I found it hard to be sure what I thought of Christianne: that is, after dismissing the idea that she was Father's mistress and accepting a less overtly sexual explanation of the way she acted, namely that she enjoyed manipulating people.

'I am afraid we have not heard any more, Robert,' she remarked as she led me down the corridor, her backside swaying captive in the tight skirt, and into her own office, which like all the others in Hartman House was unmarked by any nameplate. Her secretary worked in an adjoining room, while the access to Father was via an inlaid mahogany door which had come from a once famous country house, along with the panelling lining his sanctum.

'You've heard nothing?' I knew she treated facts like jewels, only to be revealed if the effect was guaranteed.

'Mr Stainton has the telexes. He won't keep you long. Would you like some coffee?' She seated herself behind the rosewood desk, rang the steward who was on permanent duty on the four-teenth floor, then smiled graciously, as if inviting small talk to kill the time. She was several years older than me, and unimpressed by my relatively ill-paid academic career.

'I must tell you, Robert,' she said, raising one hand to pat that shining coil of white gold hair, 'you might do more for Sir James by staying here and looking after Lady Hartman. That is my personal advice.'

'It's my mother who wants me to go to Nairobi.'

'You're determined?'

'If it will help her peace of mind, yes.'

'Then you must go, I suppose.' Christianne had always appreci-ated that her own position would be enhanced by making sure my mother had no cause to complain. The rare occasions when they met face to face were cordial.

'I'd like to know where he was staying in Africa and whom he met: or planned to meet.' Would the alleged 'Lady friend' in Nairobi be on the list? Whether or not anyone distinguishable as such was included, I expected Christianne to resent the request. She guarded Father's diary as if every entry was an inscription in the family Bible. To my surprise she was helpful.

'Provided Mr Stainton agrees,' she said. As if to reinforce this the intercom buzzed and Stainton's not quite Oxford accent demanded her presence, his tone made metallic by the tiny microphone. She scanned her desk quickly, picked up some papers, asked me to wait and left. I hesitated a moment, thought to hell with it, there was nothing she could do to me, and opened the broad door into Father's office. I had an irrational feeling that merely being in the room where he had planned this African trip might give me some ideas. I don't exactly believe in extra-sensory perception, but I do respond to the atmosphere in which people work or live.

Whereas the outer office had colour photographs on the walls to remind visitors of the Trust's multifarious activities – aircraft, beach hotels, department stores, newspaper presses, mine workings and office blocks – Father's room had only the one sepia print of him and Van Rensburg at Rukanga. It hung there on the dark panelling, precisely where he had fixed it on the memorably awful day of my twenty-first birthday, though made more incongruous now by the Old Master paintings flanking it.

In the nine intervening years I had all but forgotten that Rukanga was a codeword for Father's success. I remembered his talking to me about the world being there for the taking. Perhaps Rukanga had been more than the lucky gamble I had always supposed. The corollary, since the mine had proved the watershed in his business career, was that either it or Patrick Van Rensburg could hold the clue to what he was doing in Africa this time. The more I thought about it, the more probable it seemed.

A faint, far-off voice distracted my speculation, like a radio at minimum volume. The mahogany door to the outer office was still open. I walked hastily back, feeling half guilty at having trespassed. But there was no one there. The noise came from the intercom on Christianne's desk. She must have accidentally left it switched on and it was picking up a conversation in Stainton's room.

'Here,' Stainton was presumably back near the instrument, because his words became clearer and louder, 'give him these telexes. We'll have to go along with him. In fact he may be better out of the way.'

'And Sir James's itinerary?' Christianne was barely audible.

'Give him that too, not that he'll learn much from it.' A pause. 'What I do not want are disclosures about the takeover bid. He'll have the chance to vote if we call an Extraordinary General Meeting and that's as much as any shareholder's entitled to.'

'Sir James did specifically . . .'

My eavesdropping was abruptly terminated. There must have been an incoming call.

I was left standing in silence by Christianne's desk, wondering what those instructions of Father's might have been and why she was resisting Stainton.

'I should like to go over a few details of my trip, Miss Dessenon.'

Hartman did not wave Christianne to a chair. She automatically drew one up to the opposite side of his desk, laid down two bulky folders of papers, composed herself and prepared to take notes. She always came in with the relevant documents competently arranged, and equally invariably received no acknowledgement of her competence. So far as Hartman was concerned her monthly pay cheque constituted recognition.

'The gun has been delivered?'

She flipped open the top folder.

'The gunsmiths say it was not practicable to silver-plate the . . .' she consulted their letter quickly, 'the working parts. They say they have done the barrel, the stock . . .'

'Of course,' he cut her short. 'You have prepared the Kenyan customs declarations? Good. I do not want it impounded en route.'

'I understand, Sir James.' She was schooled to avoid asking unnecessary questions, but she remained curious. He bribed politicians habitually, and not only African ones, giving them kickbacks that were often more sophisticated than straight cash: from accounts for their wives at Harrods or tickets to Ascot races up to custom-made bullet-proof Mercedes limousines and the use of private jets. Yet a silver-plated sub-machinegun was something new by way of a sweetener, and the more challenging because she had no inkling who it was for.

'Only you and Captain Holz are aware of this gift's existence.' He was still keeping her in the dark, though. 'Captain Holz is to stow it aboard the Gulfstream personally.'

'I will tell him.'

'You have my itinerary?'

She handed over a copy. He took a gold propelling pencil from his inside pocket and made a single neat correction.

'This can be circulated. You have confirmed the arrangements for Angola on Sunday? Good. So far as the Board and everyone else is concerned, my family included, I shall be for the weekend in Kinshasa with Mr Roeyen and Miss Humphries will stay there to answer calls.'

Christianne allowed herself an almost private smile. She had not been pleased at Tina Humphries going with him. The more she was left out the better.

27

Hartman noticed the flicker of pleasure on her face and disregarded it. Women were always at each other's throats. He was taking Tina Humphries because he wanted a secretary with him who was genuinely ignorant of the risks he was taking. Christianne would appreciate too well what they were.

'As you know, Miss Dessenon, the Angolan concession is crucial.'

'I have put Mr Van Rensburg's report on Concession Twenty-Two with your papers, Sir James. The original report.' She said it coldly, thinking that his aloofness would test anyone's loyalty. The closer one was to him, the less friendly he became.

'Thank you. That was far-sighted.' For a moment he maintained his formality, then interlocked his fingers and leant his chin on them, addressing her as if seeking her advice. 'To be frank, hundreds of millions hang on this takeover and the timing is critical.' His words, superficially relaxed and slow, carried an inner urgency. 'I must be back with an agreement over Concession Twenty-Two before we make our bid. If for any reason I am not . . .'

She listened attentively, intrigued yet not interrupting.

'. . . if I am delayed the bid must none the less go through.' A guttural harshness sounded in his voice. 'There will be no second chance.'

She considered this. If Stainton or the rest of the Board wanted to back down there would be nothing she could do about it.

'I don't quite . . .' she began.

'If I am delayed you are to telephone Lady Hartman. Remind her that she has a proxy to represent me at Board meetings as well as to vote my shares.'

'Only that?' She was astonished.

'You could tell my son Robert that I hope he will act in our interests. Every dog has its day. Well.' He straightened up. 'Is there anything else?'

She went through a brief list, keeping the most promising item until last.

'There is a telegram from Nairobi.'

'From whom?' Whereas the Trust did a substantial part of its business by telex, old-fashioned telegrams were becoming a rarity.

'Madame Lohrey informs you that she is staying at the Norfolk Hotel.'

'Good.' For the first time in this session he smiled. 'Well, Miss Dessenon, we have more things than usual for you to keep quiet about. I'm sure you can deal with them.' He fell silent. 'I shall leave you a letter for my son, however. Just in case.'

When he finally dismissed her for the evening Christianne

realized that if anything did go wrong she would be in an unwontedly influential position.

When Christianne returned I was in an armchair well away from her desk making a show of reading the *Financial Times*.

'Is Frank Stainton still busy?' I asked.

'Two minutes only.'

'While I'm waiting could I see Father's itinerary?'

Her pale blue eyes quizzed me, as if suspicious. I stared back. She could think what she liked. Eventually she sat down behind her desk, opened one of the folders she had been carrying and held out a sheet of paper, forcing me to rise and fetch it.

'This was Sir James's itinerary. He would have fitted in other appointments, of course. He always does. Tina Humphries would have done up-dated versions en route.'

There was no need for her to remark that since Tina had been on the Gulfstream this was the latest available. I took it, anticipating that there would be empty spaces. There were. One thing struck me immediately. The weekend had been left completely free.

I still have that piece of paper, dog-eared from the number of times I consulted it and much annotated in my own handwriting. The original typing read:

Thursday May 20th	0800	Depart Gatwick by Gulfstream
	1200	Arrive Rhodes (refuelling stop)
	1300	Depart Rhodes
	1900	Arrive Nairobi. Met by Hon. Julius Mululu, Minister for State Enterprises and Mr Van Rensburg
	2000	Arrive Norfolk Hotel. Dinner Mr Van Rensburg
Friday May 21st	0900	Board Meeting, East African Enterprises
	1300	Lunch with local Directors
	1430	Call on Vice President Dinner private
Saturday May 22nd	0745	Depart Norfolk Hotel
	0900	Depart Nairobi by Gulfstream
	1100	Arrival Kinshasa. Met by Mr Roeyen
	1230	Arrival Mr Roeyen's residence, 17 Avenue des Arcades Dinner private
Sunday May 23rd		Private with Mr and Mrs Roeyen

Monday May 24th 0930 Call on H. E. President Mobutu
                       Sese Seko
                 1245 Lunch, Société Zaïrois
                       d'Exploitation Minière
                 1700 Depart for Gatwick by Gulfstream

There it ended. I remained standing in front of Christianne's
desk, running through the timings a second time. Some implications were obvious. Kenya was one of the more efficient countries
in black Africa and the VIP treatment would ensure there were
no delays on arrival or departure. By contrast the arrangements in
Kinshasa had allowed plenty of leeway. But the free weekend was
inexplicable for a man whose idea of a perfect day off was to
spend it reading stock market reports in search of takeover opportunities, and telephoning potential allies.

'Who's Mr Roeyen?' I asked.

'Our legal representative there. A Belgian from Antwerp.'
Distaste flickered across her face. In her prejudices Christianne
was entirely French.

'Was he a particular friend of my father's?'

'I wouldn't have thought so.'

'Therefore he probably had meetings that were not on the
programme?'

She glanced down at her nails, which exactly matched the scarlet
of her skirt, then looked up again. 'You must be aware of how
your father works.'

'Can you tell me what else he had arranged?'

'No, Robert, I cannot. In any case he never reached Kinshasa.'

'What he planned to do there might explain why he didn't.'

'Mr Roeyen does not think so. I have spoken to him already
this morning. He was worried about how to keep your father
entertained. The only change of plan he received was to say that
the Gulfstream had been delayed.'

The telex machine in the corner began clacking. Christianne
went across, watched the paper jerking through until it stopped,
then quickly tapped in a reply.

'Nairobi,' she said, glancing round. 'Mr Van Rensburg wants
to know which flight you will be on.'

'British Airways.'

She typed some more and waited until the machine spewed out
the answer, then stopped.

'He will be there to meet you. He is an old friend of your
father's.'

'I know. They were in the war together.'

'Then he may help you more than I can.'

The way she spoke left me in no doubt that she was under some kind of restraint.

'Was that all the message was about?' I asked. It seemed an extraordinary coincidence that it had come when I was in the room.

'There has been panic selling of our East African Enterprises shares on the Nairobi Stock Exchange.' She pulled the paper from the telex machine, severing it neatly. 'If there is anything more I can do, Robert, please say so. Now you must excuse me again. Mr Stainton must see this.'

I hung around another ten minutes until he was free: a wait designed, I didn't doubt, to put me in my place by demonstrating that he had more important things on his mind than placating the founder's importunate son.

Reading the telexes it became evident that our shares had begun to slide as soon as the Stock Exchange opened and that Stainton had been right. Under Father's leadership the Trust spelt strength: without him it could easily become a symbol of diffusion. Even professional investment analysts found the variety of its interests confusing. What united his companies was not so much their intrinsic commonality as that he knew he could transform them. Only a genuinely unorthodox brain could have seen that the solution to a Jersey-based aircraft firm's lack of passengers would be flying jumbo prawns from the North of Scotland to Spain. Of course, as soon as the operation started, the facts all pointed that way: Spain's local waters fished out, 'gambas' a classic item on Spanish menus, Kinlochbervie boats hauling them in to an inadequate local market, Jersey being halfway to Madrid as the crow flies and being free of value added tax. However, until Father put it together, the equation had been far from obvious.

Furthermore he was ruthless after he moved in on any company, shedding staff and selling off assets, keeping only what would yield high profit and using the sale of the rest to help cover the takeover costs.

'Come along, Bob,' he said one morning when I was on holiday. 'We've just bought a casino. We're going to raid it.'

I was mystified until we got there. What did he mean by 'raid', especially since the place didn't open until the evening? It was quite a famous upper-crust establishment, popular with Arabs and housed in an eighteenth-century mansion. The owners, whom he bought out after a fraud case when they were frightened of closure, had decorated the gaming rooms with some minor Old Master paintings of which they were proud. Father was not impressed. He arranged for us to meet an art expert at the casino and while the staff gawped he went round each room in turn, ordering pictures to be taken down and sent to Sotheby's for sale.

'Today, right? Hang prints instead. The bloody Arabs won't know the difference. What do you think they look at? The walls or the tables?'

Finally we reached the Managing Director's office, where a fine Venetian scene in an ornate gilt frame hung behind the desk.

'I'll have that,' Father snapped. 'Send it to my house.'

'But Sir James,' the man protested, 'that picture is company property.'

Father looked him up and down contemptuously. 'Do as you're told,' he said, 'or get out.'

I was acutely embarrassed and not surprised that the Managing Director shortly resigned, though not before sending Father a bill for the painting: which was settled. The rest fetched nearly £500,000 at auction. Actions like these helped multiply the Trust's assets from £4 million in 1964 to ten times as much in 1982. Yet in fairness to Father he wasn't only an asset stripper. Just as he paid for the Venetian scene, so also he cleaned up the casino's management practices, and as the word spread among gamblers the turnover increased very satisfactorily.

Effectively he did the same with whatever he acquired, whether it was a chain of High Street stores in Scotland or sisal estates in Tanzania, and the Trust's share values rose as it expanded.

'Keep the shareholders happy,' he said to me once with both cynicism and truth. 'Don't forget they are of importance. Let them know when you've made a killing and so long as the share price reflects that fact, they will respect you for it.'

The extent to which the opposite was happening became evident moments after Christianne finally ushered me into Stainton's large office. He had barely shaken hands when the phone rang, and from the conversation the caller was the company's broker.

'Your family isn't dumping shares, I suppose?' he demanded when he put the phone down. My anger at this suggestion must have been visible, because he went on quickly, 'Well, someone's running out on us. We've had twelve million pounds wiped off our market capitalization already and if the institutions join in the selling we're going to be in serious trouble.'

'Can't you make a statement?'

'Not that anyone would believe. Not until we know whether your father's alive or dead. Then we can mount a defence.'

I stared at him, realizing with disgust that he might actually prefer bad news to uncertainty.

'Mr Stainton.' I tried to keep calm. 'That's why I'm going to Africa: to get information. I asked Christianne why my father was going to Kinshasa. She either can't or won't tell me. Can you?'

'We have a small diamond mine in Zaïre. That country's so

32

corrupt there may be problems to sort out which one wouldn't want on record.'

'And would that occupy the whole weekend?' I felt sure the unoccupied Sunday was important. He evaded the question.

'We all take a day off occasionally. Not that it's easy in this organization.' The joke was forced and swiftly died, to be replaced by a dictatorial bark. 'Listen to me, Robert. How your father was or wasn't going to spend yesterday is irrelevant. Our problem is to discover what happened to his plane on Saturday. Our men out there are fully occupied with the search and I don't want them distracted. Since you insist, I will instruct them to give you full collaboration.' For a second he seemed to regret yielding. 'But kindly keep out of their hair.'

'Thank you.' However it worried me that although Mother was named as Father's alternate director, and had a proxy to vote his shares, she had never acted in either capacity. 'There is something else,' I said. 'If for any reason you call an Extraordinary General Meeting I'd like to be informed. As quickly as possible.'

He looked at me with suspicion, no doubt imagining that Christianne had been talking.

'You would of course be informed, though I shouldn't have thought you'd give a shareholders' meeting priority over finding your father.'

With that he terminated the interview and I returned to Christianne's office, feeling that overall I was the victor. She compounded my determination to join the search with a remark of doubtful sincerity.

'If you do not achieve very much, Robert, remember I advised you to stay in London. Please telephone me before you leave.'

When I recounted all this to Camilla over lunch she made a shrewd observation.

'What if Christianne really is trying to tell you something? Why do you reject what she says because she's not an outright kind of person?'

I thought what a difference there was between the two of them. Camilla trim, self-possessed and straightforwardly attractive without overplaying it, as I suppose a researcher needed to be. Christianne no less competent yet always carrying her chic too far. Perhaps Camilla understood what made her tick without needing to meet her. However that didn't answer the question. Why was I so mistrustful of her?

'She never has had much time for me.'

'Maybe she hasn't time for you because you quarrelled with your father. It's possible.'

'She blows with the wind,' I said stubbornly.

'Then think of her as a litmus paper, an acid test of what's going on. She must have a reason for suggesting you stay here.'

The eavesdropped conversation came back to me again: Stainton saying they'd have to go along with me.

Why was he confiding in Christianne? I explained my idea that he might want the search abandoned as soon as was decently possible and that I reckoned I had headed off any chance of his doing so.

'Aren't you overdramatizing a bit, Bob?'

'The Consolidated takeover is about the biggest Father's ever attempted. They're as big as we are. When hundreds of millions are on the line people get greedy. Stainton's an insider. He could have been buying Consolidated shares. He could . . .'

Camilla cut me short. 'Does your father have a controlling interest in the Trust?'

'Effectively. He has eighteen per cent. He rules because the rest is in thousands of other hands. But if they got together they could outvote our family any time.' I gave her an unnecessarily cynical smile. 'Another reason we need to find him.'

'Is there a time limit on the takeover?'

'The Trust has made an offer. It's been rejected. I can't believe Father would have gone abroad when our final bid was imminent, unless his trip was connected with it. Consolidated has mines in Africa. Could you research what they own and what he might have been after?' I reminded her of the itinerary. 'The most significant items are the blanks.'

'Now listen, Bob.' She placed both her hands flat on the table, symbolically. 'I have to ask you something. Digging into other people's lives doesn't necessarily turn up good potatoes. It can turn up rotten ones too. What if I dig up those?'

I hesitated, remembering the reporter's remarks about a woman. But I had already decided that Father's actions in the immediate past must have a bearing on where he was.

'You'll have to follow every lead you can. If you do dig up scandal, please keep it between us. I don't want Mother hurt.'

When we parted the terms had been agreed. I gave her a cheque for a month's freelance work and expenses and arranged to mail or phone through anything I gleaned. She would be available on the phone between seven and eight every morning, Kenya time being two hours later.

'Cramps your style a bit, I'm afraid,' I added, stupidly letting jealousy affect the arrangement.

'That's my problem.'

'I'm sorry.'

'Look after yourself,' she said and kissed me goodbye.

The rest of the day was hectic. The Kenyan health regulations no longer required any injections, but Christianne had told me I would be an idiot to go without them. So I had myself shot full of yellow fever vaccine in one arm and cholera in the other, collected my ticket and traveller's cheques and in no time found it was late afternoon. I called her again before the office closed and she sounded despondent. There had been no news of the Gulfstream and here in London the share price had plummeted further to £3.80, wiping £72 million off the Trust's previous market capitalization of £452 million. It was the worst day the company had ever known.

'I hope you can find him, Robert. I wish you luck.'

Her tone made it clear that she didn't think I would succeed.

CHAPTER FOUR

We were woken an hour or so before landing at Nairobi, the air-liner like a luxury hotel that had overnight become a dosshouse as passengers threw aside blankets and pillows and struggled to their feet to queue for the lavatories. My legs ached and my nostrils felt as if they had been sandpapered. It was no wonder Father avoided flying commercially. Looking out of the oval window at the dawn sky as I ate the reheated breakfast omelette, I could see tiny trails of smoke on the ground below, and realized that they must be from cooking fires: more than anything that put in context the strangeness as well as the immensity of the continent in which he had disappeared.

However, the airport formalities were polite enough, and when I emerged through the swing doors of the customs hall I immedi-ately spotted a placard with my name on it, held aloft on a stick by a khaki-uniformed African. I pushed my way through the small crowd of families and importunate taxi drivers and was intercepted by a thickset European in a safari suit, head and shoulders taller than anyone else there.

'You must be Robert,' he said, thrusting out his hand and shaking mine vigorously. 'Couldn't mistake Jim's son. Welcome to Kenya.' He nodded to the uniformed African and spoke in Swahili. '*Muthenge, shika sanduku ya bwana.*'

Muthenge took my case and led us through the throng, the taxi drivers still ambitiously trying to detach me, and we went out of a side entrance to where Van Rensburg's white Mercedes was parked. We clambered into the back seats and Muthenge drove us off.

'Good to meet you at last,' Van Rensburg said. 'Only sorry it has to be in these circumstances. Your mother must be worried sick.' He spoke in a clipped, abrupt way, yet like an old family friend. As we progressed towards Nairobi, passing the edge of the

36

National Park with road signs depicting leaping buck, I stole occasional glances at him. His voice was deep and everything about him was big. His broad face was jowled and fleshy, though deeply tanned, and his nose must have been flattened in a fight some time in his youth. He had grizzled hair, brushed back and close cropped. The forearms revealed by the short sleeves of his safari suit were hairy and muscular. He had run to fat, however: there was no disguising the bulge of his belly. I also noticed that he sat uncomfortably in the car, with his left leg stretched out almost straight.

'Old wound,' he said, catching my glance. 'Gets as stiff as hell sometimes, though this climate couldn't be better.' He changed the subject. 'Didn't come to talk about my problems, eh? Mary and I hope you'll stay with us. Thought we'd go home for breakfast, then I'm at your disposal. How d'you feel?'

'Nothing a bath won't cure,' I assured him.

'Think we can manage that. Bloody water shortage in Karen as usual.'

The driver swung left at a roundabout and the road began climbing past a small airfield, then a military barracks with a flag flying outside. After perhaps eight miles we turned left again.

'Karen,' Van Rensburg announced succinctly. 'Named after that Danish woman, Karen Blixen. Had a coffee farm in the Thirties but went bust. We're on part of what was the farm.'

The house was at the end of a long and potholed dirt drive. I stepped out of the Mercedes to find myself looking across a mist-shrouded valley with beyond a range of hills shaped like the knuckles of a hand, which Van Rensburg explained were the Ngongs. The house itself was a perfect replica of a Cape Dutch homestead, white painted with a steep roof and high decorated gables. The sun was fully risen now, slanting on the façade of the house and already warm. He ushered me inside, through a hallway into a spacious living room with polished wood floors and antique furniture.

'Mary,' he said, introducing an unexpectedly homely woman in a print dress, 'this is Robert, Jim's son.'

Mrs Van Rensburg smiled and stepped back to appraise me after she had shaken hands. 'It's a great pleasure to have you with us.' She sounded as though she meant it. 'We've put you in the main house, but you could go in the guest cottage if you prefer. It's more private if you wanted to work.'

'Wherever's easiest.'

'Then we'll treat you as family,' she declared warmly. 'Let me show you your room.'

She led the way upstairs to a bedroom suite straight from an English country house, all chintz and flower pictures, and flung open the windows. 'When the mist burns off you'll be able to see the forest.' She pointed to the left, where there was a thatched and whitewashed rondavel. 'That's the guest cottage. The whole house was a series of those in the old days before we rebuilt it.'

Since she still sounded uncertain as to whether I would prefer to be there, I again assured her that this room was fine. Then she left me to unpack and wash before having a second breakfast. It was still only seven thirty.

Over the bacon and eggs, served by an elderly African in a white uniform called Ambrose, to whom I was carefully introduced, Van Rensburg gave the first hint of the frustrations which were to obstruct my mission.

'I've arranged for us to start at the air survey firm. Your telex said you wanted to talk to all the people your father met. Correct?'

'If possible.'

'It's going to be a pretty short list. The minister is not available. No government officials will be except in the Civil Aviation. Can't blame them being cagey. So far as they're concerned your father cleared customs, had his passport stamped and left Kenya. It's not their *shauri*.'

'Problem,' Mary Van Rensburg translated.

'The authorities are facilitating the search, but no more.'

'What if he's been hijacked?' I asked, realizing that the suggestion sounded stupid, though it was not impossible. I'd heard of a Lebanese businessman being abducted in his own jet.

'Hijacked?' Van Rensburg echoed. 'Believe me, Robert, I saw them off and there were only the three crew, Tina Humphries and your father.' He paused. 'Conceivably there might have been a bomb.' He drew in his breath sharply. 'I hope to God not. Even the suspicion would cause trouble. I'm afraid you're going to find people here polite, but evasive.' He wiped his mouth with a linen napkin. 'They're expecting us at Wilson. I'll drive so we can talk freely.'

On the way to Wilson, the small airport I had noticed earlier, Van Rensburg made one further comment.

'Can't blame the politicians,' he said. 'The stakes they play for are a lot higher here than in Britain.'

'Was what Father was doing here controversial?' I hoped Van Rensburg would be more forthcoming than Stainton.

'Well, Robert,' he admitted, 'the negotiations were pretty delicate. Centred on local gemstones. Rubies and garnets. Not high value. Point is they could be marketed better if they were handled by a foreign selling organization the Kenyans trust.'

'In other words ours?'

'Naturally.'

'Is that worth so much?'

Van Rensburg swerved to avoid a bus coming head on at us, cursed African drivers in general, then answered cautiously.

'A few million dollars throughput a year. Enough for your father to come and chat up the minister.'

'Even when he had a takeover battle starting in London?'

We were passing the edge of a forest and suddenly a zebra-striped minibus shot out of an entrance gate, straight in front of us. Van Rensburg braked savagely and swore again. I had a feeling he was glad of the distraction while he collected his thoughts.

'Well,' he said eventually, 'I reckon I can tell you that we'd like to establish a wider marketing operation for African precious stones. Rubies from here, emeralds from Zimbabwe and so on. Kenya's participation would be valuable politically, even if it was small-scale. Have to start somewhere.'

'I suppose so.' We were in a queue of traffic now, waiting to negotiate a series of anti-speed bumps where the road passed the army camp entrance. Van Rensburg was forced down to walking speed. I began to realize that what he had just said didn't add up. Father simply did not think in phrases like 'small-scale' or 'not high value'. He might have night-stopped in Nairobi for the sake of the selling commission on a few million dollars' worth of rubies a year, but given the running costs of the Gulfstream and the pressure on his time he would only have done so if the trip could be integrated with a far bigger deal. Yet there was nothing to indicate one on the itinerary Christianne had given me. I tried an oblique approach.

'How do the rubies here compare with diamonds? In output I mean.'

'No bloody comparison. De Beers' diamond mines in Botswana alone must be earning a thousand million dollars a year or more. Diamonds are one hell of a big business. Our own concession in Zaïre only produces a fraction of what De Beers control and it's still a major profit centre.'

'Which is what makes Consolidated attractive?'

'You could say so. Some of their concessions haven't been developed. Be simpler to lay hands on those through a takeover than have to prospect and negotiate and go through all the hassle of new ones.'

We were over the bumps. Van Rensburg accelerated away, careered past a mud-stained bus spewing diesel fumes and continued down a long hill. Ahead lay Nairobi, spread out panoramically before us, hazy plains away in the distance. I put the question that he ought to have seen coming as clearly as we saw the city.

'Was this trip of Father's connected with the Consolidated take-over?'

'Consolidated has no interests in Kenya. Or Zaïre.'

'Then why should he come here when the takeover was imminent?' I should have known better than to lay down a challenge.

'That was his affair. Not ours.'

He swung the Mercedes off the main road, neatly avoiding Africans crossing from a bus stop. We passed a nest of air charter firms' signboards, among them incongruously the Consulate General of Costa Rica, then approached a checkpoint. A khaki-clad policeman waved us through.

'Could someone have sabotaged the Gulfstream because of the deal?'

'Not this one.' Van Rensburg shook his head firmly. 'There'll be a spot of local backbiting when old Mululu announces it. Bound to be. But nothing serious. The mines are all small and stand to gain from integrated marketing.'

He parked outside a large white-painted hangar, cut the Mercedes' engine and then paused before opening the door.

'Don't confuse the issues. Your father's negotiations here began long before the Consolidated takeover idea. Same thing in Kinshasa; or was going to be. He was tying up normal business.'

In other words, I thought, there was more at stake. Potentially a lot more. Until a few minutes ago I had never appreciated just how huge the sums involved in diamond mining were. I was fed up with having to ask questions, and I had the feeling Van Rensburg was near the limit of his willingness to answer. None the less, I posed another.

'And will our Zaïre diamonds continue to be sold through De Beers?'

'No comment.' He manoeuvred himself awkwardly out of the car – certain leg movements evidently troubled him more than others and I wondered if they affected his flying a plane – and faced me again. 'Sorry old chap. I've told you enough that's confidential already, and I mean confidential.' He gestured towards some offices alongside the hangar. 'Let's get on with what we came to do.'

The air charter company had allocated a briefing room as the operations centre for the search. Large-scale maps of the entire Nairobi to Kinshasa route were pinned to the walls. Red overlays showed areas that had already been surveyed, but more than half the 1,500-mile distance remained unexplored.

The chief pilot, a small man not much older than I was, in a neat white shirt with four gold bars on its shoulder straps, explained the details.

'We can't pretend this is exhaustive,' he said with a directness which surprised me; usually companies overstate the value of what they're doing. 'For one thing Lake Victoria is a hundred and fifty miles wide. A plane could disappear there without trace. Then in eastern Zaïre the tropical forest is so thick we often can't see the roads, let alone any wreckage. The trees are a hundred and thirty feet high.'

'You mean it's impossible?' There was no point in ducking the issue.

'Not completely. We've chartered a mining company's chopper to operate out of Kisangani and the crew are taking infra-red photographs. Those show up everything, from abandoned cars onwards.' He went to the map and pointed with his forefinger. 'Yesterday we found a light aircraft that was lost six years ago. But it's more likely that word will come in from the local population. At least that's what the British Consul in Kisangani thinks.'

'If the Gulfstream is discovered, can you fly me to the site?'

The chief pilot looked at Van Rensburg for guidance. 'He's the paymaster.'

'No problem,' Van Rensburg said, 'if you wanted to. Nothing pleasant about crashes, though. I'll be going. So will a British accident investigator, as the plane's British-registered.'

There didn't seem a lot more to say or do, so we left and drove into Nairobi. On the way Van Rensburg echoed Mother's concerns about the search.

'You ought to know we've had a telex from the Fourteenth Floor querying the costs of all this.' He was being bluff even by his standards and keeping his eyes firmly on the road. 'Wouldn't have thought the expense would matter myself.'

'From Stainton?'

'Correct.'

I'd known from the moment of shaking hands at the airport that Van Rensburg would want my position clearly defined. He was Father's oldest friend and this was no time for false sentiment.

'Father and I don't always hit things off too well.'

'I know that. He isn't the easiest man.'

'Our relationship is irrelevant now.' I had made up my mind. For better or worse I intended to find him. 'What is the search costing?'

'Two hundred pounds an hour for the chopper. Say two or three a mile for the other flying. Plus a load of overheads.'

'Would ten thousand a day cover it?'

'About.'

'And Stainton is quibbling?'

'Not yet. He's asked for figures.'

'Father earns more than that a day in salary and dividends,' I commented. 'Any executive who lands in trouble ought to be confident that the company will get him back.'

'Agreed. Unless it's a ransom.'

'This isn't. And if for any reason the Trust won't pay, then Mother and I will. We'll go on until we find the plane and him even if it takes years.'

'I'm glad,' Van Rensburg said. 'That's the way I feel. I owe a lot to Jim.' He took a deep breath, as though controlling anger. 'Frank probably only wants budget figures. All accountants are the same. The next thing is to hear what the staff here have to say.'

However, as he had predicted, nobody at the local offices, either in the city centre or out at the industrial area, had anything constructive to suggest. The managers' remarks were a liturgy. Sir James's visit had been smoothly organized and uneventful. They all emphasized that. His employees were keeping their noses clean.

Our final call, late in the morning, was at the Norfolk Hotel, where Father always stayed.

The Norfolk was something of a legend, an old colonial hotel dating from the early 1900s, Van Rensburg told me, and the traditional starting point for big game safaris ever since. Whether the fat women in over-tight khaki slacks being helped out of a zebra-striped minibus at the entrance were part of this tradition seemed debatable.

He pointed out the grey stone building of the National Theatre opposite. 'That used to be swamp, and guests could hear the lions at night. Before my time, of course.'

I looked at the hotel with greater interest, as a piece of history. The Arab settlements strung out along Kenya's coast went back a thousand years. Their names came instantly to mind: Witu, Pate, Gedi, Lamu, Kilifi, though I had never seen them. Their mosques and houses were all ruins. Now the once savage interior was acquiring a history too. I made the point to Van Rensburg.

'Bit too violently,' he remarked, indicating the left of the hotel's entrance tower, where the building was swathed in scaffolding and corrugated screening. 'Had a bomb planted here last New Year's Eve. Blew up the dining room, killed sixteen people and injured another hundred. Bloody Arab terrorist. We can do without making that kind of history.'

However, one beneficial outcome, as the young European manager explained when I met him, had been to make everyone keep a much closer eye on the comings and goings of guests.

'Sir James had no unusual callers,' he assured us. 'And to the best of my knowledge, no complaints. He left for the airport on time at a quarter to eight on Saturday. I said goodbye to him myself.' He went on to hope that Father was safe despite the lack of news, and added, 'We can do without any more sabotage.'

As he ushered us out he made a remark to Van Rensburg which was not intended for my ears.

'Sir James's friend stayed on after all,' he said in an undertone as I walked behind them. 'She's going to Treetops tonight.'

I couldn't see Van Rensburg's face, but I could tell he was caught off guard because of the embarrassed way he replied, muttering, 'Oh. Thanks for letting me know,' and not pursuing the subject.

Along the undamaged part of the hotel's frontage there was a terrace cafe, with timber beams supporting its roof and smart African waiters in dark green waistcoats. As we shook hands with the manager at the entrance, which opened straight on to this terrace, I noticed a woman of perhaps fifty sitting at one of its tables. She had blonde hair, cut short and swept back, diamonds glittered in her ears and she was dressed with a flair that stood out among the tourists in their newly bought safari clothes, all hung about with cameras. It was only an impression, because she was in the shade and we were standing in bright sunlight. But I remember a silk shirt and a brightly coloured scarf and somehow a lot of gold, like chains and a bangle on a slender wrist. However, it wasn't the clothes or the gold or the easy elegance which made me notice her, it was the fact that she was without question looking me over.

'Well,' Van Rensburg was saying, 'where would you like to have lunch?' Clearly we would not be eating here.

'Anywhere you say.' I was still conscious of the woman's eyes on me. 'I wouldn't mind a sleep afterwards. The jetlag's catching up.' Whether because of the flight or the morning's complete lack of success, I felt drained and slightly sick.

Van Rensburg led me to the car, parked opposite, and as we drove off I could see the woman on the terrace quite deliberately avert her head as if not wishing to be caught watching us.

Over lunch at an Italian restaurant I asked about Treetops. What was it?

'Hotel in the Aberdare Forest,' he answered succinctly. 'You watch game by an artificial moon at night. The Queen inherited the throne while she was at Treetops. Actually was in a tree then.'

'What time d'you have to get there by?'

He knew I was talking about the woman at the Norfolk, and he paused long enough to let me know that he knew. 'Usually people leave here around ten in the morning. Want to go?'

Therefore, he was telling me, the 'friend' could not have been the woman who had been gazing at me. Yet I wasn't so good-looking that rich women normally gave me the eye.

'Could you go later?'

'By special arrangement,' he admitted. 'Don't think we could fix it for today though. Anyway, I thought you wanted a kip?'

'It was just an idea.'

My backing down evidently pleased him, because he shifted to other subjects and eventually we drove back to the house in Karen, where I slept into the evening.

Mary Van Rensburg woke me at six, apologizing that it was later than I had suggested. 'You looked exhausted. By the way, if you're interested Patrick's just come across a spitting cobra by the rondavel.'

I forced myself awake, mildly ashamed at having fallen asleep fully dressed, shovelled on my shoes and followed her downstairs.

The round whitewashed guest house, with its pointed thatched roof, like a Chinese straw hat, had three cement steps up to the door. Standing on the grass in front was Van Rensburg, a shotgun in the crook of his arm, while two African gardeners in green boiler-suits stood back a yard or so, their machete-like pangas raised. We joined them.

'The snake's in the angle of the steps.' Mary pointed and then I saw it, coiled up exactly as cobras are always depicted, its flat head raised and immobile, and its tongue flicking in and out, its jewel eyes fixed on Van Rensburg.

'If there was time to get the boys from the Snake Park here,' he said glancing round, 'I'd let them trap the bugger. But it'll be dark in half an hour. Ever seen one before?'

He should not have turned away. The cobra's head darted forward and a spurt of spittle shot in the direction of his eyes. He recoiled, but not fast enough to stop the venom staining his shirt, while the snake, perhaps aware this was its last chance, launched into escape along the side of the rondavel. The elder of the gardeners swung his panga. A second later it had been sliced clean through into two parts, both writhing on the grass. His younger partner joined in hacking the remains into many segments. Each piece continued to squirm. I watched compulsively, disgusted and yet fascinated.

'They keep those pangas razor-sharp,' Mary commented. 'Chop each other up quite often, too. Shall we go back in?'

When she offered me a whisky I was happy to accept. Her remark would have been offensive, at least to me, if I hadn't seen the way they despatched the snake. There had been a savagery about the killing of the cobra, itself a killer, which brought it home to me that this country house with its well-kept garden gave quite an illusory impression of European order. Even the grass was different here: coarse, hard stuff that grew close enough to look like an English lawn until you examined

it. Would the search for Father prove to be an equally mis-
leading piece of European procedure, foisted on people who
worked to different rules?

Over dinner these doubts faded a little as the Van Rensburgs
told me about their life in Kenya. His parents had come to farm
here in the 1930s but after Independence – which they called
'Uhuru' – their land had been bought for African settlement. By
then the loss of the farm didn't worry them. He was a successful
geologist, employed full-time by Father, and his parents were
nearing retirement. He made no secret of the Trust having paid
for the rebuilding of his present home.

When we moved on to coffee and liqueurs in the drawing room
I asked how Father and he had first met. There were logs burning
in the stone fireplace – May evenings are cool at 6,000 feet, even
on the Equator – and Van Rensburg was relaxed and compara-
tively talkative.

'We both joined the airborne forces in the war, though at different times. Different reasons too.'

I listened more out of politeness than interest. One aspect of
Father's past I knew all about was his service in the Parachute
regiment. He never let anyone forget that its men were an élite.

'Yes,' Van Rensburg continued in a ruminative voice, 'that's
when Jim's luck took off. He'd been fortunate enough getting out
of internment after a few months, instead of years. I think the
headmaster of the school managed that by offering him a job:
schools in Britain were pretty short-staffed during the war, apparently.'

My interest stirred. This illuminated one of the haziest periods
of Father's life. Of his childhood in Germany I knew virtually
nothing, except for his admission that he had been in the Hitler
Youth. Otherwise his existence might have only begun when he
arrived in Britain as a refugee in 1937. Nor did he ever talk about
his internment as an alien under the catch-all Regulation 18b.

By contrast he made a point of acknowledging the headmaster
who gave him both a bursary and a home at the school's converted
eighteenth-century mansion near Bristol. 'Damn decent chap,'
Father used to say, and it would have been wrong to snigger at
the dated phrase because he truly meant it. Instead of being
shipped off to a camp in Canada or Australia after his internment in
the spring of 1940, as most German nationals were, he was
released to work as an assistant language tutor at the school. He
started that autumn, also helping the games master. He was nineteen and a half and suffered occasional insults from boys younger
than him who were being called up to fight the Nazis. It wasn't
until 1942 that he was allowed to join the army himself.

'Must have thought a lot of your father, that schoolmaster,'

Van Rensburg added. 'Gave him a character reference for the army. Remember seeing it in his papers once.' He grinned. 'In those days I was the officer and he was the subordinate. Well, things change.'

'Was joining the army so difficult?' I had imagined that a nation at war would welcome all the cannon fodder available.

'For a German, bloody difficult. At least without a chit from a Member of Parliament or a magistrate or some other supposedly responsible citizen. The army only started taking foreigners around 1942, and then they were drafted straight into the Pioneer Corps.' He laughed. 'Jim's luck again. Managed to join the Somerset and Cornwall Light Infantry. Well, his only home had been in Somerset. A year later he volunteered for parachute training and was accepted. Ambitious and lucky. Always has been.'

The reference to ambition intrigued me. 'How do you mean?'

Van Rensburg drank some more of his whisky and soda – he had pressed a liqueur on me but spurned it himself – and put the glass down again carefully, as though the action was part of weighing my question.

'Your father was hell-bent on more than just earning himself citizenship after the war. He had it all mapped out. He intended making his reputation.'

'You make him sound very calculating.'

'Maybe.' Van Rensburg became faintly defensive. 'On the other hand he was taking more risks than we were. The airborne forces didn't exactly fight from the rear. If he'd been captured . . . well, he'd have been a traitor as far as the Gestapo were concerned. Took some nerve to volunteer for the operation we did behind the German lines.'

'Was that when he won the medal?'

'Correct.' He heaved himself to his feet. 'Amuse you to see what we looked like then?'

He went to a cupboard and fetched a large and battered album. While he was flicking through the pages I thought of father's Military Medal, lying in a small glass-topped display case at Godstow with his campaign stars and his citation. No one had flip ideas about courage in our family. To Mother and me that citation meant precisely what its official-sounding words said. 'Sergeant Hartman . . . displayed conspicuous gallantry . . . assumed command of his detachment . . . saved the life of his Commanding Officer and led the mission to a successful conclusion against considerable odds.' We also knew the operation had a background of mystery, because the location was not precisely stated.

Van Rensburg laid the album on my knees. A black and white photograph showed a group of soldiers, all in battledress, all with an air of forced cheerfulness. He himself was instantly re-cognizable from his height.

'Bit slimmer in those days,' he remarked. 'Recognize your father?'

I hadn't done at first. Unlike the others he had his beret on straight and his tunic buttoned up to the neck. But the main differ-ence was his expression of formality. I felt that for him this was not just a snapshot, it was a record for posterity.

'The man who took that was killed the next day, poor sod.' Van Rensburg picked up the album and gazed at the pictures, reliving the past. 'Funny, we all had plenty to be serious about, but only Jim looked as though he had.'

'I've read the citation.'

'Then you know he saved my life?'

'What exactly happened?' I asked, and not only out of pol-iteness. Father himself never spoke about that.

'We dropped into Italy to join up with some partisans behind the lines. The citation left most of the story out. The truth isn't one hundred per cent pretty. Are you sure you want to hear it?'

Across the room Mrs Van Rensburg shifted in her chair. 'If you two are going to start re-fighting the war,' she said firmly, 'I think I'll be off to bed.' She got up and I hastily rose to my feet as well. 'Goodnight, Robert. It's very nice to have you here.'

'We won't be long, dear,' Van Rensburg assured her.

'I've heard that before,' she remarked amiably and left.

'Well,' Van Rensburg settled himself back into his chair, 'I only pieced it all together years afterwards, when we were down at the mine and had time on our hands. Of course there was no need for your father to have been involved at all. As I said he volunteered.'

'Surely that's no disgrace?'

'Far from it. He earned his gong. And his promotion.'

Something in the way Van Rensburg said this made me ap-prehensive. So far as I had ever heard, Father's bravery in Italy had led directly to his rising from Sergeant to Lieutenant. He'd been commissioned in the field, a rare distinction.

'You make it sound as though things were less simple,' I said.

'For political reasons the citation left out certain aspects of the operation. That we were betrayed by the partisans, for one.'

'And?'

'Jim's never been a man to fool about with. Shot first and asked questions after.'

'What exactly d'you mean?' I couldn't help feeling hostility. There were plenty of things I disliked about Father, but his war record had never been questioned. It was probably the only reason my grandfather, the upright old General, had let Mother marry him.

Van Rensburg remained bear-like in his deep armchair, his shoulders hunched, the cut glass tumbler clasped in a massive fist, and came out with an unexpectedly philosophical observation.

'What I mean, Robert, is that the value people place on life depends on how they're living. During the war life had a low price and loyalty a high one. Pretty much the same in Africa now, as it happens. You have to be either pretty sophisticated or pretty naïve to believe in live and let live. More often it's kill or be killed.'

'I'm afraid I'm not with you.'

'In a peacetime military situation, Northern Ireland for example, your father would have been charged with murder. That's another part the citation left out.'

CHAPTER FIVE

At the age of twenty-two, Captain Patrick Van Rensburg was already a veteran. Three of his four adult years had been spent on active service and the other year training to fight. His parents out in Kenya noticed the taut wariness of his face in the few photographs he sent. If they could have seen him on this particular afternoon in the autumn of 1943, they would have worried a great deal more. The colonel of the parachute battalion had just invited him to take a small group of soldiers behind the German lines in Italy and bring out as many Allied prisoners of war as he could locate. He had no need of the colonel's briefing to appreciate how tricky this was going to be.

The background was as simple as the situation it had produced was chaotic. After the American and British armies had invaded Italy the dictator Mussolini's government had collapsed. The Italian authorities agreed an Armistice with the Allies. Hitler, however, had no intention of surrendering Italy, and as the Allied troops fought their way north, reinforcements of the Wehrmacht streamed south to confront them and establish a line. That was the theory. In practice the area behind the line was in confusion. Deserters from the Italian army pillaged. Partisans, principally organized by the Communist Party, roamed the countryside. Also at large were British and American prisoners of war, released abruptly at the Armistice from Italian POW camps only to find themselves on the run from the Germans. On September the 20th Van Rensburg's battalion was ordered to organize a rescue operation.

Accordingly Van Rensburg was sitting on a canvas chair in his tent, puzzling over a map of the Pescara area while the flies buzzed irritatingly around his head, and wondering how the hell he would manage to shepherd several hundred unarmed servicemen from the mountains to the coast to be picked up by the navy under cover of darkness without the German army noticing. The mission didn't sound so much lunatic as suicidal, quite apart from the partisan leadership being communist. A soft cough interrupted his thoughts. In the doorway of the tent stood a soldier in shirt-sleeves, sergeant's stripes visible on his arm. He saluted stiffly.

'Excuse me, Sir. Permission to speak, Sir.'

'What is it, Sergeant?'

'I wish to volunteer, Sir.'

'So Mr Robertson told me. Why?'

Another fly settled on Van Rensburg's cheek. He tried to swat it as he looked Hartman over. The sergeant remained rigidly at attention, his sunburnt forearms firmly against his trousers, fists clenched with the thumbs forward. His red beret was correctly pulled down to one side over closely shorn dark hair. His face was impassive, the mouth set in a hard line, the eyes fixed resolutely on a point a foot or so above Van Rensburg's head. He might have been parading for a CO's inspection.

The quick rundown Van Rensburg had been given of the man's character fitted his appearance.

'Disciplined, yet aggressive. Talks as if he'd like to take on Hitler personally. Last he heard of his mother she was in a concentration camp. The lads call him "Lucky" because he came down safely once on a parachute with its canopy ripped from top to bottom. Too educated for a sergeant, really.'

'Why d'you want to volunteer?' Van Rensburg repeated sharply. 'You don't even know what the mission is. At least I bloody well hope you don't.'

'I heard there's to be a drop, Sir.'

'Don't tell me you just want a buckshee job. How many operational jumps have you done?'

'Only two, Sir. Tunisia and Primosole.' The dissatisfaction showed in Hartman's voice and he shifted his gaze down to meet Van Rensburg's. 'We ought to be making drops behind the enemy to clear the way, Sir, not footslogging on with everyone else.'

Van Rensburg grunted. He agreed. Because two thirds of the men parachuted in to seize the Primosole bridge in Sicily had been dropped in the wrong place, there had been no airborne operations since. But the principle was right. However, he did not propose to let a sergeant criticize their superiors.

'The generals have their reasons, Hartman. Anyway strategy's irrelevant to the operation I'm leading. It's to bring out prisoners of war. We won't fight unless we have to. There won't be any glory and we won't be proving any theories. Sure you want to come?'

'Yes. Sir.'

'If we're caught and the Gestapo discover you're a German

you'll be tortured and shot. Doesn't that worry you? It would me.'

Hartman shook his head doggedly. 'I have joined the army to fight the Nazis. I know about the risks. I speak some Italian.'

'I'll consider you,' Van Rensburg said levelly, wondering how long this soldier's inflected English would deceive an interrogator. 'You may dismiss.'

As Hartman saluted and marched off it occurred to him that a German speaker might be useful.

The next evening, when two Dakotas of the United States Air Force took off from Bari to drop the thirty-eight men, Sergeant Hartman was on board the second plane.

During the flight in an arc over the Adriatic, avoiding as much German-held territory as possible, some of the men dozed, their equipment piled around their feet, comatosely anaesthetizing fear. Others sat so deeply wrapped in their own thoughts that they might as well have been asleep, only an occasional frown or twitch of the facial muscles revealing otherwise. Waiting to jump was the worst part of the entire operation.

Hartman himself held a map up to what little light there was from the window behind him, trying to imprint the details of their dropping zone on his mind. He wanted to be able to re- cognize the features of the landscape instantly during the thirty seconds of his descent in the twilight. He felt quietly exultant at being on the operation. The dangers he had already discounted. He'd had a philosophy about risk since he was fifteen and he was twenty-two now: risks were justifiable in proportion to the po- tential gain. The gain from this was that it would add lustre to his military record. If he could win a decoration, even better. He knew he might never break through into the officer corps, but he could earn the respect of his regiment. When peace came his ex- ploits with the airborne forces would give him the status he had so grievously lacked before the war as a refugee.

As the plane rocked and the soldier next to him lolled sideways, he wished he could have explained these plans to his mother. It was 'Muttilein' who had arranged his escape from Germany de- spite the restrictions which prevented any boy approaching military age from leaving the country, let alone taking money with him. Germany under Hitler was as tightly sealed a cage for its citizens in the 1930s as was Russia under Stalin. The first inmates of the concentration camps in 1933 and 1934 had not been the Jews: they had been the leaders of the Communist and Social Democratic parties. It was through a Social Democrat sympathizer who cap- tained a Rhine barge that Hans Hardtmann, then a lanky fifteen- year-old, had reached Holland, hidden in a load of coal.

The joke, and it had been a wry one, was that he had been

51

visiting Koblenz with the Hitler Youth from his school when he slipped away via a lavatory window at the back of a canteen to meet the bargee. In consequence the official in charge had been held responsible for his disappearance, not his parents. The risks had been colossal. So far as he was concerned they had been rewarded when he stepped off the ferry at Dover. He didn't know that only the down payment had been made.

For a time after his escape his mother and he had corresponded successfully. '*Liebstes Muttilein*', his letters always began, and continued with an innocuous account of life at the school near Bristol where a generous headmaster had given several refugees free places. Her replies, sometimes mysteriously posted from France, were full of conventional expressions of affection and concern, but otherwise extremely guarded. Then in 1938, after the Munich conference, from which the British Prime Minister came back assuring the world of 'peace in our time', Hans made his mistake. Miserable at not having seen her for a year, he had managed to telephone her from the school and said he wanted to come home. Caught unprepared, she forbade him to return.

'Then can't you come here? Can't you somehow, Mutti?'

'*Nein*,' she had said, and he could hear the break in her voice and the tears. 'No, *meine Liebe*, I cannot.'

'Not even for a visit?'

'I have things to do here, Hans. Things I could not do anywhere else. We can only hope that times will change.'

The operator interrupted to say their time was up. Hans shouted 'goodbye' and the line went dead. He did not hear from her again, or from his father, who had seldom written anyway. Seven months later roundabout enquiries brought word of their being taken away by the Gestapo. He never became reconciled to the fear that his telephone call had caused their arrest. It lent a cold ferocity to the way he fought which even the most hardened of his British comrades lacked.

Movement inside the Dakota jerked Hartman out of his reverie. The narrow door to the cockpit had opened. The second pilot's head and shoulders appeared and he displayed both hands, fingers and thumbs outstretched, in an emphatic gesture to the despatcher in the rear. Ten minutes to go. The despatcher shouted 'Prepare for Action' and heaved open the aircraft door. A roar of slipstream and engine noise swamped the cabin. Hartman fastened his equipment container to his left leg, got up and checked the attachment of his static line to the cable that ran along the fuselage. He would be first to jump. The despatcher beckoned him forward and he stood, swaying by the doorway. Outside it was dusk. He could distinguish fields and the dull silver snake of a river below. A red light came on by the door. He moved forward and tensed, balancing himself with one hand around the opening. The green light came on, the despatcher thumped his shoulder and shouted 'Go'. He was out, whirled away by the slipstream, held as if in an invisible chair. His legs jerked up in front of him, then swung down again. It was very quiet. Above he saw the dark shape of the parachute comfortingly open, released the kitbag to hang below him on its cord and thirty seconds later thumped, feet together, on to hard ground to roll over, partially winded.

Others were gathering their equipment and parachutes, then running towards the corner of the long field near the river where they had dropped. When Hartman reached it he found Van Rensburg checking men in at this RV and audibly wondering where the hell the partisans meeting them were. To the west the outline of the distant Gran Sasso mountains was just visible against a rose-tinged sky. The drop had been accurate. The partisans were supposed to rendezvous with them here. If that failed, the alternative was at a lone farmhouse among olive groves in the foothills. The one thing Van Rensburg did not want to do was hang around.

'Prepare to move.' He gave the order in an undertone, conscious of the way the darkness seemed to magnify sounds.

The other officer, Lieutenant Jack Robertson, positioned himself in the centre so that the group could split up into two fighting patrols if they met opposition. Hartman brought up the rear and they set off in loose single file along a track towards the hills, walking a yard or so apart.

The moon had not yet risen and Van Rensburg halted frequently to check his bearings until they reached an old stone bridge, visible only as a dark hump above the subdued luminosity of a stream. This led to the farm. As he approached the outline of it a man moved and Van Rensburg froze.

'*Buona sera*,' a voice said quietly. 'Welcome.'

A second man emerged from the shadow beside the bridge and flashed a torch on himself. He had greasy black hair, no hat, and was dressed in grey German army trousers and a green Italian army jacket. A leather bandolier of rifle ammunition was coiled across his chest and a long knife protruded from his belt. He looked like a stage brigand. He saluted.

'I am Luigi,' he said in over-simple Italian, and called softly to the one on the bridge to join them. 'He is Zito. We lead you.'

Zito did not trouble to identify himself, though Van Rensburg could see he was in some kind of uniform and wore an Italian army forage cap.

'*Andiamo*,' Van Rensburg suggested, automatically checking that his revolver was in its canvas holster on his belt. He had been warned that the partisans were a law to themselves.

53

From the rear of the small column Hartman saw nothing of this, simply receiving the order to halt as it was whispered down the line, and eventually the order to continue. In the darkness he could see no more than the shapes of the two or three men ahead of him.

The track they were following entered the olive groves and slowly steepened. After an hour the moon came up and its cold light revealed that they were ascending a valley. They left the shelter of the olives and saw a straggling group of farm buildings ahead up the slope.

'There is no village,' Luigi told Van Rensburg. 'Only the farm. The owner is old.'

A dog barked as they approached, then was subdued to ferocious growling. Van Rensburg halted to look around and mistrusted what he saw. The buildings were ranged round a walled yard, with the wall facing them. Broken wooden gates hung open in a stone archway. He moved closer. Inside there were a barn to the left and a house opposite. Behind, the hills reared up steeply. The only escape would be into the mountains. It looked as much a potential trap as a sanctuary.

'No Germans here,' Luigi remarked, neatly reading his thoughts. 'For the men is the barn. Zito will show them. I take you to the owner.' He gave a low whistle, the unseen dog burst into a frenzy of barking and a crack of light appeared at a downstairs window in the house.

'Sergeant!' Van Rensburg called Hartman forward and gave him instructions in an undertone, then turned to Luigi and asked, 'Is there food?'

'There are bread and olives and wine from the owner.'

'No wine, thank you. Water.' He turned back to Hartman and said loudly, 'Get the men in the barn.' He hoped Hartman would be able to follow his orders without the Italian noticing. They might misinterpret the elementary precautions he was taking, but he had a gut feeling that something was wrong. He hoped the owner would settle his doubts.

The owner proved to be a wizened man in his seventies, as gnarled as the trunk of one of his own olive trees, dressed in a dirty collarless shirt and an old waistcoat. A dull-coated, underfed Alsatian snarled as they entered and sniffed at their legs. The room itself was large and the old man sat at a long scrubbed table, on which stood the only source of light, an oil lamp with a smoky glass chimney. The whole scene could have been a nineteenth-century conversation piece painting.

Van Rensburg guessed that the homestead had changed little in a hundred years. He remembered the briefing about this part of Italy, the Abruzzi. It was one of the most deprived and primitive parts of the entire mezzogiorno, where banditry had been endemic for centuries.

'We are very grateful to you,' he said in laboured Italian.

The old man muttered something, reaching for a bottle on the table, and poured four glasses of wine. As he gestured at them to drink, and raised his own, his movements cast grotesque shadows on the whitewashed wall behind. They all drank.

'The padrone hopes you will eat with him,' Luigi said. 'He asks how long you stay.'

'That depends. Where are the nearest of our men?'

'Some are near Cepagatti.' The Italian seemed evasive. 'They are in many places. We bring them here.'

'Then we will stay two nights.'

The old man spoke argumentatively to Luigi.

'He is poor,' Luigi said blandly. 'Bread costs money. Also he is taking much danger.'

They hadn't taken long to start begging, Van Rensburg reflected, but at least he had come prepared. The local funds for the operation totalled one hundred and fifty thousand lire, and for safety he had parcelled it out among several men. He ferreted inside his smock, withdrew a small wad of notes and counted out eight thousand.

'The owner,' he said firmly to Luigi, 'can have the silk from our parachutes.' The material would be readily saleable. So would the cords and webbing straps.

'Ten thousand,' Luigi demanded, staring flatly back.

Van Rensburg agreed with reluctance. The old man smiled craggily, revealing a gap-toothed mouth, the skin tight over a protruding chin. 'Maria,' he shouted in a cracked voice.

'They are honoured to welcome British soldiers,' Luigi said with little conviction. But as if to back up his words he unslung the sub-machinegun from his neck and placed it on the table.

Half a minute later a peasant woman appeared. She wore a long skirt and shawl and looked at least as aged as the man. She was carrying a steaming bowl of spaghetti, which she set on the table. Then she fetched plates from an old dresser and served them.

'To victory,' Van Rensburg said, raising his glass. 'Soon our army will be here.'

'But now you make escape for your men?' Luigi commented.

'Because we do not want them to be caught and taken to Germany before we arrive.' The explanation sounded weak even to himself.

'We all have our own country,' Luigi agreed and began eating with noisy pleasure.

When they had finished Van Rensburg and Robertson were

shown to a room which had been prepared 'for the officers'. It was spacious, simply furnished and smelt antiseptically clean. In the flickering candlelight they could see that the stone floor had been washed. There were three beds with blankets. A table stood beneath a flimsily curtained window, which proved to face towards the mountains.

'Is OK?' Luigi asked in unexpected English as he watched them investigate.

'Fine,' Robertson remarked. 'Like the Ritz after where we've been.'

Van Rensburg waited until the Italian had left. 'I wouldn't trust that fellow further than I can spit,' he said. 'Go and see how the men are while I do some planning. And bring back Hartman with you.'

While his subordinate was gone Van Rensburg spread out his maps, lit a cigarette and began taking stock. He traced the route they had taken, identified the farm and decided that Luigi's ideas were completely unacceptable. His plan was not to gather together a powerless, unarmed group of POWs, but to contact as many as possible through the partisans and order them to find their own way to the coast to be picked up in a week's time at an RV which his own small force would establish and protect. Luigi and Zito must lead him to the escapees, not vice versa, and the sooner they left this valley the better.

He was on his third cigarette and had clarified his mind when Robertson and Hartman returned. They told him the men were fed and would sleep in their combat clothes, ready to move at short notice. The sergeant, as ordered, had posted a ten-man standing patrol down in the olive groves to ambush the track.

'I don't think the Italians saw them go, Sir,' Hartman assured the captain, then said suddenly and urgently, 'Would you mind putting your cigarette out, Sir.'

'Don't like the smoke, eh?' Van Rensburg was about to add a more caustic comment to the effect that if he wanted a fag he would damn well have one when he saw the expression on the sergeant's face. Hartman was standing immobile except for quick turns of the head, sniffing like an animal. Mystified, Van Rensburg ground out his stub alongside its two predecessors and waited.

Certain scents have the power to transport one into the past. Hartman was back in his parents' old house in Düsseldorf, breathing the sanitarily efficient smell of the soap his mother used and the distinctive odour of his father's shoes, when they were on the kitchen table for cleaning. The smells were as distinctive to him as the vinegary tang of fish and chips in an English street, and they could only be German. He glanced around the room, saw a closet and went to it. The doors were locked. Lifting his boot against one, he wrenched the other open, splintering the wood.

'What the hell are you doing?' Van Rensburg came to life.

Hartman took no notice. The cupboard was empty, but the smell was stronger. He flashed his torch over the interior, bent down, picked something up and turned back to the two officers holding out a small rectangular packet.

'Germans have been here, Sir.'

Van Rensburg took the packet. It was a fraction less than three inches long and an inch wide. It bore a crude picture of camels in front of the Egyptian pyramids with the initials EFKA and above that the words '*Feinstes Zigaretten Papier*'. Inside there was a single thin cigarette wrapping left. Jesus, he thought, we've walked straight into it. We're just a bunch of adolescents. The operation's been betrayed. This valley is a trap.

Hartman reacted faster. Without waiting for an order he dashed out to the farmyard. The light in the house had been extinguished. He hammered on the door. There was no reply, not even a bark from the dog. He ran across to the gates, scanning the moonlit landscape for movement, and could see none. But the partisans could not have been gone more than fifteen minutes and the old couple were infirm. They must either be a short way into the hills, in which case they could be caught, or have followed the track down the valley. Hoping to God the corporal in charge of the standing patrol had been alert, he ran on down to the olive groves, halted among the trees, cupped his hands and gave an owl's hoot.

A crouching figure emerged from the shadow of a wall and gave a password. It was the corporal.

'Any of the Eyeties come down here?' Hartman demanded.

'One did.' The corporal's eyes shone white against the camouflage paint on his face. 'It's OK. We grabbed him like you said to. He's further down, arguing his bloody head off.'

'Which one is he?'

'Says he's Luigi.'

'Bring him.' Hartman touched the corporal's arm. 'And one thing, I may take his side. Don't worry, just shoot him if he tries to run.'

They went on down through the olives a couple of hundred yards to find the Italian squatting in the grass beneath a tree, guarded by two soldiers. Hartman flashed the torch on him. It was indeed Luigi and his face showed fear and truculence in about equal proportions. He immediately launched into a *sotto voce* diatribe against his detention.

'I am sorry, my friend,' Hartman said quietly in Italian. 'There is a misunderstanding. The captain wants to see you. Please come to the house.'

57

'Why do you stop me? Without us you can do nothing. We are your allies. How dare you threaten me?'

Hartman rounded on the corporal, simulating fury. 'What the hell are you doing, arresting a partisan? Don't you understand orders, you fool?' He continued for half a minute, overplaying the anger, hissing out the words, turned back to Luigi, all friendliness. 'Come with me. The officer needs your advice.'

There was not much the Italian could do except comply. Hartman led the way, with the corporal behind, until they were within the farmyard and close to the officers' room, when he ordered the corporal to go ahead. The corporal knocked, Van Rensburg's voice told him to enter, he swung the door inwards and Luigi moved into the rectangle of lamplight. What followed took Hartman unawares, even though he was expecting trouble.

In one continuous movement Luigi lobbed a grenade through the doorway, shouldered them both aside and bolted for the gate.

Later, recounting the event, Hartman decided that the Italian must have pulled the pin out while the opening of the door momentarily distracted his own attention. By the time he had recovered his balance and flipped off the safety catch of his sten gun, Luigi was halfway across the moonlit open space.

Many soldiers would have instantly opened fire, spraying shots at the fugitive. Hartman dropped on to one knee, raised the submachinegun into his shoulder and took deliberate aim. The first shot missed and ricocheted whining off a wall. The second scored. Luigi tumbled a few feet short of safety, a dark shadow rolling over in the dust a moment after the grenade detonated indoors, its explosion made thunderous by the confined space of the room.

As paratroopers rushed out of the barn, imagining they were under attack, Hartman followed through an almost intuitive assessment of priorities. Behind him three men might be dead or dying, must certainly be wounded. By definition they were out of action. Ahead, crawling to the gate, was the traitor, whose knowledge might save the whole group. He sprinted after him.

Luigi was already hauling himself round the stone gatepost by his hands, groaning from the exertion. Hartman could not see his gun, but still stopped short out of prudence.

'Stay where you are,' he shouted, and when the order was not obeyed, fired a shot into the ground, close to the man. He wanted Luigi alive.

A soldier's voice sounded behind him. 'Sarge, come quick. Mister Robertson's dying.'

'Send Corporal White,' he snapped, without looking around. 'First help me. Take the torch.' He pulled it out of his pocket and handed it over. 'Shine it on the bastard.'

The soldier fumbled, then a narrow beam illuminated Luigi,

lying on his side, one hand clutching his stomach, the other out-stretched.

'Stand up!' Hartman yelled.

'I cannot.'

Hartman fired again, the dust spurting alongside the Italian, who struggled on to his knees, moaning.

'Get behind him. Pull him up,' he told the soldier.

When Luigi was semi-erect, pinioned from behind, Hartman relieved him of his gun and a knife, then undid his belt and yanked his trousers down around his ankles. In the intermittent flashes of the torch the flow of blood was visible pouring down the Italian's legs.

'OK,' Hartman told the soldier. 'Keep him until I come back.' He doubled across the yard, only pausing when, above the general clamour, he thought he heard a dog howling somewhere up the valley.

The room was a shambles. The window had been blown out and the ceiling had fallen, showering everything in fine dust which was still settling when he joined in trying to extricate the officers. Lieutenant Robertson was dead. From the position of his body it appeared he had been trying to throw the grenade out again through the window when it went off. Captain Van Rensburg was alive, though unconscious. He had flung himself flat and had been partially protected by the table, but blood was staining his clothes from wounds in his back and thighs. The corporal had been more fortunate. The blast had catapulted him out of the doorway into the yard and he was merely concussed.

Hartman took charge, sent men to look for hurdles or ladders that could be used as stretchers, and ordered the contingent to be ready to move in an hour. His plan was to retreat into the hills and bury the dead officer there. Meanwhile he wanted everything that could betray a British presence gathered together, from empty food tins to his own spent cartridge cases.

'I'm going to have a talk with that wog bugger,' he told the senior corporal. 'And the others, if I can find them. I think I heard the dog. Now, see there?' He pointed to a slope rising to the northwest which was largely in shadow. 'If I do not return in one hour, you're to move up the hill. Is that understood? I will join you, then we'll cross to the next valley.'

Having given his orders Hartman walked back to the gate, tied Luigi's hands behind his back, hauled his blood-soaked trousers round his waist again and hobbled his ankles with a piece of rope. Then he stood him against the farmyard wall and asked softly, 'Where did the others go?'

The Italian spat in his face.

Hartman wiped the spittle away and quite deliberately hit him so hard in the mouth that he crumpled backwards against the stone. Then he stood over him, and thrust the muzzle of his sten gun against the Italian's chest.

'Take us to the capo.'

Luigi struggled briefly on the ground until Hartman pulled him up again by one arm.

'Ten seconds,' he said.

'He is in the mountains.'

'Where? Eight seconds.'

'I do not know exactly. He moves often.'

'Find him and I will ask for your life. What is his name?'

'We call him Barba Nera.'

'*Prima!*' Without thinking Hartman lapsed into his native German at this success. 'And the farmer?'

Luigi hesitated, confused. He had recognized the German exclamation and the wild thought crossed his mind that his interrogator was some kind of spy. Anything was possible. That meant he held a card, meant he might get out of this alive.

'There is a small barn higher up,' he muttered, 'for cattle in the summer.'

'We will go there.' Hartman half carried, half marched him away into the darkness.

Half an hour later the standing patrol heard a dog barking up the hill, followed by five shots, two fired rapidly, the others separately over several minutes.

When Hartman reappeared at the farm with his prisoner, he was carrying a bundle of clothing. He put it on the ground as he addressed the men gathered round him in the yard in the eerie light.

'We've been lucky,' he announced curtly. 'The Germans round here are rear echelon troops. They didn't fancy a night attack. They're coming at dawn. All they're going to find is a farmhouse where a grenade's exploded, plus a lot of footprints. I do not think they will follow us into the mountains. This one,' he indicated Luigi, 'will take us to the partisan leader. Until the captain's able to give orders, I'm in command. Are there any questions?'

There was one obvious question but the iron in Hartman's voice deterred them from asking it.

'Then we get going,' he said, and turned to the soldiers carrying Van Rensburg, strapped to an improvised stretcher and covered with a blanket. 'Be careful how you carry him. Take it in turns.'

A log crackled and spat sparks on the carpet. Van Rensburg hauled himself laboriously from the armchair and flicked the embers back into the hearth with his fingernails.

'Still get stiff from that wound,' he commented. 'One reason I stay in Kenya. Dry climate helps.'

'What happened in the mountains?' I asked, half afraid of the same question his men had shrunk from forty years before.

Van Rensburg leant against the fireplace, as though the warmth comforted his aches.

'I was only conscious intermittently. Broadly, that part went as the citation said. Your father led the group into the hills and established contact with the partisans' boss, then he went down another valley, caught up with several batches of POWs and a week later reached the coast to make the RV with the navy. He only brought out a few dozen of the hundreds who were milling around. But it was a conspicuous achievement. He was actually commissioned in the field before the award of the Military Medal came through.'

'And the partisans?' The question had to follow.

'There were various stories,' Van Rensburg said cautiously. 'All the men knew was that after they had buried Jack Robertson on the hillside your father and two others kept watch on the farm until first light. Odd thing to do when he was in command. Suppose he wanted first-hand confirmation. The Germans came all right. Burnt the place down. After that there was no sign of anyone around. But your father made that shivering bastard Luigi take us to Barba Nera, as he called himself.'

'What did he say? I mean, his own men had betrayed you.'

'Remember him clearly. One of the moments I wasn't delirious. Big bloke with a black beard, as you'd expect. Your father and he carried me down to a village to see a doctor.'

'In broad daylight?'

'Must have been. Quite a character, Barba Nera. His boys ambushed a small German convoy and hijacked the medical vehicle, complete with doctor. Your father spoke to the medic in German, told him I was a partisan and if he treated me well he'd be released and if he didn't . . .' Van Rensburg lifted his right hand and drew it across his throat. 'Between them they saved my life.'

'But he must have known you were British.'

'I kept my mouth shut and we were both in the right kit, bits and pieces of German and Italian uniforms. Your father knew what he was doing when he kept that stuff.'

I stared at the fire, embarrassed. The implication was obvious: Father had used Luigi as bait for the others on the hillside and killed them all, the old woman included.

'Remember it was war and we'd just been betrayed,' Van Rensburg commented matter-of-factly. 'Your father would have been pretty hyped up, as the expression goes. And Barba Nera didn't object. Communists like him had very few scruples.'

61

'And Luigi?'

'Him? He was a rat. He killed Jack Robertson and he damn near killed me too. Must have thought he could save his skin by taking us to his headquarters. He was bloody wrong. They put him on trial at the village. I was a bit better by then. They brought me along as a witness. Couldn't follow it all though, my Italian wasn't up to the subtleties.'

Barba Nera presided over the People's Tribunal, conducting the proceedings from the steps of the church. All the approaches to the village were guarded. Luigi, unshaven, stood on a low wooden platform between two partisan soldiers. The crowd formed a horse-shoe around them, completely filling the little piazza. Watching from a chair to their side of the church steps, Van Rensburg strained to understand the proceedings.

'What have you to say?' Pointedly not calling him 'comrade', Barba Nera read out the charges of treachery. People in the crowd murmured and pushed for a better view.

'He promised me my life,' Luigi shouted, pointing a finger dramatically at Hartman, who was also on the steps, 'and don't Germans always keep their word?'

Uproar followed. Barba Nera looked momentarily pole-axed. The crowd surged and swayed, its attention wholly distracted from the accused.

'Does he say he is not German?' Luigi yelled. 'He's a liar.'

Hartman stepped forward, and raised his hands for silence, a young and powerful figure even in battledress that was now filthy and torn. Miraculously the crowd obeyed.

'I was born German, but like you I fight the Nazis.'

Barba Nera took the cue immediately, clapping his hands with great sweeping gestures. For a few seconds no one responded. Then, tumultuously, the mood changed. Barba Nera allowed time for the applause to die down, then addressed Hartman, though loudly enough for the benefit of the audience.

'This traitor says you promised to spare his life. Is that true?'

'No.'

Startled, Van Rensburg looked at Luigi, whose swarthy face became noticeably paler.

'I told this man if he brought us here he could put his life in my hands. He agreed.'

'And now?'

'Now I pass him to you.'

'Do you recommend mercy?'

'He should be shot.' The cold contempt in his sergeant's voice shook Van Rensburg. What had Jack said about him before this operation? He'd kill with his bare hands if necessary. He'd saved that bastard Luigi for just so long as he was useful.

'Does anyone want this traitor to live?' Barba Nera shouted and the crowd roared back its condemnation.

The sentence was carried out at once, in a field by the village, and Luigi was buried on the spot, without a headstone.

In the evening, suffering a recurrence of pain and half-drugged, Van Rensburg lay on a bed while Hartman and Barba Nera shared a meal. The next morning the paratroopers would leave with some thirty POWs whom the partisans had assembled. It was clear that during their brief acquaintanceship the sergeant and the partisan capo had established an effective rapport.

'Comrade,' Van Rensburg heard Barba Nera say, 'you have solved a problem for me. The general situation is too fluid to control. Discipline has become difficult. Your attitude was correct and already the word has gone round. There were very few like Luigi and after today there will be none.'

'I would like to thank you,' Hartman replied with laboured formality as if addressing a senior ally, 'for saving the captain's life. I hope that after the war the British authorities will recognize what you have done.'

'I shall not expect it. After the war, when we have thrown the Nazis out, we shall no longer need the Americans and British. We have better friends.'

Angered by what he could understand of this reply, Van Rensburg struggled to lift his head and intervene. Before he could speak he was astonished to glimpse the Italian clapping Hartman on the back in the most friendly way.

'But you, comrade, you will always be welcome in the Abruzzi.'

'I'm not sure I took in all the Italian words,' Van Rensburg said. 'I was pretty much under the weather. But that was the gist of it. Your father and he seemed to have an instinctive understanding, though Barba Nera must have been several years older. He was damn right about after the war too. Togliatti, who was the top communist, dropped all contact with the Allies who had helped him in spite of its being us who'd given him radios and money, not the Russians.' He kicked a log which was threatening to fall out of the fire. 'Well, it was all a long time ago and I'm lucky to be alive to tell the tale. Thought you might be interested to hear how I got to know Jim. The curious thing was that Barba Nera turned up here once. Late 1963 it must have been; a few weeks before Uhuru; sorry, Independence. He'd been visiting Somalia and came on down to talk to some trade unionists. He'd heard Jim had interests in Kenya and looked us up in the phone book.'

'So you did meet him again?' I had guessed as much.

'Don't forget it was he who kidnapped a doctor for me. I owed him a pretty solid debt of gratitude, whatever his politics.' Van Rensburg swallowed another healthy swig of whisky. He was enjoying this chance to reminisce. 'Since your father wasn't here I gave him the standard trip to Rukanga with a night at Kilaguni in the Tsavo on the way back. Weren't so many game lodges then. Intelligent bloke. He'd gone into politics. Didn't know any of the Italian settlers here though and didn't want to. My other idea'd been to show him Lake Naivasha. Quite a few Eyeties around there.'

'And after that?' I prompted.

'He went on to Tanzania. Something to do with the AGIP refinery contract in Dar. I offered a report to the Special Branch, but they weren't interested. Too busy handing over.' He grunted again. 'Stupid of me, I suppose. The Africans he'd been meeting were all public figures. Taught me to keep out of politics after Independence, if nothing else.' He hauled himself out of his chair. 'Time to hit the sack, I think. We've an early start. None of your English getting to work at ten here. The office opens at eight fifteen.'

I would have liked to ring Camilla, except that my one immediately relevant discovery of the day, namely the mysterious woman at the Norfolk, could not prudently be discussed on Van Rensburg's phone. However I did speak to Mother at Godstow and reassured her that I was receiving every assistance. She was being very brave, though I could sense the closeness of tears from the slight trembling of her voice. I no longer had the slightest doubt that coming out to Africa had been the right decision. I was already meeting too many evasions for comfort.

Van Rensburg then escorted me upstairs, though I disregarded his advice about going straight to bed. His story had left me feeling almost physically winded, once I realized that when he was in Italy Father had been eight years younger than I was now. He must have been as hard as hell: and did men like that mellow with age? Stalin chucked children under the chin in the same months that he was ordering mass murders. The cruelties of Middle Eastern rulers merely became more refined as they grew older, though they also showed more benevolence on occasion. The answer to my question was 'No'. Father would remain as ruthless at heart as he had been in Italy, right through to the time when senility crippled his mind.

I could not precisely see how Van Rensburg's story might relate to our present search, but I wanted it on tape none the less. So for twenty minutes, sitting on the side of my bed, I dictated quietly into the cassette recorder I had brought with me, concluding with

Van Rensburg's comments about the difference between such actions in wartime and in peacetime. I didn't agree with them. In fact I reckoned that if the Germans had won the war Father would have deserved to find himself on trial as a war criminal as well as a traitor. It was small wonder there had been official silence about precisely where and how he earned his medal.

As I undressed an extraordinary noise from outside made me open the window and look around. It was a croaking, rasping sound, half like a bark, half like old floorboards creaking. There was a nearly full moon, but I could see no creatures in the garden. The night was still, the Ngong Hills a dim outline, and as I listened I became aware of many other sounds: faint African music, insects, all kinds of cracklings and movements. This continent was as strange as it was immense. When I eventually fell asleep it was with the thought that I should take nothing here for granted.

CHAPTER SIX

I slept badly and woke the next morning out of a bad dream to the accompaniment of some tropical bird crying raucously outside. The nightmare was straight from a psychoanalyst's casebook. I was driving a car in which everything functioned in the opposite sense to normal. If I braked, it accelerated; if I tried to turn left it went right. When I came to, sweating profusely, I was about to hit a wall head-on.

Lying in bed as this dream faded, I found myself afraid that the search for my father was going to be similarly illogical: that people would insist his trip had been normal when everything, including Van Rensburg's 'no comment' and the mysterious woman at the Norfolk, shouted the contrary. A superbly equipped jet like the Gulfstream, flown by a pilot of Captain Holz's experience, could not just disappear. But today was Wednesday, May 26th, four days since the plane had lifted off the runway at Jomo Kenyatta airport and headed west. If it had crashed the likelihood of anyone being found alive must be decreasing hourly.

The bird outside screamed again and my mind switched back to the execution of Luigi, as Van Rensburg had described it. The ferocity of Father's response to betrayal did not square with the best way out of the fix he and his men were in. Nor did this apparently bitter hatred of anything connected with the Nazis tally with his postwar indifference to having his membership of the Hitler Youth publicized. He was an enigma.

Then, shaving, I found his image looking back at me from the mirror: softened by my being younger, yet still what he would have called 'a chip off the old block'. In his place would I in fact have acted as he had? Van Rensburg had talked about war's harsher realities. What if Africa's proved to be equally as harsh? What if Father had been kidnapped, as that newspaper suggested? There wouldn't be much room for sentiment in my own actions then.

Over breakfast I would have liked to ask outright whether everyone was going to maintain the pretences about Father's trip. But the bright and early atmosphere of the household made such an accusation out of place. Ambrose, the major domo, broad-faced and beaming, brought the bacon and eggs and coffee like a scene from the good old days and the only questions it was possible to ask centred on the various disturbances from the garden.

'I expect that bird was the Hadada ibis,' Mrs Van Rensburg said in a consoling voice. 'Look, there he is.'

She pointed out of the window. A large, dark brown bird with a metallic green glint in its body feathers and a long curved beak was strutting along, occasionally pecking at the grass in a discriminating kind of way.

'Searching for spiders,' she added. 'They do make a dreadful noise. They're related to the sacred ibis. What you heard last night must have been the hyraxes. There's a family of them. Furry things the size of a rabbit, though actually they have the same ancestor as the elephant.'

'Robert doesn't want a natural history lesson, Mary. He wants to know what today's programme is, eh?' Van Rensburg cut in. He must have sensed my unease. 'Is there anything you particularly want, old chap?'

'Yesterday didn't really make sense,' I remarked, circumspectly putting down my knife and fork to emphasize my point. 'I mean, if everything went so smoothly on Father's visit here, why should everyone be so noncommittal?'

'I warned you they would be cagey.'

'Father often changes his destination in mid-air. Could he have decided to visit another country instead of Zaïre?'

'Possibly.' His tone of voice did not welcome the idea. 'We've checked with the aviation authorities in Angola, Zambia, Zaïre, the Congo and the Central African Republic, as well as the other East African states. The Gulfstream has definitely not landed at any recognized airport.'

'Aren't there any clues?'

'What do you expect us to do?' Van Rensburg demanded, anger beginning to show. 'Search every bloody mile of bloody Africa? D'you realize the size of this continent?'

'Patrick! Please!' Mary Van Rensburg was looking genuinely distressed. 'The poor man's hardly been here twenty-four hours.'

'I'm sorry,' I interjected quickly, 'I didn't intend to be critical.' Which was nonsense, because I had, though not necessarily of him.

'Believe me, Robert,' he said, calming down, 'if I had any convincing leads I'd follow them. But it needs to be more than a wild goose chase.' He paused to drink some coffee. 'D'you want to phone your mother again?'

I considered the idea. I had spoken to her before going to bed last night and although taut and worried, she had sounded basically under control. 'It will come right in the end, Bob darling, I just know it will. I'm sure something quite simple has stopped him letting us know where he is.' Given her teeth-clenching optimism and the inhibiting effect the telephone always had on me, I could see no point in ringing again so soon. Besides it was only six fifteen in England, not that Mother would have minded. She must have been becoming desperate for news and feeling terribly cut off.

'I'd rather wait until this evening. The person I would like to call is my secretary.'

'Must be an early riser.'

'She gets paid.' I wasn't going to be hassled, even though his comment was good-humoured.

'Well, it's a good time for getting through,' he admitted. 'Come along to the study.'

Camilla sounded understandably sleepy. I asked her about progress, wondering if Van Rensburg would have picked up an extension to eavesdrop.

'Wait while I fetch my notes.' A pause, then more fully awake. 'Facts first. Hartman Trust shares fell again yesterday, closing 16 pence down on the day at £3.64. Consolidated were steady. The newspapers were full of the Falklands war – we lost two ships. But the City pages did carry a stonewalling statement from Stainton saying that in your father's absence the Board were reviewing the position and would meet again at the end of the week. Are you still there?'

'Yes. Try to speak slowly.' There was a kind of echo on the line, not surprising I suppose, given that our words were being bounced to and fro by a satellite.

'That's what's public, Bob. But the City's full of rumours about both companies. A friend of mine on the stock market says Consolidated's overvalued.'

'Why?'

'He's heard it could lose one of its most valuable diamond concessions on June 1st because the mine isn't producing enough.'

'Which country?'

'In Africa somewhere. He wouldn't say.'

I felt the familiar sick grip of apprehension in my stomach. Africa might be huge, but it could not be coincidence that Father had been here at a crucial time for his prey.

'Consolidated's Chairman has said any uninvited bid will be regarded as hostile,' she added.

So neither side would be choosy about its methods. Each would do everything to decry its rival's worth whilst trumpeting its own. How far would Father go to win?

'Camilla, listen. You must find out more.'

For heaven's sake, Bob, d'you know what time it is? You said seven or eight o'clock, not six.'

'Find out everything you can about Consolidated's problems.' Stupidly, I found myself half shouting, as though that would diminish the distance. 'How's your friend advising his clients?'

'To hold tight. His firm's economists are certain your father knows something no one else does.'

'Ask him why.'

The operator cut in, saying three minutes was up, asking if I wanted to extend.

'I'll phone again tomorrow,' I said, never imagining that the action might have been transferred to my end by then. 'Keep at it.'

When I left the study Van Rensburg was in the hall, ready to leave. Evidently he had respected the privacy of my phone call. He might be uncommunicative on occasion, but at least he was straight.

'Let's go down to Wilson and see what's up,' he suggested briskly. 'I keep a plane there myself. Thought if there's time to kill you might like to see Rukanga.'

'If there's time.' I would be intrigued, of course. That photograph of Father standing in the bush at Rukanga was part of the Trust's folklore. None the less, legend or no legend, it ungenerously crossed my mind that Van Rensburg might have reasons to want me out of Nairobi for the day. The woman watching us from the terrace of the Norfolk was still a puzzle. Had his presence dissuaded her from speaking to me? Jumping to conclusions, I guessed she would be back from her overnight safari by lunchtime.

'How far is it?' I asked.

'An hour and a half in the Cessna. We could take a packed lunch and be back in the early afternoon.'

I dismissed the conspiratorial fantasies. 'If nothing else is happening, I'd like to go.'

'Good.' He sounded relieved. 'Don't expect too much, though. The mine may have made Jim a millionaire, but it's basically just a hole in the ground.'

'So was Kimberley,' I said.

He grinned, and I felt we were getting on the same wavelength at last.

As I had feared, there was no news at Wilson airport. The search programme was continuing.

'Will you be speaking to the consul at Kisangani?' Van Rensburg asked the chief pilot.

'If we can get through. He's only there in the mornings. After one o'clock calls are put through to some lady running a school of English. All she ever tells us is to call again tomorrow between nine and one. It's a Catch 22 situation.'

'You can't dial from here?' I asked.

The pilot looked at me. 'To Zaïre? You must be joking, Sir. We're routing our calls through Brussels as it is because that's quicker. The mining company telex is OK, but they're not in phone contact with Kisangani.'

'Surely,' I persisted, 'the Zaïre authorities must be able to do something.'

'Robert.' Van Rensburg cut in curtly. 'What you read in handbooks and what's real are unrelated. Officially Zaïre is divided into provinces administered by governors whom the President appoints. In practice the provinces are private fiefdoms. Until we can establish a working relationship with this particular governor's Swiss bank account our best bet is the consul. He isn't around much but at least he's on our side.'

'You mean you have to pay the governor?'

'No option. And we won't know his price until we find the plane.' He drew in his breath. 'I'll say one thing for Kenya. Some of the politicians may be corrupt, but we wouldn't have this hassle.' He clapped his hand on my shoulder. 'Don't worry. It won't stop us. Just holds things up.' He turned to the pilot. 'We'll be back around four. Keep our fingers crossed, eh.'

The pilot cheerfully held up two intertwined fingers, but the confidence didn't deceive me. Even if by a miracle Father had not been injured, the tropical rain forest was still a dangerous and unhealthy environment, especially for a man over sixty, while if he was injured . . .

'Let's be on our way then.' Van Rensburg did not want to prolong the scene. He led me out to the tarmac, where his sleek red and white Cessna 210 was parked in a line of other planes. 'Best of the perks your father gives me,' he commented, as he did various external checks. 'Flying's the only way to get around Africa.'

Fifteen minutes later we took off, roaring low over the game park and then climbing on to a course roughly parallel to the Mombasa road, which threaded through the arid landscape like a black ribbon, the single track of the railway visible alongside. Although there had been murky cloud around Nairobi, down here it was clear.

'See a hundred miles on a day like this,' Van Rensburg remarked over the intercom, pointing out landmarks that meant nothing to me, except when he indicated the snow cap of Mount Kilimanjaro. Then the road slid away to our left and we circled with the wings

70

steeply tilted above an isolated and precipitous-sided hill, with great slides of exposed rock plunging into the vegetation of its lower slopes. There was a village of corrugated roofed huts, which glinted in the sun on either side of a dirt road. 'Rukanga,' he explained and began repeating, 'Rukanga, do you read, Rukanga mine, do you read' over the radio. There was no answer.

He swung out of the dizzying turn and headed over the bush, losing height rapidly. This was my first experience of such flying and I didn't even recognize that the short scrape of bare earth ahead of us was an airstrip until it became obvious we were landing. He stopped at the end to park by a small building and when he opened the aircraft's door the heat flooded in. We were three thousand feet lower than Nairobi and suddenly this felt like Africa in a way the city never had.

No one seemed to be around. With its engine stopped, the plane made small whirring and ticking noises, as though reluctant to be grounded. The iron-roofed building had its door heavily pad-locked. I noticed a tattered windsock hanging limp from a pole. There was no breath of wind.

'Have to wait until someone comes,' Van Rensburg said. 'They'll have heard us overhead.'

I walked a few yards away to relieve myself. What had appeared to be low scrub from the air was in fact close-packed bushes and small trees, though few had any leaves. Something stabbed my leg, making me wince, and I found it was a thorn three inches long, as sharp as a miniature stiletto. The ground was hard and dry and the puddle I made was instantly absorbed, leaving only a damp stain. I realized with shock that the land was dying.

'No rain.' Van Rensburg echoed my observation as I rejoined him, wishing I had brought a hat for the broiling sun. 'No rain for two years down here. Believe it or not this is a ranch.'

The rumble of an approaching vehicle interrupted him and a moment later a much dented dark green Land Cruiser drew up in a cloud of dust, which hung in the air as a paunchy African in fawn slacks and a short-sleeved shirt jumped out. He greeted Van Rensburg like the lost prodigal, grasping his hand between both palms with such ebullience that I thought the black and white checked cap perched on his head would fall off.

'Hey Patrick! Long time you haven't been here. Too long. Too long. Who's this you've brought? Aaiah! The bwana mkubwa's son!' He turned to me and pumped my hand in turn. 'Jackson is my name. Jackson Magugu. Have you come to see what makes the world go round? I don't need to tell Sir Hartman's son. Pretty stones make the world go round, don't they Patrick? Pretty stones and pretty women.'

'Keeps his own wife tucked away safely in Machakos, though,' Van Rensburg roared. 'Wouldn't trust her not to start prospecting on her own, would you bwana?' He slapped Jackson on the shoulder. 'An old rascal, he is. Prettiest lady in Kenya and he keeps her under lock and key.'

'Oh women!' the African chuckled. They were obviously great friends. 'He is right. With women too many problems. Too many.' He grinned at me, teeth flashing. 'So you want to see what your father bought from the *serikali*. I will show you.'

He drove us with surprising care along narrow tracks through the bush, interspersing comments on the dangers of a breakdown with cheerful gossip until we reached a high barbed-wire fence, enclosing buildings and a watchtower.

Two languid security guards in brown drill uniforms and construction site hard hats eased themselves to their feet and let us through the gate. Jackson took us first to his house, a stone bungalow with a corrugated iron roof. Close to it was a small patch of garden with unfamiliar bright bushes sprouting from the reddish earth.

'Pawpaw,' he said with pride, 'and I have crossed orange with grapefruit. Very fine.' He waved his hands vigorously at the flat landscape and sighed. 'No water. No water here. If there is water you can grow vegetables for the whole world. But we have to bring water by truck, every drop.'

'You need something other than money to care about in this wilderness,' Van Rensburg commented.

I tried to imagine him and Father camped here all those years ago and failed to come up with a vision. How did they decide where to dig?

'If it hadn't been for the water,' he explained, when we were indoors sipping squash made from Jackson's special fruit, 'no one would have found the rubies. This area's on the border of Tsavo National Park. The Game Department were digging a dam on a dry riverbed, we call them luggas, streams that only flow in the rains. Hardly dug a few feet before they began turning up garnets. They're often found along with rubies. One of the local game wardens was a friend. He tipped me off and I pegged our concession ahead of the rush.'

'Frien's.' Jackson remarked. 'All a man needs in life is frien's. Tell Sir Hartman's son how much you pay your game warden frien'.'

'Case of whisky.'

'But for the concession, much more?'

Van Rensburg shook his head firmly. 'Standard government fees. It was different then.'

'Oh, those fine days,' Jackson observed, with cheerful irony. 'Do you tell me there was no chai? No chai for the *serikali*?'

72

'The *serikali*,' Van Rensburg explained, 'is the government and chai doesn't only mean tea. All right, bwana,' he admitted, 'in those days we knew the right people. And in 1957 the Mau Mau was keeping everyone busy up in the Highlands so the administration weren't too bothered. Until Independence. Then it began.'

'After Uhuru we were not so stupid, eh?'

'Come on Jackson.' Van Rensburg rose to his feet. The two men's bantering relationship had reached an unspoken frontier with those questions of corruption.

We left the house and walked across the red earth of the mine compound to where a primitive system of wooden scaffolding and pulleys rose at the edge of a vast pit. Stopping, Jackson scuffed the dust with his foot and picked up several tiny stones, all a dull raspberry colour. 'Rubies,' he said. 'Too small for cutting. For cutting they must be one gram weight.'

'The surface ones are alluvial.' Van Rensburg explained. 'Left by a river millions of years ago. Further down there's a primary deposit.' He pointed into the pit, the sides of which had been cut into galleries down to a depth of perhaps seventy feet. The drill marks for explosive charges had left channels in the greyish white rock. Down in the bottom labourers were shifting stone on to primitive hoists. 'The host rock of the rubies is formed from limestone which has been metamorphosed into a kind of marble. Bloody hard. The veins run through it. We were lucky. A rich one ran through our concession and they've gone on digging it out ever since. Each year the hole gets wider and the Trust gets richer. The government too.'

'Last week,' Jackson said proudly, 'we have one and a half million shillings of uncut stones.'

'Seventy-five thousand pounds, give or take exchange rate fluctuations.' Van Rensburg translated. 'Four million quid a year. Or would be if production kept level. Doesn't of course. But there's still a healthy turnover. And look at the overheads! Peanuts.'

I stood and surveyed the mine, the sweating labourers shifting earth and rock with an unhurried rhythm, the buckets and ropes and wooden poles. The basic methods could not have changed in hundreds of years, thousands even.

'Pretty much of a gamble, this kind of mining,' Van Rensburg said. 'Several of the adjoining concessions went bankrupt. Not like copper in Zambia or alluvial diamonds in Guinea, where you can assess the yield in advance and justify all the infrastructure, excavators and dump trucks and housing. With rubies you make an initial investment and hope for the gamble to pay off.'

'The big win,' Jackson said. 'That is what I call the big win.'

A shout interrupted him. An African was waving from beside a truck which appeared to have broken down. He apologized and left us.

'Great bloke that, the whole operation would grind to a halt without him.' Van Rensburg clicked his teeth despondently. 'And we only pay him a pittance. Typical. Jim insists we don't spoil the market by paying expatriate salaries to locals.' He glanced at me, no doubt remembering Father's much publicized support for a campaign to increase black wage levels in South Africa, where we had no interests. 'In fairness, the government here pays officials lousily too.'

'And what's this mine worth?' I watched the men rhythmically labouring in the deep hole.

'Today? Around eleven million on the Nairobi Stock Exchange. Was capitalized nearer twenty. Your father floated the shares during the coffee boom in the late Seventies. Damn good sense of timing, Jim.'

None of this fitted the pioneering image. 'Where did you start digging originally?' I asked, to change the subject.

'Long time ago. Memory plays tricks.' He looked around, then gestured at a clump of leafless, thorn trees near the manager's house. 'Over there I pitched a couple of pukka safari tents. Scrounged some old army ones for the labour. Hired most of the men up in Wundanyi. They've a long tradition of mining round the Taita Hills. Had a three-tonner to bring in supplies. First big improvement was buying a diesel generator. I was able to do that after your father took over the concession.'

'You both lived pretty rough, even so?' I commented, still remembering the photograph.

He gave me a quizzical look. 'You might say so. I was out in this bloody bundu for two years. Jim had other fish to fry.'

'I thought you did the pioneering together.'

As I spoke memories stirred, telling me the legend could not be true. In 1957 I had been five. Mother never took me to Kenya and Father, although he was away for long periods, had certainly not been abroad for two years.

'If you'd like to hear the story,' Van Rensburg eyed me intently again, 'I'll tell you the gist of it while we're waiting for Jackson. Let's go back to the house anyway. Might as well have some more of that squash.' He wiped his brow with his forearm. 'Doesn't get any cooler down here, that's for sure.' He led the way across the hard ground.

We went inside, to the living room of the house, with its simple wooden table and chairs and a large radio transmitter on a shelf by one wall. He took a glass jug from the refrigerator.

'I would like to hear about Rukanga,' I conceded, accepting the drink he poured. 'But I'd like even more to know if Father was visiting any of Consolidated's concessions on his present trip. You said yourself that it's cheaper to take over existing mines than prospect for new ones.'

'Can be,' he corrected me. 'Certainly was down here.'

Van Rensburg possessed a buffalo-like obstinacy. He seemed as determined to tell me about Rukanga as not to talk about Consolidated. I tried again, obliquely.

'You mean there are parallels?'

'Between what?'

I gave up. Perhaps the past would illuminate the present. In a sense anything I discovered about Father would. I asked him to tell the story.

'May not be quite the version you heard at home.' He allowed himself a reflectively inward smile and chuckled. 'But it's how your father made what old Jackson calls the "big win". Put him on the map as a businessman. He founded the Hartman Trust out here, you know. Protected my interests and chiselled me at one and the same time.' He leant his arms on the rough table. 'Tell you something, Bob. Saving a man's life puts you under a kind of obligation. It was your father who kept in touch with me after the war, not the other way around. Then, one day in March 1957, he cabled that he was arriving . . .'

CHAPTER SEVEN

The Colony and Protectorate of Kenya had no international airport in those days. The civil terminal at the Royal Air Force's Eastleigh aerodrome was a low wooden building with a verandah, like an oversized sports pavilion. The runway was dirt surfaced and clouds of red dust rose from it whenever aircraft landed or took off. As Van Rensburg waited for the passengers arriving from London a middle-aged woman in the small crowd of settlers displayed a little pearl-handled revolver to a friend, made an abrasive remark about 'no bloody Kuke's going to catch me napping,' and holstered it in her handbag. A white police officer standing near them grinned.

This was the height of the Mau Mau terrorist Emergency and there were more soldiers and police in the terminal than civilians. Van Rensburg carried a gun himself whenever he was up-country. Now he stood, gently sweating despite his loose-fitting safari suit, and wondered how Jim Hartman would react to a colony in ferment. Come to that, would they recognize each other? Yes, he decided, Hartman's was a face one could not forget.

The low whine of a plane's engines sounded in the distance and Van Rensburg thought of the loyal yet sporadic correspondence Hartman had maintained with him over the ten years since their demobilization. The first Christmas card had come from Germany. Odd that Hartman should have accepted a posting to his homeland in the circumstances, with his parents dead. Possibly it had been a way of staying on in the army longer. No-one could blame the poor bugger for that, when he had no family. But Germany? There must have been a reason.

Interspersed with the Christmas cards there had been occasional letters. Van Rensburg sensed that each marked a definite step in his friend's progress. They were like pegs staking out the ground of a career: though not of a career that had any conventional or specific direction.

The first, forwarded to South Africa, where Van Rensburg was completing a degree in geology at the University of the Witwatersrand, mentioned that 'after some difficulties' Hartman had established a property company.

The second reached the family farm up at Molo in the Kenya Highlands early in 1951. It wasn't so much a letter as a note attached to an invitation printed in formal script on thick, crisp, expensive paper. The note read, 'I am a very lucky man, as always. I hope one day you will meet Anne.' The invitation was to attend the marriage of Anne Felicity, daughter of Major-General and Mrs C. J. Hewlett, to Captain James Hartman, late the Parachute Regiment, at the Church of All Saints, Dogmersfield, Hampshire.

Van Rensburg read this looking out over the broad landscape of the farm and laughed his head off at the rascal using a temporary military rank as if he'd been a regular officer. At the club on Sunday he asked various ex-army friends if they'd heard of General Hewlett. Quite a number of soldier settlers had gone to Kenya after the war. His acquaintances all produced different answers. Hewlett had been a cavalryman, a sapper, a Guards officer. He'd been tall with a bristling moustache and a temper to match; he'd been fat, pompous and far from competent. They only agreed on one point: namely that major-generals had been two a penny at the end of the war. Van Rensburg bought them Tusker beers and laughed some more at his ambitious sergeant fixing himself a place in society by marrying a general's daughter.

When he was next in Nairobi he called at Rowland Ward's shop and arranged for six cut glass tumblers engraved with wildlife scenes to be delivered in England in time for the wedding. He asked the retired major who ran the firm about General Hewlett, and he thought that was the feller who'd won a DSO in the western desert commanding a gunner regiment.

A year later Hartman cabled asking him to be godfather to his son. The telegram reached Van Rensburg in the wilds of Tanganyika, where he was working as a geologist at the Williamson diamond mine. He declined with genuine regret, on the grounds that he so seldom came to Britain. After that he effectively forgot about Hartman for several years, though maintaining the Christmas card ritual. He was fully occupied launching his own mining career.

In 1956 Van Rensburg quit Tanganyika, took his own destiny by the scruff of the neck, and raised the money to exploit a claim he staked at Rukanga. Venture capital wasn't easy to come by at the height of the Emergency. Business confidence was low: so, however, was the price of the concession. He found rubies, but not enough. The mine drank money as fast as the dry bushland absorbed rain. By early 1957 he had only enough resources for

another four months' operations and it was then that he remembered part of Hartman's third letter, received long ago and
disregarded.

'I am now connected with an Italian industrial group and have
colleagues interested in Africa. If you know of any long-term investment opportunities, send details. You would receive a normal
commission.'

A pretty uninspiring communication, he had thought at the
time. He didn't want to be associated with Eyeties either. It was
as a last resort, after two days of painful discussions with the
accountants, that he sent a telegram to Hartman. The response
had been immediate. Now, as he watched the airliner land in a
trail of dust and turn sedately off the runway, he wondered what
kind of business relationship could be established with the man to
whom he owed his life. On one point he was determined. He
would accept an investment, but he himself must remain the boss.

The airliner was huge, a turbo-prop newly introduced to the
route by BOAC. They called it the 'whispering giant'. Van
Rensburg watched with interest from his place in the crowd as
it taxied slowly towards the terminal building.

At the periphery of his vision a British army officer, immaculate
in service dress and bedecked with the gold aiguillettes of a
Governor's ADC, walked out in front of the verandah, as Africans
in white overalls hurried forward with the aircraft steps. Yet another important person must be on the plane, one of the stream of
officials and MPs from Britain whom the Emergency attracted.
Bloody parasites, Van Rensburg thought, if they'd only turn the
spotlight off we settlers might have a chance.

The plane's door opened. The ADC was standing at the bottom
of the steps. A stewardess's blue-hatted head appeared briefly,
then withdrew and the first passenger came down, a tall man in a
grey pinstripe suit carrying a briefcase. The ADC saluted and was
ushering him away before Van Rensburg recognized the face he
hadn't seen for so long. Hurriedly he pushed his way back through
the crowd to the entrance, fearing that Hartman would be gone
before he could reach him.

A potentially humiliating chase was only averted when he heard
his name called over the primitive public address system. Outside
the building, where his battered Land-Rover was parked, he found
the ADC, who saluted with something less than enthusiasm.

'Mr Van Rensburg? How do you do, Sir. I believe you are also
meeting Captain Hartman.'

'Correct.' Although aware of how crumpled his safari suit
looked, because he had started from Rukanga in the early hours,
he still nearly choked at the use of Hartman's wartime rank. He
was just as much Captain Van Rensburg.

'His Excellency has invited the captain to stay with him at Government House. Unless, of course' – here the young ADC's polished voice became deprecating – 'you have made other arrangements.'

In fact Van Rensburg had booked rooms for both of them at Muthaiga, the settlers' club, intending thereby to demonstrate that Hartman would be socially acceptable in the colony. That made a pretty sick joke now. He muttered that his plans were flexible.

'His Excellency will be delighted.' The ADC's face cleared. 'If you have no other plans he hopes you can dine at Government House tonight.'

Van Rensburg accepted with as much good humour as he could manage. The settlers seldom saw eye to eye with the Governor of the time and never had done, often with reason.

At this point Hartman himself walked across, having checked that the driver had retrieved the right suitcase from the customs.

'Good of you to meet me, Patrick.' He shook hands firmly. All trace of his former German accent had vanished. 'My father-in-law insisted on telling the Governor I was coming. Didn't know how to get hold of you at the last moment.'

Van Rensburg clasped his hand in return, mollified and at the same time noticing how much the ex-sergeant had changed. His thin face had filled out. He was self-assured and, unlike normal passengers emerging from the overnight flight, he looked fresh and must have shaved and put on a clean shirt before the landing. He wore a regimental tie and his suit was expensively hand-stitched round the lapels. Everything about him announced that this was a man to reckon with.

'You couldn't have got hold of me anyway,' Van Rensburg said. 'I've been at the mine. Thought we'd go down there tomorrow.'

Hartman glanced at the ADC. 'How does that sound?' He was obviously sticking with the more influential of his two hosts.

'Will you be needing transport, Sir?' The ADC was cautious. 'I'm not certain that we could fly you down. Operational requirements up-country and all that.'

'No airstrip anyway,' Van Rensburg said, adding, 'Yet,' as an optimistic afterthought. 'If you don't mind the slipway to the sea I'll drive you myself.'

The Mombasa road, very little of which was tarmacked, was notorious. However the ADC seemed relieved and so was Van Rensburg. He had already guessed that Hartman's trip would be short and he needed time alone with him.

That evening, uncomfortable in a borrowed dinner jacket because his own was at his parents' farm, Van Rensburg joined the party at the white colonial mansion which was the Governor's residence. The eighteen guests were a mix of officials, elected members of the colony's Legislative Council – known as the 'Legco' – and prominent settlers. The only Africans present were the servants, in starched white uniforms and red tarboosh hats, scurrying to bring food and wine to the long polished table, set with silver and flowers.

During the meal Van Rensburg was seated away from Hartman, though he caught snatches of conversation.

'Shot the gang, shot their own cook, even shot the bloody dog!' A middle-aged settler was relating a tale about two women defending their farmhouse against raiders. 'Hell of a pair, deserved a medal, not that they'll get one.' He lowered his tone. 'Don't take any notice of those bloody politicians at home, Stonehouse and that Castle bitch. This is a white man's country and it's going to stay one.'

'What about Kenyatta?' Hartman asked.

The question cut into the conversation like ice. It was nearly five years since the veteran black politician Jomo Kenyatta had been jailed for managing the Mau Mau insurrection. The settler's wife glared. The Governor paused in mid-sentence, not grateful to his guest for singling out this explosive topic but prepared to deal with it.

'The Gold Coast will be independent soon,' Hartman said quietly. 'Won't you have to come to terms with the Africans here?'

'There is really no question of Kenyatta being released,' an official remarked with strained casualness. 'I agree there are acceptable younger leaders like Mboya who might be given some responsibility. In time. Does that concern you?'

'Stability does.'

'Quite right.' A Legco member named MacDonald intervened to defuse the unwelcome tension. He was a paunchy, balding man in his sixties who effectively represented Nairobi's business community. 'We have to put the economy back on its feet before anything else. People at home don't appreciate the Mau Mau's basically a Kikuyu affair. No problems where Patrick has his mine, I promise.'

'Only elephant and lion,' Van Rensburg said. The last thing he wanted was to have the conversation revolve either around terrorist atrocities or politics.

'For investment, stability is essential.' Hartman sounded weightily Teutonic, good though his accent was. 'As I have learnt,' he continued without changing his tone, 'having recently had my Egyptian property confiscated.'

As the implications of this deadpan remark sank in there was a buzz of sympathetic comment. The British, French and Israeli attack on Egypt and capture of the Suez Canal the previous autumn had split public opinion as seldom before. The withdrawal from Suez, under American pressure, was just beginning to be seen as a watershed of British influence and power. Hartman had made his point.

'Can't blame you being cautious,' MacDonald agreed. 'Once bitten, twice shy. What did they take off you?'

'A cotton estate. By a miracle I've been given compensation.'

'You were damn lucky,' the official remarked. 'Can't be many who have.'

'I am lucky,' Hartman said.

With that the Governor's wife steered the conversation on to the less dangerous subject of racing. However, when the ladies withdrew and the servants brought brandy and cigars, Hartman resumed his discussion with MacDonald, flatteringly asking for his opinion on local conditions, until to Van Rensburg's annoyance they arranged a meeting in the morning.

'Come to my office in Delamere Avenue, everyone knows where I am,' MacDonald offered, adding cheerfully, 'No problem that can't be solved with a spot of good will.'

'Jim,' Van Rensburg interrupted, 'we have to leave early. It's a full seven-hour drive.'

'We went over the accounts this afternoon. The geological survey I read before dinner.' Hartman blew out cigar smoke in a luxurious, almost insolent way. 'Do we need to spend so long at the mine?'

The implication was obvious. Why go at all? Van Rensburg gripped his temper, though the blood still came to his face.

'You must see the concession,' he said tightly, choking back the years of labour, sweat and frustration he had already invested in it, the hopes, the money and the fears.

'Certainly ought to,' MacDonald chipped in tactfully. 'People have bought land here off prospectuses before and lived to regret it.' He winked studiously at Van Rensburg. 'No offence meant, of course.' He paused, his tone became sly. 'On the edge of the Tsavo Reserve, isn't it?' He glanced at Hartman again. 'Need any introductions in the Game Department, Captain?'

'What for?' Van Rensburg demanded. 'The Tsavo Warden's as jealous as hell of every inch he owns.'

'The whole eight thousand square miles?' Hartman asked. 'How well is the boundary marked?'

'Your guest's been doing his homework.' MacDonald commented.

'They'll never let us prospect inside the Reserve.'

'Far be it from me . . .' MacDonald said, and let the matter drop.

The next day had an infuriating inevitability about it: at least from Van Rensburg's point of view. He hung around drinking coffee in the New Stanley Hotel while Hartman's private meeting with MacDonald dragged on. Then his visitor had no suitable clothes. They had to acquire a bush shirt, trousers and hat from a safari outfitter. When they finally drove out to the Princess Elizabeth highway and headed southeast for the long, dusty Mombasa road it was nearly three o'clock and they had less than four hours of daylight left. Van Rensburg was so angry that he remained tautly silent for the first part of the journey.

An hour out of Nairobi it began to rain as they were descending a long escarpment. In places the rutted road became greasy and treacherous. Instead of being blinded by red dust as they overtook trucks, they now had the windscreen splashed with mud, the wipers clearing only a narrow arc of vision. Further on, near an African village called Kiboko, the Land-Rover juddered and began shaking rhythmically. Van Rensburg swore and pulled into the side. The rear offside tyre was flat. In the course of changing it they were both splattered with mud by passing vehicles.

'Should have brought a boy with me,' Van Rensburg muttered, straightening up after tightening the last wheel nut. 'Better stop the night at Mtito Andei. Get a bed and a meal.'

'Is it possible to reach Rukanga tonight?'

'Anything's possible.'

'Then we go on.'

'Could be awkward if we run into trouble. It's only a track through the bush for the last forty miles.'

'We should go on.' Hartman released the jack and stowed it in the back of the vehicle, for the moment reverting to the role of subordinate. 'You want me to drive?'

'Fine.'

Van Rensburg climbed in the passenger seat, saying nothing more as they drove on, in the way they used to in the army. The sun came out and began to dry the land. On either side of the road a haze of steam rose from stunted grass that was already tinged green with fresh growth. He slid open the window and smelt the air, clean from the rain, thinking about Africa and that there was nowhere else he wanted to be. He was thirty-seven and he had everything he needed from life. Almost. Everything except the capital to develop the mine, and a wife. He wondered why Hartman had lunched with the banker. Maybe he didn't have so much money either. You could pay too high a price for money, he reflected. He wasn't going to wind up working for his ex-sergeant after the experiences of the past twenty-four hours. He should have remembered that Hartman took men as far as they could go; and then further. That had always been the secret of his 'luck'.

Mtito Andei was a short line of petrol stations, African huts and primitive tin-roofed shops. While the tyre was being mended they had beer and sandwiches at the Tsavo Inn and the light faded with the disconcerting speed that night falls on the Equator. When they set off again Van Rensburg drove. After another hour he turned right off the main road and eventually left on to a farm track.

'Going through a ranch,' he said. 'More game than cattle. Pity you can't see the country.'

For mile after mile the track ran bumpily straight, the headlamps occasionally reflected back from the twin pinpricks of the eyes in the surrounding bush.

'Buck,' Van Rensburg said once. 'Tell from the colour.'

The track became winding and sandier and they came to a stretch littered with thorn bushes that forced Van Rensburg first to slow down to walking pace, then to stop altogether. Piles of dung lay among the strewn thorns.

'Elephant,' he said matter-of-factly, reaching down to detach a rifle from its mount behind the seat. 'They tear down the bushes. Have to clear the way, we don't want another bloody puncture. You bring her forward, slowly.' He got out, gun in hand, and began dragging the branches to the side.

He was still pulling away thorns by the light of the headlamps when Hartman saw him straighten, half turn, then quickly transfer the gun to his right hand and work the bolt. A second later, from alarmingly close by, came a squealing, trumpeting roar. Van Rensburg retreated to stand alongside the Land-Rover. As he reached it a cow elephant lumbered on to the track, a calf a quarter her size trailing behind. She faced them, her huge ears flapping, her dark bulk made more menacing by the single source of light, reared up her trunk, her small tusks dimly white, and trumpeted again. Beyond her other shapes appeared, only partially visible, waving their trunks like distant ghosts. Then as Van Rensburg raised his rifle to his shoulder, Hartman involuntarily revved the engine.

The cow screamed a third time, infuriated, ready to charge. Then, for whatever reason, she swung her massive head angrily around, turned and lurched away into the bush, the calf following close to her flank. Further off, with ponderous deliberation, more elephant crossed the track. Van Rensburg lowered his rifle.

'Stay quiet. Give them time.'

He stood still, looking away from the headlights in the direction the elephant had come. Even without the noise of the engine to mask their movement he would barely have known they were there. Only the crack of a snapping twig had alerted him. Despite their size they passed in silence through the scrub. This was their country. Men were the intruders. Chancing on game at night, when the wildlife was so active, always made him feel like this. Tomorrow, in daylight, he would again be wholly absorbed by the demands of the mine. He waited until he was satisfied that the whole herd had passed, then finished picking up the branches.

'How many were they?' Hartman asked.

'Thirty, fifty, God knows.'

'And the price of ivory?'

'Too bloody attractive. Not a business I want to be in.'

They reached the concession shortly before eleven to find the nightwatchman wrapped in an old army greatcoat, sitting in a chair by the gate, and fast asleep. Van Rensburg shone a torch in his face and he jumped into wakefulness, making a great fuss over welcoming them and stumbling away to rouse a young African overseer named Jackson. Hurricane lamps were lit and the camp fire revived.

'We have believed you are not coming, bwana,' Jackson apologized. 'You want *chakula*?'

'What'll you have, Jim?' Van Rensburg asked. 'Bangers, eggs, beans. Pretty basic, I'm afraid. Like the camp. We eat in the open. My tent doubles as an office.'

Hartman decided on the lot and checked his own tent over while they were being cooked. He hadn't slept on a camp bed or used a hurricane lamp since the army. When the sausages arrived, spitting hot in the pan, they reinforced the memories.

'Like old times,' Van Rensburg echoed.

'Here.' Hartman planted a bottle of whisky on the table. 'A contribution. Keeps the cold out, as they say.'

'Let's have some then.'

Hartman poured a generous slug into each of the cheap tumblers and raised his. 'To our cooperation. Prosit.'

'Cheers. Could have used more of this in Italy. Not so clever to drink here, though, by oneself.'

Hartman made no comment and they began to eat. The table stood only a few feet from the fire and as the flames took hold of the fresh wood they cast more light than the hurricane lamp. A distant grunt signified some unseen animal. The night had an atmosphere of its own, and after a while Van Rensburg began to relax, as though he had come home. He noticed Hartman watching him covertly and that he drank very sparingly. For him this was purely business. He would never get sentimental about Africa. There would never be any choice if there was conflict between the interests of wildlife and the interests of the mine. Whereas, Van Rensburg reflected, for his own part he was motivated as much by enjoyment of pioneering as by money.

'You get lonely?' Hartman asked.

'With all these rubies around!' The truth was he got as lonely as hell these days. It wasn't the conditions. He knew how to live in the bush. What he could not do was bring a wife here and he wanted to get married. Christ, you could look at being thirty-seven two ways. You were young or you were getting old. With the war and working down at Williamson's, he had delayed long enough. Now he'd found the girl, Mary Roberts, and she wouldn't wait for ever. There were too many hungry men in Nairobi: army, businessmen, hunters. He needed to buy a house and marry her, before someone else did. But his entire capital was committed to this hole in the ground.

'Plenty to keep me occupied down here,' he said. 'Another year and Rukanga'll be in full production.'

'You have decided a price?'

'A value. I'm not selling. I'm looking for a partner.'

Hartman poured himself more whisky, and cradled the glass in his hand. A giant moth brushed past his cheek, fluttering and dancing around the fire until its wings were incinerated and its fat body hissed in the ashes.

'You make a living, Patrick? The accounts suggest not.'

'Within limits.'

A puff of wind drifted wood smoke in their direction. Van Rensburg rubbed his eyes. His moment of contentment was lost anyway, his features looked strained in the flickering light. Hartman noticed and said nothing.

'Why don't we talk figures tomorrow, when you've seen the mine.' The figures were the weak spot, open to be exploited.

'As you like.' Hartman leaned back in the canvas chair, his elbows on its wooden arms, his feet stretched out towards the warmth, sipping the whisky contemplatively and very slowly; deliberately adopting the mood of relaxation which Van Rensburg himself could no longer maintain.

'There is one thing,' he said. 'I do not want unfair advantages. You should not feel under an obligation for the past.'

'Saving my life, you mean?' Van Rensburg stared into the fire. 'Fact is, you did.' Even though he'd been under morphine much of the time during their escape, he knew that.

'You can as well say that I did not.' Hartman looked at his host. 'I saved you only when you had survived already. The blokes gave you first aid.' For a moment he lapsed into the almost forgotten language of an NCO. 'After that bastard threw the grenade I had to knock the shit out of him. No fucking option.'

'Why didn't you simply shoot him?' By the time Van Rensburg had recovered, Hartman had been promoted away from the unit and no one discussed the incident.

'Shoot him? He was the only one who could take us to the partisans. My problem was persuading him he wasn't the walking dead. Which he was, the lousy bugger. Lucky he was such a shit he believed he could get away with it.' Hartman gave a guttural grunt, aware he was losing the moral supremacy of a moment ago, knowing also that this ghost had to be laid for the sake of the future. 'I suppose you want to know if I killed the old farmer and his wife? Of course. They'd betrayed us too.'

'They must have been forced into it.'

'Forced? They knew bloody well who was who in the mountains. They knew who was collaborating with the Germans, and who wasn't. It's only in cities you don't know what the neighbours are doing. They betrayed their own organization. For me, that was enough.'

Van Rensburg shivered, feeling suddenly cold, and drained his whisky. He stood up.

'Past history. The citation says you saved my life.'

'History is what the authorities want believed. You owe me nothing.'

'At least you gave the right orders.'

'True,' Hartman grunted again. 'That was something I discovered I could do.' He hoisted himself upright and clapped Van Rensburg on the shoulder self-confidently. 'The debt, my friend, is from me to you. Remember that tomorrow when we talk. You gave me the chance. A strange place, the Abruzzi.'

'Don't imagine you'd ever want to go back.' Van Rensburg twisted the cap back on to the whisky bottle. 'In the circumstances.'

'On the contrary. I took Anne during our honeymoon.'

Van Rensburg was about to express astonishment when he recalled lying on a stretcher and overhearing the partisan leader's parting words. 'Your action was correct. You will always be welcome.'

'Barba Nera must have been quite a character,' he said.

'If he should ever come here, make him welcome. He's given me useful introductions.'

'A communist in business?'

'The dichotomy is more apparent than real.' Hartman moved towards his tent, where a hurricane lamp stood on the grass by the pole. 'Through him I represent two Italian corporations. Goodnight, Jim.'

Van Rensburg re-opened the whisky, threw another thorn branch on the fire, and sat for a long time staring into the flames. He didn't know how the hell Hartman had managed it, but the man certainly had a soldier's gift for landing on his feet; and for exploiting every opportunity. He tried to imagine introducing a young British general's daughter to a guerrilla chieftain like Barba Nera and failed: let alone emerging with a business agency afterwards. Small wonder that after ten years Hartman was a rich man. When he eventually retired to his tent it was in the sorrowful and yet relieved knowledge that tomorrow would be his last day as sole owner of the Rukanga mine.

Next day Jackson woke them at dawn with mugs of strong tea. Sunlight slanted in as Hartman opened the tent flap. He swung himself carefully off the low canvas bed, realizing that he had slept more soundly than for months, pulled on his trousers and went outside. The air was cool, the sky blue, birds sang in the bushes. Van Rensburg joined him, dressed in khaki shorts and a faded bush jacket.

'Like to take a look around straightaway?'

Hartman delayed long enough to shave in a bucket of hot water. Then they set off round the concession. There was not a great deal to see. The main pit, irregularly rectangular and in places twenty feet deep, stopped some fifty yards short of a barbed-wire perimeter fence. Van Rensburg scuffed the ground with his boot and showed off tiny, dull dark red stones that had been lying in the dust.

'Don't become clear until they're cut. A lot of alluvial stones on the surface.' He threw the specimen away. 'All too small to cut. The good ones are in the limestone underneath.'

'The vein runs that way?' Hartman pointed to the fence.

'I think so. Pretty narrow where we've dug so far. Veins can go wider in a fold of rock or a fault, which is what we seem to be reaching now. Should widen a lot before the fence. You could take the stones out with your bare hands, or just a hammer. Problem is the rock above.'

'And beyond the fence?'

'Game Department. Fence is for my benefit, not theirs. Had a hard time making them agree where the boundary runs.'

Hartman surveyed the flat landscape on the other side, the sun gilding the branches of the thorn trees.

'The vein will be wider inside the Reserve?'

'I told you, the Game Department won't part with a square inch.'

They turned back, examining the ropes and pulleys serving the main pit, into which diggers were now descending, hammers slung from their belts.

'Labour's cheap enough,' Van Rensburg said, 'but I could use better drilling gear and trucks, not to mention a generator.'

'Let's talk over breakfast,' Hartman said abruptly. 'You are without question under-capitalized.' His expression was critical and Van Rensburg guessed from the way he tested a strand of barbed wire fence with his fingers that he thought the security poor.

They ate in the open again, with rock samples and maps covering most of the table, scarcely leaving room for their plates and a dented aluminium coffee pot.

'So,' Hartman asked eventually, 'how much have you in mind?'

'Twenty thousand. With twenty I can buy equipment, increase the labour force, extend up to the fence.'

Hartman checked the figures, scribbling calculations on a pad with a gold propelling pencil. 'You said you want a partner? What percentages do you suggest?'

'Sixty forty. I'm putting in the expertise, remember?'

'And you've spent twenty thousand to date.'

'Of mine and the bank's.'

'What about the Emergency? What does the bank feel?'

Van Rensburg shrugged his shoulders. It was futile making pretences.

'Nearly half the colony's budget being spent on prisons and security. The manager considers further investment too risky.'

'I agree. Until this can become an independent African State.'

'For God's sake, Jim, you're talking about thirty years, if ever.'

'You do accept the principle, however? Would you train Jackson as a manager?'

'I am training Jackson.' He was on the verge of losing his temper. 'If you want to play politics, go back to London.'

'Tomorrow I shall.' Hartman's deep voice became incisive and unyielding. 'I'll make you an offer. I will buy you out for thirty-five thousand, appoint you Managing Director at three thousand a year on a two-year contract, give you an option on five per cent of the new company and guarantee sixty thousand for expansion. Take that or leave it.'

Van Rensburg gritted his teeth, asking himself why he ever imagined any man would come all the way from Britain except to buy him out. At the same time the salary was fair, and even after repaying the accumulated interest he would be in credit to the tune of ten thousand, enough to buy two large houses in Nairobi in the present depressed market.

'There is one condition,' Hartman added.

'Go on.'

'You will finalize any arrangement I make for us to mine inside the Game Reserve.'

'If you succeed. I suppose you have got the capital?'

Hartman slid a document out of his briefcase. It was a bank guarantee for £100,000. 'I take it you accept?'

'Yes.'

Hartman gripped his hand with genuine pleasure. 'I think,' he said, 'that for public consumption my wartime citation can remain correct. I saved your life.'

'Not far off it anyhow.'

Hartman consulted his watch. 'We have an appointment with lawyers in Nairobi at four.'

'Jesus . . .' Van Rensburg all but exploded, then cut himself short. 'Well, you're the boss.' It wasn't going to be an easy situation and he was still shell-shocked at the speed of Hartman's decision.

'Don't worry,' Hartman remarked, reading his mind, 'I shall not be here often. You keep the production going up and the overheads down and there will be no trouble.'

'What if you fail to extend the concession?'

'The member of your Legislative Council whom I met will not receive a new Mercedes.' He allowed himself a contemptuous smile. 'On which his wife is very much determined.'

Van Rensburg had never paid a bribe in his life. He stayed quiet for a moment longer, then squared up against it.

'I don't operate like that, Jim. Never have and don't intend to start.'

'I am not asking you to.' Hartman stared straight back at him, his jaw set, his hands on his hips, his whole attitude almost insultingly nonchalant. 'I will do the dealing, you develop the mine. If you wish to back out of our agreement, back out now. We shook hands, but you may forget that.'

'If we don't play straight, how can we expect the Africans to?'

Hartman laughed. 'How little you know about them. Now, do we continue, or do we not?'

For a few seconds Van Rensburg wanted to argue. Then he capitulated. 'We continue,' he said.

'Good.' Hartman turned, cupped his hands and shouted his first order at Rukanga. 'Jackson! Jackson, come here. I want you.'

The young African came running and sensed what had taken place. He could see it in the way the white men stood and he could smell Van Rensburg's defeat.

'Excuse, bwana,' he apologized and approached the new owner.

'Can you use a camera, Jackson? Wait.' Hartman went to his tent and came back with a Leica. 'Here.' He demonstrated looking through the viewfinder. 'Like this. Now you take a photograph of us, right?'

'*Piksha*,' Van Rensburg said, unnecessarily.

The two of them posed, side by side. The expression of triumph on Hartman's face owed little to pioneering. Van Rensburg set his own features in a determined grin.

'One thing else,' Hartman said. 'I want the first fine stone from this mine for Anne.'

'You can have it now.' Van Rensburg took a small cotton bag from the pocket of his bush jacket and extracted a modest-sized ruby. 'Three carats uncut. I was taking it with a few others to a dealer in town.'

'Have a jeweller set it in a ring instead. If my information is correct you will be needing one. But I'll have the next.'

Jackson's return interrupted the story, though I was by no means sure Van Rensburg had told me the whole of it. I reckoned he had deliberately softened the edges of Father's image. Even so, the pioneering legend enshrined in the office photograph had bitten the dust, though I had been glad about the ruby subsequently reserved for Mother. It had been incorporated in a pendant she still treasured. There were many other questions I wanted to ask, like how Father found the money for the mine. They had to wait until later, after Jackson had driven us to the airstrip and we were bumping and rocking our way back to Nairobi in the turbulent heat of the afternoon.

'Must have been hard for you,' I suggested. 'I mean watching Father's hundred thousand turn into several million.'

'The vein got a lot wider inside the Reserve. Most of the production comes from there.' Van Rensburg spoke flatly through the intercom, stolidly watching the instruments and the horizon ahead. He had on a sort of red mesh baseball cap, with the earphones over the top and the spindly arm of the microphone across his mouth. What with sunglasses as well his facial expression was largely obscured. 'Anyway, what does it matter? Maybe I did feel bitter for a time, but I'm happy enough now. Worked out for the best. Jim made his coup, I kept five per cent and I've been advising him ever since. Jesus, I never had his knack with politicians. I was a geologist. Better have five per cent of a decent business than one hundred per cent of a bankrupt one.'

I sat silent for a time. Jackson's phrase 'the big win' had been circling in my mind like a vulture over a corpse. Father had been generous when he bought Rukanga, by his standards, undoubtedly because of his unique relationship with Van Rensburg. But suppose that last week he'd had the chance to move in on Consolidated's undeveloped concession, wherever it was? What then? I had no need to tell myself the answer. He would have been as single-minded as ever and he wouldn't have cared a damn who got hurt in the process.

A whirling red brown spiral rose from the bush below and ahead of us, snaking upward, moving slowly sideways. Van Rensburg banked the plane to fly round it, breaking my concentration.

'Dust devil,' he said. 'A tornado in miniature. We don't have real ones, thank God.'

'Like Father, uprooting everything in his path.'

'You could say so.'

'He was after another big win on this trip, he must have been.' I tried to make it a statement not a query. 'Was he lifting a concession off Consolidated?'

'Not in Kenya.'

'They have a concession lease which runs out next week,' I persisted. 'If they lost it their share price would take a beating just before the Trust makes its bid.'

'Not for discussion. Sorry. If I thought it relevant to what's happened to the Gulfstream, I'd tell you. Will do if it turns out to be. That's a promise. OK?'

Back in Nairobi there was no further news, though both Patrick and Mary insisted that the Gulfstream could not have simply vanished, even in central Africa. When I rang Mother in the evening I relayed the details of how many more square miles had been searched and Mary talked to her afterwards. She was being pestered by the Press again and, to his credit, Stainton had provided security men for Godstow. Nonetheless the strain was intensifying. When I then rang Camilla, I suggested she visit Mother, just to give her someone to talk to.

'If you really think it would help. Are you sure she'd want me there?'

'She always liked you. She doesn't change her opinion of people.'

This was the kind of elliptical remark, leaving more unsaid than said about how she should make the approach, which Camilla always complained about. With the next subject I was more direct. During the flight back in the afternoon Van Rensburg had deliberately killed the conversation about concessions, so I had not asked where Father found the money to buy Rukanga originally. £100,000 had been a lot of money to slam down on the table in 1957. He must have had exceptionally strong motivation for such an instant investment, not to mention substantial backing. So I asked Camilla to start researching financial reports and mining news of that period.

'As long ago as that?' A recurrence of echoes on the line seemed to emphasize her disinclination.

'Rukanga has been the touchstone in Father's life ever since I can remember.'

'But twenty-five years, Bob!'

'Yesterday for him. He almost went bankrupt around then. It's not something he or Mother ever talk about now.'

'Well. If you say so.' Her agreement was grudging.

'I'd be very grateful. I'm sure he's had a plan ever since.' I didn't like being too explicit, even though Van Rensburg had left me alone to make the call. 'In theory I think Father put some sort of compensation he'd received towards buying the mine.'

'All right then.' Camilla switched the subject. 'I spoke to your Professor Muhsin. He says not to worry. In your place he would be doing the same. "It is a son's duty," he said. Nonetheless I thanked him again on your behalf.'

Westerners think Muslims' behaviour is erratic and wayward if they don't put business first in life. More often it's because they regard family and religious obligations with a respect which we have lost. Camilla maintained similar priorities, though for reasons of individual conviction more than faith. Perhaps that was why she consented to call on Mother more readily than she agreed to extend her researches.

When I eventually went to bed, it was in the realization that our relationship was changing yet again. But I fell asleep speculating on the plan which had brought Father back to Africa and what his long-term ambitions might have been.

CHAPTER EIGHT

For what felt like minutes, but can only have been seconds, I listened to the hammering and splintering noises downstairs and wondered what the hell was going on.

Then there was a crash of breaking glass and Van Rensburg shouted along the corridor. The furious barking of the dogs outside was partially cut short by a shrieking howl, which drained off into nothing. From overhead an alarm siren's eerie wailing began to mount in intensity.

I leapt out of bed, pulled on a dressing gown, paused to think long enough to take a torch from the bedside table and ran out on to the landing.

Van Rensburg was at the head of the stairs, wearing only a kind of red loincloth. He had a knobkerrie in his hand.

'Help Mary with the guns,' he yelled. 'They've cut the phone.' He pointed to his own bedroom door and as I ran behind him, I caught a glimpse of several Africans at the foot of the stairs, brandishing the same kind of pangas with which the gardeners had so literally chopped the cobra into pieces. As I watched one swung his up and smashed the hall lantern, leaving us illuminated by the landing lights and the intruders in the shelter of darkness.

'Get the bloody gun,' Van Rensburg repeated, then raising the knobkerrie above his head, launched himself straight down among the intruders.

In the bedroom Mary was on the floor in front of an open cupboard safe, struggling to load a shotgun. As I reached her she managed to slide the second cartridge in. I could see her hand tremble.

'Get the other,' she ordered, stood up and dashed for the door. A moment later there was a deafening bang from the landing followed by screams.

I loaded the second shotgun, snapped the twin barrels locked and ran to the landing, puzzled that she hadn't fired her second barrel.

'Shine the torch,' she said and I appreciated why.

The beam illuminated Van Rensburg inert at the foot of the wide staircase, his body streaming blood, and an African with a panga raised above him. The hallway seemed to explode as Mary did fire again, and the African fell, dropping the weapon. I flashed the beam around, saw two more men in the shadow and decided it was now or never. If I didn't get there they would finish Van Rensburg off.

I thrust the torch into her hands, fired once in the direction of the two remaining Africans and rushed down, half-expecting to have my legs chopped at as I descended, jumped over Patrick's body and blasted off again just as other sirens and car horns sounded outside. One African screamed, the other fled and then the shouting of rescuers demanded attention.

I turned to the front door, uncertain how to open it in the dim light, shifted an iron bar, and was being confounded by a chain when there was a cry behind me.

'Quick!' Mary was kneeling by her husband, examining him with the torch. There was blood all over the floor. 'The bathroom,' she shouted. 'There's a first aid box in the cupboard. Be quick, please. I daren't move him.'

I ran upstairs, found the box and hurried down again. Cradling Patrick's head with her hand, she was talking in Swahili to an African security guard in a thick khaki overcoat and a knitted balaclava helmet. He nodded vigorously and then ran out to the kitchen.

I followed the security guard and lit a hurricane lamp, discovering that the back door had been broken down. The rock with which it had been splintered lay abandoned on the threshold. This must also have been the thieves' line of retreat. I took back the lamp and held it up for Mary's benefit.

Patrick was grievously hacked about the arms and legs, but alive and fully conscious, as Mary bandaged the appalling wounds. The hall was a battlefield, the windows shattered and the floor slippery with blood. The African who had fallen to my second shot lay in the study doorway, his hands clasping his face. Mary's victim was sprawled on his back, very definitely dead.

Moments later an African police inspector appeared, wearing a military camouflaged smock and carrying a sub-machinegun, a constable at his heels. After a brief conversation with Mary he turned to me. 'You shot them?' he demanded.

As a Kenya resident Mary would surely be jailed. As a visitor, I might be excused in some way.

'Both, I think,' I admitted. 'I was firing in the dark.'

'You should have shot more,' he said curtly. 'We have caught only two outside and there were many.'

This matter-of-fact response decided me to confess as much as possible while he was in a receptive mood. At home in Britain self-defence was no excuse for killing a burglar. However, for the moment he wasn't interested, and perhaps rightly if there were other attackers still around.

'We must get Patrick to hospital,' Mary pleaded. 'Can someone please help?'

I hurried out to the drive, where a number of vehicles were parked in the moonlight, but no ambulance yet. A European in a sweater and slacks introduced himself as a neighbour and offered to take Van Rensburg to the city. We carried him out with Mary's help and laid him on a blanket in the back seat of the man's car, while the squat, troglodyte security guards made subdued comments on his wounds and a police constable stood to one side, as if this was not part of his duty. Van Rensburg was conscious and must have been in great pain, but contrived to crack a joke as we shifted his position.

'For Christ's sake don't pull my leg again, it'll come off.'

'I must go with him,' Mary insisted, glancing round wildly for support.

'You go,' I said. 'I'll look after things.'

'But you can't speak Swahili . . .' She was beginning to sound distraught.

'Don't worry,' the neighbour assured her, 'I'll see Patrick safely there.'

'I'll be fine,' Van Rensburg's voice came from inside the car, though he was only speaking with great effort. 'You stay, Mary.'

The neighbour wasted no time leaving and for the first time I became aware that I was still in my dressing gown standing on the gravel under a bright moon while the residual drama of the raid continued to be played out around me. The security men, clumsy in thick boots and sweaters and woollen balaclava helmets which made them look as much like robbers as guards, milled around apparently searching for tracks. The driver of the police inspector's car was talking on the radio, the other police constable glowering at the two captured men, who were squatting, handcuffed, in the dust by the corpses of the two dead, which had been carried out. The constable had a rifle and whenever the captives shifted he jabbed at them maliciously. The night air felt moon cold and the unreality of the whole scene equally chilling.

I walked indoors to get dressed. Although the time was just after three, there was no sign of the activity abating.

In the hall the inspector stopped me again.

'How many thieves?' he asked.

'Five or six, I think. One ran away.'

'Two dead.' He counted on his fingers, the sub-machinegun tucked under his arm, 'two more...' Abruptly he cocked the weapon, drawing back the bolt with a grinding click. 'Who said they all run?' he demanded, more of himself than me, turning slowly to survey the various exits from the hall until the darkness beyond the open study door seemed to beckon him. He went through and flipped on the light.

What followed happened extraordinarily fast. A ripping noise came from the study, as though cloth was being torn, there was a shriek and the next second an African cannonaded out through the doorway straight towards me, terror written all over his face.

The man tried to dodge, I flung myself at him, slipped on the blood-wet floor, took a violent kick in the face and lost him. The inspector pounded past, shouting in Swahili. As I picked myself up, shots rang out from the garden and I reckoned they had caught up with this last intruder. Suddenly I was alone and intensely curious about the man who had hidden in the study and why. I went in there myself.

Papers strewed the floor, some concealed beneath a heavy velvet curtain which the inspector had evidently yanked down. A filing cabinet by the desk had all its drawers open, but an antique brass carriage clock on the mantelpiece was untouched. So was a videotape machine. I began wondering if the purpose behind the violence of the raid could simply have been to ransack this room. The thought led naturally to examining some of the documents, but I had barely picked one up before I heard Mary's voice and returned guiltily to the hall.

'*We na penda chai?*' She was saying to the inspector, then seeing me explained, 'Before we do anything else, we're going to have some tea. You'd like some? Good, I'll go and make it.' She seemed glad to have something positive to do.

'You are on safari?' The inspector asked me.

I agreed. It seemed simpler than trying to explain about Father.

'Let me tell you, Kenya is not like this; not at all. Do not be afraid. It will not happen again. You have lost some things?'

'Thanks to Mr Van Rensburg they never got upstairs.'

'And that man he stays until I was here.' He shook his head in puzzlement and continued with a chain of rhetorical questions. 'And what do they steal? What have those ones we catch in their pockets? Nothing. When gangs come it is for money or guns or televisions. In and out, too quick. Maybe these men want more? What do they want? I do not know.' He grunted. 'I like to know their reasons because I think these ones will say what they think I like to hear, even very clever things, they will say.'

'Won't the one who was in there talk?' I suggested, indicating the study. 'He was frightened enough.'

'He ran too much.' The dismissive words required no gloss. He was dead too. 'But we will learn his name. In the end I will know them all.'

I remembered the man's terror and the whites of his eyes bright against the black skin and I also remembered thinking, in that fraction of a second as I tried to grab him, that he seemed somehow different to the others.

'He didn't look like a burglar,' I said, feeling surprised that I could be so sure about an African face. But I was sure. Furthermore the fear in his expression had been so overwhelming that he could not have been an experienced criminal.

'Even educated people can be thieves. Too many have no job. I shall find out their reasons.'

I had little doubt he would.

When Mary came back with three mugs of tea on a tray the questioning inevitably turned to what was missing. Since going round the house was going to be an ordeal for her I excused myself to go and dress quickly and rejoin her. When I returned, the police had roused the servants and were interviewing them. It wasn't difficult to guess why they hadn't come on the scene earlier. They would have been scared stiff, if not actively intimidated by the thieves in advance. This preliminary investigation confirmed the inspector's doubts about the motive. The only item stolen was a cheap transistor radio from the kitchen, presumably grabbed by one of the thieves as he fled, and then dropped. It would be found in daylight. Why nothing else?

In the meantime a tracker dog, a magnificent Alsatian bitch, had been brought in a van. She was shown the rock used to break the door down, sniffed it thoroughly, then surged off round the house and across the lawn towards the river valley at a pace which kept her handler running.

It was four thirty before the inspector left, promising to return if the dog's chase was successful. At Mary's insistence I did then go to bed for what little remained of the night, my eyes gritty, my thoughts absorbed by there having been something strangely out of key about the raid. I was as determined as the inspector to find out what it was.

The servants themselves could not have gone back to bed at all, because when I came down for breakfast at eight, the house had been thoroughly cleaned. In daylight, with normality restored, the night's events assumed the detached aura of a dream. If it had not been for the broken windows and a carpenter at work replacing the back door, I could almost have imagined the whole drama had never taken place. There was also a note from Mary, who had gone to the hospital.

Dear Robert, I am dreadfully sorry this should have happened on top of everything else. If you want to go to town tell Ambrose to fetch the driver. I hope to be back for lunch.

In her absence the temptation to go through the papers scattered around the study floor became irresistible, even though Ambrose was liable to report back on my snooping and I had no precise idea of what I was looking for. Indeed I might as well have been fishing for diamonds in a bran tub. I could find nothing related to any new deal or contract, although as I fingered through the piles of documents which had been pulled out of filing cabinets and drawers, I became more and more curious about what the thieves had intended to achieve. Had they hoped to isolate the family upstairs while the study was searched? If so, they were badly misinformed, both about Patrick's character and his wife's. Mary's matronly, slightly fussed, manner did not square in the least with the way she had unhesitatingly shot a man dead, even if her hands had trembled. While I would have expected his bravery, I had thought of her as an unassuming English suburban housewife. In fact she was nothing of the sort. Wrong continent, wrong suburb.

Yet even allowing for this fatal miscalculation on the part of the thieves, the man in the study would still have needed to know what to look for. At the best he would have had only a few minutes before the security men arrived, because they were not summoned by phone but by radio. Indeed a metal plaque announcing the protection of 'Ultimate Security', with a symbolic lightning flash, was nailed to a tree trunk in the drive as a deterrent.

Presumably he had hoped to escape through the window. I walked across to it, lifted the fallen curtain and noticed for the first time the unobtrusive steel bars which had imprisoned him. Then I saw a document which the curtain had concealed. I picked it up, immediately recognizing Father's scrawl of a signature and an identifying reference 'JH/cd'. Dictated by him, typed by Christianne, a clear indication of confidentiality. Was this what the thief had been after? I began to read '. . . will bring both contracts with me on May 20th . . . assumption is that the Minister will sign at the weekend. Takeover bid will then be . . .'

The noise of a car halting outside made me jump. I thrust the memo into my pocket and hastily left the room.

Standing in the drive were two vehicles, which must have arrived together. One was a telecommunications van with a ladder on its roof, whose African crew members were already examining the severed phone wires. The other was a black and yellow Kenatco taxi, out of which stepped a woman in a pale blue linen suit, her eyes and expression hidden by fashionably large sunglasses. It was the woman of the Norfolk Hotel terrace.

98

I gawped for a moment, then pulled myself together and walked to greet her, wondering what to say. I need not have worried. She put on an immaculate show of non-recognition, asking if this was the Van Rensburgs' house in a voice that was detached and masculine, yet sexy: like Marlene Dietrich, whom I'd often heard on the old records Father cherished.

'Unfortunately we had a break-in last night,' I said cautiously. 'Mr Van Rensburg's in hospital and Mary's gone down there.'

'I heard they have trouble. That is why I came out. The telephone was always engaged.'

'The thieves cut the line.'

'Ah, so!' Her voice lapsed into a more guttural pitch. 'Patrick, he is not badly hurt I hope?'

So much for his pretences at the Norfolk, I thought, as I told her briefly what had happened.

'I'm Robert Hartman, by the way,' I concluded. 'I'm staying with them for a few days. Would you like to come in?' I couldn't see this earning me any brownie points from Patrick, but I could hardly turn her away. In any case, I was full of curiosity.

'Lohrey,' she said in the same businesslike tone, and extended her hand, long-fingered and elegant, though I noticed the heavy gold bangle was missing from her wrist. She must have been conscious of its absence herself because she immediately gave an explanation. 'The hotel warned not to wear jewellery going out of town. I suppose this man is okay, but who knows . . .' She shrugged her shoulders, glanced at the driver, then smiled at me disarmingly. 'I think I accept your invitation.' There was a distinct air of conspiracy in the way she said this, and when we reached the front door she stopped and added, 'You must be Sir James Hartman's son, no?'

She had given herself plenty of time to reach that question, but I wasn't deceived. She hadn't come to see the Van Rensburgs at all. I was the target of this visit and the realization annoyed me. I showed her through to the drawing room, asked Ambrose to bring coffee, and we settled down to an edgily stilted conversation.

'You are worse than barbed wire,' she said suddenly. 'How can I get through such defences?'

'Why do you want to?' I was becoming convinced that she must be an old flame of Father's and felt I had enough trouble on my hands as it was.

'I like to know if I can help.' She answered softly yet insistently.

'Who?'

'The son of Sir James.'

So she knew he'd disappeared. I was rapidly losing what was left of my patience, and anyway feeling faintly sick after the night's events.

'I was very sad to hear. Truly.'

'Then maybe you can tell me what he was doing? I'd appreciate *someone* telling me.'

The heavy sarcasm was a mistake and she took no notice, simply shaking her head. 'Our meeting here was chance, nothing more. Just chance. Yes, I have known him many years ago, in Germany after the war. For a time we exchange letters, then no more. Of course I have read about him in the newspapers. Even in Switzerland, where I live, they know about him. Last week I came for the first time to Africa and there he was in the same hotel.'

I listened, not seriously believing a word. Except that coincidence always did seem to have played a large part in Father's life.

'Was he going to Kinshasa? Or somewhere else?'

She smiled again, tolerantly, maternally, quite unruffled.

'Young man, when old friends meet after a long time they talk about yesterday, not tomorrow.'

The phone began to ring in the hall. Thinking it might be the workmen testing the line, I left it to Ambrose to answer. But the thread of conversation was broken and my own nervous tension must have communicated itself to Mrs Lohrey, because she sat up attentively, with her head inclined towards the door. The attitude made me notice the wrinkled flesh of her neck. She was older than I had thought. Perhaps she had been telling the truth. Perhaps she was just an old friend of Father's.

Ambrose appeared in the doorway.

'*Kwa bwana*,' he said, beckoning. I rose hastily and followed him to the phone.

A woman was on the line whose voice was familiar, yet out of place. It took me a second to realize that it was Christianne speaking from London. She sounded equally surprised to hear me.

'Is that you Robert? We have a telex message about some trouble Mr Van Rensburg has. Can you fetch him please.'

'I'm afraid he's in hospital.' This was a morning of explanations.

'Oh my God. I must tell Mr Stainton.'

'Wait a minute.' I could not lose this opportunity. 'What's happening at your end?'

'There is no news of Sir James, I'm afraid.' A fractional hesitation. 'Mr Stainton has called an emergency Board meeting.'

'So I heard.'

'I think you should come back.' She spoke hastily. 'Oh. He would like to speak to you himself.'

'Robert? I want to know precisely what has happened.' Stainton was more incisive than usual. 'The telex was unclear.' He sounded as though he was blaming me. 'What was this gang after?'

'Documents, apparently.' I repeated the story.

'What documents? You've no damned idea I suppose.'

He was vexed and also, I thought, worried. I dismissed the possibility of revealing what I had found.

'Is Patrick badly hurt?' he asked.

'He was pretty cut about. Mary Van Rensburg's at the hospital now.'

'Now listen.' His tone changed to one of near-avuncular concern. 'I admit I was opposed to your trip.' The line echoed his words, as if anxious to underline their insincerity. 'But in the circumstances you have my full authority to take over direction of the search. And if you can also find out what's been stolen, I should be deeply grateful.'

My reaction to this was so cautious that he reiterated the offer, then fairly brusquely ordered me to let him know as soon as possible. He wasn't sure how to treat me, whether as an employee or a potential co-director, and I might have sympathized if his motives had not been so transparent. I had no right to attend the emergency Board meeting, but my mother did, and she would be easily outwitted if no one gave her advice beforehand.

I was still pondering this when Mrs Lohrey touched me on the shoulder like an affectionate relative.

'I think perhaps you are deciding whether to return home or not. May I give an advice? You should go to be with your mother.'

'You think Father *is* dead?' This was Wednesday, the fifth day since his disappearance. None the less, what justified her assumption?

'Who has said so? Ah, no.' She gazed at me with compassion. Her eyes were a beautiful greyish blue, with all their vitality undiminished. Looking straight into them I felt that a single look from her could command a lifetime's allegiance: probably had commanded it. 'No, Robert, I make the advice that you go home because you can do nothing here. How can you tell if these pilots search in the right place? Think for your mother. For a woman waiting five days can be eternity. You should go back.'

'Are you staying yourself?'

She gave a tiny shake of her head. 'I shall leave tonight. Here.' She handed me a visiting card. 'If you need to find me sometime.'

'Dr Lotte Lohrey,' the print on the white pasteboard announced. 'Conseillère Relations Publiques.' The address was in Geneva.

'Sometime could be never,' I said. 'Can we have lunch today?'

'If you like, sure. That would be a pleasure for me.'

With Patrick incapacitated, I had to find out for myself how the aerial search was progressing. I arranged to meet her at the Norfolk, then escorted her to the waiting taxi. She held her hand out elegantly in farewell, having to restrain herself, I felt convinced, from kissing me, and she waved through the car window as the taxi driver accelerated away. I waved back, pretty well hooked.

There remained the document from the study, now slightly crumpled from having been in my pocket. I smoothed it out with care.

From: Sir James Hartman.
To: P. Van Rensburg
Date: April 30th, 1982
I will bring both contracts with me on May 20th. Before then require your assessment of the attached production and cashflow estimates. The decisive assumption is that the Minister will sign at the weekend. Takeover bid will then be made not later than June 4th. From takeover to an operational consortium will be six months. All the above top secret. Locally if Mululu insistent then leak basis of the ruby deal to the media in advance, telexing me 'Ministry satisfied'. Important to remember this is the official reason for my visit.

Clearly the Kenya deal was subsidiary to a far greater one on which an unexplained consortium depended. Very soon too. I turned to the single sheet of projections clipped to the memo and gasped, though they would have meant far less if Van Rensburg had not explained about the value of diamonds. Whichever mine these figures referred to was scheduled to produce two million carats a year. A sixth of that output would be 'close goods', which I recalled meant gemstones, and he had told me the trade value of those was $3,000 to $5,000 a carat, as against an 'average' figure of $10 for 'industrials'. Eventually I found some reconciliations among the figures which confirmed that the mine would be earning over $1,000 million a year. The location of this treasure trove was another question. It was simply referred to as Concession Twenty-Two. I thought, idiotically, of the novel *Catch 22* and wondered if there was something wrong, some hidden snag. But there couldn't be if Van Rensburg had checked it out, and since these documents were a month old, I assumed he must have done. It also seemed entirely plausible that this was what the thieves had been sent to steal. Men would kill their grandmothers to exploit such inside information, let alone if they had interests in the concession itself.

Reasoning the scheme out and recalling figures that Camilla had researched, I began piecing together a scheme that would have appealed as much to an Arab slave or ivory trader as to a modern tycoon. It was all a matter of parcelling out Africa, of political balances in tipping the scale of influence one way or the other. When people spoke of this Concession being the pivot of Father's intended bid for Consolidated they were failing to see that it might go a great deal further than that.

He must see future competition in the diamond business as being between South Africa and black Africa. De Beers produced 21 million carats a year, of which 12 million came from Botswana, an independent African State. On the other side, Zaïre's output was 19 million, and it probably mattered less politically that these were mainly low-value 'industrials' than that Zaïre had broken with the De Beers selling organization. If Father could bring a major Angolan concession back into production he might easily cajole all the black States into his consortium, even eventually Botswana. That must be his game and it was a very great one: if he could finance it.

My speculations were cut short by Mary Van Rensburg's return. I had been so absorbed that I never heard the Mercedes outside and was caught *in flagrante delicto*, standing in the hall with the memo in my hand. I immediately handed it to her, explaining that I had been doing some amateur sleuthing. She was not much interested, and said that she would put it in the safe, then turned at once to the subject of her husband. Patrick was 'comfortable', in the soothing term that hospitals use. He was not seriously injured, despite all the blood, and his wounds would heal. I was greatly relieved and said so.

'Who was the lady visitor?' she demanded suddenly. 'We passed a taxi down the road.'

Women don't miss a trick where their own sex is concerned, even the nicest.

'She was a friend of Father's. A Mrs Lohrey. In fact she came to see Patrick.'

However Mary's blank expression revealed that the name meant nothing to her and reinforced my feeling that I had been the objective of the visit. I changed the subject by mentioning Stainton's phone call.

'Frank's a snake,' she said with unexpected vigour. 'Patrick never has trusted him. If he wants you here it's most likely because he's up to some chicanery in London. Anyway, what can you do here without Patrick? I don't mean to be rude, but the flying people down at Wilson are perfectly efficient.'

'I thought I'd go and see them, if the driver's still available. You think I should go back to London?'

'I don't want to force you, you're more than welcome to stay as long as you like. You earned your keep this morning.' She smiled in a motherly way. 'Thank God you didn't panic. In fact thank God you were here. But it does sound to me as though you ought to be back in England.'

'If there's no news, I'll go.' I agreed with her assessment, adding as an afterthought, 'Who would you trust on the Board?'

That was a trickier question than an outsider might have realized. Although I had met all the directors socially at one time or another, uncertainty surrounded Father's relationships with every single one of them. He kept the top management of the Trust involved in a perpetual power play, distancing himself from one man or drawing others closer without apparent logic, constantly maintaining his own autocracy. In a sense Lord Watson, being so long-standing an acquaintance, was the obvious one to approach. But he was too much the opportunist politician.

'Andrew Ferguson?' Mary suggested and I admired her shrewdness. Andrew was not merely the youngest director – and therefore the one with the most incentive to play his hand long. He had charge of our newspaper interests and they were losing money. He might well be my best ally. I asked if I could phone him.

The operator obtained the call remarkably quickly, so much so that I barely had time to prepare myself before his soft Scots voice came on the line. After a brief exchange of courtesies, I mentioned the emergency meeting.

'That's entirely correct,' he admitted. 'Frank called for it yesterday and the minimum notice is forty-eight hours, so it'll be tomorrow afternoon. I'm surprised you should know.'

'News travels fast.' I was learning to bluff. 'What hasn't reached me is the agenda.'

'To consider the Directorate.'

'But there is no evidence that my father's dead.'

'A company needs direction, you can't leave it rudderless in a storm.' He made the remark apologetically and I had no doubt he was reflecting Stainton's line.

'Did you know my mother has a proxy to vote as my father's alternate?'

'Is that so?'

'Someone should brief her beforehand. I'm flying back tonight. I hoped we could have lunch tomorrow.' I allowed time for this polite request to register fully, then added, 'It is for example common knowledge that one or two Divisions of the Group are making unacceptable losses.'

'That will not be on the agenda, Mr Hartman. There is only the one item.'

Since he was reluctant to be pressured, I made the threat more direct.

'If another Chief Executive is appointed before it is confirmed that my father is dead,' I almost spelt the words out, 'our family will demand an Extraordinary General Meeting and every single Board appointment will be challenged.'

There was complete silence for perhaps fifteen seconds: so long that I thought we had been cut off.

'I shall be glad to advise Lady Hartman,' he said.

'My father will appreciate that. Thank you.' I asked him to transfer me to Christianne and told her I was returning.

'I think that is a wise decision, Robert,' she commented, and I imagined her sitting behind the rosewood desk, sexily cold, smoothing her hair and trying to evaluate where the balance of advantage lay, exactly as Father would have taught her. Or was I being too cynical? Either way my thoughts were interrupted by Mary.

'There's something else you ought to know if you're going back.' The worry in her voice was unusual. 'One of the thieves was a clerk in Patrick's office.'

'Are you sure?'

'I'm afraid so. I saw his body after the police shot him. I can still hardly believe it. We trusted him. He's been out here. His name was Moses.'

The terrified African, bursting out into the hall, his eyes wide with terror, came back to me again. Now I knew why he had been in a panic. He was more scared of losing his job than of the police. Perhaps thieves never expect to be shot until they are.

'I've been thinking about the raid,' Mary said. 'They didn't really try to come upstairs, did they? They were all at the bottom stopping us from coming down.'

'While Moses ransacked the files?' Or more likely took what he knew was there and strewed the rest around for the sake of appearances.

'Moses must have had the right keys. Someone must have forced him into it.'

She could only be right. The whole affair began to smell of conspiracy. Could Consolidated have organized the raid to obtain documents affecting our takeover? It was probably never intended to end in bloodshed.

'Africans have loyalties we don't always understand,' Mary said. 'Their clan loyalties are terribly strong. They can be under enormous pressure to help even the remotest relations. For all we know Moses could have owed his job to some kind of family deal that Patrick was completely unaware of. You simply can't tell.'

Since this sort of hypothesis could lead anywhere, I headed her back on to more immediate questions and soon after left with the driver for Wilson airport, having tactfully assured her I would find myself some lunch in the city.

The young captain at the air charter firm had become markedly more despondent. He stood in front of an array of maps lining the briefing room walls and stubbed with his forefinger at the minute proportion of Father's route which had been flown over yesterday.

'Frankly, Sir, the further one gets from the point of departure, the wider the circle of uncertainty becomes. We're searching close to eight hundred miles from Nairobi now. A five-degree error in the Gulfstream's heading would have put it sixty-five miles off track at that distance and five degrees is nothing: if the pilot's in trouble, I mean.'

'Are you saying we should abandon this?'

'No, Mr Hartman. We'll continue so long as you want. Unfortunately it isn't only the chance of finding the wreck that's lessening. It's the chance of Sir James still being alive.'

I stared at the maps again; at the 1,500-mile-wide chunk of Africa that the Belgians had arbitrarily delineated as the Congo and was now the Republic of Zaïre; the same country that contained Conrad's heart of darkness and some of the greatest copper mines in the world; crocodiles and jungle; pygmies and modern cities; witchcraft and a national assembly. Full of the paradoxes which Father liked, not for their own sake, but because he could so adeptly exploit their tensions. It would be a kind of poetic justice if, in revenge, it had swallowed him up. I told the captain I was going to London briefly and he should only suspend the search on my personal authority. Then I went to the Norfolk and told the driver to come back in two hours.

As before, Mrs Lohrey was seated at a table on the Lord Delamere terrace, idly observing the flow of people and presumably watching for my arrival. She held out her hand and gave me a warm smile. As if by magic an African waiter immediately appeared, causing mutterings at the next table. I guessed she gave handsome tips.

'So,' she said, as if she had just triumphed by guile over a rare species. 'I am glad you suggest lunch. But first I must ask, have you any more news?'

I shook my head. 'It isn't too hopeful.'

'Do not despair. James is one who survives always.'

'You have no idea if he was going to some other country than Zaïre? Surely, you met him, you talked to him, he must have said something about his trip?'

'I have told you, when old friends meet they talk about the past.' Whether purposely or not, she had ceased emphasizing that they had met here by accident. She leaned towards me a little. 'I am anxious for him as you are, Robert. All I can tell you is he was full of excitement. I have the feeling he had big plans.' She laughed lightly. 'Whenever did he not?'

'Did you meet the Van Rensburgs with him?'

'He has told me the name. I remembered it.'

The waiter interrupted us with the drinks and I dropped the challenge. She was too confident a fencer for me to succeed and she immediately turned to enquiries about my career and our home, as if trying to construct a mental picture of Godstow and the surroundings in which Father lived. She pressed for obscure details like how the cat, Agapanthus, acquired its admittedly unusual name. Eventually, in self-defence, I countered by asking how she had first met my father.

'You know he went back to Germany after the war? I was there also.' She laughed at herself. '*Natürlich*. How stupid I am! It is where I was born, after all.'

'He went back with the army, didn't he?' He had talked about that occasionally, though never about a girl.

'The army was the means, I think.' Those compelling grey eyes conveyed innocent wisdom. 'It would have otherwise been hard at that time. It was for everyone a hard time, 1945. But he must go. Your grandparents had been taken by the Gestapo. You know that? No. The story was terrible. He went back to find if he had still a family.'

My interest was caught at last. 'Surely after the war he wanted to stay in England?'

'Perhaps.' She shrugged off the possibility. 'Perhaps he had some doubts. I tell you something, Robert, we Germans are very strong for the fatherland and for the family. That is very important to us. In any case, he must come. He must come to search, as you come here yourself.'

She had a point there, though I didn't warm to the parallel. 'He never found them?'

'Never. He searched very long but no. Instead he found me. She allowed herself an introspectively gentle sigh, as though recalling a miracle. 'I was in those days fifteen and how could he know it was for me he was looking?'

CHAPTER NINE

It had been different during the fighting. In those hard months after the Allied invasion of Europe Hartman saw nothing of civilians or his homeland's devastated cities, because they were an obstacle to the army's advance.

During the fighting he discovered that war offered rewards as well as hazards. He dropped with the Sixth Airborne Division in Normandy in the early hours of June 6th, 1944 and was promoted twice as he fought with it through the bitter winter battles in the Ardennes forests and on to the final three-hundred-mile race across the north German plains to reach the Baltic ahead of the Russians. Towards the end streams of refugees clogged the roads, their few possessions piled on handcarts and barrows. But the shattered civilian world to which they belonged, like the cities, seemed irrelevant to the vast panorama of military victory.

Then, abruptly, it was all over. As soon as he was able to Hartman scrounged three days' leave and took his driver and jeep back to the town where he had been born twenty-five years before.

Düsseldorf, the once vaunted *elegante, gastliche Stadt am Rhein*, the playground of the industrial Ruhr, was the corpse of a city. Whole streets and squares had been demolished and the warm sun brought out the unmistakable smell of death from bodies still buried in the rubble. The survivors had become moles, scratching shelter from the basements and cellars beneath the empty-eyed shells of houses. A packet of cigarettes would buy a woman for the night and a pound of coffee a week's labour. Hartman had supposed he would remember the way through the city, but when his driver brought him to the tumbled stone blocks which had been the Opera House he found the other landmarks had gone and they had to trace their route out to the suburbs with the aid of a map.

It took them nearly an hour to find the Hagedorn Strasse, where his family had lived, by which time he was mentally prepared for an emotional shock, though not for the person, aged almost beyond memory, who would transmit it.

The devastation was less complete here. The shops at the end of the Hagedorn Strasse were recognizable, their windows planked over, though the street itself was gap-toothed. Fireplaces and tattered wallpaper hung out of blank walls three storeys up, where bombs had struck through roofs and floors, as though a demolition gang had left its work unfinished. They drove slowly along, searching for number 14, to find it was a pile of dusty debris. Hartman got out and for a few minutes scrambled over the remains of his home, knowing in his heart that the search would be futile. Anything resembling personal property would have been looted long ago. In any case, he didn't know when his parents had last been there. He turned away and began calling at each inhabited dwelling in turn, always asking the same question.

'Did you know the family Hardtmann?'

Perhaps the way he spoke had some unintended overtone of threat, though he tried to sound friendly. Perhaps they were scared of the foreign uniform. Either way, he could see fear veil people's eyes as he approached and he met only with shakes of the head and denials.

Then, having descended the cracked steps to the entrance of a basement, the only viable remnant of what had been a small working-class apartment building, he found himself confronted by an old woman who looked him up and down with contemptuous familiarity.

'*Wie geht's, Hans?*' she asked with a grunt. 'You have grown! Quite the big man, eh. A soldier too!'

He stared, not recognizing her yet knowing the voice, while she held the door tight with one wrinkled hand, demonstrably keeping him out.

For a few seconds longer he stood bemused, then the past stirred and he knew who she was: the owner of one of the shops on the corner, where he had bought his weekly few pfennigs' worth of sweets as a boy.

'Frau Winkelmann?' He could hardly believe this gaunt old woman was really her.

'So now he remembers,' she crowed, still clutching the door.

'What happened?' He meant what had happened to her, but was misunderstood.

'There was a war. Ran away from that, didn't you? Changed sides too, eh.'

'I hated the Nazis,' he said coldly. 'I'd do the same again.' This sudden harshness frightened her and she cut short whatever comment she had been going to make, saying instead, 'I suppose you're looking for your parents?' She moved forward into the doorway and peered up at the street, darting her head in and out like a bird, as though afraid of being overheard. 'They were taken away before the war. They and the Lohreys the same night.'

'They never came back?' That was an unnecessary question. Prisoners of the Gestapo seldom returned.

'If they did we never saw them. Communists. That's what we were told they were. Undercover communists. The Lohreys, who knows? But not your father, he wasn't that kind.' She began to withdraw again into the basement.

'You never heard anything?' Hartman persisted.

'The Lohrey girl was sent to an orphanage. In Berlin, I heard.'

Hartman recalled the daughter vaguely, playing on the pavement outside the shop. Frau Winkelmann must have been aware of all the goings on.

'But we hardly knew them,' he said. 'Why together?'

'Lotte,' she remarked pensively, disregarding him. 'Pretty little thing. They'd have educated her there, right and proper. She wouldn't tell anything even if you did find her.' What was left of her pride reasserted itself through this piece of minor spite and she began to close the door. 'Well, I can't stand here gossiping all day!'

'Wait!' He dashed back to the jeep, returning with a packet of coffee. She might be an old bitch, but at least she'd given him a lead. 'Thank you, Frau Winkelmann.' He held out the packet, but she didn't take it. He fumbled in his battledress pocket, found a slip of paper and scribbled his military address. 'Please, if you hear anything, write to me.'

She accepted the paper, but her eyes were on the coffee and when he pressed it into her hands they were quivering. Suddenly she began to cry and shut the door quickly in his face.

After that Hartman went and sat in the jeep for a minute in silence, shaking his head and swearing to himself, until he ordered the driver to go to the City Hall. There was one way to trace the girl, if she came back that was. Every German needed documents, residence permits, labour permits. To get them she would have to register with the police at the City Hall, where his uniform gave him instant attention despite the long queues. Two packets of cigarettes went to the functionary who promised to notify him through the Allied Control Commission. It only occurred to him years afterwards that this was the first occasion on which he gave a bribe to an official. At the time he reckoned it was justified.

This done, he made an unconventional and unauthorized move. The Allied Control Commission was a four-power military government, hastily being established to run occupied Germany.

A request for volunteers to staff it had recently been circulated in the army. He knew its British element was being established at Minden, 140 miles to the north of Düsseldorf. He told his driver they would billet themselves there for the night and set off.

'Trying to short-circuit the system, eh Captain?' the officer who interviewed him remarked. 'You know you ought to apply through channels, eh?'

'I was passing here. Don't you need German speakers?'

'We do.' The officer eyed him curiously. Most applicants seemed to be motivated by uncertainty about their futures. This one was exceptionally positive. 'What's in it for you?' he asked.

'I want to find my parents.'

The naïve straightforwardness of the reply caught him off-balance.

'At least that's honest,' he conceded. 'You'll have one hell of a job, you know. There are displaced persons all over Europe. And it'll be strictly an off-duty enterprise.'

'What would you do?' Hartman demanded.

'In your shoes, Captain, I think I should get back to my unit and persuade them to put forward your name, quoting the appropriate Army Council Instruction. It's this one, by the way.' He handed across a small printed leaflet. 'We'll see you here in due course, I expect.'

A few weeks later Hartman was posted to the Control Commission, with a warning that he would eventually have to go through the process of being demobilized from the army and re-engaged. That might happen in a year, or might happen later. Mentally he allowed himself twelve months.

This private, spare-time task was formidable. During the six years of war hundreds of thousands of political prisoners, Jews and slave labourers had been moved around the Continent by the Gestapo and the Todt Organization. There had been hundreds of different camps. Hartman did not even know which his parents had been consigned to first. He set in train the documentation and made regular visits to the central search bureau down at Friedland where a card index was being collated from interviews with concentration camp survivors. The months passed. Then in July 1946, when his demobilization was in sight and he had begun applying for management trainee posts in Britain, a message came from the Düsseldorf City Hall. The girl Lotte Lohrey, aged fifteen, had registered her return and was staying with an aunt and uncle.

By mid-1946 many restrictions had relaxed: the anti-fraternization rules among them. He could legally make friends in Germany. When he retraced the route to the city he wore a tweed coat and flannels. The clothing was still unmistakably British, but at least it wasn't uniform. If Frau Winkelmann had been right, and Lotte's re-education had been successful, she would be loyal to Hitler at heart and burningly resentful of defeat.

Düsseldorf still had an air of apathy and despair, but less so than before. A plodding determination to resurrect the city was evident everywhere. On the bomb sites men and women crouched by piles of rubble, methodically chipping the mortar off old bricks so that they could be re-used. They began at one end of a street and rebuilt house by house, so that there was every stage of construction from ruins to finished dwellings within a few hundred metres. Most significantly, Hartman learnt that one of Düsseldorf's priorities was to reconstruct its Opera House, symbolic of both past and future. He found this confidence strongly expressed in the attitude of the Lohrey family, who insisted he joined their Sunday meal of potato salad and sauerkraut, spiced with a few slivers of sausage as a luxury, and made no apology for the shabbiness of their apartment. Now it was his turn to be embarrassed at bringing gifts of food, though they were accepted willingly enough.

As for Lotte, he would not have recognized her, except that the leggy, blonde girl selfconsciously helping in the kitchen could be no one else. She wiped her palm on her apron, curtsyed and then shook hands, but remained shyly silent.

'Well,' her authoritarian aunt prompted crudely, 'I hope he knows your parents were arrested because they helped him escape. If he doesn't he ought to.'

'Is that true?' Hartman was shocked, his worst teenage fears justified.

The girl nodded unhappily. 'They told me the first time they beat me at the orphanage. "I suppose you wish you'd run away like the boy who caused all the trouble," the matron said. "One decent German is worth ten of such filth." When I tried to answer she only hit me harder. "Forget your parents. Grow up to serve the Führer," a lot more like that.'

'I'm sorry,' Hartman said lamely, relieved that the re-education had failed, but shattered at what he had been innocently responsible for.

'It wasn't your fault. Anyway those women were so stupid. I pretended to believe what they said and I got away with it.'

Probably because of her Aryan blonde hair and blue eyes, Hartman thought. She spoke with such self-assurance that he decided to plunge straight in with the questions which mattered.

'Have you any idea what happened to our parents?' he asked. 'Were they sent to the same camp?'

'How could I know!' She tossed her head, suddenly angry and tearful. 'I was told to forget them, that they were traitors, I should never speak of them again. How could I find out? During five years I was in the orphanage by the Kaiserin und Königin hospital and never once allowed out alone. When the Russians came all the staff were raped. Serve them right. I was too young. I found an officer and told him my parents had been against Hitler. He believed me. They needed nurses so after that I did nursing. They said if they found nothing bad about us, we could go home to our relations one day. Last week they gave me the permit. Here I am.'

'Stop talking, girl,' the aunt interrupted sharply. 'Uncle is hungry. We must eat.' She evidently disapproved of her niece's attitude.

They ranged themselves round the living room table, though 'Uncle', a portly man, lay on his side on a settee, propping himself up with one arm, like a Roman emperor, while his wife and the girl served him from cracked china dishes.

'Six days he works. Sundays not,' the aunt explained with finality.

The only point that emerged from the stilted mealtime conversation was that Lotte wanted to find a place in the *Gymnasium* to qualify for university.

'If you are with the Control Commission, you can help,' the aunt argued, and Hartman agreed.

The girl smiled. 'That would be wonderful.' The smile transformed her freckled face, making it radiant. Christ, Hartman found himself thinking, she's going to be a stunner one day.

When he left, he gave instructions on how to get in touch and she curtsyed goodbye, her good temper fully restored, a grateful schoolgirl.

The visit left Hartman in mental turmoil. He had caused the arrest not only of his own parents but also of hers. Yet she had never attacked him for it. He owed her all the help he could give. On the Monday he began the process of finding the right official in the Control Commission's sprawling educational network. Directly or indirectly the Allies had power over every aspect of Germany's civil administration. Eventually, in the autumn, Lotte Lohrey was allocated the *Gymnasium* place she wanted, though he did not see her again because he had been sent back to Britain for demobilization: a Britain where the nearest he had to relatives himself were the schoolmaster who had sponsored him before the war and that rapidly dispersing band of brothers, his regiment.

Lotte wrote that winter of 1946/47, thrilled at being in the *Gymnasium*, and mentioning that things were difficult because the canals had frozen and the coal barges were unable to get through. He replied in German, solicitous as a godfather, aware that in their different way his own out-of-date phrases were as awkward as her orphanage-instilled formality. Gradually the correspondence developed and as she grew older her personality emerged, strong and vivacious, not afraid to make fun of the ambitions he began to reveal. After he was demobilized in 1947 he found a job with a merchant bank and those ambitions became more focused.

'I see you with a bowler hat and umbrella, walking through the London fog,' she wrote at the end of that year. 'Is it possible? Do you really want to be like those stuffy English? When you say you and a friend are buying a house are you serious? A whole house?'

'*Meine liebe Lotte*,' he replied, half charmed and half piqued, 'the lodging house is entirely a business proposition. Our bank gives special low interest rates on loans to employees, so instead of paying rent to a landlord, we pay off the loan.' He didn't bother to describe the house, every room separately let off with a gas burner and a sink behind a curtain in the corner, one soap-rimed bath and lavatory on each landing.

Their correspondence continued in a desultory way, with him enquiring mechanically about her aunt and uncle, while she indulged her fantasies about his becoming an English gentleman and his 'London house'. He omitted to mention that he had now let the basement to someone who paid an exorbitant rent for having a private entrance and was all but paying off his loan for him single-handed.

Then in the late summer of 1949, when he had not set eyes on his protégée for three years, she wrote in jubilation.

'Can you imagine? I am going back to Berlin! The Free University has accepted me. You see, some good came from those terrible years in the orphanage. They were a Berlin qualification, as well as the school work here of course. I am so excited I could dance. Promise you will visit, promise please.'

That autumn, as the Berlin blockade declined into history, he took up the invitation. The trip was an absurd extravagance. Although he had been promoted twice by the bank, he was saving every penny and normally would not cross London to see a girl, let alone Europe. But Lotte was now like a sole surviving relation, the only link with his upbringing. So he took a flight from the miserable Nissen huts of Heathrow North, changed planes at Hanover and eventually reached the concrete-columned Hitlerian splendour of Tempelhof airport in the beleaguered city, marvelling at his own folly.

This time Lotte greeted him with an impulsive hug and warm kisses on both cheeks, in place of the institutional curtsy.

'How wonderful that you've come!' She linked her arm through his. 'Now we can explore Berlin together. We're going to make the most of your few days here. I've borrowed a room for you in the University, a friend is away. I hope that's all right? So stupid to spend money on a hotel. I'm sure you'll like it. We can eat in the canteen. They've hardly finished the buildings, but already the place has a fantastic atmosphere, like being reborn.'

Her enthusiasm inspired him. In the leafy suburb of Dahlem, where the Free University had been established, he discovered a student world which the war had excised from his ambitions. Instantly he became immersed in its informal way of living. He listened, with tolerance, to impassioned political arguments. He even attended a lecture out of curiosity, until he decided that this venture into what might have been was a waste of time. He knew where he was going, which was more than most of the students did.

Then, continuing what amounted to their joint education in each other's interests, Lotte led him into a chance meeting with a man he had never really expected to see again. 'I'd like to go to the theatre,' she announced on the Saturday. 'You've heard of Brecht? No? Well, he's just the greatest living German playwright, that's all. They've given him a theatre of his own in East Berlin. Will you come?'

'What's the play?' He tried to sound enthusiastic, anxious not to break the spell of the visit.

'*Mother Courage and Her Children*. We may not get in. At least we can try.'

They went through one of the crossing points – this was a dozen years before the wall was built – and into the bleak, deprived Russian sector of the city. But the Theater am Schiffbauerdamm was well maintained, the same theatre where Brecht had made his name in 1928 with *The Threepenny Opera*, and they were able to get seats, ironically among the best.

However for Hartman the climax did not come in the performance at all, though there was a universality about Helene Weigel's portrayal of Mother Courage, the camp follower of the Thirty Years War, which stirred his memories of the refugees on the roads in 1945 and of Frau Winkelmann mocking his own uniform. For him the climax of the play came in the interval.

As the lights went up after the first act he saw rising from a seat three rows ahead a figure that he thought he recognized. Seizing Lotte's hand, he pushed his way towards the aisle until he was close enough to call out '*Buona sera, Capo.*'

The man swung round, while his dark-suited escorts moved instinctively to protect him.

'The Abruzzi, remember?' Hartman shouted.

A huge grin spread across the man's bearded face. He waved the escorts away and pushed aside members of the audience to clasp Hartman's hand.

'*Mamma mia! Come sta?* The Inglese sergeant!' He seized on Lotte. 'Is this your wife? She isn't? Too young and pretty for a soldier like you anyway!' He roared with laughter, still pumping Hartman's hand. 'We must celebrate after the performance. That's an order, understood!' He turned to one of the Germans with him. 'This was a man to have with one, I can tell you. A real Nazi-killer.' Unperturbed at the escorts' embarrassment he thumped Hartman on the back. 'We shall celebrate.' Then he allowed himself to be led away.

'A partisan leader I met in the mountains,' Hartman explained to Lotte. 'D'you mind?'

'Of course not. He must be important. Those can only be Party members with him.' She was wide-eyed and impressed.

'Perhaps. I wonder what he's doing here.'

The play was long and ended late. When they met in the foyer afterwards Barba Nera's hosts were unenthusiastic and the celebration never got beyond a couple of glasses of schnapps. In any case Lotte was anxious to catch the S-bahn train back to West Berlin. But the men did exchange addresses, which revealed Barba Nera as being a Deputy in the Italian Parliament named, most inappropriately, Carlo Angelino.

'Pay us a visit,' he assured Hartman. 'Any time.' And as the couple departed they distinctly heard him remark to the officials, 'You're too suspicious, comrades. That one is worth knowing, whatever his origins.'

'What did you do for him?' Lotte asked as the train rattled back towards West Berlin. 'It must have been important.'

'Oh,' Hartman did not want to elaborate, 'I helped him and he helped me. It's a long story. A different side of war to Mother Courage.'

'War is so futile,' she said. 'Brecht is right. The ordinary people always suffer.' She did not return to the subject of Barba Nera, though she could tell that her companion remained abstracted.

The Sunday was his last day and she took him for her favourite walk through the woods towards the Havel River and the Wannsee, where sailing boats once again flitted across the water, like dragonflies reappearing after winter. They lay on the grass in the sun and picnicked, their bodies almost touching, and she stroked the thick hair on his forearm with a fingertip, feeling both content and sad at the same time. He would so soon be gone.

'We should be blood brothers, you and I,' she said softly. 'Well, brother and sister.'

'Why not?'

'Come on then. Here.' She found a pin in her bag and solemnly made a tiny scratch on the soft inside flesh of her arm, then did the same on his and rubbed the two together. It left a messy red stain on both their skins. 'Now, don't we have to swear an oath?'

'True unto death,' he suggested, half joking.

116

'True unto death,' she repeated, and leant across to kiss him on the cheek, but he turned towards her and the kiss came full on his lips instead.

'I think you can guess the rest.' Dr Lohrey smiled across the table at me. 'It was inevitable I suppose.' He was so attractive and strong. My imagination was in love with him before he had even arrived. But we were completely star-crossed. He was making his career in London, I wanted to remain in Germany. Berlin was always a city like no other. Well, one part of me would have given up everything, the other part began to see that he had a plan and there was no place for a wife yet. Of course I did not discover this at once. We met during holidays, he paid my ticket to England. Very slowly, oh God, very painfully also, we came out on the other side, like through a thorn hedge, being torn all the time, until in the end we had the friendship a man and a woman cannot have unless first they have been lovers. Can you understand?'

Intellectually, the only possible answer was 'Yes'. I could well imagine Camilla and me ending up as lifelong friends. But physically I could not imagine Father and this woman together, elegant as she was. Worse, they must still have been lovers for at least a year after his courtship of Mother began in earnest.

'We have all been young,' she said, misinterpreting my embarrassment, 'and you will be old one day also, Robert.'

'Somehow I always thought Mother was his great love.' It was the first excuse that came into my head, though true in its way.

'She was, of course, she is still.'

Anxious to escape from this emotional morass I asked if she had ever married herself.

'To a Swiss. That is why I live now in Geneva. Rudi died of cancer a few years back.'

'I'm sorry.'

'Let us talk of other things.'

I did my best, unable to escape from the story she had told me, which had raised a host of questions, far more than it had answered: among them Father's 'plan' and where Barba Nera fitted into his life.

'What was my father's plan?' I asked. 'You said he had one.'

She laughed with relief. 'It was so simple. He would be a millionaire before he was thirty-five. And by thirty-five he was.'

'But he almost went bankrupt?'

'About that I do not know.' She brushed it aside like an irritating insect. 'In any case, he is the kind who succeeds again. Always.'

'You said that last week he was "full of excitement"?'

'With any big deal he became, how can I say it in English, full of tension.' She qualified the statement quickly. 'In the past it was so and he was like that here.'

'Did he or Van Rensburg ever talk about a Concession Twenty-Two?'

The trap in that question was unintentional, but in any case did me little good.

'I am sorry, Robert. I recognize the symptom, I do not know the cause. As for Mr Van Rensburg, he is only a name your father gave me.'

There seemed little point in challenging her evasions further, so I let her steer the conversation where she wished. Predictably she continued asking about how I grew up, as if we shared an undeclared family bond. Perhaps she attached real significance to that childish ritual of mixing her and Father's blood, in the Berlin park so long ago. The only slight surprise came when she mentioned Carlo Angelino again.

'Barba Nera, you mean?'

'*Natürlich*. Did your father not speak of him? For a young girl that night at the theatre was an unforgettable occasion. I had not before that time seen former comrades in arms together.'

'I only heard about him from Van Rensburg. Didn't Father and he have some business association?'

'It is possible.' She backed off, as though her only interest was in wartime allegiances. 'Perhaps. In Italy Angelino was much respected.' She laid a distinct emphasis on the past tense. 'So people have told me.'

'Was?' I queried.

'He is now dead. One of my business clients knew him.'

I let that subject drop. The more dead ends of enquiry I could identify, the better. Van Rensburg's stories about Barba Nera had cast a savage light on a forgotten aspect of Father's past, but if the man was dead he was irrelevant to the present. Indeed I might equally be wasting my time on Mrs Lohrey. Her reticence could simply be due to having met Father here fortuitously, as she said. Given her own obsession with the past and the secrecy of whatever plan he was pursuing, their conversations might easily shed no light on my search. She was being evasive because she wanted to hear about the life Father had created for himself in Britain and didn't want me to lose interest in talking to her. When the coffee arrived I made a show of looking at the time. She instantly echoed my thoughts.

'I am afraid I talk too much,' she remarked self-deprecatingly, 'and after a certain age that can be boring. But I hope you keep me informed if your father is found. You will do that? I like you to promise.'

I swore to keep in touch and she walked out with me into the bright sun, shading her eyes against the glare until we saw my driver waiting a few yards off. She kissed me on both cheeks, then stood back. 'You asked many things, Robert. I am glad to answer. But one I am surprised you have not asked. Do you not want to know what happened to your grandparents?'

'They died in the Sachsenhausen concentration camp. Father told me.' I was unlikely to forget the bitterness in his voice when he related how he had eventually found out, a full seven years after the war ended.

'Mine also,' she said with quiet intensity. 'Sometimes people can be held together in such ways.'

I flew back to London that midnight, after lounging away the afternoon and evening at the Van Rensburgs' house, trying to sleep off accumulated exhaustion and only achieving disembodied fantasies of Father being found in some remote African village and this unwanted commitment ending.

We had been airborne long enough for the cabin crew to have dimmed the lights, and Africa was slipping out of my life as fast as it had enveloped me three days ago, when a steward touched my shoulder.

'The captain would like you to come to the flight deck, if you wouldn't mind, Sir.'

I pulled on my shoes and followed him forward. There was less space in the crew's isolated world than I had expected. The two pilots sat in their shirt-sleeves, with various control levers mounted between them, while a third officer worked at a tiny desk behind them, facing a high panel of instruments. I stood awkwardly by him while the captain rose from the left-hand seat and gripped my hand.

'My apologies for dragging you out, Mr Hartman, but it's more private here. We've just received a radio message for you.'

He had no need to warn me of bad news. It was implicit in his manner.

'I'm sorry to have to tell you,' he went on, 'that the wreckage of Sir James Hartman's jet has been found in southern Zaïre.'

For a moment I floundered, gazing inconsequentially at the pad on which the message had been taken down, as though it might tell me more. I wished to God I was in a private jet, able to change course as Father himself would have done in an emergency, and go straight to Zaïre. Then I pulled myself together.

'What about survivors?' I asked.

'The message was passed to us by Nairobi. There was no information about survivors. You have my deepest sympathy. If there is any message you would like to send yourself, we shall be glad to help.'

The captain stood attentively, while the airliner drove on through the darkness. There was a faint humming noise in the background. I tried to think.

'If I give you a telex number can you get through to my father's office? I want them to keep this from Lady Hartman until I'm home and can tell her myself.'

'No problem.' He scribbled this down and I looked up the telex number in my diary. 'If there is anything else . . .' he offered.

'You did say southern Zaïre?' The maps ranged around the briefing room out at Wilson airport came into my mind. The Gulfstream's route ought to have passed straight across the centre of that huge country, not the south. 'Do you know where?'

He consulted his notes. 'Approximately 300 miles south-west of Kinshasa. They didn't give a latitude and longitude.'

'You have a map?'

'Only the radio navigational charts, I'm afraid.'

He reached for a large black document case, extracted several folded maps and spread one out on the engineer's table. It was white, dominated by straight black lines between circles representing radio beacons and heavily annotated with figures. The outline of Zaïre was faintly visible as a background. He made a quick measurement, then with a pencil described a light arc southwest of Kinshasa.

'Pretty approximate, you understand Sir.'

There was no need for him to say more. The pencil mark was at least 200 miles south of the normal airline route which the Gulfstream would have followed.

'They were flying from Nairobi,' I said. 'Would a professional pilot stray so far off course, even in an emergency?'

'Frankly, Mr Hartman, speculation seldom helps.' He sounded unwilling to speak ill of the dead. 'There must have been some major failure to cause a crash at all.'

I left it at that, thanked him and returned to my seat, where I lay stretched out in the darkened cabin, wondering whether the crash might have been survivable and how long it would be before we had definite news. Nothing was clear-cut, except that in Father's absence I should have to start making decisions. My role as a spectator was over, if it hadn't already ceased since the burglary.

A week ago, if asked, I could have provided a straightforward biography of Father's career. Now, it seemed characteristic that his death – if dead he was – should be surrounded with unaccountable circumstances. Images of him came to me as I tried to sleep, and strangely they were all photographic ones: the false pioneering of Rukanga, the bland optimism of that personally disastrous topping out ceremony, the snarl at whatever media man had angered him just before his disappearance. I could not pluck a single sharp picture from my own memories. It struck me that in talking about the emotional bonds and commitments of the past Mrs Lohrey had unwittingly spoken with more relevance than she realized.

CHAPTER TEN

Camilla gave me a quick, anxious kiss. To my pleasure she was standing by the barrier when I emerged from the Heathrow customs hall at breakfast time on Friday morning, May 28th.

'The least I could do was come and meet you after such dreadful news,' she said, taking my briefcase.

'Which news?' I stopped dead, letting other passengers jostle past. A man bumped his luggage trolley into my ankles. 'What do you mean?'

She guided me out of the way. 'It was on the ten o'clock news last night about your father's jet being found. The Trust made a statement. I know you didn't like him all that much, but I'm still terribly sorry.'

'But I radioed Stainton to hold any announcement until I was back!' I was tired, but not so tired as to miss the implications.

She looked puzzled. 'It said the next of kin had been informed.'

'The bastards,' I muttered, reasoning this through.

'Rather a lot has been going on, as a matter of fact.' She glanced around the crowded concourse as though wary of eavesdroppers. 'We can talk in the car.'

When we reached her white VW Golf in the multi-storey car park the likely effects of the Trust's statement were already clear in my mind. No time had been allowed for me to react or influence what the Press was being told. The natural assumption would be that Father had perished in the crash. The Trust's share price would drop sharply the moment the Stock Exchange opened, with the brokers marking the price down automatically on the news. Stainton's own hand would be strengthened at this afternoon's Board meeting.

'The bastard,' I repeated, as I explained this to Camilla. 'Quite apart from all that, how could he be so inconsiderate to Mother?'

'I phoned her at once. I was to have gone down to see her today. Stainton had just broken the news. He'd apologized and said it would have been impossible to wait for clarification because the news agencies would have picked it up. That could be true.'

'Possibly. How did Mother sound?'

'Very upset and determined not to show it.' Camilla's fingers strayed to the ignition key, as though she'd had enough of talking. 'How would you expect her to be with an ex-girlfriend of yours? It wasn't very easy for me either.'

'I'm sorry. But I'm glad you spoke to her. Personally I shall only believe Father's dead when I see his body. We have to fight our corner today on the assumption that he's still alive. Plane crashes sometimes have survivors.'

'What do you mean "fight our corner"?' She gave me a sidelong glance, her hand no longer hovering around the key. 'You're not involved with the takeover.'

'I wasn't when I left. I am now.' I told her briefly about the burglary and the document and remarked with a harsh humour, 'A hack historian would call the whole business Byzantine. If anyone had told me last Monday that within three days I'd be shooting a man I'd have laughed at them. Even if Father is dead I still intend to find out what he was doing. And I don't want Frank Stainton dictating my family's interests. You said a lot has been going on. It certainly has.'

'Well, well. So you don't like hocus-pocus after all!' She was teasing, yet I sensed an undertone of relief. 'In that case, you ought not to be sitting gossiping. I can tell you what's been happening at this end on the way home. Lady Hartman's coming up from Godstow this morning. I'll take you to my place for a bath and breakfast and you can go on from there.'

On the way into London she told me that rumours were being spread around the City about Father having a discreditable past. A reporter she knew had been tipped off by Consolidated's Press Officer about the near-bankruptcy in 1957.

'But that's no secret!' I exclaimed.

'My friend seemed to think it was.'

'Well, I agree it's not Father's favourite subject. Surely the important point is that he did NOT go broke?'

'Not to a journalist. The scandal is what matters for the story.' We were reaching the part of the M4 where it narrows from three lanes to two and she didn't say any more until we were safely on the flyover. 'What I suspect, Bob, is that Consolidated want their shareholders to be frightened of your father's reputation. "Ever since 1956," they want the papers to say, "Sir James Hartman has been taking enormous risks in Africa. And what's happened now? He's disappeared there! Would you trust a man like that with your money?" I did warn you research might lead to unpleasant discoveries. And there's also the 1949 court case.'

'1949?' I hadn't even been born then. 'How far back does this go, for God's sake?' Was it something Lotte Lohrey had concealed?

'The details are at the flat. You ought to read them for yourself. Even if he has survived, I don't think he could stop them being republished.'

She refused to say more until we were at Pelham Court and I had washed and changed. Then, over breakfast, she gave me a folder to leaf through. The first item was a cutting from a London evening newspaper of November 1949, or rather a photostat of one. It was only a short report, but the headline gave it spice.

BANKER ACCUSED.
Banker James Hartman, 28, of Lexham Gardens, South Kensington, appeared at Rochester Row Magistrates Court yesterday accused of living off immoral earnings. The prosecution claimed that he had received rent from a prostitute, Jane . . .

'To be honest,' Camilla said, 'it does sound pretty damning. He must have known what was going on in his own house.'

'Do you plead guilty or not guilty?' After the clerk had put the charge the stipendiary magistrate looked across the courtroom at Hartman with curiosity rather than severity. He was a man of about fifty, handsome in a reclusive way, dressed in a businessman's pinstripe blue suit and without the disfigurement of a judge's curled wig. Above him the royal coat of arms on the wall was a heraldic reminder of his ultimate authority, the Crown. James Hartman faced him in the dock. Between the two sat the clerk of the court and the two solicitors, one representing the police, the other the defendant.

'Not guilty, Sir.' Hartman stood stiffly to attention as if on parade. To his left a policeman took notes, while another, the dock officer, watched.

'You may sit down Mr Hartman.' Something caught the magistrate's memory. He consulted his papers. 'Captain Hartman,' he corrected himself, and glanced at the lawyer. 'Your client prefers to be known by his former rank?'

'Yes, Sir.'

'Not always an advantage, I should have thought.'

'It was hard earned, Sir.' The young lawyer named Curtis whom Hartman had hired intended to emphasize his client's wartime record: he was slightly in awe of it himself.

'Now, Mr Stanley.' The magistrate turned briskly to the police prosecutor, who appeared frequently before him. 'The defendant has already been remanded twice at your request. Is there any reason this case should not be brought to trial today?'

Seated. Hartman prayed the answer would be negative. It was vital to get this over with.

'The police would have appreciated more time, Sir.' Stanley was an ageing solicitor, his skin the dead colour of parchment, long versed in the wiles of petty crime. He had back trouble and stooped as he confronted the magistrate. He was convinced of Hartman's guilt, first offender and war hero or not. He was less sure about the quality of the evidence, and whether the police had been prudent in charging him with living off immoral earnings rather than the lesser offence of allowing his premises to be used for prostitution. They were a shade too keen to have him jailed, not merely fined.

'My client has recently become engaged to be married, Sir,' Curtis intervened. 'He is anxious for the charge against him to be heard as soon as possible.'

'Understandably.' The magistrate was equally in a mood to go ahead. The police asked for remands too often. They ought to complete their homework before issuing a summons. 'The charge against the defendant,' he summarized, 'is that between March 25th and October 30th this year Captain Hartman accepted rent for the basement of his house, knowing that it was being used for the purposes of prostitution. In other words, that he was living off immoral earnings. We have heard his plea of not guilty. Kindly proceed, Mr Stanley.'

'First, Sir, I shall call evidence to prove that the tenant of the basement, Miss Jane Newell, has regularly solicited in the Cromwell Road area and that she takes clients back to the rooms she rents from the defendent.'

As one by one the prosecution called its police officer witnesses, each going through the routine of being sworn in, Bible in hand, and then entering the wood-panelled witness box to give evidence, Hartman's confidence declined. A next-door neighbour was called to state that men could be seen going in and out at all hours. The magistrate nodded agreement. He was clearly satisfied that Jane Newell was a prostitute and using the basement for her trade.

Hartman remembered what his lawyer had said before this, his first ever appearance in a court of law. 'They can prove anything they like about the tart. What matters is whether you knew what she was up to, or the beak can infer that you did.'

The next witness was a police sergeant who had interviewed Hartman and quoted his saying that since the basement had its own entrance he had been able to charge more than to others lodging in the house and that he was trying to pay off a mortgage.

'As many people are,' the magistrate observed, then addressed the prosecuting solicitor, who had let his mouth twitch fractionally in appreciation of the remark. 'But on what grounds do you submit that the defendant knew from what source his mortgage was being paid off?'

'From the great size of it, Sir.' He turned to the sergeant in the box. 'Did the defendant make any statement as to the exact amount?'

The sergeant consulted his notebook. 'Twenty pounds a week, Sir. I couldn't believe it, Sir. I asked him if it was correct twenty pounds a week was paid' – both the policeman's expression and his tone underlined how vast a sum this was – 'and he admitted that was the case.'

'And what would a normal rental in the area be?'

'Three to four pounds, Sir.'

'Surely a policeman is hardly an expert witness on rental values, Mr Stanley,' the magistrate interrupted.

'I hope that if the defendant consents to give evidence I shall be able to elucidate the point further, Sir.'

'I hope so. Do you wish to call further witnesses, Mr Stanley?'

'No, Sir.'

There was a moment of silence. Two women in the public gallery whispered, the clerk of the court shuffled papers, Hartman tried to assess the mood and was uncertain. A great deal more than a sentence was on the line for him. A verdict of guilty spelt the end of any engagement to Anne, the loss of his job, the cutting off at the roots of his career in Britain. He wished he had not closed his eyes to Jane's profession. Normal rents would have paid off his bank loan in the end. He tried to keep his expression anxiously unemotional, the stalwart yet human hero. Even so, his own lawyer's next words horrified him.

'I accept the prosecution's case, Sir.' Curtis, conscious of being greatly his opponent's junior, enjoyed exploiting such drama as a drab police court offered. 'The case that Miss Newell plied her trade from the basement of Captain Hartman's house. But I submit that the defendant was totally unaware of it and that so far as he is concerned there is no case to answer. He has, of course, already evicted Miss Newell from the building.'

There was a further pause. The dock officer eyed Hartman, deciding he was not as innocent as he protested. The two solicitors stood almost alongside each other, waiting while the magistrate pondered, rubbing his forefinger against his cheekbone. Hartman himself sat immobile in the dock, already thinking beyond the verdict. Whichever way it went he would be a fool to keep the house: the police would watch every single lodger. He would have to sell, repay the loan from the bank he worked for and find somewhere else. The thought of the bank's attitude worried him most of all.

The magistrate looked up, his cogitation over, and addressed the defence. 'I regret, Mr Curtis, that I am unable to accept your submission. I should like to hear the prosecution's case answered. Does the defendant wish to give evidence himself?'

Hartman swore to himself. Curtis had briefed him on his 'right of silence': to refuse cross-examination in case he incriminated himself. But the solicitor had advised him not to insist on the right because it would look so bad on the part of an ex-officer. Curtis caught his eye and he gave a little nod.

'The defendant is happy to give evidence, Sir.'

Remembering the army phrase 'you can't win 'em all', Hartman wondered what kind of an image he did present to the magistrate. When he answered questions should he abandon the laborious middle-class phrases which he still did not speak quite correctly? Should it be obvious that he'd come up from the ranks? He was still uncertain as he listened to Curtis open on his behalf, stressing his war record and then moving smoothly on to the questions they had rehearsed beforehand.

'Tell me about your house, Captain Hartman.'

'The house has four floors and a basement. I rent out seven rooms, apart from the basement, and I live on the top floor myself. I am studying for banking. It is more quiet there.'

'Now tell me, Captain Hartman, when you decided to let the basement of your house, how did you go about it?'

'I advertised it in the evening papers.'

'And you had a large number of replies?'

'A large number, Sir.'

'And what did you do?'

'It was difficult. I did not exactly know what a self-contained flat should be worth.'

'So you accepted the highest offer?'

'That is correct.'

'I presume you asked for references?'

'Mr Curtis,' the magistrate interrupted, 'you may not lead the defendent. He must answer for himself. How did he decide which potential tenant to accept?'

'I asked for a bank reference and a personal reference. Miss Newell provided both.' Hartman thought of the basement: dark and damp, with thick pipes running along the passage wall, a chipped china sink in the kitchen and a flaring gas geyser to heat the water, its living room equipped with thin curtains and stained furniture. The flat was shabby even by the standards of postwar austerity. 'I also asked for a deposit against damage,' he added. 'Miss Newell was willing.'

A quick smile transformed the magistrate's solemnity. He had little doubt that the tenant was willing in many ways. 'Thank you,' he said. 'Please continue Mr Curtis.'

Having been reprimanded, Curtis became more circumspect. He was learning his profession as a barrister and the low fee Hartman was paying reflected the fact. He took note of the smile and responded. 'Captain Hartman, I should like a straight answer. Were you aware of Miss Newell's profession?'

'No, Sir. She told me she was a fashion model and well paid.'

The magistrate nodded. He knew that 'model' was the new euphemism. But could the police prove that the defendant knew?

When the turn came for Stanley to cross-examine for the prosecution this was the point he pursued, setting out to trap Hartman in his pedantic, world-weary manner.

'How long have you been in London?'

'Since I left the army in 1947, Sir. Two years.'

'You said you rent out seven rooms. To seven people?'

'There is a married couple, Sir.'

'Eight people? A busy house!'

'I try not to interfere with their private life, Sir.'

'Captain Hartman, how much rent does each of these individuals pay?'

'Two pounds a week, Sir; the married couple pays three.'

'And did Miss Newell pay the same?'

'She had two rooms and her own bathroom and she paid more.'

'How much more?'

When he was first interviewed by the police, Hartman had considered lying, then realized that Jane Newell might have given him a kiss and wink when he told her she had to leave, but that was no guarantee of her discretion. What if she'd done a deal with the police?

'She paid twenty pounds a week, Sir.'

'What is your own salary as a trainee banker, Captain Hartman?'

'Four hundred and fifty pounds a year, Sir.'

'Four hundred and fifty?' Stanley's tone expressed dry surprise. 'And this lady paid you in excess of one thousand in rent? She was a valuable tenant, Captain Hartman. Did you not wonder how she could afford so much?'

'She told me she was well paid. Rents for self-contained flats *are* very high.'

'Not often higher than salaries, surely. Are you aware Captain Hartman that a Member of Parliament's salary is fractionally less than twenty pounds per week: one thousand pounds per annum to be precise?'

'I was not, Sir.'

'Perhaps you can tell me what a second lieutenant in the army now receives. That would set a standard you appreciate, would it not?'

Hartman did know. 'Four pounds ten shillings a week, Sir,' he admitted.

'I think you have made your point, Mr Stanley,' the magistrate cut in. Only a prostitute or a criminal would pay £20 a week for a basement near the Earls Court Road. But had Hartman been in London long enough to know that?

'Thank you, Sir.' Stanley inclined his balding head towards the bench, then resumed on a different tack. 'Captain Hartman, how often did you see Miss Newell?'

'Very seldom, Sir. She had her own entrance. I have said, I lived on the top floor. How should I see her?'

'You were friendly perhaps?'

Hartman remembered the soft, provocative kiss on his lips. 'No, Sir.'

'But you knew she had a lot of visitors?'

'No, Sir. She had her private entrance. I might not see her for weeks running.'

'Come, come, Captain,' Stanley's tone was incredulous. 'Are you telling this court that she pays you twenty pounds per week and you do not even meet her to collect the rent? The cash, Captain. How do you receive the cash? Do you not sign her rent book?'

Hartman glanced across at the magistrate, who was leaning forward intently and seemed both interested in the line of questioning and unhappy with it.

'Mr Stanley,' he interrupted, 'sarcasm is inappropriate in this court.'

'Tell me, Captain Hartman.' Stanley was unperturbed. He was winning. 'Did you receive the rent in person every week as is normal or did you not?'

'Not in person, Sir.' Hartman glanced at Curtis and was answered with the ghost of a smile. This was the question that Curtis himself had planned to ask in his concluding examination. Far better that the prosecution should have it blow up in their own faces.

'Then how did you receive it?'

'Through a bank by standing order.'

The magistrate stiffened in his ornate chair, amazed at the conclusion this appeared to be reaching.

'But you told the police that your lodgers paid in cash?'

'My lodgers do pay cash. Sir. That is normal. Miss Newell rented the flat for one year. For such a rental a monthly bank order is normal. Also it makes my accounting for tax more simple.'

'For tax! You can provide proof, I take it?' the magistrate asked.

'I have the bank statements here, Sir.' Curtis handed a folder to the clerk of the court, who stood up and passed them on. After a brief perusal the magistrate handed them back.

'Thank you.' With his long experience of prostitutes and pimps being brought before him the magistrate was satisfied. Few professions dealt more exclusively in cash than the oldest. Jane Newell was a prostitute. But if she paid the defendant monthly by banker's order he could be excused for believing models were highly paid, as genuine fashion models were. 'These bank statements seem clear enough to me. Have you any further questions, Mr Stanley?'

'Confronted with such a model landlord, Sir, I have not.' Stanley resumed his seat, annoyed at being outmanoeuvred. Whoever had advised Hartman to accept the prostitute's rent by standing order was exceptionally shrewd. The Inland Revenue probably wouldn't get far with him either, though they'd be certain to examine his accounts as a result of this prosecution being reported in the papers.

'Does the defence wish to make a final submission?' The magistrate extended the traditional courtesy of the last word to Curtis.

'Only to emphasize that it is not customary for those who live off immoral earnings to make voluntary returns to the Inland Revenue, Sir.'

'Captain Hartman.' The magistrate had come to his decision and the dock sergeant hissed at Hartman to stand up. 'The point at issue has been whether you knew that you were to some extent living off immoral earnings. I find there is insufficient evidence either to prove that you did or for me to infer beyond reasonable doubt that you did. The case is dismissed.'

'Thank you, Sir.'

Hartman stood to attention, thanking his stars for having refused to accept Jane Newell's rent in cash, his eyes fixed blankly on a point a foot or so above the magistrate's head, just as the army had taught him to look at commanding officers. Too late, the magistrate recognized this unfocused stare for what it was: the badge of the guilty soldier.

'I suggest, Captain Hartman,' he said, 'that you be more selective over your tenants in future.'

Camilla turned another page of the folder and showed me that evening's headline: 'WAR HERO ACQUITTED'.

'The man your father worked for was not impressed.'

'How do you know?'

'I spoke to him yesterday. He retired ages ago, of course. But he hasn't forgotten the scandal because the two of them had a pretty stormy session as a result.'

When he left the courtroom Hartman had been aware that the real trial was only just beginning. He could write a cheerfully innocent letter to Lotte Lohrey in Berlin, making light of the whole affair. That would be easy. She never read the London papers. His boss and his intended fiancée's father did. Somehow he had to gain the initiative with them and he went about this with a single-mindedness comparable to that of a man who has to cut away his own flesh after a snakebite because he has no serum: the serum in this case being a birthright of social advantage.

From the court in Rochester Row he went straight to a firm of estate agents in South Kensington and gave instructions for the sale of the house. Then, in what remained of the afternoon, he returned to the merchant bank where he had only recently been promoted an assistant in the investment department and requested an interview with the director to whom he was responsible. However Gerald Anderson, the ex-Guards officer who had given him his chance, was not available. Hartman forced himself back into his ordinary routine, disregarding the ribald comments of his colleagues, and waited.

Discretion was the bank's watchword, and Hartman himself would later emulate its approach. Its name did not appear on the writing paper used by the directors, nor did their names: all that the heavily embossed heading gave was the street address in the City. Its dealings were as unobtrusive and as influential as they had been when the original Huguenot partners made their fortunes out of helping to finance the Napoleonic wars.

Gerald Anderson was given to remarking cheerfully that he himself was 'not of the blood', but that was a pose. His own family was more distinguished, if less rich, than any of the bank's founders, and when their descendants recruited him, in the 1930s, they knew they had found the rare combination of a gentleman with an instinct for finance. He had reached colonel's rank during the war. Now, at fifty odd, he had the relaxedly brusque manner of a person born to rule. Hartman both admired and envied him. Eventually, on the afternoon after the court case, when he did consent to receive Hartman in his mahogany-panelled office, he came directly to the point.

'Sit down, James. Well, what are you going to do next?'

'Sell the house and repay your loan, Sir.'

'Given that we granted it on condition of owner occupation, you have very little alternative.'

'I have been living there myself.'

'In very undesirable company, too.' Anderson referred quickly to the single file on his uncluttered desk. 'You appreciate that it's out of the question for you to continue working here.'

'But I have been acquitted!'

'I understand the case was dismissed for lack of evidence. So far as I am concerned that is not an acquittal. You've a great deal of commercial acumen, James. Possibly too much. We cannot be seen to employ anyone involved in scandal.'

Hartman's temper was rising, fuelled as much by fear of what Anne's parents would say as by anger at the bank's readiness to ditch him. If he'd been 'one of them', the self-assured, patrician City network of friends and relatives would have closed around him like a human stockade, protecting and excusing. Because he was an immigrant and an outsider – which the bank's founders themselves had been when they started – he was being dumped. He decided to fight back.

'You cannot fire me for something I have not done. That is wrongful dismissal.'

'Don't play the barrack room lawyer.' Anderson gave him a hard look. 'The fact is, James, we can sack you for any reason we like, including breaking the terms of the loan.'

Hartman stood up, his cheeks flushed. 'I'll sue you,' he said. 'I'll take you to court.'

'And never work in the City again? Don't be so bloody stupid. Sit down and answer my question. What are you going to do next?'

An undertone of friendliness in Anderson's words made Hartman obey. He could not challenge the power of the bank. At least, not yet. Furthermore a disregarded proposition had come into his mind, one that would show he could survive without patronage if he wanted.

'I have been offered a business,' he said. 'Since you ask.'

'In what?'

'Import export.'

'Lot of government restrictions, you know. Exchange controls. Customs duties.'

'Imports will grow.' When he had adopted an idea, Hartman defended it, and he thought fast. The same project which he had turned down some months ago because of Britain's postwar economic austerity reassembled in his mind as he spoke. He elaborated for a minute or so.

'You'll need capital.'

'Because I was happy here I did not go into that. I refused the idea.'

'Well,' Anderson was only temporarily discountenanced, 'I appreciate loyalty. Send me a funding proposal and if it looks right we'll back you.' He stood up himself and extended his hand.

'I shall expect to hear from you. In the meantime you can collect three months' salary from the cashier.'

Hartman shook hands with deliberate formality and departed. He had reached a turning point. He would take the bank's conscience money and when he returned to the City it would be to give orders, not accept them.

'Did Anderson tell you what Father's proposition was?' I asked Camilla.

'He remembers it was connected with Italian imports, that the bank did back it and your father repaid them a year later. What the business was seemed less relevant now than the scandal.'

The final items in her folder were clippings from a long defunct newspaper, the *Sunday Pictorial*. The first was a sensation-mongering interview with Jane Newell, along with a photograph of her provocatively half dressed. The second was a paragraph apologizing for any misunderstanding the previous story might have caused and stating that the newspaper never intended to suggest Captain Hartman had lived off the earnings of Miss Newell and that a settlement had been agreed. I could imagine the cold fury with which Father must have pursued the paper. However, Camilla's diligent research only really posed further questions.

'Why should Consolidated want to rake this muck over thirty-three years later?' I asked. 'Do they seriously think their shareholders will take any notice?'

'They're out to destroy your father's character. They announced that a bid from him would be regarded as hostile.'

'He'll sue them. The air will be thick with writs.'

'If he's alive,' Camilla said gently. 'The dead can't sue and you couldn't on his behalf, even if you wanted to.'

She had a strong point there. The more we probed into Father's past, the more clear it became that his character was an extraordinary blend of brilliance and opportunism, often despicably amoral if not immoral. The only reason for defending him would be to protect my mother.

'Why not phone the office?' Camilla suggested. 'It'll be open now and there might be more news.'

I took the advice and was eventually connected to Andrew Ferguson, who sounded as raw and tired as I felt myself.

'Yes, we have heard something. I was called in early and I'm waiting for Frank Stainton to arrive. We've had a telex from Kinshasa. An incomprehensible one. There's some fracas with the authorities about identifying the bodies.'

'You mean there was a fire?' An empty pain caught my gut. To be burnt alive was a medieval death.

'I don't think so. Roeyen has sent a man down to the crash site. Apparently he'd never met Sir James and because he can't be positive they've arrested him. They're demanding someone from London. The whole business is insane.'

'If necessary I'll go myself.'

'You'd be taking a risk.'

I refrained from remarking that risks were what paid his salary and that his division of the Trust had been notably unsuccessful in taking the right ones. Instead I confirmed our lunch appointment.

'There'll not be much to talk about.' His native Scots accent surfaced, as if brought out by my demands.

'I don't agree,' I said bluntly and asked to be transferred to our Press Officer, who proved not to be in yet, forcing me to leave a noncommittal message. I wanted him to remind the media that Father's death was unconfirmed and that until it was they'd better be careful. But I could hardly relay that through a secretary. During a crisis like this the Press Officer should have been in early too, damn him. If I were in charge I'd have fired the man.

Camilla then ameliorated my ill-temper by driving me to Westminster, which was nice of her even if she was being paid.

'Don't mention those old scandals to your mother, will you Bob,' she counselled as she dropped me off at the grandiose Edwardian entrance to our block of flats. 'She's had quite enough on her mind without ghosts from the past. And if she'd rather have the Board meeting postponed, support her. She may not want a showdown with Stainton, even if for some inexplicable reason you do.'

I kissed Camilla on the cheek and thanked her. She was astute as well as sensitive. The Board would have to defer to us, superficially at least.

Mother greeted me with a warm hug and a kind of controlled relief, as though I were a soldier back on leave from a war to which I had to return.

'It is nice to see you, darling.' She embraced me impetuously again. 'Not that I was worried. But the last few days haven't been much fun and that burglary sounded quite frightening.'

'You heard about it?' I had deliberately not told her.

'Frank Stainton thought I might want to send a message to the Van Rensburgs. I did, of course. Poor Patrick. I'm thankful you weren't hurt.' She paused and held my shoulders. 'Here, let me look at you. You must be exhausted. Come along and I'll make you some breakfast.' She led the way to the kitchen and I had not the heart to say that Camilla had fed me already, because she needed to mask her anxiety about Father with the activity of laying the table and cooking. She raised the question as she was beating eggs without looking up.

'The office rang again before you came. They said your father's . . .' She choked on the next word and had to start again. 'They said he hadn't been identified. Is that good or bad?'

'It must be good.' I had to be positive.

'You mean he could have survived and gone for help?'

'Possibly.' His struggling injured through the bush was hardly a line to pursue. 'What occurred to me was that he might have stayed on secretly in Kenya.'

'Bob, darling.' She put down the pan and looked at me reprovingly. 'You're talking nonsense. He's been gone for a whole week. He would never be out of touch for as long as that. Don't try to console me with stupid inventions.'

She sounded so miserable that I got up and gave her another hug.

'I don't understand about this identity thing.' She dabbed at her eyes. 'We just have to hope, don't we? There's nothing else to do.'

Inevitably, though, our conversation circled around the subject the whole morning, if only because Mother wanted a full account of my doings. But I left out the document I had discovered in Van Rensburg's study and the meetings with Dr Lohrey. Omitting them detracted from my secret deal theory, which she was inclined to dismiss. Her thinking was completely straightforward, like my grandfather the General's. I suppose most people either look at things that way, with chance pulling out the jokers from the pack, or else they see human affairs as controlled by a series of conspiracies, as Father did. Thus, unlike me, she saw nothing odd in Frank Stainton telling her about the burglary, whereas I was doubtful of his motives for no definable reason.

The one outcome of our long talk was that Mother decided against asking for a postponement of the directors' meeting. She thoroughly mistrusted the single agenda item 'To consider the Directorate'.

'If they are lining up against us,' she said with a robustness more like her usual self, 'then the sooner it's out in the open the better. I just pray Andrew Ferguson can explain this takeover business to me clearly. I don't want to look a complete fool this afternoon.'

We lunched at the Savoy Grill, a favourite spot of hers. 'When I was a girl,' she told Andrew Ferguson with a little smile, 'I used to dream about staying at the Savoy: the impossible dream in those days.' However, the surroundings did not distract her attention from what he had to say.

'What Sir James was planning, Lady Hartman, was to launch

his bid for Consolidated Diamond Concessions next week. We'd have been printing the offer papers to send their shareholders this weekend and it was an attractive offer too, very cannily pitched.'

'How exactly?'

'We'd have been offering two of our shares for every three of Consolidated's with a pound in cash on top. Before Sir James went to Africa our shares stood at 452 pence each, which was a lot more than Consolidated's were at 290.'

Mother quietly slipped a tiny calculator out of her handbag and to Ferguson's astonishment did the sums herself. It wasn't hard to guess that he had a low opinion of women in business and her competence unnerved him.

'So our offer totalled £10.04 for each £8.70 worth of their shares?'

'Entirely correct, Lady Hartman, as ye say.' He was a humble Scot again.

'Not over-generous,' I suggested.

'Sir James had some kind of a trick up his sleeve, I believe. He was certain the Consolidated price would fall. He could have arranged for institutions abroad to buy into our stock. That would push our own price up, you know.'

'A concert party?' I asked.

'That's the slang the brokers have for it.'

'But Consolidated would fight back, wouldn't they?' Mother observed.

'They would indeed, Lady Hartman. They'd tell their shareholders it was a pitiful offer, and their company was being undervalued: they'd be producing glowing forecasts for the next five years and all the rest of it. Sir James wasna' worried. He told us he had them by the short and curlies – forgive the expression – and we'd win in a fortnight.'

'And what has actually happened?'

'The Trust's shares are down to 328 pence and Consolidated's up to 340.'

Mother was busy with the figures again. 'So we couldn't possibly make a bid on the basis my husband planned?'

'Worse I'm afraid, Lady Hartman. They could take advantage of the drop and his absence to mount a raid on us.'

'I see.'

Being fairly sure that she didn't, at least not fully, I prodded Ferguson.

'If they managed to take over the Trust – if they got the necessary 51 per cent of shares or voting pledges – would Father be removed as Chief Executive?'

'I should say almost certainly, Mr Hartman. Every one of us would be in danger. They'd give no quarter if the tables were turned.'

'You mean they could simply throw my husband out?' Her alarm began to show. 'They could dismiss him in spite of his having created the Trust?'

'Not only could, Lady Hartman. Most likely would. Even your size of shareholding cannot guarantee a seat on a company's Board.'

We all three sat quiet for a moment. My mind ranged over what this meant. We would always be rich, of course. They couldn't deprive Father of his existing wealth or of his dividends. But his one million salary plus bonuses would dry up. Worse, he would be cut off from the back-up of the Trust's resources: the jets, the cars and chauffeurs, the lawyers, the vast expenses, our London flat. His international influence would collapse. A tycoon without a power base is like a beached whale.

'Dear God,' Mother murmured, injecting a wry and brave humour into the prospect. 'I always complain that I'd like to see more of Jim at home, but he'd be impossible to live with. Quite impossible.'

Ferguson laughed, not altogether easily. 'Fortunately it hasna come to that yet, and Sir James is a man of truly exceptional resource.'

'What was the trick he had up his sleeve?' I asked. 'The one which would defeat Consolidated?'

'That I cannot tell you. Frank Stainton may know.'

'Or Van Rensburg?'

'I could not say. It sounds to be connected with mining.'

'Well, Andrew,' Mother had heard enough. 'I really am most grateful to you.' She slipped the pocket calculator back into her handbag. 'Now I understand what the Trust is facing, and between ourselves I do not like this afternoon's agenda. I hope you will support me.'

'I certainly shall, Lady Hartman.'

Ferguson was a poor dissembler. I reckoned Stainton had been doing some quiet whipping-in during the morning to line up the votes for whatever he had in mind, which was most likely his own promotion. There wasn't a great deal of logic behind my presentiments: I just felt that Father had trampled on his ambitions too often in the past. My guesswork was reinforced when Ferguson excused himself before the waiter brought coffee, saying he had things to do before the meeting began. He probably didn't want to be seen arriving at Hartman House with us.

'Listen, Ma,' I said after he had gone, 'whatever happens, don't let them appoint a new Chairman or Chief Executive. Plump for an executive committee, if they insist. This agenda item "to consider the Directorate" could be turned into anything.'

'Robert, darling, there's no need for you to be so protective. I shan't let them stampede me: although it would be nice if they let you attend as well.'

'You can always ask.'

'Perhaps I will,' she said and left it at that.

Half an hour later I was accompanying her up the steps into the building and an obstinately optimistic greeting from one of the commissionaires.

'Don't worry, m'Lady. Sir James'll be back. If he ain't been found dead, he must be alive. Only stands to reason, don't it?'

They always were as loyal as family retainers, and I could never quite comprehend why Father inspired such devotion. We were ushered to the lift and escorted to the fourteenth floor with great solicitousness, there to be met by Frank Stainton, sombrely dressed and smiling with an appropriate degree of restraint.

'Anne, my dear, it's good of you to come, very good indeed.' He pressed her hand, obsequious as a courtier, then shook mine. 'How are you, Robert? Good to see you.' This tiny burst of effusion over, he turned back to Mother. 'The afternoon's formalities will not last long. During the present uncertainty someone has to take decisions.'

'I appreciate that. Do I have to provide proof that Jim nominated me as his alternate?'

'Good heavens, no.' Stainton made an attempt at light-heartedness. 'The proxy's been on file with the Company Secretary for years.'

'Could Robert attend as well?'

'Robert?' He was momentarily off-balance. 'As an observer? Only by invitation of the Board. It would require a vote. On another occasion, perhaps. Well,' he dismissed me, 'the others are waiting, Anne. Shall we go through?'

He led her along the deep carpets towards the Boardroom's double rosewood doors, above which a tiny light glowed red, warning against unwarranted intrusions. No sign indicated what lay beyond, and I reflected how typical that was of Father's approach to business. Everything at Hartman House concealed, rather than revealed. Even the Trust's Annual Report, fulfilling the legal requirements for a quoted public company, left unstated the activities of a string of holding concerns which spanned the world from Liechtenstein to the Dutch Antilles and back via the Bahamas to Jersey, every one of them as blank-faced as those doors. I wished I could be a fly on the wall at the meeting, then turned away and went along to visit Christianne, hopeful of clues to the power struggle in the Trust, if only oblique ones.

'So you came back, Robert,' she remarked, indicating an armchair. 'I think that was wise.'

'You warned me not to be away too long.'

'I would not say warned. Advised perhaps.' She smoothed her impossible gold hair and sat back behind the desk, waiting.

'A week can be a long time. What's been going on here?'

'They have been getting cold feet,' she said with contempt. 'Suddenly they do not like risks any more.'

'And Father had taken one too many?'

'I am afraid so.'

'Do you know who he was really visiting in Africa?' I thought of that over-simple itinerary, with its neat timings and ministerial appointments: and the blank weekend in Kinshasa. 'What wasn't on the list?'

'He did not tell anyone.' She gave way a fraction. 'Except that he was going to the capital of Angola last Sunday to discuss a deal.'

'Concession Twenty-Two?'

She gave me a sharp look. 'You are very well informed, Robert. But he never had those talks, so how can they have a connection with the crash? The only result is to embarrass the Board, who do not know everything he planned.'

I fell silent, speculating on how much she knew and where the burglary at Van Rensburg's house fitted in. Then the telex machine in the corner began clacking and she rose to read the incoming message, gave a tiny whistling exclamation of '*Zut alors*', tore the paper out and came back to stand beside me.

'You read French? Maybe it's easier I translate in any case. This comes from Roeyen in Zaïre. They have found only three bodies on the plane, not five as there should be. There is no woman's body and no man with the description of your father, although one of the three corpses is older.'

'That could be Captain Holz?'

'I suppose.'

She hesitated, which was unlike her, and eventually seemed to come to a decision, going to open a walnut-faced cupboard which concealed a small safe, carefully twirling the rings of the combination lock and lifting out an envelope. She balanced this briefly on her palm as if still uncertain then gave it to me. The envelope was thick, crisp and embossed with Father's crest on the flap, the kind he reserved for private correspondence.

'Sir James left this for you, Robert. I think you should have it now.' She moved away. 'I am going to take in the telex.'

She left and I slit open the heavy envelope with a paperknife, as apprehensive as if I were receiving a message through a medium. The letter was in Father's neatly assertive writing and began in the customary cold way he had maintained even after our quarrels were settled.

Dear Robert, I have been taking a calculated risk. Christianne

139

will only give you this if I am delayed longer than a week, in which case you must assume something has gone wrong. Do not panic. Keep your head. We are involved in a complex and most important takeover bid, which could turn into an attack on us. If this happens call an Extraordinary General Meeting and vote the family shares in our defence. Various fund managers ought to support you. I enclose a list. Tell them I have been detained in secret negotiations abroad and will return as soon as possible. Bring Van Rensburg back from Kenya. He understands the position. Finally look after your mother. We both owe a great deal to her.

The letter was signed simply, 'Father'.

I was re-reading this, thinking that he hadn't even wished me well, when Christianne returned.

'Who did you give the telex to?' I asked.

'Lady Hartman was nearer to the door.' Her right eyelid fluttered in the suspicion of a wink. 'I gave it to her.'

'Thank you very much.' For the first time I felt some warmth in her expression, and on an impulse gave her Father's letter to read, adding the comment that I could hardly call on Van Rensburg when he was in hospital and that overall the instructions were as imprecise as they were condescending. Being told to 'keep my head' angered me. 'Is there anything else I should know?' I asked.

She made a moue and pondered a moment. 'I have to tell you, Robert, your father did not confide in anyone about this trip. We know he hoped to meet the President of Angola last Sunday and that is all we know.'

'How could he keep the Board in the dark?'

'Often he would reveal things only on the day decisions had to be made. I think on this trip the only person who knew must be Mr Van Rensburg. Will you go to Zaïre yourself?'

'Tomorrow, if they'll let me have one of the Falcons. I must confirm that Father was not on board the Gulfstream. And there could be documents.

'Then there is a small thing you should know, which could cause problems. Sir James had a sub-machinegun with him.'

'A what?' Father's deals might be nefarious, but he laid down the strictest rules about what was carried on his plane. He had sacked one of the crew for trying to smuggle a gold watch.

'It was not an ordinary gun at all,' Christianne said patiently. 'It was for a present and completely silver-plated, except what they call the "working parts". The make was Heckler and Koch.'

'Who on earth would want a silver gun?'

'Truly, Robert, I have no idea. Sir James always takes gifts, but never before such a bizarre thing. I only tell you because it could cause problems.'

'Well, thank you again.' She obviously could not elucidate this curiosity further and I was glad to be forewarned. 'I think I owe you a present myself.'

She affected a demure confusion. 'Really, Robert, that is not necessary. Perhaps we can have a drink when this is all over.' She changed the subject, tactfully describing the atmosphere at the Board meeting during her brief interruption of the proceedings, and commenting, 'It is not so easy for a woman to hold her own against so many men, that is why I gave the telex to her . . .'

CHAPTER ELEVEN

The prospect of facing the assembled directors had intimidated Anne Hartman more than she cared to admit, even to herself. She rationalized her fears by telling herself that if only Patrick Van Rensburg had been here she would have someone to confide in. She was worried as much by the meeting's unfamilar procedures as by the shrewdness of the men she must confront.

Frank Stainton had welcomed her on the fourteenth floor with a ritual of concern which over the next weeks was to become a routine.

'Anne, my dear, it is good of you to come. Naturally we are all praying for the best, but as I explained, in any Chief Executive's unexplained absence someone has to take decisions.'

If anything his phrases made her confidence dwindle further. She touched the knobbly wool of her Chanel suit for reassurance and decided she must immediately assert the position she intended to maintain.

'So far as I'm concerned, Jim is alive until he's proven dead.'

'Of course, my dear, of course.' He opened one of the rosewood double doors of the Boardroom. 'Perhaps I should remind you none the less that since he is not here we shall have to elect a Chairman for today's proceedings.' He inclined his head towards her, lowering his voice as if in confidence. 'Strictly between ourselves, though the others may not agree, I think Arthur Watson would be the best man. A non-executive director can be more truly impartial.' He smiled, a knowledgeable smile from which benevolence was absent, then courteously swung open the door and stood back, ushering her into the unfussily elegant room. As she entered the eight men seated around the long table rose to their feet. She glanced around, noting with brief pleasure the flower arrangements between the french windows and the fountain in the courtyard beyond them. She had told Jim the fourteenth floor garden would be the room's greatest visual asset.

'Lord Watson is an old friend, of course.' Stainton began the introductions, reminding her of the names with tact. She shook hands with Watson, thinking that he moved with noticeable laboriousness. Arthur was getting old. 'Jack Cunningham looks after our home manufacturing interests; Hans Bertels flew back from Florida last night to be here, he's only recently taken over the hotel division.' Bertels was a thickset man of around forty-five who looked every inch the Teutonic manager. 'Andrew Ferguson needs no introduction . . .' Was there a hint of acidity in the way Stainton said that? Did he know Andrew had been briefing her? 'Nor do I think does Ramesh Gupta.' A thin, dark Asian wearing the best-cut suit in the room took her hand limply. She did indeed know Ramesh, a Hindu of great astuteness responsible for everything they owned in India, from jute mills to computer technology. Next Stainton introduced the two remaining directors, Hugh Clarke and an American named Carl Hoffman, rounding off by regretting the unavoidable absence of Patrick Van Rensburg, who was still in hospital in Nairobi and had not named an alternate. Finally, the Company Secretary, an accountant called Plowright, greeted her.

After this brief ritual she was shown to a seat between Watson and Ferguson, while Jim's leather-upholstered chair at the top end remained conspicuously unoccupied.

'Well,' Stainton said, clearing his throat, 'there's no need for me to elaborate on the unhappy events which have brought us here today. We all offer our deepest sympathy to Lady Hartman in her ordeal and admire her courage.'

A murmur of agreement confirmed this statement, which she acknowledged with a tight smile.

'Our first concern must be to elect a Chairman for this meeting and I suggest that we should ask Lord Watson to accept the duty, if he is agreeable.' Stainton turned his gaze on the peer and waited. There was silence.

Why? Anne asked herself, not for the first time. The question had been buzzing in her brain while the introductions were going on, and now Stainton had made the suggestion so directly that for anyone to dispute it would be difficult. But why? True, Arthur was an old friend of Jim's; true his recently acquired title outranked everyone else. Yet what had his peerage been for? Long service on the Parliamentary backbenches and a few undistinguished years as a minister. Neither was a qualification here. So why had Frank pushed him forward? Money: that was the explanation. Apart from his attendance allowance at the House of Lords and his Commons pension, Arthur probably did not have much money. He needed his directorships. He would be obedient and Frank knew he would. With horror she realized that she had been outmanoeuvred before the meeting had properly begun.

'I should say there could be no better choice.' Bertels broke the silence and Stainton shot him a glance of thanks.

'Go on then Arthur.' Anne was surprised to hear herself speak. 'Move to the head of the table.' As he gathered up his papers and transferred himself, she felt Andrew Ferguson touch her elbow. Beside her hand was the scribbled words 'watch out' on a scrap of paper. In the same instant she realized that with Watson removed, she and Andrew were effectively isolated at their end.

'Thank you,' Watson said, straightening his back, though the tiredness showed around his eyes. She thought he looked like an ageing owl, wondering if it could still catch mice. 'This is a privilege, albeit that I deeply regret the circumstances.' He had chaired countless meetings before, the phrases came to him instinctively. 'We have only one item on the agenda today: "To consider the Directorate", and I think we all know what that means. We must, however reluctantly, accept that until we know what has happened to Jim Hartman his role as Chief Executive ought to be assumed by someone else.'

Stainton said nothing, though he let his eyes wander from face to face.

'I guess that's indisputable,' the American Hoffman said. 'At a time like this the Trust has to be seen to be strongly managed.' He represented the interests of an American bank which was heavily committed to co-financing a vast new coffee estate in Brazil and he had tough-minded superiors to keep sweet.

Several others nodded and murmured their assent.

'There is no reason to believe my husband is dead.' Anne again took herself unawares with her own determination. 'In fact to the contrary. Surely all we need during the short time until he is found is a caretaker. Couldn't two or three of you form a temporary executive committee? I believe such a thing is quite usual.'

She saw surprise and annoyance in Stainton's eyes, and his look hardened further when Ferguson spoke.

'I think Lady Hartman has a point there. Suppose you, Frank, and a couple of other executive directors formed such a committee. Under its direction we could run our Divisions as normal.'

Suddenly Stainton broke his silence. 'Normal? We had been expecting to make a formal offer to Consolidated Diamond Concessions' shareholders within the next fortnight, based on payment with an issue of our own shares. Since Jim disappeared those shares have collapsed.' He directed a contemptuous look at Ferguson. 'I would hardly call that situation normal.'

'Will the Consolidated Board fight?' Bertels asked. His hotel chain was far removed from this other battleground.

'They emphatically will now,' Hugh Clarke interjected in his well modulated upper-class voice, 'and I doubt if we could win.'

'Apart from anything else,' Stainton cut in, 'our bid preparations include committing $60 million to a diamond concession in Angola on June 1st, which is next Tuesday, or at the latest by the end of next week. We could have difficulty raising it.'

'Then why the hell wasn't that on the agenda?' Hoffman said.

'Please, gentlemen,' Watson intervened, raising his hands for silence, wounded pride sounding in his voice, 'I for one have not been briefed on this Angolan project.'

'Only the working directors concerned have,' Stainton said frigidly, 'namely myself, Hugh Clarke and Patrick Van Rensburg. With respect to the others any leak could have been disastrous for negotiations which Sir James was conducting.'

Anne glanced around, aware that they had abruptly come a lot closer to the real crux: and to what Jim had really been doing in Africa.

'Why are we committing $60 million to an Angolan concession?' she demanded.

'It was part of Sir James's preparation for taking over Consolidated. But it depended on his concluding a deal with the Angolan government last Sunday, under the cover of his trip to Zaïre. From the location of the crash he might have decided to fly there direct on Saturday.'

'But surely the Angolans would have told us?'

'Unfortunately not. The negotiations were highly confidential.'

Anne steeled herself, wanting to scream that these mysteries were absurd and instead digging her fingernails into her palm. Trying to keep her voice steady, she repeated the question. She had to understand what was so special about this Angolan concession.

'Hugh is the expert on these particular figures.' Stainton brought Clarke back into the arena. 'You explain, Hugh.'

'Only the details are complicated, Lady Hartman, and I won't trouble you with those. The essence is simple. Consolidated have a very large diamond concession in Angola, where they've invested over $200 million in buildings and equipment. But the lease had a condition. They had to achieve production of a million carats a year by a certain date. That date is next Tuesday, and they have failed. Nonetheless they believed the lease would be renewed and they only wrote off half the investment in their books. They reckoned without Sir James persuading the Angolans to sell us the concession when the lease expires.'

'Holy cow,' Hoffman exclaimed, 'that's a snatch. We get $200 million of plant for $60 million.'

'I'm terribly sorry,' Anne felt confused and foolish, 'I'm afraid I don't see the relationship between buying this concession and making a bid for Consolidated.'

'It's really very simple Anne.' Stainton permitted himself a faintly superior smile. 'Once Consolidated's loss of that lease became public knowledge their shares would take a beating. The Trust's offer would have been in the post next day. At the same time various friendly organizations would have been buying our stock in order to boost our price.'

'A very clever plan,' Gupta murmured, 'very nice indeed.'

'Except,' Stainton spoke with quick brutality, 'that Jim himself has made the coup a non-starter. Unless he reappears and our share price recovers, we cannot bid for Consolidated and the concession ceases to be of interest.'

He stopped speaking as the door opened and Christianne appeared, holding a telex message. She looked around quickly.

'Excuse me, this is perhaps most important for you Lady Hartman. I have written a translation.'

Anne took the paper, her hand trembling, read the few words and felt a relief that was agony as well, because this news did not end the uncertainty.

'My husband may not have been on the plane.' She passed the torn-off sheet to Stainton. 'I think this means we can assume he is alive.'

'Does it say where he may be?' Andrew Ferguson asked.

She shook her head, trying to force her thoughts into order. None of this made sense. Had he survived and gone for help or had he never been on the flight at all, as Robert suspected? The only clear thing was that she must continue to protect his interests.

'Surely,' she insisted, addressing Watson as Chairman, much as it riled her, 'if this diamond concession is so valuable we ought to buy it just to keep our options open? Sixty million dollars isn't an impossible amount of money ... surely.' She found her conviction wavering. When Jim had been nearly bankrupted all those years ago the figures involved were comprehensible. Nowadays when he or acquaintances from the City talked money over dinner, they talked in colossal sums and made them sound like entrance fees, and when he spoke people listened, believed and participated. But where those huge sums came from, she had no idea, and Stainton was easily able to demolish her protest.

'Anne, my dear. In itself, as you rightly suggest, sixty million dollars is a manageable sum: under normal circumstances. These are not normal, as I have said. Despite this telex, unless Jim is found in the next few days and our own share price recovers, the Trust itself could be the target of a bid.'

A murmur of agreement around the table made her appreciate that she was outnumbered.

'For that reason,' Stainton continued, 'we need to appoint an acting Chief Executive in Sir James's absence.'

A tap on the table made them turn to Watson, who took control with an incisiveness that surprised her.

'In the circumstances,' he was visibly unhappy at having to take sides, 'I favour appointing a single temporary Chief Executive.' A flicker of satisfaction shadowed Stainton's face. 'However, in my opinion he should report to the Board more frequently than has hitherto been the case.'

Anne found herself wondering if any member of the Board was more than a fair-weather friend. Arthur had been happy enough to accept a substantial retainer for consultancy when he was a backbench MP and to arrange Jim's knighthood when he was in power as a Cabinet minister. In the days before Members of Parliament had to declare their interests, he had attended innumerable conferences and congresses abroad at the Trust's expense. But now his loyalties were shifting. He was like the Vicar of Bray in the old song, high church under Charles, low church under Cromwell, 'and so obtained preferment'.

'Since that is settled,' Andrew Ferguson said at last, adding fuel to her thoughts by also changing sides, 'I propose we elect Frank Stainton. If we are up against a financial crisis he is the obvious choice.'

Watson glanced around. 'Would anybody care to second that?'

Automatically Bertels and Clarke nodded.

'Then we can continue to the second issue,' Watson reminded them. 'Should the Trust drop this Angolan concession or should we attempt to re-establish negotiations?'

'I repeat,' Stainton insisted, 'its value was as the pivot of the bid. As a mining operation it has disadvantages.'

'What do you mean?' Anne asked.

'The area is not fully under government control. There have been rebel attacks on the mine. We do not know how Jim intended to deal with this problem.'

'Can we now vote?' Watson demanded tetchily.

This time Hoffman raised his hand against. 'I guess Sir James never bid for an asset that he couldn't do something with.'

Stainton was thus defeated, though accepting the setback with good grace. 'Believe me,' he assured them, 'whatever happens I shall act in the best interests of the Trust. I must warn you that Consolidated will be taking defensive action: organizing share support, briefing brokers, probably issuing revised profit forecasts. They're not going to wait for Sir James to be found.'

'Then we should reconvene this meeting as soon as more information is available,' Watson cut in, reminding them that he was Chairman of the meeting. 'How long have we, Frank?'

'Over this concession? Until June 1st, next Tuesday. Four days.'

'Let us meet on Tuesday.'

'By which time, God willing, we shall know where my husband is,' Anne said, relieved that to some extent they had boxed Stainton in and deciding to exploit the advantage.

When they rose from the table she had extracted agreement from him on several points, including the provision of a company jet for Robert to go to Zaïre the next day.

During the drive down to Godstow through London's unending southern suburbs, Mother was reticent about what had taken place, presumably anxious to avoid saying anything the chauffeur could retail as gossip. When I reached out and squeezed her hand she gave me a look pleading for silence, which was only explained after we were safely home and the butler had brought tea to the drawing room.

'Is there any news, m'Lady?' he enquired as he laid down the tray, stiff as a penguin in his black coat. Even in summer he suffered from arthritis.

'I'm afraid not, Hooson.'

'We have had reporters on the telephone again, m'Lady.'

'You didn't speak to them, I hope?' She glanced sharply up at him from the sofa.

'Certainly not, m'Lady.' He stiffened even more, if it were possible. 'Only to the operator.'

Evidently my instructions, given in the world ago of last weekend, were being strictly followed. The procedure of the exchange intercepting calls was to have unintended consequences, as precautions are apt to. For the moment, though, it gave us protection.

'I'm glad to hear that,' Mother remarked with uncharacteristic asperity. 'We have nothing to say to the Press, nothing at all.'

'I quite understand, m'Lady.' Hooson retreated, dignified, thin and angular, his mourner's back as straight as he could keep it.

Gradually Mother became more like herself, seeming to regain her shattered, wavering confidence as she went through the familiar ritual with the silver teapot. Then, calmly, she raised the subject which must have been on her mind throughout the drive down.

'This could easily be 1957 all over again.'

'Nineteen fifty-seven?'

Had Camilla warned her that past scandals were being resurrected?

'When we nearly went bankrupt, when we had the bailiffs in. Did no one ever tell you about that?' I shook my head. 'I suppose not. You were only a child then ... I'm not sure I could cope with it being repeated.'

'Why should it? Father's an extremely rich man, even if the Trust's shares have taken a beating.'

She recounted some of the Board meeting's discussions and except that Stainton's success was bad news, I couldn't spot immediate danger.

'Robert, darling,' she concluded, 'before your father left he did something else quite unusual.'

She rose and went to the meticulously polished Queen Anne walnut bureau in which she kept her own correspondence. 'He left me some codewords to be used if he was kidnapped. He must have known something could go wrong on this trip. The codewords explain how urgent things are or aren't. I'm beginning to think that's what could have happened.'

'Do you mean we should stop searching for him?'

'No!' As I had expected Mother instantly rejected the idea. 'No!' she repeated. 'We are going to find him.' Then she let her guard slip a little. 'This deal may have been what that American Hoffman called "vicious". I simply don't care. Your father's still the one and only man in my life and he's still your father. After 1957 he promised we'd always be provided for. There must be something more we don't know about yet.'

She could only be right. Father did have something close to a fixation about ensuring her comfort: perhaps the result of whatever went wrong in 1957. I remembered him striding restlessly to and fro in this same room five years ago, after we had at last agreed to differ about my career, dictating what amounted to the terms of his own surrender. His voice was more guttural than usual, through having to control his emotions.

'Very well, then, Robert. You exploit what you believe is your own ability. Take your own road.' He had swung round and paced back in front of the great stone fireplace. 'It is the talent that matters, not the vehicle. I will back you, in spite of everything. What you want arranged, tell me.'

His words evoked an absurd vision of his suborning the Dean of the College on my behalf. He would have sounded ridiculous if there had not been such force in the way he spoke.

'We must both think forward, Bob. Always think positive. Never look back. Follow your star.' He had continued for some minutes, moulding the phrases of his own pragmatic philosophy – in which he believed like a faith – towards supporting my right to my own life. After four years' refusal to speak to me it was an extraordinary turnabout. But so equally had been the circumstances of our reconciliation. Then, quite suddenly, he stopped his pacing and raised a finger in warning, his expression set and serious, as though everything he had said before was merely an exercise in face-saving and he had arrived at what mattered.

'One thing, Robert. I do not want your mother hurt any more. Is this understood?'

That had been the key. Now, sitting in the same armchair, with the intensity of his words a vivid memory, I realized that on this principle of protecting Mother he had always been consistent. The letter he had left for me with Christianne reiterated his concern. Furthermore, both the letter and the document she had found implied risk and his absolute confidence in overcoming that risk. I took the letter from my inner pocket and showed it to her.

'I was afraid this might upset you,' I explained.

She read the brief note. 'I'd much rather know everything, darling,' she said. 'One can be protected too much. If you don't have any success in Zaïre,' she went on, 'then we'd better request one of these Extraordinary Meetings when you get back.' She allowed herself a small smile. 'Not that they could be more extraordinary than ordinary ones are.'

I laughed dutifully. 'Was it so odd today?'

'Frank is determined not to buy this concession. He makes excuses about rebels in the area stopping production.'

'How long have we got?'

'Four days.' Mother gave a sidelong glance. 'I know exactly what's going through your head. Please don't try. I don't want you disappearing in Africa too. Promise? All I want is to know whether your father was or was not on the aeroplane.'

I promised not to go off on any wild goose chases and let the subject drop. Besides I wanted to confirm that Mother must have known about the ancient court case scandal. If she did, she was to some extent vaccinated against being hurt. First, however, it would be wise to find out from Camilla if publication seemed imminent. As had happened before, Mother's intuition took her halfway there as soon as I mentioned a phone call.

'Do you see much of Camilla these days?' she asked.

'She's helping me with research.' I tried to be unspecific.

'I'm glad. I like her and it was especially nice of her to telephone me last night. Well,' having declared her sympathies Mother tactfully broke away, 'I need a rest before dinner. And I'm sure you need a bath.' She kissed me and left to go upstairs.

Camilla was less consoling. She had spent most of the day chasing facts about Concession Twenty-Two and come up with very few.

'No one wants to talk about that mine. Consolidated will not even admit where exactly it is, just "in eastern Angola". The one point they can't conceal, because it's in an old annual report, is that at the start the Angolan government received a 51 per cent share for no investment. I have a feeling Consolidated know they've lost out and don't want to risk any more.'

'Well, Father was prepared to stake capital there, though mainly to embarrass Consolidated. His disappearance, the takeover and this raking up of his past must all be interconnected somewhere. It occurs to me that Stainton might have reasons of his own for keeping the Trust's hands off Consolidated's concessions. What's been happening with the Press coverage?'

'My media friends expect the papers to be full of the Falklands war until it's over. You might get off lightly.' She paused. 'You're probably right about there being linkages. The question, Bob, is whether you're able to influence them.'

'I shall have to.' Ten days ago, if she had asked whether I would interfere with Father's affairs while he was on a trip to Africa the answer would have been very different. I was immersed in the summer term, giving lectures, tutoring, counselling final year students on their futures. Ten days ago, for that matter, she wouldn't have asked, because we weren't seeing each other. Our relationship had foundered on what she referred to as my retreat into the ivory tower and I called pursuing my own career. Ten days ago was another world.

'Father left me a letter,' I said. 'He mentioned risks which he didn't explain and the action he wanted taken if his return was delayed.'

'How extraordinary. Like a voice from the grave, almost. So you'll do as he asks?' There was a hint of disbelief in her voice.

'Some of it. I want us to keep control of the Trust as much as he does. Whether I could handle a shareholder's meeting without knowing precisely what he was doing in Africa could be another question.'

'I don't see why not,' she said encouragingly, and then re-quested orders. 'So what's next on the list? More about this Angolan mine or are you still haunted by the past?'

'Did you have any luck over who else was involved in Rukanga originally?'

'I simply haven't had time.'

'Well, hire an assistant if you need to.'

A short cough sounded down the line. 'A little less peremptory, if you please Mr Hartman. Taking up the cudgels for your father doesn't mean you have to behave like him.' She accepted my quick apology. 'No, if you haven't spoken to Professor Muhsin, I think you ought to. He's been exceptionally decent over your absence.'

'Concerned about my career?' I asked, unable to resist a dig at her changing attitudes.

'About you, idiot that I am. Please look after yourself in Zaïre. It doesn't sound a very pleasant place. You can buy me dinner when you get back.'

I rang off feeling happier. At least one thing was going right. Then I had a long chat to the Professor, discussing how my problem students were progressing and saying that as the Gulfstream had been found it could not be long before we located Father.

'Alive and well, inshallah,' Muhsin said.

'Inshallah,' I echoed, out of politeness more than conviction. Ten days ago I would have accepted God's will in the matter, as in the last resort we all must do. Now I intended to exploit whatever chances might be available on the way to the inevitable.

Partly because of these conversations, mainly because of Mother's determination to look on the bright side, dinner that evening turned into a more cheerful occasion than was truly justified. She put on an informal black evening dress, the table sparkled with silver in the candlelight, we talked as though Father must be safe somewhere. Not surprisingly, her optimism became gradually transmuted into reminiscence. The past offered a safe avenue to the subject that preoccupied her, and she responded sentimentally when I asked about her engagement and marriage.

'We waited two years before your grandfather would let us get engaged. It was an eternity.'

'When did you meet?' Some of Dr Lohrey's remarks came back to me. Wasn't it in the autumn of 1949 that Father had gone to see her in Berlin? And continued seeing her?

'The first time was in the spring of 1949. At a dance. Then, just as we were getting to know each other, Daddy had a ridiculous incident with the police. I'm sure it was only because he was a foreigner.'

I looked the question, rather than speaking it.

'He was accused of renting the basement of his house to a, well, to a prostitute. He was completely cleared, of course. He went straight to my father and told him. He even insisted we didn't meet for a year, while he established his own business. Daddy was very sceptical, but Jim did make a success and we were married eighteen months later, in May 1951.'

In the circumstances my grandfather's doubts were justified all round. Perhaps more perceptiveness lay behind the old General's bushy white eyebrows and military manner than I had supposed. However, my main emotion was of relief that the old scandal would not catch Mother by surprise if the Press did rake it up, so I asked the obvious next question about the honeymoon.

She laughed, the tender and kind laugh of remembered happiness. 'Jim told everyone it was Florence. And we did stop at Florence for a night, by making a huge deviation. As you say, Grandfather does have rather fixed ideas and both he and Mummy would have died if they'd known where we really went.'

'So where did you go?' What would have been daring in 1951? Capri, perhaps.

'You'd never guess, so I'll tell you.' She gave a tiny little shake of the head, as though still amazed. I thought how radiant she looked in the candlelight and was puzzled at how a memory of the past could completely overlay a present disaster, at least during the telling of a story. Then the story itself caught up with me.

'We went to the Abruzzi,' she said. 'I don't suppose you've even heard of it.'

All those connections of Father's past which Van Rensburg and Lohrey had revealed clicked through my mind, yelling at me that I should have guessed.

'Tell me more, Ma,' I asked. 'What was the Abruzzi like?'

'We flew to Rome – that was quite an adventure, in those days people usually travelled by train – and stayed a few days in a big hotel near the top of the Spanish Steps. It's funny, I can hardly remember any of the sights, they're all jumbled up in my mind now, except the Colosseum I suppose because it is so huge. But I can see every detail of the little restaurant where we met your father's friend one evening.' Mother smiled with inward pleasure at the memory. 'It was a lovely place, though quite unpretentious. There was a courtyard with vines growing round where it was cool, and red check tablecloths.' She sighed. 'A man played a guitar in the corner and as it got dark they lit candles. It was so romantic. Then this tall, bearded mysterious-looking man came up to us and suddenly produced a bouquet of red roses from behind his back, with a marvellous flourish. I nearly fainted.'

CHAPTER TWELVE

'For the prettiest girl in England.' The Italian bowed, waited for
Anne to take the flowers, then gently caught her hand and kissed
her fingertips. She felt the thick hair of his beard brush her skin,
wondered if she was dreaming and glanced at her husband for
reassurance.

'Darling, this is Carlo Angelino, the only man I know in Italy.'

'The only Italian he trusts enough to present so beautiful a
wife. This is what he means.' Angelino beamed at his own
command of English. He slapped Hartman on the shoulder
affectionately. 'You told the truth in your letter. You are a lucky
man. I congratulate.'

'Please,' she blushed, 'you're making me embarrassed. But the
roses are glorious. Thank you so much.'

'Here.' Jim reached for a spare chair from an adjacent table. 'I
didn't tell Anne you were coming because I wanted it to be a
surprise.' He turned back to her. 'Carlo is an important man,
darling. A deputy in the Assembly, representing Pescara. I was
afraid he might have been caught up with more important business.'

'What is more important than old friends?' Catching Anne's
enquiring look, Angelino explained, 'We have been comrades in
the war.'

'He was known as Barba Nera then,' Jim said, in apparent explanation.

'A stupid codename!' the Italian chuckled, stroking his thick
beard, which was flecked with grey, making Anne think he might
be older than he seemed. 'Everybody knew.'

'Since the Germans could never catch him, what did it matter!'
Jim's admiration was unconcealed.

'You were comrades?' Anne was confused. 'Carlo was in our
army?' She sipped the bitter-tasting Campari which Jim had
persuaded her to try, hoping to mask her embarrassment.

154

'No, darling! He was a partisan. We met when I was on an operation in 1943. Without him we would never have escaped. Surely I told you?'

'Where exactly was it you met?'

'Of our country it is a most beautiful part.' Angelino made a gesture of kissing his fingers. '*Bellissima*. But neglected. No one goes there.' He lunged across the table to punch Hartman playfully on the shoulder. 'Except crazy men like him. It is the Abruzzi. In the Abruzzi you make a friend he is a friend for life.' He gazed at them both in turn with sudden earnestness. 'You would like to visit there? I go tomorrow for the weekend. I am honoured for you to come.'

Anne hesitated. She wanted to get to know her husband, not strangers, on her honeymoon. Besides, they had other plans. They were going to Florence and Siena.

'If you're serious, Carlo,' Jim said, 'that would be our honour. Wouldn't you like to, darling? We can't spend the whole time looking at paintings and ruins. I never expected to see the Abruzzi again.'

'I show you an Italy tourists never see,' Angelino assured her, and she smiled nervously. She had begun to realize that this invitation was not impromptu at all. By refusing she would risk offending both of them.

'It would be lovely,' she said, trying to catch Jim's eye to make him understand. 'Just for a weekend.'

'*Molto bene!*' Angelino seized on her agreement. 'We go tomorrow. And, please, you must call me Carlo.'

Once the details were settled, she sensed a definite relaxation in her husband's mood and reflected, not for the first time since their engagement, that it really was quite futile trying to block his desires. He was as obstinate as a mule over getting what he wanted. But then his relentless energy was half his attraction.

As they ate and drank Carlo probed how the two of them had met, sometimes lapsing into Italian with Jim acting as translator, constantly making sly jokes.

'So your father make you wait two years,' he grinned through the thick beard. 'He does not trust you, eh? Or he does not trust Jim?'

'Daddy thought I was far too young.'

'In Italy any father say the same. For a father his daughter is like a jewel.'

'Beyond price,' Jim added. 'And she is!' He touched her fingers. 'I never thought she'd accept me.'

Anne blushed with pleasure. When he paid compliments, Jim made her whole being melt. They might be platitudes. She didn't mind a scrap, because she knew they were sincere.

'So you meet in which place?' Carlo asked.

'At a dance.' She smiled tenderly across the table. 'He was hopeless on the floor.'

She could no longer remember why the dance was being held, but everything else about the occasion was as vivid as last night. Her parents lived near Aldershot and she'd been invited by a would-be boyfriend to join a party at the Officers' Club. The Club itself had a curious aura of glamour, with its sprung dance floor and crowds of young officers: curious because the building itself was a 1920s mock Tudor house, completely out of place in a military town of Victorian brick barrack blocks, though appropriately smelling of carbolic soap and changing rooms. At eighteen, and only just out of school, she had never been to a London nightclub. Perhaps, she decided later, her parents had been a little too protective. At all events, Jim was in the same party and as out of place as a veteran among recruits. None the less he managed to monopolize her increasingly, cutting out her young escort with the same bull-like insistence that less happily characterized his dancing.

'If it hadn't been for the Abruzzi,' Jim said, 'I'd have never met her. I'd have wound up the war as a sergeant.'

Anne found herself inexplicably shocked. 'I didn't think of that,' she said awkwardly.

'To us the rank is nothing,' Carlo commented, launching into a description of the region which Jim translated, though he was too slow and literal for the mixture of humour and passion which illuminated the Italian's expression.

'Carlo says the real Abruzzi is in the mountains, where we shall go. There the peasants are brave, independent and tough. But they are also very poor. Little has changed in two thousand years. He is trying to alter that, so they can afford kerosene for their cooking instead of charcoal, so they have more to live on than polenta and legends and their sons do not have to emigrate to America.' He paused, listening carefully to Carlo's flowing speech. 'The Abruzzi may be the countryside of Ovid, but you cannot live on poetry and fountains of love.'

'We shall,' Anne joked, 'at least for the next week. Perhaps your Abruzzi is the place to start after all.'

They left the restaurant very late, sauntering hand in hand through the narrow streets to the Spanish Steps, then climbing happily up the great sweep of stone stairs to their hotel at the top. Staying at Hassler's Villa Medici was a wild extravagance, and Anne loved Jim the more for having chosen it. When they reached the room a vase was standing ready for the roses Carlo had given her. She arranged them carefully, then hugged Jim and kissed him.

'Darling, you're just a wicked old conspirator, aren't you? Why didn't you tell me about him before?'

156

'How could I be sure he was in Rome?'

'How could I be sure he would be . . .' she corrected tenderly. 'Anyway, I don't believe a word of it. You knew perfectly well he would.' She kissed him again, affectionately teasing. 'And since we're on the subject, how did you come to be in the same party as me that evening at the Club? I've always wondered. You didn't have a partner, did you?' She almost added that it was unlike him to be the odd man out when it occurred to her that the 'odd man out' was precisely what he had been most of his life.

'You think you're old enough to know?' He kissed her nose.

'Not only old enough: married long enough.'

'I will let you into a secret.' He grinned disarmingly. 'Ted Johnson told me he knew the prettiest girl in Hampshire with the fiercest father.'

'You're a wicked liar, James Hartman, even if you are my husband.' She remembered Ted, a young banker like Jim, though renowned for always being short of cash.

'So I bet him a fiver I could be asked to tea by her family within a week. He accepted. Naturally he lost.'

'You beast! Just because I felt sorry for you!' She hardly knew whether to believe him or not.

Later, after they had made love and she was lying in his arms in bed, stroking the thick hair on his chest, she asked him, 'You didn't really think of me as a challenge, did you darling?'

'No, *meine Liebe*,' he murmured. 'I fell in love with you, of course. Being equal with your family was the challenge. Are you happy, my sweet?'

'Very,' she said, deciding that past dramas were best forgotten, 'very, very happy indeed.' She cuddled closer and fell asleep trying to decide how to dress for the journey, anxious to look her best and wishing she had a clearer idea of what they would be doing.

The next day they set off early in Angelino's new Fiat, driving east towards Tivoli and the Apennine mountains. Anne was offered the front seat, but decided to sit in the back so that the two men could talk, though as they progressed she began to feel this was unkindly symbolic of her role in the expedition. Occasionally Carlo would throw her a remark over his shoulder, as they zigzagged up into the hills.

'This is the route the King took for escape after the Armistice. How can he think he will rule Italy when he has been Mussolini's puppet?'

She didn't understand the references, and anyway the question was rhetorical, so she tried to content herself with watching the sun-seared countryside go past. Meanwhile the men's talk became an increasingly political, if bantering, discussion.

'Our party has a great wartime leader also,' Carlo said at one point, apropos of Churchill, and she became more attentive. Churchill was her mother's hero. 'You hear of Togliatti? Like Churchill he lose the election after the fighting. Not the same reason. Togliatti tells the people they have been on the wrong side in the war and must give Trieste to Yugoslavia.'

'You mean the Russians ordered him to,' Jim said.

'Togliatti believe they were right. The truth is sometimes not popular.'

'In other words, pragmatism is of more use than orders from Moscow?'

'Heresy!' Angelino erupted with laughter. 'Do priests refuse to obey the Pope?'

'As a partisan, you made your own decisions.'

'True. Now I take orders of the Party again.'

'Which Party is that?' Anne leant forward, clutching the back of Jim's seat.

'The Communist Party, darling,' Jim answered for him. 'They were on the same side as us in the war.'

'I suppose they were.' Her father regarded the communists as the source of the world's troubles. Her uncle had even gone abroad when the Labour Party took power in 1945, though she had always thought that rather idiotic. She stared at the handsome outline of Carlo's leonine head and jutting beard in confusion. How could he be a communist? He was such a pleasant man.

'Don't worry, my darling.' Jim twisted round to look at her. 'I'm no Marxist. I take things as they come, which is what any entrepreneur has to do. In practice even communists bend with the wind.'

Carlo said something in Italian, Jim replied and, not understanding, she retreated from the conversation again, feeling both apprehensive and excited, as if sampling a kind of forbidden fruit. Her father always insisted on the importance of moral behaviour. Whatever would he say if he knew she was going into the wildest part of Italy with a communist?

They stopped for lunch in a village, the name of which Anne never learnt, and ate in the courtyard of an inn, under a primitive straw awning. The sunlight filtering through made a lined pattern on the wooden table and glinted on the glasses. The warmth of the day enveloped her. She broke the crusty bread, tried the rough wine and quite unexpectedly knew she had found all she had imagined of Italy. Jim was affectionate and Carlo poured compliments at her.

'I like to see you together.' He kissed his fingertips and smiled hugely through his beard. *'Bellissima.'*

'Are you married, Carlo?' she asked, because it seemed natural.

'Before the war.' Some past event shadowed his expression and all the happiness of the moment was fractured. 'In the war she die. A man learns to live again.'

She felt like answering, 'So does a woman.'

'One must adjust,' Jim intervened. 'Nothing is pre-ordained. You interpret life the best way you can.'

'We all have different ways,' Carlo said abruptly.

'In the army we called it "playing things by ear".'

'Sometimes, sometimes not. In the Abruzzi we have a saying: *"Una bugia ben detta val più di un fatto stupido."*'

After some discussion the two men agreed an exact translation of the proverb for her benefit.

'A believable lie is better than a stupid fact.'

'A reasonable motto,' Jim observed.

'In politics, yes,' Carlo said with finality. 'In business, not.'

'If you say so.' Jim was so defensive that Anne wondered why. 'But with me a deal is a deal.' He turned to her. 'Carlo has given me some very good introductions. He's helped my business a lot. On politics we agree to have different views.'

'Oh!' The revelation caught her completely off-balance and she blushed. 'I'm afraid I don't know a thing about business.'

'For women, is not necessary.' Carlo dismissed the confession with a shrug, then leant across and punched Jim on the shoulder, a favourite gesture. 'Crazy, eh? The communist and the capitalist, like the lion and the lamb. But we know each other from the war. That is what matters.'

Anne felt incredibly stupid. Why hadn't Jim told her? In retrospect all she really knew about his activities were that the bank had financed his import export firm when he left after that vindictive police prosecution. Her father had given him a grilling on his prospects. She hadn't asked a lot of questions herself. Her married friends like Mary and Sarah never bothered themselves with details of how their husbands earned a living.

'I like to give a present for your wedding,' Carlo beamed benevolently. 'It is this. Your husband will be the representative of our car company.'

It was Jim's turn to flush, though with pleasure. He leant across the table and gripped Carlo's hand. 'Can we drink to that?'

'*Certo.*'

Both men raised their glasses and Anne joined them.

'To the future,' Carlo said solemnly. 'You have help me. I am glad to help you.' Quite suddenly he began scolding himself. 'But you two are on honeymoon, why should you talk about things like this? Let me tell you a story about where we shall go. In the mountains there was a wolf . . .'

When eventually they continued the drive Anne was content to doze in the back of the car, although the lunchtime discussion stayed in her mind. Whether intentionally or not, Jim had touched the roots of his philosophy. He was a pure opportunist, and the more she thought about the friendship between the two men, the more puzzled she became. Physically they had much in common. Both strongly built and handsome, though Carlo was running a little to fat and Jim stood a head higher than he did. She could easily imagine them fighting side by side. Intellectually, though, they seemed quite different. Jim would never take orders from a rigid Party hierarchy, except perhaps in a war. He was a loner. She could understand his fellow feeling for partisans. She asked herself why she was confident he would always look after her and any children they had and found no real answer. She just knew he would, like the mountain wolf in Carlo's folktale, outwitting pursuers in the snow.

As the twisting road climbed the air became colder. Anne slipped on a cardigan. Finally they seemed to cross the last crest of the Apennines and Carlo stopped the car on the verge. They all got out. To the east was a magnificent though hazy panorama across a valley, cut by rivers, to a vast plain stretching out below.

'Popoli,' the Italian pointed to the smudge of a town. 'Up there, Gran Sasso.' He indicated a massive peak crowned by cloud, then swung round to face east. 'Down that way, far down by the Pescara River, is where your husband jump from his plane to join us.'

She gazed at the bare mountain sides, thought she smelt the scent of herbs amongst the parched grass of the roadside, saw a beech forest below, and began to understand Carlo's passion for his homeland.

Two hours later, after a tortuous descent, they reached an *albergo* in the foothills. The Gran Sasso stood outlined against the early evening sky. Smoke trailed limply from a bonfire. She was unable to imagine fighting in such a quiet place.

'You dropped only a few kilometres from here,' Carlo said.

'God, eight years is a long time.' Jim turned to her. 'We jumped at last light. I remember the river shining like a ribbon.'

'You remember more tomorrow. Tomorrow we go to the farm, before the lunch.'

Anne assumed 'the' lunch was a grammatical mistake and only began to appreciate that their visit had local significance when two peasants arrived at the inn next morning, evidently in their best clothes, to act as an escort. They saluted Hartman and clasped his hand, greeting him volubly. Then they all crammed into the Fiat and set off, jolting along a track up a valley. The peasants leapt out to open occasional gates until they passed through a last olive grove and she saw they could go no further into the hills. Ahead lay a ruined farmstead. They all got out.

'Here your husband earn the right to a General's daughter!' Carlo announced theatrically.

'When Robertson was killed and Patrick Van Rensburg was wounded I had to take over.' Hartman took her hand and led her the last few yards, stopping at the remains of the farmyard wall. 'Hell,' he muttered, 'they blew the place up, as well as burning it.'

The buildings were more than abandoned: they had been tumbled into piles of rubble. Nothing stood more than four or five feet high. The black marks of fire showed on many fallen stones. Not a wall or gatepost was left intact. Weeds infested the yard so thickly that they could not pass through.

'What happened?' Anne asked, and was surprised when Jim hesitated.

'This was our rendezvous after the drop. Had a bit of trouble here.' He glanced at Carlo as if for support.

'Your husband is a modest man. The truth is there was an ambush. This was when the officers were kill. He defeat the traitors and bring his men to me in the hills.'

'It must have been a terrible battle.' She looked at the fallen walls.

'This is not from the fighting. The next day the Nazis come. They kill the farmer and his family. They burn the house. After the war I decide: what happen here shall never be forgotten. I myself give the order to pull down everything. Now it is a memorial.'

'To the dead, you mean?'

Carlo was having problems with his English again, needing Jim to translate. In the jumble of sentences she caught the words '*Una bugia ben detta*', and thought she must have misheard, since that funny proverb could hardly be relevant to this.

'What Carlo means,' Jim explained, 'is that the ruins are a memorial to the local people's resistance against the Nazis.'

Anne found herself shivering in spite of the sun's warmth. There was an unnerving brutality about these remains and their history, not least because so much was being left unsaid. Why hadn't relations been allowed to inherit the property? If this was a memorial why was there no plaque?

'Now, we've seen it, can we go?' she asked. 'I think we should try to forget the war.'

'Today we are remembering,' Carlo rebuked her with none of his former good humour. 'Your husband and his *Inglesi* parachute far, far behind the German lines to join our partisans. To the *Abruzzesi* he is a hero.'

She apologized, convinced none the less that she was right, and they walked back down the track to the olive grove where the car had been left. Jim dawdled, examining the landscape and stopping to stare at the hills, as if reliving the past. Then they drove down to the road again and by a long and circuitous route to a village high in the hills.

The first thing she noticed were the flags. Bunting was draped between houses and flags hung from all the windows. Many bore hammer and sickle emblems. Carlo slipped on an armband before they reached the tiny piazza in front of the church. A band was drawn up beside the steps. As they arrived it began to play a strident anthem.

'The *festa* is for your honour,' Carlo whispered and led them to be introduced to the mayor, standing at the head of the church steps, with the parish priest next to him in a long black cassock. Grouped behind them were a number of men and women wearing the same armbands as Carlo, some dressed in remnants of military uniforms. They saluted raggedly, while two officers of the Carabinieri, far smarter, with polished leather belts and guns, also stood to attention. She longed to ask how the priest came to be alongside the communists, but had no chance. They were overwhelmed with introductions and hand shaking, while the brass and drums of the band deafened conversation.

After this official reception there was a lunch served at tables in the open air, with piled dishes of pasta and bread and olives and wine. At the end Carlo himself rose, held his hands high for silence and began an emotional speech of welcome, which she could not understand, though her own name 'Anna' brought a gust of applause and Jim was clapped repeatedly when he delivered a formal reply. The whole proceedings took so long that she felt fuzzy from the wine and the heat and was afraid she might faint. Mercifully, an observant peasant woman brought her a glass of water.

'Were all these people partisans?' she managed to ask Carlo in an aside, when the speeches were over.

'Oh no. And some are even so foolish not vote for me. But I must tell you about these people of the Abruzzi. They hate authority. They fight anyone who comes. They fight the Germans and they hide Inglesi and Americani who escape from the *campi di concentramento*. Very few they betray. You count the traitors so, on one hand.' He held up his right hand and made a chopping motion with the other, across his fingers. 'Those we cut off.'

Anne fell silent, not trusting herself to speak. She had no doubt he would kill traitors without thinking twice. His character was the most disturbing mixture of geniality and ruthlessness. If Jim let him down in business, would he be equally vengeful?

The celebration continued unabated towards the evening. She pleaded exhaustion and was allowed to rest for an hour in the simple, whitewashed bedroom of a village house. Then, with dusk, there was dancing in the piazza, which Carlo insisted on leading

162

off with her, to enthusiastic cheering. Midnight was past before they were driven back to the inn.

'Darling,' she protested when they at last reached their room, 'it was lovely, it was out of this world, but why didn't you warn me?' She was so tired she hardly knew whether she was elated or angry. 'You must learn to tell me what we're doing.'

'I didn't know myself.' He kissed her, and though she smelt wine on his breath, she also realized that he was remarkably sober, more so than she was. 'Carlo sprang it on me too, darling. Can't you take life as it comes?'

By the next morning she was afraid she had been churlish. She accepted the offer of the car's front seat, and told Carlo how touching and unforgettable the ceremony had been.

'But why didn't you call Jim by his rank?' she asked. 'He was a captain, after all.'

'When we know him, he is sergeant. We like sergeants, more than officers.' He threw back a comment at Hartman. 'Pragmatic, eh?'

'I didn't expect history to make so much of what we did.'

'History, comrade, is what we decide afterwards. It is enough you help me.'

'By attacking, you mean?' she asked.

'Something like that. I'll tell you all about it one day.' Jim touched her shoulder. 'Look at that view. Italy is magnificent.'

Eventually, inevitably, the men's talk drifted back to politics.

'Africa,' Carlo remarked. 'You know Africa? Many things are the same in the Abruzzi and in Africa. They are poor, they are backward, their resource is people, they will develop. Recently I have been there.'

'You mean I should be doing business in the colonies?' Jim asked, leaning forward between the front seats. 'Are you serious?'

'Your British Empire will fall. India is gone. There are independence movements everywhere.'

'So?'

'Make friends with the revolutionaries. Help them. They will not forget when they are the government.'

'Come on, Carlo.' Jim sounded sceptical. 'I'm not a bloody philanthropist.'

'Africa.' Angelino took no notice. 'When the blacks have power they want men who are *simpatico*. It will be good business.'

'One day, maybe.'

'More soon than you think,' Carlo said.

The drive back seemed shorter than going out. When they reached the hotel in Rome Carlo kissed Anne on both cheeks and demanded that Jim should not wait another eight years before returning, handing him an envelope.

'Before you leave, give half a day to see this man. You will not regret the time. Write and tell me.'

They shook hands and parted. That evening, over dinner, Jim clearly still had the Italian's advice on his mind, because he said apropos of nothing, 'You know, darling, Carlo could be right about Africa. I ought to go there one day.'

'Your father never switched off, as you say.'

Mother smiled at me, affection and regret mingling in her expression. 'He lived for work. Five years later he was a millionaire. Well, on paper.'

'Had he become an agent for Italian cars?'

'Oh yes. He was involved in all sorts of things, especially property. He started by converting decrepit old houses into flats and in no time he was buying and selling whole mansion blocks. We lived in one of his conversions ourselves, it was the bottom two floors of a monstrously ugly Victorian house in Phillimore Place. He had so much going on I couldn't follow it all, though I wanted to.' She smiled again, her face still lit by memories. 'That wasn't so easy after you came along. Anyway, he always used to say "By the time I'm thirty-five I'm going to be a millionaire." And so he was.'

'Fast going,' I commented, though I was beginning to recall shreds of conversation which suggested that the actual ride had been bumpier than the official version. The Trust's standard biographical Press release presented his progress as a kind of seamless robe, every piece woven naturally into the next. 'After distinguished war service in the Parachute Regiment, being demobilized in 1947 as a captain, Sir James joined the merchant banking house which was subsequently to partner so many of his business ventures. In 1957 he acquired the Rukanga ruby mine in Kenya and in 1958 the Rukanga company was amalgamated with his existing interests in property and manufacturing to form the Hartman Trust.' And so on. Not a word about trauma in 1956 or any other year.

'Then all of a sudden we were in Queer Street. He'd taken a gamble I only discovered about afterwards.' Mother sighed. 'The awful thing is it's so like this diamond concession now.'

'In Africa too?' When Father used to talk about Rukanga, he mentioned that it was not his first venture there. Quite apart from Barba Nera's advice, the dark continent held a near-mythical attraction for him. 'Out there you can feel you have made the first footprint,' he once said with quite poetical intensity. 'You can touch the clay of life waiting to be shaped.' He wasn't putting it on either, though I'm sure he had borrowed the phrases. The concept of pioneering did inspire him.

164

'I suppose Egypt is Africa. I always think of it as the Middle East. Anyway he flew out to Cairo early in 1954 and bought a cotton estate cheap off a Lebanese who was worried about the future because of the King being overthrown. What was his name?' Mother tut-tutted at herself. 'I shall forget my own next. Farouk. But your father had met some minister in the new government who gave him a lot of assurances. Huge fortunes had been made with cotton in the past and it was still Egypt's main export.'

'Suez?' I asked.

There was no need for her to go on. The ill-starred Anglo-French attempt to seize control of the Suez Canal after Egypt's President Nasser nationalized it had been the subject of contention ever since.

'The cotton estate was expropriated after Suez, presumably.'

'Your father had paid for it by mortgaging his property developments in London. When he had to sell in a hurry the market was very weak – I think the crisis had caused a frightful run on the pound. He couldn't clear the debts. He managed not to worry me with it at all until one day, out of the blue, an official came to Phillimore Place to value everything.' Mother shook her head despairingly at the memory. 'I don't expect being declared bankrupt means any more to you, darling, than it does to most people. Unless you've experienced it, I don't think you can understand what it means. I had no idea this man was coming. When he told me, "You'll be allowed to keep the clothes you're wearing, a bed, a chair each, a table and enough cutlery and dishes to eat off," I couldn't believe him. I rang the office in a complete panic.'

I could imagine: and that most of what Mother knew of this catastrophe had been learnt afterwards.

'Your father told me to keep calm. "The proceedings won't be heard in court for a fortnight. We have a little time, my love. The flat's in your name, so they can't take that. We won't be homeless.' Then I had to watch the wretched bailiff listing all the furniture in case we tried to smuggle it away.'

'But you were saved?' By whom, I wondered. Hardly Barba Nera, hardly the merchant bank. Yet actual bankruptcy had been averted. It must have been, or Father would have been banned from holding a directorship. Nor, of course, could he have bought Rukanga.

Mother laughed nervously, mirroring the relief she must have felt. 'The miracle happened. He flew to Cairo and Nasser's government agreed to compensate him. The first payment came three days before the proceedings, we kept the furniture and he started again. I don't think I'll ever forget the date: February 17th, 1957.'

'Well, Ma,' I said stoutly, trying to convince myself as much as her, 'we're going to get him back from Africa again and this time without having the bailiffs in.'

She gave me a quick kiss. 'Thank you darling, thank you for all you're doing. Would you awfully mind staying here tonight? I just don't want to be alone.'

Naturally I agreed and went off to the study to phone Camilla. I hadn't even told her I was going to Zaïre tomorrow.

'Rather you than me,' she commiserated. 'What can I do for you while you're away?'

'Can you find out about the expropriation of British assets in Egypt after Suez? Cotton estates in particular.'

'So you're still on 1956?' I could hear her amusement down the line. 'You don't give up, do you Bob?'

CHAPTER THIRTEEN

Travelling to the crash site in Zaïre was a saga in itself. Told as an after-dinner story it would have provoked disbelieving chuckles. Despite Van Rensburg's warnings about the corruption and inefficiency there, I was still unprepared for that extraordinary country.

True, I didn't help myself by arriving at Kinshasa without a visa in a symbol of affluence – a company jet. I had imagined humanitarian considerations would have entered the equation somewhere, while telexed diplomatic clearances for the flight had been obtained before we left. In practice it was as if my father's name, now that he was presumed dead, provoked deliberate official obstruction.

We took off from Gatwick early that Saturday and landed at Kinshasa in the early evening, local time, but come eleven I was still being detained at the immigration. Worse, neither of the African officials who interrogated me on the reasons for my visit would let me telephone the British Embassy.

The senior of the two men was fat, smelt rankly of sweat, and chain-smoked, while his junior, a lanky beanpole with an adolescent moustache, lounged and fingered his gun, saying little. The small office where they held me was stiflingly humid. An electric fan merely stirred the fumes and my eyes had begun to sting and water after less than an hour. The room had bare walls and a scratched Formica-topped desk behind which the senior man dumped his bulk when he wasn't striding around, throwing staccato questions at me in a parody of an American TV detective's procedure.

At five past eleven this man had just returned from a long absence, evidently to eat, since he burped prodigiously when he sat down, and I again demanded contact with either the consul or Mr Roeyen.

'*Non!*' He slammed down his fist as he shouted, making the telephone I had wanted to use shake and tinkle. '*Non. Ecoutez. J'ai dit non. Non, non, non. Taisez-vous, crapaud.*'

As he glared at me, his black flesh bulging around heavy-lidded eyes, there was a tap on the opaque glass door. He nodded at the youth, who opened it with a jerk.

Standing facing us, looking urbane and no whit surprised, was a young European in a beautifully pressed light grey suit, a plastic airside pass clipped to its lapel. The impossibly cool look of this man and his white shirt, defying the oppressive heat, astonished me. He had a keen, aristocratic face with a short, close-trimmed beard, and his entire appearance radiated confidence. It was only later that I realized that he was actually narrow-shouldered and physically unimpressive.

'Forgive my intrusion, Captain,' he said with manicured politeness, stepping into the room. 'Allow me to present myself. Maître Roeyen, a friend of Colonel Bombolo.' He extended his hand and to my amazement the African accepted the gesture, reaching out across the table, though not going so far as to rise to his feet. I almost laughed.

'I believe there has been a misunderstanding. This English gentleman's documentation is in order. If I may give you the papers . . .' He held out a cardboard file cover and handed it across.

It was like watching a comedy of manners. The captain made a show of seating himself more squarely behind the table, opened the file and after a brief inspection removed a fat envelope. He lifted this envelope's unsealed flap, glanced inside and with a leisurely movement thrust it into his tunic pocket. The contents crackled as he did so.

'On account of the emergency,' Roeyen continued, 'the diplomatic applications had to be transmitted by telex. They were given special approval this evening.'

The captain spread the telexes and other documents on the table, perused them, withdrew my passport from the drawer in which he had placed it two hours previously, and went through a pantomime of inking a rubber stamp, testing the imprint, and then certifying every single piece of paper involved. The stamp and his rotundly scrawled initials occupy a whole page of my passport to this day.

'Next time,' he said to me sternly, 'do not expect us to be so lenient.'

'*Vous fumez, mon capitaine?*' Roeyen asked, cigarettes appearing in his palm as if by sleight of hand. He could have hardly doubted that the African did smoke, the room being as fetid as a nightclub at dawn, and I concluded that this was a further part of the ritual. The captain accepted the offer without a word, keeping the pack, while Roeyen tactfully gave the younger man another.

Finally, after a brief exchange of pleasantries and handshakes, the captain ordered his junior to escort us through the airport. We followed his slim figure, his buttocks protuberant inside absurdly tight trousers, reminding me vulgarly of Christianne, and his revolver bouncing on his hip, until we reached, of all places, the VIP lounge.

There we found my suitcase and Maître Roeyen made a further discreet payment, answering my curiosity about the division of the spoils. But although there were a few army officers lounging in the easy chairs, there was no sign of my crew.

'On my advice they left immediately for Nairobi,' Roeyen said, reminding me as we walked to his car that he was the company's lawyer and adding a sharp question as we drove away. 'Tell me, Mr Hartman, what precisely was your father doing on this ill-fated trip?'

'I wish I knew. I was hoping you or the manager might have some idea.'

'Your manager is under arrest. The police searched the offices today.' He glanced across at me, his face only an outline in the dark, and I sensed he was summing up my reactions. 'I was lucky to be able to arrange your visa. To be exact, it was only possible because other clients of mine still retain good will'.

'I'm very grateful. I was afraid they were going to lock me up.'

'If you'd offered them money, they probably would have. Those fellows won't dance to every tune.' He paused. We were driving down a broad boulevard, apparently towards the city, and I wondered what our destination was until he answered my unspoken question. 'I shall be honoured to have you as my guest. It will be a pleasure for me and also safer for you. This crash, so far south of the correct route, has aroused suspicion about your father's activities.'

'But he habitually changed his plans in mid-air,' I protested. 'Don't they understand that?'

'They are paranoid about security, especially in the diamond areas of the Kasai. They already believe your father was attempting an illegal landing.'

'In the bush?' The idea was absurd. Or, to be more exact, I thought it was.

'In Africa European logic is not applicable.' Roeyen swung sharply left to avoid a man on a bicycle without lights, dark against dark. We were on a side street now. 'I have heard people here claim that if they had become independent earlier they would have invented the jet. In practice all they've achieved in twenty years is ninety-nine per cent corruption.'

He sounded so bitter that I queried the assertion.

'Don't think I am a racialist,' he continued, concentrating on the potholed road surface. 'It takes two to make a deal. We are all guilty to some degree. But personally I do not set out to corrupt. I only pay if I have to: like tonight.'

'Whereas others?'

'We are nearly there.' He changed the subject. 'You must be tired and tomorrow we have an early start.' He eased the car to a halt in front of some gates and hooted. A nightwatchman opened them and I caught a glimpse of a whitewashed villa in the headlights.

Inside the atmosphere was completely continental, the odour, the furnishings, even the floor tiles. However I had barely time to reflect on how thoroughly each colonial power had exported the ambience of its culture to Africa before Roeyen was pressing a cut glass tumbler of whisky into my hand and explaining the next day's programme. To my amazement he had obtained a helicopter.

'We have paid a price for the police authorization of course, but this time an acceptable one – we shall take the official accident investigators with us. Your British man arrives from London in the morning. The Zaïrois is of course already here. He preferred to avoid the road journey and I do not blame him.'

Trying to appear relaxed, I studied my host as he told me something of his life as a bachelor in Kinshasa. Although French influence had greatly increased in this former Belgian colony and the Americans had poured in money, the number of Belgians was actually greater than at independence. 'The Africans prefer the devil they know,' he observed.

'That's Father's principle,' I commented.

'Principle?' His fine features wrinkled with amusement and I remembered the silver gun that Father had taken on the plane. Possibly 'principle' was not the most appropriate word.

'One should not speak ill of a man who may be dead, Robert.' Roeyen stroked his trim beard. 'On the other hand, if we encounter problems tomorrow you must know the reason. Sir James paid enormous bribes here. The Minister of Mines was his poodle absolutely. This week they were due to sign a most controversial deal on the marketing of gemstones. But when the master dies, such dogs run scared. A denunciation of the Trust's activities in Zaïre is imminent. That is why you are staying at my house and why I am coming with you tomorrow.' He sighed and shook his head sadly. 'I do not wish the sins of the father to be visited on the son.'

Why the hell are you telling me this, I thought, feeling the blood rise in my cheeks. Since leaving London I had been mentally steeling myself for tomorrow's search through the

170

wreckage: there would be nothing pleasant about that, or about confirming the identity of the dead. But I was not prepared for character assassination as well.

'Most international companies operate slush funds,' I remarked coolly. 'If Father bought politicians I'm sure it was only because he had to. What was so special about this deal anyway?'

Again Roeyen shook his head. 'I'm sorry. That must be kept secret.'

'Then why mention it?'

'If we meet hostility tomorrow, you will understand why.'

'You mean he was after the Kasai diamond output?' The conclusion was inevitable, after everything said earlier. 'Or else what?'

'I'm afraid I cannot comment.' Roeyen drained his own 'petit whisky' and stood up. 'We should go to bed,' he said firmly but kindly. 'Let me show you to your room.'

'Who markets the Zaïre diamonds now?' I persisted, remembering Father's list for his consortium and realizing with a moment of shock how fortunate it was that I had not kept the letter. The interrogators at the airport would have seized on it as evidence of a conspiracy, which in a sense it was. It's only after conspiracies succeed that they turn out to have been legitimate planning operations all along.

'The marketing was done by De Beers until recently,' Roeyen answered. 'Now matters are in a flux. In theory anyone could buy under government supervision, as they were doing before from a few inferior mines. In practice...' he made an elegantly dismissive movement of his hands. 'Listen, my friend, we have more immediate worries than discussing a battle which I personally do not believe Sir James could have won.'

With that, he showed me upstairs and I had to admit, though I would like to have argued further, that to reach the air-conditioned bedroom was a relief. Even at midnight the atmosphere was stickily humid. I was tickled to find that Roeyen, the prudent lawyer, did not rely on the air-conditioner to protect his guests against insects. The bed itself stood beneath an old-fashioned canopy of mosquito netting. He was not in business to be bitten by anything or anyone.

We drove out to the airport after breakfast on Sunday. The idea was to join up with the accident investigator from London when he arrived. Roeyen insisted that I take my belongings with me, and while we were waiting he reserved a seat on the evening flight to Brussels.

'In case you wish to leave tonight,' he explained.

'I'd rather bring our own jet back from Nairobi.' A night's sleep had left me better able to assess matters. I felt he had overreacted on my arrival.

'This is a time for discretion. Why draw attention to one's movements?'

I would have argued, had not the British Vice Consul joined us and passengers started coming off the inbound flight. I wondered what the investigator would be like, particularly when the diplomat assured us he was one of the most highly regarded men in the Accidents Investigation Branch in London, which itself sounded like part of Scotland Yard, though it wasn't.

'They have wide powers,' the Vice Consul explained, in a tone of veneration. 'They're responsible directly to the Secretary of State.'

He made it sound like having a hot line to God.

In the event the man who emerged ahead of the other passengers was an unobtrusive-looking forty-five-year-old carrying a Burberry raincoat over his arm and wearing a tropical suit with a striped RAF tie. He had pleasant, regularly formed features and a neat moustache. He could have been an insurance salesman, except that he had very keen pale blue eyes.

'Donaldson,' he said, putting down the briefcase and grip he was carrying and sticking out his hand firmly, 'Jim Donaldson,' and followed up the introduction with an immediate, 'Well, how's the transport situation?'

Half an hour later, having joined up with his African opposite number, we were lifting into the air, the helicopter tilting into forward motion, like an athlete straining to gain speed. The noise made conversation difficult and during the two-hour flight I concentrated on getting some impression of a country I should probably never see again, as we left the tropical surroundings of the capital and headed southeast over scrub and bush. It was well past midday before we reached the area of the crash. The pilot suddenly began pointing and with apprehension gripping me, I gazed down as we hovered over the site.

In its last moments, the Gulfstream had gouged a rough channel through small trees and the long, yellow-brown elephant grass, breaking up as it ploughed into the ground. I recognized the wings, and knew there must be smaller pieces of debris which I could not see. At the end of the littered trail lay the wreck of the cabin, with a group of Africans staring up at us.

'Fly along there,' Donaldson ordered the pilot. 'I want to see where it hit first.'

The pilot eased the helicopter forward, while Donaldson scanned the bush.

'Lower. Bring her down.'

We descended to perhaps thirty feet, so that the grass below was flattened by the rotors' downwash. Ahead of us was more wreckage.

'That's the tail all right,' Donaldson said and turned to his African opposite number, with whom he had rapidly assumed Christian-name terms. 'You want to see any more Paul? You're the boss.'

'I think not.' He was half shouting above the din. 'I want to know the time of the crash, the names of the dead, what cargo it carried, things like that.'

Donaldson gave him a curious look, but made no comment and told the pilot to land.

Moments later we were being greeted with distinctly qualified enthusiasm by an official who announced himself as the District Administrator and might have been the twin of my interrogator at the airport. He looked fat and mean and listened impatiently to Paul's explanation that he and Donaldson were respectively the Zaïre and British government's official investigators.

'There is nothing for you to do,' he announced in volubly imperfect French but with total conviction, Roeyen translating. 'I myself have solved the mystery. It is perfectly simple. This plane crashed while attempting to smuggle diamonds from the Kasai.'

'Please tell him,' Donaldson said to Roeyen, 'that we are here to determine the technical reasons for the accident, not whether the crew were breaking the law. Tell him the law is his business, we don't dispute that, but we also have a job to do.'

A long confabulation ensued, conducted with much gesticulation and excitement, Roeyen acting as interpreter. What emerged was that the bodies had been removed to the mortuary in the nearest town and that while 'safeguarding' the baggage, the police had found a parcel of uncut diamonds. They had telephoned this information to Kinshasa, which was presumably why our manager had been arrested. When Paul, who at least knew what his job ought to be, pointed out that the Gulfstream could not have been taking off when it crashed because there was no airstrip nearby, his intervention was brushed aside.

'All that is irrelevant,' the administrator insisted. 'This plane was carrying illegal diamonds.'

'For God's sake,' Donaldson muttered. 'What is this?'

'As I feared, Sir James is being framed,' Roeyen said quietly in English. 'Let me talk to him alone.' He turned to the administrator, but I caught only his opening words. 'These officials are of course prepared to pay the normal inspection fees, they have asked me . . .' Then he drew the African aside.

Ten minutes later we were allowed access to the wreckage, albeit under guard. Donaldson changed into yellow overalls, put on a red armband with the letters 'AIB' on it and then handed me a similar one.

'Highly irregular,' he said, 'but you'd better put it on. You may need official British status. From now on you're my assistant. What we do first is make a plan of where the pieces are lying and photograph them.'

Together with Paul we walked through the high grass to the nearest part of the wreck, a policeman following us, sub-machinegun in hand.

This was the moment I had been dreading most, the moment when although Father's body had not been found, I might discover some irrefutable indication that he was dead, like a shoe, or one of the flamboyant spotted silk handkerchiefs he favoured. But even seeing the remains of the plane from the air had not prepared me for the reality.

As executive jets go – apart from converted airliners – the Gulfstream was large and roomy. When you came up the steps you entered the plane just behind the flight deck, passed a closet for hanging coats and came through a door into the main cabin. The interior was panelled in rosewood, like Hartman House, and the first section contained six large and comfortable armchairs, three on each side of the aisle. Full-sized tables came out of the wall panelling beside these chairs. Beyond them the cabin had a long, three-place sofa which could be used as a bed, two more armchairs, a closed-circuit TV, and a telephone. Aft again was the galley, and beyond that a washroom which extended the whole width of the plane while finally, through a smaller door, there was access to the baggage compartment, with its own exterior cargo hatch. Now I gazed at what remained of this luxury with horror.

The nose had been savagely crushed, and as we came closer I saw that it had collided with a termite hill, a rock-solid pinnacle of hardened red earth. The rest of the once gleaming fuselage was crumpled and torn open at the rear, with the engines and tail missing, while the side we were approaching from – the opposite side to the door – had been crudely hacked open with axes or machetes. A coating of dust lay over everything. As we stood trying to obtain a general impression of what had happened, Donaldson pointed to a heap of debris in the grass. Visible among splintered pieces of the rosewood panelling was a single badly damaged armchair, its upholstery ripped.

'That wasn't "safeguarding",' he said angrily. 'That was plain bloody looting.'

'If it was left so many days in your country, what would take place?' Paul demanded defensively.

'Much the same, I suppose,' Donaldson conceded. 'But not after the police had arrived. Let's take a look inside.'

He led the way, crouching to scramble through the jagged hole, and the three of us entered, leaving the guard standing uncertainly outside. The cabin was a ruined shell with the oval windows broken and virtually all the furnishings gone. The front bulkhead had buckled and the door was off its hinges. We moved slowly forward to look at the flight deck.

The impact with the anthill had compressed the crew area into half its normal length. The pilots' seats were up against the instrument panel, the radar screen in the centre of the console was shattered, as were many of the dials and gauges, and there was dried blood in several places. It must have been a hell of a struggle to get the bodies out.

'Was this survivable?' I asked. 'For anyone?'

Donaldson twisted round in the narrow space. 'Realistically,' he said, 'I can't pretend it would have been. Think of the deceleration. Down from a hundred and twenty miles an hour or faster to a standstill in, what, eighty yards? This was a strongly built aircraft, it took a lot of force to tear the wings off. Hitting that anthill would be like running into a stone wall. The only good thing was that losing the wings with their fuel tanks probably saved the rest from catching fire. I'm sorry old chap, but if you had hopes your father might be alive and wandering in the bush somewhere, you should forget them.'

I backed away, feeling sick, stopped by what had been the curtained-off hanging cupboard and as I stood there, trying to stop myself retching, noticed something on the cupboard floor. I reached down and found a dark grey summerweight overcoat, which the looters must have missed: it was my father's, one he always travelled with. No discovery could have been more conducive to believing that he must be dead. I was about to call out to Donaldson, when instinct urged me to search the pockets first. Although outside there was strong sunlight, the only illumination here came from the axe holes in the fuselage further back. I moved that way, fumbling in the pockets, felt a piece of paper and held it up. The paper was a message form headed 'Norfolk Hotel'. On it was written, in a strong yet feminine hand:

'Good luck, my dear. If you cannot do this, no one can.'

The message was not signed, and it took me a full minute to decipher for a simple reason: the writing was in German.

'What have you found?' Paul's voice sounded behind me, and I swung round, startled, shovelling the message into my trousers.

'An overcoat.' At least I had the presence of mind not to identify it as my father's. I seemed to be purloining more documents in a week than in the rest of my life.

'We must give it to the police,' he said, 'or there will be trouble.'

'You take it,' I suggested, grateful for his sympathetic attitude. All the government wanted from him was confirmation of the accusations. But what about the silver gun? Had that been found already?

Donaldson reappeared, holding out a large reeled tape measure. 'You might as well make yourself useful,' he said briskly. 'Get the exact distance to the first impact will you. Do a sketch plan but keep it simple. And take that damned guard with you. I want to take photographs here undisturbed.'

I did as instructed, leaving Paul with him, and after struggling through the scrub established the distance as 84 yards. Then, with the policeman watching suspiciously, I made a plan showing the position of the engines and wings relative to the cabin. One thing perplexed me. Where the end section of the tail lay, with the high fin partially wrenched off, there was no sign of the cargo door, only torn metal and ragged edges. In fact the body itself seemed to have broken open at that point, if such a construction could.

When Donaldson rejoined me I pointed this out, and he spent a long time examining the tail section, while I scoured the surrounding bush for the missing door. There was no trace of it. When I came back, he prepared to take more photographs, but the guard rushed forward and held a beefy black hand against the lens. He tried polite bribery by taking a photo of the man himself, achieving a huge grin as the instant print emerged from the Polaroid camera, but nothing more. Pictures of the wreckage were forbidden. Then the administrator came across and suggested, uncompromisingly, that we had enjoyed enough time. He wanted to confirm the identification of the dead. Furthermore, perhaps not trusting us to stay around, he insisted on coming in the helicopter too. Or perhaps he only wanted to boast of having been in one. Luckily there was a spare seat.

'I've had problems overseas before,' Donaldson said to me under his breath as we strapped ourselves in, 'but, believe me, seldom like this. Now I understand why our African colleague isn't bothering much. He has to live here, poor bastard.'

The town, more of a trading post than a town proper, was a fifteen-minute flight away, though by road a two-hour drive. The helicopter rocked in the afternoon heat and I began steeling myself for this further ordeal, shouting questions at Donaldson to take my mind off coming face to face with the dead.

'Did the instruments tell you anything?'

'Yes and no.' He leant across and spoke in my ear. 'The plane wasn't carrying a flight recorder. I don't like jumping to conclusions.'

'But you must have learnt something!'

'No rpm on either turbine. The fuel gauges read a third full. Something stopped the engines and probably cut the electrics. Could be why no distress call was picked up.' He paused. 'Another thing. The instrument panel clock showed 1019. If it was local time, that might make sense. If they were on GMT, it cannot.'

I was about to ask him why and demand a less technical explanation – the Trust was paying for this expedition after all – when our helicopter landed on a patch of waste ground, close to some low tin-roofed buildings, with a faded red cross painted on them. Dust swirled up all around, the rotors' clattering diminished and we got out. Waiting police ran up and we were escorted straight to the hospital mortuary, Roeyen commenting wryly that he hoped the refrigeration was working.

Happily the mortuary was relatively cool, though the smell of death if not of actual putrefaction, hung in the air. In the principal room were a series of slabs, four with the low humps of corpses showing under soiled shrouds.

'There were four?' I asked, my heart almost stopping.

'From the aeroplane, three,' said the attendant.

'Show the faces,' ordered the administrator, his eyes on us as the first was revealed.

I breathed in, told myself not to be squeamish and stepped forward.

There, pallid as ivory and tinged with a day's growth of beard, his eyes black-ringed as if he had been in a fight and his forehead deeply gashed, was Captain Holz. Yet his face looked quite calm and gave a feeling of detachment, perhaps because his skin colour was so different to that of a living man.

'The chief pilot,' Roeyen confirmed. 'I met him several times.'

The second body was unveiled down to the shoulders and I gasped involuntarily. The face was hideously disfigured under a bandaged forehead.

'I have tried to clean the mess,' the attendant said apologetically.

'Is he Sir Hartman?' the administrator demanded of me.

'No.' I turned away, only to be forced to look again as the third corpse was displayed. Having seen the flight deck, I wasn't surprised at the terrible injuries. The remains of this head had a moustache caked in blood. 'I think he is the co-pilot,' I said.

'Not Hartman?' The administrator had only one interest.

'Definitely not,' Roeyen assured him.

'The second man must be the flight engineer,' Donaldson said.

'Where is Hartman? Where are the passengers?' The administrator became bullying. He confronted us, his countenance as nearly purple as a black skin could get. 'You!' he shouted at Donaldson. 'You who spent so much time examining the plane. Why are there no passengers?'

If he wanted to intimidate, he had picked the wrong person. Donaldson looked straight back at him and said calmly to Roeyen, 'Tell him that if I am allowed to make a full investigation, I might find out what happened. Otherwise I shall lodge a formal complaint.'

It was a brave stand, and rendered more effective by his asking Roeyen to translate, so underlining that he was a foreign official. The administrator glowered and said nothing.

'The baggage might indicate how many people were on the plane,' I suggested, wanting to know if my father's cases were there and if they had discovered the ludicrous-sounding silver gun.

'The baggage is impounded.'

'We would like to see it,' Donaldson backed me.

For a moment I thought this demand had taken the African beyond boiling point and he would arrest the lot of us. But instead of shouting, he laughed: a high-pitched cackle of a laugh. Then he strode across to the fourth mortuary slab and stripped off the sheet. The body was of an African, its chest and stomach gouged with bullet holes, the black skin smeared with blood. I stared with disgust, realizing that these were all exit wounds. The victim had been shot in the back.

'This one tried to escape last night,' the administrator said, prodding the corpse disdainfully with his swagger stick. 'I give you warning. No one plays games with my authority. No one. Be careful.' A look of cautious cunning came across his face. 'If you wish to see the baggage, you may also assist the law. Come with me.'

He led the way out of the mortuary and a short distance across the dusty compound to a newer building, where a trio of armed police lounged in the sun, smoking. They roused themselves and saluted languidly. In the corner of an office stood two black leather document cases of the sort aircrew use and three small suitcases, battered and dusty but apparently intact.

'Monsieur . . .?' The administrator beckoned me across.

'Robert,' Roeyen prompted.

'You know these, Monsieur Robert?'

I shook my head. There was a trick in this. It was obvious from the way he had so abruptly turned our request into a challenge. I wondered if Holz had packed the gun in one of the cases, though from Christianne's description it had been in a presentation box of some kind.

'But you know what is in these baggages?'

'I have never seen them before.'

'I will show you.' The administrator went to a large green-painted safe and unlocked the door, taking out a little transparent plastic bag and dumping it on his desk. 'These were in the brown case.' He opened the bag and tipped it up. A stream of dull, dirty-looking stones cascaded out. 'You think we people of the Kasai cannot recognize an uncut diamond? You think we are stupid? Sir Hartman is a smuggler.'

'Where did you find the cases?' Donaldson asked with unexpected urgency.

'In the aeroplane, of course.'

'Not in the bush?'

'Are you trying to trick me? I warn you again. I warn you solemnly.'

'The cases were in the aeroplane?'

'I have said so. Do you call me a liar?'

'Thank you, Sir.' Donaldson relaxed a little. 'Please excuse my questions. May we examine them?'

His main point accepted, the administrator gave an order and one by one the cases were put on his desk and opened. The locks had already been broken. From the labels and the white uniform shorts inside it was clear that the small ones had belonged to the crew. The leather briefcases contained aeronautical maps and technical manuals.

'And now,' the administrator demanded, 'where is Sir Hartman?'

Donaldson again asked Roeyen to interpret.

'Please apologize for my doubting his perspicacity. Tell him, that as a stranger I was bound to ask unnecessary questions. Say that his deductions are obviously correct and that when the plane landed for the purpose of smuggling the diamonds, the passengers must have stayed behind. Since this is the administrator's own district, I am sure he will find them.'

I listened to this performance incredulously, wondering what on earth Donaldson was playing at with such pompous nonsense when we had agreed there was nowhere the Gulfstream could have landed secretly. However the purpose of the flattery became clearer when he explained that the British government would want a more detailed examination of the wreckage than he had been able to make so far.

Roeyen promptly offered to send the helicopter back in a couple of days' time and handed over a liberal advance for the cost of local transport and accommodation. The administrator became genial and offered us bottles of local beer.

After some polite conversation and the giving of assurances on both sides, we were escorted back to the helicopter. I shook Donaldson's hand warmly, thanking him for his efforts.

'All part of the service,' he smiled. 'I like to get to the bottom of things. The manufacturers will be worried as hell too. We ought to take the entire wreck back to a hangar and try to reassemble it, but I can't see that being feasible.'

'I have to ask you this again,' I said. 'Do you seriously believe my father and his secretary can be alive?'

He looked at me, the sun slanting into his eyes and making him blink, while Roeyen and the helicopter pilot listened, then he took my arm.

'I'd prefer to talk to you alone.' He guided me a little distance away. 'I don't want to pre-empt my own conclusions. It's against our code of conduct for good reason. But I do understand your concern, so all I'll ask is your word that you're not going to repeat what I say. All right?' I nodded. 'Well, there are two possibilities. One is that your father was not on the plane at all. The other is that he was in the lavatory and was sucked out along with the baggage when the bomb went off.'

I stared at him. 'Bomb?'

'Cargo doors don't come unlocked towards the end of a flight. If they're going to fail, they fail during the climb. The loss of the door had every sign of being caused by an explosion in the hold. When a bomb detonates in a pressurized aircraft the air inside goes out through the hole like a whirlwind. The reason the crew's suitcases didn't go with it is that the crew members like to have their own bags accessible. They would have stowed them in the hanging cupboard, not the hold. But your father's baggage would have been sucked straight out and so, possibly, would anyone in the washroom adjoining the hold. What I find hard to believe is that a second passenger in the main cabin would have been dragged out through two bulkhead partitions. There should at the least have been a fourth body in the wreck.'

'The other person could have gone back to find out what was wrong.'

'No time. The whole chain of events would have been over in seconds. The decompression's like an explosion itself. The fall in pressure would burst everyone's eardrums. They'd become unable to breathe properly. Any passenger who didn't put on an oxygen mask would pass out.'

'So Father's body or Tina Humphries' should have been found in the wreck?'

Donaldson laid a hand on my shoulder. 'I don't wish to be quoted, privately or publicly. But to my mind the balance of probability is that neither of them was on board at all.'

On the helicopter flight back to Kinshasa I began to realize that this dispassionate analysis posed more questions than it answered. Could there be any connection between the burglary at Van Rensburg's house and a bomb? For that matter, who could have wanted to kill Father? Above all, how had he and Tina Humphries contrived to vanish before the attempt and where were they? I recalled Roeyen's refusal to comment on the deal Father had been involved with in Zaïre and his lack of surprise at the packet of diamonds in the plane. When the helicopter dropped us off at the airport I declined to be delivered to the Sabena check-in.

'As you wish.' Roeyen absorbed the refusal, arching his eye-

180

brows and miming regret. 'I merely point out that if that madman down in the Kasai makes further accusations, you would be the obvious target.'

'Which was why you let him think my surname was Robert?'

'Africans often assume the first name is the important one. Such a small misunderstanding hardly merited correction.' He smiled delicately. 'None the less, you would be wise to leave.'

We compromised on a breakfast-time flight to Geneva, which fitted my purposes very well, and returned to his house. Despite having been overruled, he remained a meticulously courteous host. My former room was instantly prepared, though I noticed the servants had not changed the sheets on the bed, presumably by way of an economy in case I did come back. Roeyen had not been completely confident that he could pack me off home at once. Encouraged, I pressed for information over the ritual whisky before dinner.

'I am here with the Board's full authority,' I reminded him, 'and I would appreciate full collaboration. What exactly was my father negotiating on his last visit? Did he make enemies?'

'You seldom make friends of men by buying them.' Roeyen surveyed his spacious reception room, the sofas with their cream-coloured loose covers, the polished mahogany tables and the heavy ornaments, as if summoning back the past. 'I sat where I am now.' He gestured towards a chair. 'Van Rensburg there, Sir James there, the Minister facing him, the Chef de Cabinet . . .'

'You mean he gave bribes to a minister in front of others?'

'This is a sophisticated country in its own way.' He allowed himself the ghost of a smile. 'The percentages are well understood. Of course, Sir James normally takes care to save face, much as he despises politicians. Envy is the greatest enemy of ambition. But last month, *au contraire*, he was exceptionally direct. For myself I doubted if that was prudent.'

CHAPTER FOURTEEN

'Our arrangement will depend upon confidence. Mutual confidence. All business does. Your Excellency knows that as well as I do.'

Hartman's negotiating voice, dead of emotion, cut across the Minister's demands. Translating, Roeyen tried to ameliorate its impact.

The Minister was a small, neatly dressed African in his forties, with an enquiring expression intensified by professorial gold-framed spectacles. He was proud of being a graduate of Louvain University in Belgium, and the fact that Roeyen came from Louvain gave him an illogical confidence in the lawyer. He listened carefully, then protested.

'*Mais vous avez proposé un rayon d'action exceptionnel . . .*' He spoke for some minutes, reminding them that Zaïre was the world's largest producer of industrial diamonds and he could not re-orient that export trade without 'reasons of the greatest validity'.

'The validity is commercial or nothing,' Hartman growled. 'We're all in this to make money.'

Van Rensburg sat on the sofa quietly making notes. Jim's scheme was bold, almost visionary: to create a marketing consortium for black Africa's diamond producers which would challenge De Beers' South African-controlled Central Selling Organization head on. Zaïre had broken with the CSO last year, thus contributing along with the recession to a 46 per cent slump in the CSO's sales. The moment was right to exploit that slump and Zaïre would be the key participant.

'What price per carat are you proposing?' the Minister enquired, via Roeyen.

'A floor price of eight dollars and ten cents on a five-year contract with review procedures.' Hartman laid the terms down with finality. This was the price Van Rensburg had advised. Not generous, but competitive.

The Minister exchanged a few words with his Chef de Cabinet, the portly, egregious African civil servant who ran his office and was not so much the shadow of ministerial power as its substance. Deals like this could only be implemented with his collaboration. He appeared to agree and both men then sat back, waiting for the aspect of the proposal that counted.

'In addition,' Hartman said crisply, 'three cents per carat paid wherever His Excellency wishes.'

Van Rensburg nodded imperceptibly. He had been afraid Jim would go higher. Zaïre's production was around 19 million carats a year. This would give the Minister upward of $570,000 personally. It damn well ought to be enough.

'Five cents,' the Minister said, his dark eyes cloudy behind the gold spectacles. 'You are asking me to have confidence in an unproven organization.'

This was far too much in Van Rensburg's view. The Minister's cut would have to be added to the consortium's trading mark-up. Even assuming the success of their planned takeover of Consolidated, which would give the consortium valuable diamond production of its own to swell the profits, there would be fierce reactions from the CSO with its £1,000 million stockpile. They would have to undercut the CSO's prices and when the CSO fought back the margins would be paper-thin.

'Frankly, Your Excellency,' Hartman spoke with greater cordiality, aware he had been somewhat abrasive, 'five is too much. I suggest Zaïre cannot afford *not* to join our consortium. Ghana, Liberia and Sierra Leone have agreed. They will be represented on its governing council.' This was an enormous political advance and he underlined it. 'They believe the independent States of Africa should control their own trading destiny. So, Your Excellency, do I.'

'*Sur le plan politique . . .*' Roeyen began explaining.

Van Rensburg thought of last week's negotiation in Sierra Leone, where corruption was completely institutionalized. Seventy per cent of the diamond production vanished before it reached the Government Diamond Office. Jim had arranged with a half-caste Lebanese government adviser for it to reappear. At a price. That price had owed nothing to African political aspirations. Why should this minister be more sensitive?

'We are all concerned for Africa,' Hartman concluded. 'This consortium will be powerful. It will handle close to half the world's production of diamonds. The days of exploitation are over.'

Van Rensburg blinked. Black Africa did not yield even a quarter of the world's production, at least not while Botswana remained under De Beers' control, while in value terms it yielded far less. By weight, as measured in carats, Zaïre produced 29 per cent of world output: by value in dollars only four or five per cent. He was not surprised when the Minister asked from what other source supplies would be drawn.

'The Ashton and Argyle mines will make the Australians major producers. Their government seems more worried about apartheid than you are.'

'*Ah, non* . . . We are of course concerned. How else will you expand this consortium?'

Hartman laughed. 'Who knows, the Russians might come in.' He spread his hands, eloquently suggesting vistas of opportunity. 'Another eleven million carats. I ought to go to Moscow.' He cut himself short. 'However, at this moment we are talking about the West and the faith we have in Africa. Three and a half per cent.'

'Not enough. Certain percentages are accepted practice.'

Having translated, Roeyen intervened. He wished this negotiation to succeed. He lived in Kinshasa.

'Possibly, Your Excellency,' he suggested, 'one of those famous British compromises may resolve this. A percentage and a guarantee.'

Thirty minutes later Hartman and the Minister signed a Memorandum of Understanding, prepared beforehand, with the blank figures hastily typed in place by Christianne, working next door in Roeyen's study. Then they stood up and shook hands, an incongruous pair, the European physically predominant, stooping because he stood a head taller, the African erect and formal.

'As I have always said,' Hartman retained the Minister's hand in his own longer than was customary except among Africans, 'Your Excellency can have confidence that arrangements I make will be honoured.'

'Will Angola join us, Sir James?' The African did not relax his rather limp grip. 'You did not mention Angola.'

The juxtaposition of the two men was absurd. They continued clasping each other's hands, as if in public for photographers, while the barbed question forced them apart. Angola was Marxist and riven by civil war. Though neighbours, the two countries were seldom in agreement. Hartman withdrew his hand, stood his full height and smiled beneficently down at the African, joking his way out of this embarrassment.

'If the mines in the northeast could be brought back into production. If the Angolan Liberation Front permitted. There are many "ifs". What is Your Excellency's view?'

'They are our brothers.' The Minister replied in English with disquieting promptness. 'Some of them.'

For some reason a sign I once saw in a French bar came into my mind '*Profitez-en,*' it had read. '*Le Patron est en bonne humeur.*'

'The Minister's good humour didn't last long,' I remarked to Roeyen.

'Since the crash his percentage could not be guaranteed. Further in my opinion, Sir James was unwise to have mentioned the Russians, even in passing.'

I recalled Van Rensburg's telling how the Russians were the joker in the diamond marketing business. Their eleven million carats used to be marketed through De Beers, then they broke away. Sometimes they sold through the Antwerp market, sometimes through the CSO again. They pursued exactly the kind of pragmatic approach that Father admired. But politics must have come into it.

'The Minister wouldn't want to be associated with communists?' I said.

'Labels.' Roeyen dismissed the idea. 'In the West you label everything "communist" or "capitalist". In Africa we do not. Ideologically the Minister would not care. Ethnically, he would.'

'Ethnically?' I was lost.

'The Soviet Union supports the Angolan government. Ever since independence the government has been fought by two movements: UNITA in the south and the Angolan Liberation Front in the northeast. The Minister was born in the Kasai and his tribe is divided by the frontier. He calls his relations in Angola "brothers". We would call them cousins. Distant clan members. The difference is purely semantic. Whether they are brothers or cousins they are the enemy of the Angolan government. Therefore, at heart, so is he.'

That gave me pause. How far would it go? To promoting a burglary on the other side of Africa? To planting illicit diamonds in the wreckage? To planting a bomb on the plane itself? Roeyen knew nothing of the bomb theory and I did not want him to. My final question was circumspect.

'Would the Minister have sabotaged the agreement while Father was alive?'

'You ask impossible questions, *mon ami*. How can we penetrate the mind of an African, a mind steeped in millennia of tribal loyalty and superstition and merely overlaid with a deceptive few decades of French or British culture? Sir James excelled in his dealings with Anglophone leaders. He was the devil they knew and they trusted him. Perhaps you British created a deeper impression by giving orders than the French achieved with their cuisine. Who knows? Here, through the neglect of my own Belgian compatriots, the veneer was at its thinnest. Here we have a saying, "You can buy a minister for the morning, but he will not be yours for the afternoon." The Zaïrois have remained true only to themselves.'

This explanatory tour de force closed the conversation. Maître Roeyen's eloquence was invincible. More, I suspected he was correct. Father had bought one politician too many.

Before dinner I risked asking for a phone call to Geneva. We had finished eating before it came through. To my relief Roeyen accepted my explanation that since I had to change flights in Switzerland I might as well look up an acquaintance. After that I was glad to go to bed. I was exhausted. As I fell asleep it struck me, mordantly, that if Father at twice my age had the stamina to survive jetting around Africa as routine, he probably had the reserves to survive whatever he was going through now.

At the airport next morning Roeyen smoothed my path through the formalities, an island of elegance in the hurly-burly of departure. A shrewd operator, I thought, once I was safely cocooned in the comfort of the airliner, who could have more urgent reasons for hustling me out of Zaïre than he was prepared to reveal. But my leaving was now a fait accompli. It was more important that he had provided a clue as to where Father's grand strategy had gone wrong.

Even so, as I gazed out of the tiny window at the hazy green landscape of Africa, I began to feel that if I rubbed my eyes the whole visit might turn out to have been a dream, or a television film about someone else. In a day and a half I had spent as much money as my university salary for a year. For the first time in my life I understood how super-rich Father was, not so much in physical assets like houses or pictures, or income, but in the human resources he commanded through the Trust. Wherever he went pilots and chauffeurs stood waiting while advisers like Roeyen shepherded his movements. I had never fully appreciated this before, nor that he bribed as a matter of course, taking corruption for granted. At home he did not throw money around. Despite the size of Godstow, we lived unostentatiously. Any servant who cheated us would be instantly sacked. I found the dichotomy extraordinary. However it was no longer surprising that someone should have wished him dead. Many people might have done.

The realization brought little reward. Quite apart from not knowing how a bomb might have been secreted on to the Gulfstream, why, assuming that he and Tina Humphries had escaped death, should they then choose to vanish? Father loathed being out of touch. Whether it was day or night in London, some company he owned somewhere would be at work and he kept tabs on most of them. In one of her very rare outbursts Mother had commented that being married to him was worse than being married to a Cabinet minister. Any voluntary disappearance would be completely out of character. Might he somehow have been kidnapped? A host of wild ideas began running through my brain. The hijacking of private jets was not unknown.

However, if he had been kidnapped there would have been a ransom demand. So that theory made no sense. Then I remembered Donaldson's observation about whether the aircraft clock had been on Greenwich Mean Time when the impact stopped it at 1019. I foraged in the seat pocket for the in-flight magazine, hoping it would have route maps. It did. I began making approximate calculations and was so worried by the results that I rang for the stewardess and asked if pilots worked on GMT. She was not sure but after a short delay took me up to the flight deck, where I pretended an interest in other matters as well and rapidly received my answer.

'Well, Sir,' the Swiss captain said, swinging round in his seat, 'all position reports and arrival and departure times are given in GMT.' He smiled. 'You may notice we sometimes convert it wrongly before landing and inform the passengers incorrect local time. It is easy done. I would say any professional pilot keeps his watch on GMT while flying.'

Back in my seat the information quickly assumed an authority of its own. The Gulfstream had departed Nairobi at 0600 GMT and should have reached Kinshasa at 0900. It had crashed one hour and nineteen minutes later than that, off course, and still forty minutes short of its destination. In other words it was running two hours late.

In two hours the Gulfstream would fly 1,000 miles, or further. Captain Holz could not conceivably have got that far out of kilter. They must have landed somewhere: presumably south of the original route because the crash had been to the south. That was the only tenable explanation for Father's and Tina's bodies not being in the wreckage. I juggled with the scale indications on the map and realized that such a stop could have been made in Tanzania, Zambia, Angola or Zaïre itself. If we alerted the authorities in those countries a second time, what would we say: that they should now search for two illegal immigrants?

Eventually Donaldson, that irreducibly calm and British investigator, might deduce whether the bomb had been planted in Nairobi or at my hypothetical en-route landing. Meanwhile I decided to work on the assumption that Father had made a characteristic change of plan during the flight and thereafter things had

187

gone desperately wrong, though he was more likely to be alive than dead.

My thoughts switched to the Tuesday Board meeting. Tuesday was tomorrow. If I was to extract anything from Dr Lohrey I should have to stay overnight, which in turn meant telling Mother a white lie. My own life was becoming as convoluted as Father's.

Accordingly I rang Godstow from Geneva airport. Mother sounded more than happy to hear me, though distressed by the explanations.

'So long as you think he's alive, darling. I simply don't understand all these technical things. What are you doing now?'

I began to say that I had something to follow up in Switzerland, but behind her words she sounded terribly hurt.

'Frank has postponed the Board meeting until Wednesday and you can come to it . . . I suppose there's no hurry.' She broke off for a moment so that I thought the line was cut. 'Please darling, get back tonight if you possibly can.'

She didn't say why, but was obviously so generally unnerved and upset that I agreed. I was going to have to extract a great deal from Dr Lohrey in a very short time.

Lohrey had said she would meet me outside the terminal building, some ten metres from the bus stop sign. It was raining, a light drizzle of the kind that soon soaks into your clothes, and the afternoon was grey, not like summer at all.

'Taxi M'sieur?' a man offered. I shook my head and resolutely stood firm, watching for her face as cars drew up.

'Robert!' Her voice came instead from behind. I spun round to find her a couple of yards away. She might well have been watching me from inside the terminal while I was intent on the traffic.

'I keep you waiting? I hope not. I find it a stupid privilege for women to be late.' Her voice was so huskily vibrant that I thought she must have a cold, despite which she looked even more soignée than she had before. She wore a light spring coat cut with a dash that only just stopped short of the theatrical, and it occurred to me how much easier it was for a woman to shine against this dull background than under the harsh light of Africa.

'You know, Robert.' She released my hand. 'I have thought we can go to my apartment for a tea and afterwards I drive you back. But have we time?'

'Whatever you prefer. I've three hours.'

'And there are things to talk about from Zaïre?'

'Yes.'

'Then we go.' She touched my elbow and began guiding me towards a car park. It was a relief. That initial encounter had felt as brittle as icing.

We reached a small, bright red, Volkswagen, identical to

Camilla's, except for its colour. 'Very practic,' she commented, compounding German and English. 'I have no need for impressing clients with a car, as a man would. I can be my own advertisement.'

She elaborated a little on her public relations business as we drove towards the city, past the large villas and solidly nondescript office buildings typical of Geneva, until she swung left up a hill and halted outside an elderly apartment house.

'If I had children,' she remarked unexpectedly, 'I would live further out, with a garden.'

The reasoning was tinged with wistfulness and seemed out of character for such a self-possessed person. I agreed hurriedly. I hadn't stopped over to discuss her lifestyle.

Her apartment, however, demanded admiration. It was high-ceilinged, spacious and ornamented with many small objects of *vertu* and a variety of pictures. Among them was a reproduction of a Rouault, so strongly and almost crudely painted as to be out of place, yet seeming familiar. Suddenly I realized that the original was at Godstow.

'A gift from him,' she said following my gaze. 'Since many years.'

In fact Father had only acquired the Rouault in the late 1970s, but I let that ride. There were more significant matters to attack her over. She showed me to the spare bedroom, allowed me time to wash and change my shirt, then brought the promised tea and settled herself on the gilt-legged chaise-longue, sitting necessarily upright and attentive. I began to realize that the confrontation I had planned might not be simple.

'So.' She was friendly, but more poised than relaxed. 'You have come a long way. You told me very little on the telephone. It was awkward, I suppose. How can I help?'

I slipped the crumpled Norfolk Hotel message from my wallet and handed it across.

For a moment she stared at this relic as though I had no right to be in possession of it, then put it down beside her and took a sip of tea.

'What did you mean by "If you cannot do this, no one can?" What was my Father trying to do?' I'd had enough of her playing the *grande dame*.

She disregarded the question. 'Where have you found this?'

'In the wreckage of the plane. In the pocket of Father's coat. If you wished him luck,' I insisted, 'you must have known where he was going.'

She picked up the message again and frowned: I imagined in annoyance at Father not having destroyed it. Her next words showed me I was wrong.

'It is in his coat?' she asked perplexedly. 'And his body is not there?'

'Definitely not. Listen, Mrs Lohrey, if you know something I don't, for God's sake tell me. A plane doesn't get sabotaged for no reason.'

She seemed forced to a decision. 'I know a little of what he was planning. Yes, that is true. Where he was going that day except for Zaïre, I do not know.' She laid down her cup and saucer carefully. 'I want to help you, Robert. I have said so. But let us be honest with each other. You speak as if you accuse me of something. What is exactly in your mind?'

'You weren't in Kenya at the same time as Father by coincidence.' I felt angry with myself for having gone along with the pretence before. She was his other woman, had been throughout his married life. Whatever she might claim, men do confide in their mistresses. 'You came out to the Van Rensburgs' house because the Gulfstream was missing and you already knew it was. Otherwise you'd never have gone near Patrick and Mary while I was there. When you found me alone you put on a great piece of acting.'

'Oh, Robert.' She gave a tiny shake of the head, as though it was a waste of time trying to explain. Then she reached for her handbag and took out her diary. 'I want as much as you to find where he is. Maybe there is something he said which gives us a clue. But I told you, we did not speak about business. We spoke about what he still wanted from life.' She looked me straight in the eyes. 'As old friends do. Now,' she flipped the pages. 'I come back from a safari on Thursday, May 20th and stay in the Norfolk. That evening to my astonishment he is standing in the lobby, with Patrick, before dinner. He tells me the only time he would be free is the next afternoon and maybe the evening.'

Remembering Father's itinerary, this made sense. He had called on the Vice President after lunch and would have been free thereafter. 'Dinner private' was, I knew, a euphemism to protect last-minute arrangements.

'I suggest we go to the Game Park.' Her tone was disarming. 'And so we did, like children going to the zoo.'

I smiled in spite of my annoyance. Only two things would persuade Father to gawp at wild animals: a business deal or an attractive woman. I began to believe what she was saying.

'We had only one problem,' she went on. 'The driver talked too much.'

'Look bwana! You see that one?' The khaki-uniformed driver of the open-topped hunting car slowed and gesticulated. A lithe, long-legged leopard-like cat with a spotted coat was loping along the verge of the dusty road ahead of them. 'Cheetah, sah. You are very lucky, sah.' The cheetah, disturbed by the vehicle, vanished into the long grass. 'Now he is hunting. Soon he will kill. Very lucky to see cheetah, bwana.'

Lotte Lohrey gazed obediently at the part of the bush where the cheetah had disappeared, thinking she saw movement, until mercifully the driver guide fell silent. The hunting car was big bodied, with wide leather cloth-covered seats. She pulled at Jim's sleeve and they both stood upright, their heads and shoulders projecting through the roof. Her hair blew back in the wind.

'Maybe it's better we talk in German,' she suggested.

'*Jah. Gut.*' He raised his binoculars, resting his elbows on the padded side of the roof opening, and made a perfunctory show of observation, though the bumping of the car over ruts in the dirt surface made it difficult. 'Why did you come?'

'Carlo has died in Rome.'

'But he was recovering.'

'On Monday he had a second heart attack. In the evening he died.'

Hartman lowered the binoculars, and continued staring at the landscape, his face set. He rubbed his eyes, as though dust had blown into them.

'That's bad news.'

'I came as soon as was possible.'

He turned to her – they were close together – and kissed her cheek. 'Thank you, Lotte. I can always trust you. What about the arrangements Carlo made?'

The vehicle slowed and a shout from the driver interrupted them. 'Buffalo, bwana. On the left.'

At the edge of the woodland a small herd of buffalo were grazing. They were big, dull-coated, beasts with broad, heavy horns. They raised their heads. A bull pawed the ground, snorted and took tentative steps towards them. Lotte snapped a picture for the sake of appearances.

'Damn the bloody animals,' Hartman muttered, then called to the driver, 'Is there any place we can get out and walk around?'

'There is Impala Point, bwana.'

'Take us there.' He couldn't carry on a discussion like this. Equally he couldn't wait. 'Is the bank doing its part of the bargain?' he asked. 'Will they still support us in the bid?'

'Thirty million has been deposited. When you make the bid their nominees will buy heavily to push up the Trust's price.'

'*Prima.*' He grunted with satisfaction. Consolidated would be savaged, caught between the value of his offer rising and its own assets falling through the loss of Concession Twenty-Two. The

London Stock Exchange had rules to prevent this kind of manoeuvre, but no one nominee would hold enough of the Trust's shares to transgress those rules. 'They'll make a killing, too,' he added. 'The price will go on up.'

'They know that, Hans.' She drifted back into calling him by his real name when they spoke in German and she didn't trouble to correct herself.

'Carlo's undertakings about Angola will remain?' he asked.

'In principle.' She had to keep this businesslike, because she had a message to deliver: one Carlo would have sent direct had he been alive. This was why she had come. She looked sideways at Hans, thinking she was a fool to have agreed. His hair, ruffled in the breeze, was greyer than it had been, the lines round his eyes deeper. If she hadn't been involved with this so long ago she would never have agreed to be a courier. 'There has been a change,' she said. 'One you will not like.'

The vehicle skidded slightly. They were on a bend and the track was wet after rain. They were clear of the woodland and driving along the top of an escarpment, below which the green plains lay in a vast sweep, stretching towards distant hills.

'Impala Point, bwana,' the driver shouted as he stopped near a small stone observation post with a conical roof. 'You can walk to the look-out.' He dismounted and opened the doors for them.

Hartman thanked him and guided Lotte to the rondavel, thankful that it was unoccupied. They went inside and leant on the stone parapet, conscious of the immensity of the landscape, the silence and the fresh earthy smell of the recent rain.

'We don't have to fool with each other,' Hartman said. 'What do they want?'

'Angola will give you the concession. But they wish for a guarantee of production.'

'They'll have one. How I keep the Liberation Front off my back is my affair. The diamonds will go out and the foreign exchange come in.'

'Do you not think that is a little naïve, Hans? They are tired of losing face and they could lose more. They want the counter-revolutionary leader captured. Even if you can only meet him in Lisbon or Paris they will do the rest.'

'They know damn well Edmundo never leaves the bush.' Hartman stopped his ostensible gazing at the view and pivoted round. 'Nor am I going to be a stalking horse just because the Cubans can't win the war for them. If they want their diamond industry revived I'll do it my way. Tell them that, Lotte. Say they'll have a guarantee next week.'

'Hans.' She touched his arm. 'I only repeat what I was asked to tell you. Do not blame the messenger for the message.'

192

The noise of the hunting car being restarted shattered the quiet.
'We'd better talk over dinner, if you're free.'

'I am, of course.' She was watching his expression carefully, absorbing both the anger and the strength. 'As a friend, Hans, I think you should withdraw. You have created an empire in Africa, but with this deal there are too many dangers.'

The driver revved his engine impatiently.

'I'll think about it,' Hartman conceded. 'Let's go back to the hotel before that damn man feeds us to the lions.'

After their return they sat outside in the dusk, listening to the cicadas and comfortable in the mutual silences that long friendship made possible.

'Lotte, *meine Schatz*,' he said at last, thinking how rarely he could talk to anyone in confidence, with no need for explanations, 'are you serious that I should withdraw from this?'

'For your own sake, yes. Without Carlo things will not be the same.'

'But his death doesn't alter the plan? Apart from anything else we'll give the Angolan government credibility in the eyes of Western banks and the IMF. We'll bring one of their most important industries back to life. The political and business interests still run parallel.'

'No, Hans.' She spoke very quietly. 'To them the politics matter more. They may have an economy which is in chaos, we know the reasons. But they are not stupid. They can guess a lot will follow from this concession so they make a very simple condition for selling it: that you bring them their enemy.'

'If I do that, no African leader will trust me again. In any case, his followers would continue fighting. They have to defeat him militarily. For the moment the only solution is a compromise.'

'Oh Hans, be honest with yourself.' She laughed lightly. 'Your kind of compromise will make him richer and they want him dead.'

'I could have sold out on African leaders a hundred times in the past twenty years. I never have. I've withdrawn support, but that's the most.'

'You remember when you were betrayed in Italy?'

'That was war.'

'Carlo told me you killed the whole family, even the old woman.'

Hartman shifted in his chair, and stretched his legs, though his discomfort was not physical. 'They were collaborators.'

'This is war also. You did not compromise then. Why should they compromise now?' She reached out and touched his arm, wishing to soften what she was about to say. 'People change, my dear. You have changed. You have become too pragmatic.'

'Too capitalist, as well?' He made a joke of it. 'But in seriousness, Lotte, whether you are the President of a company or a country you have to compromise. A man of action can avoid it only on the most simple issues, like betrayal.'

'Wasn't there an expression in English you told me? "Playing the ends against the middle"? I think this time it is not possible.'

A long silence followed.

'Stay on a few days,' he suggested. 'Patrick will pay the bills. I'll be back on Monday.' He sat quiet, reflecting. 'You think I'm getting too soft?'

'No, Hans. Too ambitious.'

'To talk during a game drive is not so practic.' She smiled. 'And in the evening we . . . Well, we have not met for five years, after all. There were many things to catch up with.'

'Like?'

'What he has done.' She tried initially to be dismissive. 'Africa. Your father had always an understanding for Africans. Twenty years ago they won political freedom, most of them. Next they needed economic independence. He was sympathetic to that. He helped them from the beginning. That was why they trusted him.' She checked herself, just as she was becoming impassioned, and I caught the distinct unease in her eyes, as though she had let herself go too far.

'The people in Zaïre didn't have much faith in him,' I argued. 'They're accusing him of smuggling diamonds.'

'He could have been, how do you say . . .' She hesitated delicately, and I felt sure she was exploiting her imperfect English. 'Somebody could try to frame him.'

'Why?'

'He could have enemies.'

'Please,' I said, sick of this pussyfooting. 'If you know something, come clean with it. A plane doesn't get blown up for no reason. You keep saying he was trusted. With the help of Swiss bank accounts? Or what?'

'I told you, Robert. All those companies of his, they worked for development.' She silenced my attempted interruption. 'Of course he put Government ministers on his Boards. Maybe he gave backhanders. But they believed in him, he had vision, he was a pioneer.'

'Oh, come on!' I felt like quoting the carefully fostered image of Rukanga. 'Those companies made him a multi-millionaire. Look at this diamond marketing consortium.' I mentioned the few details Roeyen had revealed. 'All he's really doing is exploiting black hatred of South Africa to create a vastly bigger business for himself.'

'And for the Africans themselves. You have understood, at last.'

She laughed, though without humour and instantly became serious again. 'Now you know as much as I do. For this consortium he must visit several countries. But when I have no idea.'

'Not at all?'

'I am sorry. Truly. I told you, when old friends meet after a long time they talk of the past, not the future.'

It began to strike me that like the character in Shakespeare she was protesting too much. However, all I had managed to extract from her before I had to leave was a promise that if she heard anything more she would let me know. She also cautioned me obliquely against running unnecessary risks, as though she was an aunt.

'Diamonds are a dirty business, I think. Like gold. Men stop to be themselves when they find them.'

The last thing I anticipated was that this warning would be echoed by others within hours of my return home. In fact, apart from deciding that Lotte Lohrey was basically a friend, despite her equivocations, I dismissed it from my mind. I was much more concerned that I had failed to respond to whatever had been worrying Mother.

How overwrought Mother had become was obvious from the moment she embraced me in the hall at Godstow, though the reason did not emerge immediately. Late as it was, I recounted my bizarre experiences in Zaïre. Then it tumbled out.

'One of those filthy gutter Press papers had a story about your father yesterday. I suppose they've nothing better to print on a Bank Holiday.'

I had completely forgotten that this weekend was Whitsun, and asked to see the newspaper.

'I was so upset I burnt the beastly thing. Why should they drag up the past just because he's missing?'

As tactfully as possible, I drew her on. The paper proved to be the same one whose reporter had made innuendoes about 'the woman in Nairobi' nine days ago. Yesterday, it had rehashed the story of the prostitute in the basement. The campaign to destroy Father's character had been launched.

'Did they mention anything else?' I asked, anxious not to be specific.

'Only the inevitable "other woman".' Tense as she was, Mother managed to throw the remark away. 'Was Lotte Lohrey your "someone" in Geneva?'

'You know her?' I was so taken aback that I was unable to make pretences.

'Not very well. To speak to. But you'd met her before, hadn't you?' The statement was almost flat, neither a question nor an accusation, though of course I felt it was both.

'She came to Patrick Van Rensburg's house in Nairobi. I had no idea who she was until then.'

'You went to Switzerland to see her though.'

'I thought she might . . .' I flushed and broke off. 'The last thing I was trying to do was go behind your back.'

'I never imagined you were.' Mother was holding herself in, trying to sound casual. 'As a matter of fact, Lotte rang me after you left. Don't look so amazed, Robert darling. Why should your generation be the only one that knows what makes the world go round? Your father has always been the only man in my life, but I know I haven't been the only woman in his. In any case, Lotte is different. She rang because she was worried about you: more exactly about how you go about things. She is afraid you might walk into something more than you can handle.'

'You can tell her I'm perfectly capable of looking after myself. I'm sorry, but it isn't any of her business.'

'None the less, darling, you thought it might be?'

'Yes.' I was neatly caught out. 'I couldn't decide if she's involved or not.'

'She could be. Really I don't know. Jim is so unpredictable.' Mother faltered. The hurt was showing, in spite of her self-control. I moved across to the sofa she was on and held her hands in mine. She shook her head and made a moue, as though annoyed with herself, then said huskily, 'Lotte Lohrey is one of those shadows from the past that one has to live with. Did she tell you about your father's and her parents dying in the same camp? It had the most enormous effect on him. He told me it all before we were married, he said there was this one woman in his life whom he couldn't drop.'

'But they didn't stay lovers?' I realized too late that was a crude and perhaps offensive way to phrase it.

'Oh no.' Mother laughed edgily. 'She just had a great influence over him and always has had. Actually she wanted him to marry me. I remember he told me that once, in a roundabout way. She said he'd adopted Britain, he should forget about Germany and marry an English girl. I just happened to be the girl . . .' Her voice began to crack.

I held her hands more tightly. 'There's nothing between them now,' I said to be comforting. 'I'm sure there's not.'

She dried her eyes. 'Men do have a genius for missing the point,' she said, trying to sound more cheerful. 'Really I shouldn't complain. I was very, very happy for the first few years, when I could still share what he was doing, and after that I had you.' She kissed me fondly. 'The trouble with your father isn't other women, it's that for most of our marriage he's been away so much.'

196

There was nothing I could answer to that, and I had shifted the subject to the Board meeting on Wednesday when the phone rang, distantly. We both stopped talking, which was a measure of the tension we were feeling, because Hooson was sure to answer it. Half a minute later he entered as smoothly as ever. 'The operator is on the line m'Lady,' he announced. 'She has a call from an unidentified person.'

'I'll take it in the study,' I said quickly, forcing a smile. 'Probably just another reporter.' In fact, I had a suspicion that it might be Lotte Lohrey, deciding to come clean after all.

'Is Lady Hartman there?' the operator demanded sharply, sounding piqued at being kept waiting, like an impatient shopgirl.

'This is her son. I can accept the call.'

'The gentleman won't give a name. D'you want the number traced?'

'Please.' So it wasn't Lohrey. A couple of clicks followed, then silence, though the line sounded live. 'Robert Hartman speaking,' I said, challenging the void.

'If you wish to hear something to your advantage,' a flat, middle-class voice cut in, 'you will provide a number on which we can talk in privacy.'

'Who are you?'

'Legal representatives.'

'Then surely you appreciate why our calls are being intercepted.'

The reply was frigid. 'We are not empowered to speak to third parties. Of any sort.'

I had no option. 'Phone me on six six nine, two two one.' That was one of Father's private lines in his study. A click decreed the end of the conversation and immediately the operator came on again, asking if I wanted anything done. 'Not yet, thank you,' I assured her, realizing that if this was some kind of threat I was already distancing myself from official action. However, the phone in the study was connected to a recording machine. We used to tease Father that if he insisted on taping all his conversations, he could end up with a mini-Watergate. Now I was glad the system functioned automatically. I hurried there.

As I sat waiting, Mother appeared. I told her what little had happened and had barely finished before the private line shrilled. I let it ring twice, then picked it up as calmly as I could, switching on the loudspeaker.

'Mr Robert Hartman?' enquired the same flat, hard voice.

'Speaking.'

'Mr Hartman, I am a lawyer. My name is Lewison. My Swiss correspondents have asked me to pass you a message from Sir James.'

'Go on.' Mother edged closer to me, listening.

'He is alive and well, but detained by circumstances beyond his control.'

'What do you mean? In prison?'

'Not technically.' There was a lifetime's legal caution in the voice. 'Sir James is in a part of Africa which fighting makes it difficult to leave.'

'Difficult or impossible?'

'Difficult without great organizational effort.'

'And what will that effort cost?'

'I will read his words as we have today received them, greatly delayed. "Am with Angolan Liberation Front. They can provide military escort to neighbouring country of choice in exchange donation sixty million dollars their party funds Switzerland. War situation fluid please advise soonest. Jim."'

For a few seconds I could hardly believe the figure. I glanced at Mother. Her face had gone dead white.

'Mr Lewison,' I said, shaken, but making the only sensible response. 'Our family hasn't access to that sort of cash.'

'I am not a principal in this matter, Sir. My function is to pass on the message. If you prefer to contact my Swiss correspondents direct, you are free to do so.'

He was definitely keeping on the right side of the law. I took stock for a moment. 'Can I phone you tomorrow? We shall have to take advice.'

'Speaking personally, Mr Hartman, I think that would be wise.' He gave me a London number and rang off. Curiously, by the end of the conversation I felt he might almost be on our side. But that did very little to alleviate the chill of this being a very thinly disguised ransom demand. Furthermore, the amount was the same figure Father had offered for Concession Twenty-Two, and it was in dollars not pounds. That could not be a coincidence.

Mother interrupted my thoughts. 'Bob darling, the message had the phrase in it.'

'How do you mean?'

'The code I told you about. If he was kidnapped any genuine message would either include the word "clear" or the word "fluid". If he said "clear" we were to negotiate. If it said "fluid" he wanted us to pay. We must tell Frank Stainton at once.'

'But . . .' Stainton was the last person to rely on so far as I was concerned. Confrontation with him was becoming inevitable.

'Darling.' She silenced me. 'Your father was insured and now we know where he is. Frank must speak to this lawyer immediately.'

I had not the heart to point out that we did not in fact know where Father was at all. No place had been named. All we knew was the price demanded for his release.

It was only while Mother was talking to Stainton, urging him to come as soon as he could, that I remembered tomorrow was originally significant for another reason. It was Tuesday June 1st, the day Consolidated's lease on the Angolan concession expired and Father had been due to launch his takeover bid. Wherever he was, Father must be in mental turmoil. For the first time in years I felt sorry for him.

CHAPTER FIFTEEN

For all the many times Frank Stainton had been to Godstow he was still in awe of us on our home ground. Mark you, it was a magnificent place, a vision of age mellowed stone glowing in the late sun, of mullioned windows, wide lawns and smooth clipped topiary. Most visitors were impressed.

Stainton no longer needed to be. Yet when he arrived on Tuesday morning and I went out to greet him, I noticed how carefully he straightened his tie and checked himself over after stepping out of his Mercedes. He never felt comfortable here and invariably compensated for the feeling with undue pomposity.

By contrast the younger man with him, dressed in a blue blazer with regimental buttons, merely glanced squint-eyed at the façade, like a professional valuer making an instant appraisal, gripped my hand firmly and remarked that it was a pity to be spoiling a fine day with business like this.

'John Timmins,' Stainton explained, 'is a specialist in kidnaps. He has cancelled another engagement in order to be with us. As have I.'

'That's very good of you,' I said formally, though I was taken aback by the nakedness of the word 'kidnap'. 'Please come in.'

Mother had tried unsuccessfully to rest during the afternoon. She had endured too many sleepless nights and this latest twist, though welcome initially, had only increased her worry. She looked drawn and older. None the less she settled the two men down in the drawing room, told Hooson to bring whatever refreshment they wanted and listened attentively while Stainton made a fuller introduction.

'I should perhaps explain that John's firm specializes in handling, er, cases of this sort.'

'Ransoms you mean?' The way she plunged straight in showed how uptight Mother had become.

200

'Superficially,' I said, 'it wasn't a ransom demand.'

'Pretty thin legal fiction,' Timmins commented. 'My guess is that the lawyer will drop out of the action pretty soon. If he doesn't he'll have the police round his neck. Have you told them yet, Lady Hartman?'

'No.' She glanced at me for guidance. 'We weren't sure.'

'You must do.' Timmins was completely cut-and-dried in his statements. 'They may not be able to do much if Sir James is in Africa. But they must be in on the act if we're to negotiate for you.'

'For us?' I asked.

'As you know, Anne,' Stainton cut in, ignoring me, 'Jim was insured against any such unfortunate eventuality as this. The insurance underwriters have nominated John Timmins's company to handle the negotiation. They insist, in my view rightly, that any member of your family who negotiated would be subject to impossible emotional pressures. Equally any director of the Trust, such as myself, would be known to have the authority to make large financial commitments. John on the other hand can correctly say that he has to refer back to us if things become difficult.'

'Given time,' Timmins said, 'most ransoms can be settled for around a fifth of the demand.'

'But Jim's message had the codeword.' Mother's distress surfaced. 'He wants us to pay, why must we argue?'

'I'm afraid the message contains no proof of Sir James having sent it voluntarily.' He saw Mother shiver. 'Don't worry, Lady Hartman, this isn't some mafioso kidnapping, even if they are making a huge demand at the start and hoping to jump you into paying.'

'Which Anne, you would in no case have to do yourself,' Stainton said, and I wondered, cynically, whether now that Father was definitely alive, he would start backtracking. 'Jim approved these arrangements in principle some time ago and he gave specific instructions which we are obliged to follow.'

'I suppose that's right.' Instead of relief, confusion returned to Mother's expression. During the restless afternoon, she later told me, she had agonized herself into the conclusion that even if we ourselves had to sell everything in order to pay, rescuing Father was all that mattered. 'But,' she repeated, 'Jim also arranged a codeword system with me and he's sent the one which means "pay". Surely we ought to do that?'

'I am afraid, Lady Hartman, that is the reaction these kind of people count on.' Timmins was tough, yet sympathetic. 'As I pointed out, Sir James could be under duress.'

'Mr Timmins,' she said abruptly, 'how can you negotiate with this Angolan Liberation Front? Who are they?' She was sitting as bolt upright as her armchair allowed, and I thought how much more sensible it would have been to talk around a table.

'Why don't I get a map?' I suggested, and went off to fetch one of the many Father kept – he had a stock the CIA might have envied – and when I returned spread it across the round library table at the end of the room, forcing the others to join me.

'Leaving aside the colonial history,' Timmins began, tracing across the map with his forefinger, 'Angola has a Marxist government which is supported by Cuban troops. Even so it only controls about half the country. The southeast is all in the hands of UNITA, a movement helped by South Africans, and there's another, smaller, outfit called the Liberation Front. This one, the ALF, maintains a guerrilla army in the northeast, where most of the diamond mines are.' He circled a yellow brown patch of the map with his finger. 'No one knows how far their writ really runs – the government denies they're a serious force at all. The best guess is they effectively hold thirty or forty thousand square miles.'

'The size of Ireland?' I queried.

'Correct,' Timmins answered sharply. 'And it's no easier to catch a guerrilla in the bush than a gunman in Belfast.'

From the way he spoke, I knew he must have done just that, or something very similar. He didn't look much more than thirty-five, but everything about him created an image of experience.

'Are you saying,' Mother interrupted, 'that you have no idea where my husband is?'

'I'm afraid, Lady Hartman,' Timmins quickly modified his tone, 'that we have only this solicitor's word for it that Sir James is in Angola at all. The message is no proof. In fact the ALF allegedly has a training base in Zaïre.'

Wheels within wheels, as with everything Father did. Yet that would explain the hostility I had encountered there, the absurd accusations and our manager's arrest.

'Looking at the map,' I suggested, 'the Gulfstream was found only a few hundred miles from where this Liberation Front operates.' I turned to Stainton, with a loaded question. 'Could Father have landed first at Concession Twenty-Two?'

'The present management would scarcely have made him welcome.' He dismissed my detective work.

'In this game,' Timmins emphasized, 'you have to be very careful not to jump to conclusions: particularly ones the other side wants you to. If the plane had been fitted with a flight recorder we might know a lot more.' He gave me another of those squint-eyed glances. He must have been keeping a watching brief on Father's disappearance from the start.

202

The reason Father refused to have a flight recorder in the Gulfstream was basically no different to the reason truck drivers hate having tachographs in their cabs: the tape would reveal where he'd been, and when, and for how long. Captain Holz knew, of course, and his crew. But they were dead now, and when they were alive they had been too well paid to talk.

So what construction did Timmins put on the Gulfstream's last flight? He made no further comment and it came home to me that he simply might not be interested. His fees were paid by the insurance underwriters and their aim was to minimize their loss. Our identity of purpose was confined to getting Father back in one piece. The diamond deal was at best tangential to his purposes.

'It would be highly unusual for any organization holding a hostage to indicate his whereabouts.' He turned to Mother. 'I'm sorry, Lady Hartman, but we do have to assume Sir James is a hostage even if he may not have been kidnapped in a conventional sense.' He paused just long enough for us to take in the implications of that remark. Personally I was becoming certain that Father had been in eastern Angola voluntarily, though I was hardly going to say so in case it prejudiced the insurance.

'What we ought to do,' Timmins went on, 'is insist on some positive kind of identification. Your codeword could have been coincidence. It's happened before.'

'I see,' Mother said, sounding a long way from convinced. 'How do we do that?'

'The simplest method is to ask a question only he can answer.'

'A question of no significance in the negotiation, I presume?' Stainton asked and it struck me that the time schedule of ransom bargaining was now crucial to the battle with Consolidated.

'Correct, Sir. The date of a godchild's birthday for example.'

'He could give that under duress, though,' I suggested.

'That's not the point, at least at this stage. The point is to establish beyond doubt that he is alive.' Timmins let the sharpness die out of his voice and went on quietly, 'Photographs can be faked.'

Subsequently he told me that the body of one Italian kidnap victim had been frozen and posed holding an up-to-date newspaper to make it appear he was still living.

'Alexandra Stephens had a birthday three weeks ago,' Mother interrupted. 'Jim never forgets to send a present.'

'Are you sure?' Stainton queried.

'Positive. This year it was her twenty-first.'

'Then I think we should start the ball rolling.' Timmins gave a cheerful impetus to the words, knowing that what we wanted above all was action. For Mother the worst aspect had been the waiting. I picked up the phone, but he laid a hand on my arm.

'Better not risk that lawyer overhearing other voices, if you don't mind. I try to keep it one to one.'

I led him to the study and rang the number Lewison had given. The lawyer must have been hanging around for the call because there was a perceptible jumpiness in his reply.

'Ah. Mr Hartman. I take it you have a reply for me to transmit.' He did not sound happy.

'Yes.' I rehearsed Timmins's advice in my mind. 'Yes, we have. But I'm rather out of my depth. I'd like you to talk to a representative of my father's company, if you don't mind.'

'My instructions are to accept messages only from your family.'

Timmins shook his head.

'Well, he represents us too of course. As I told you, Mr Lewison, we don't have the sort of money you're talking about. Only the Trust could raise so much in a hurry.'

'Not which *I* am talking about, Sir. The sum my clients have quoted for a rescue.'

'To avoid any misunderstanding,' I insisted, 'you must deal with our authorized representative. He is with me now.'

Timmins picked up the cue beautifully, saying at once how he appreciated the delicacy of the solicitor's position. 'We do have to be satisfied that Sir James and Miss Humphries are both with your clients. As a simple form of verification, could you say his family need to know the dates of her birthday and of his god-daughter Alexandra's?'

When, eventually, he put the phone down again he gave me an amiable grin.

'Exit Lewison, I reckon. He'll come back with directions to contact someone else. Won't want to risk being implicated in blackmail. Did you notice he never once referred to the police? Normally kidnappers give tough warnings against going to the Law. I draw two conclusions from that. First, he's nervous. Second your father may genuinely be out of reach.'

'In other words, in Angola?'

'Or an adjoining country.' Timmins certainly did not rush to conclusions. He gave me another of those sideways looks. 'Could your father have got into this situation voluntarily?'

My immediate instinct was to deny the possibility. However, he read my fears.

'If you're worried about the insurance, don't be. How he came into the ALF's hands doesn't alter the fact that he is now being held to ransom.'

'Well,' mentally I took a deep breath, 'we have to assume he landed somewhere en route in the Gulfstream and the obvious place is the concession, even though Mr Stainton rules that out.'

'Personally, I rule nothing out. This might not even have been planned in advance.'

'In that case what about the bomb?'

'Assuming that there was one, it could have been smuggled on at Nairobi and timed wrongly. For the moment I'd prefer to keep an open mind about that too. All it really tells me is that your father's captors may behave irrationally as kidnappers sometimes do and that we must be very careful.' The measured way he spoke was comforting. He paused. 'You made the right decision just now.'

'How d'you mean?'

'Deciding to come clean. Our task can be incomparably more difficult if the family doesn't cooperate. I was afraid you might not. Believe me, it is essential to have only one negotiator.'

'Would you do me a favour in return?'

'If it's a reasonable one.'

'Keep us fully informed. The Trust may have paid the premium but my mother and I are rather more deeply involved than Frank Stainton is.' I watched Timmins's face to gauge if he appreciated my irony and decided he did.

'I will of course do that,' he replied evenly. 'But you must keep it to yourself. Secrecy is essential. Shall we rejoin the others?'

This cool reaction seemed a definite retreat from the friendliness of the moment before. I was glad not to have let honesty carry me further. It would be safer to puzzle matters out and decide on tactics with Camilla. However, when he left he shook my hand warmly and told Mother, 'Don't worry, I've tackled many worse cases than this.'

Stainton left with him, asking whether we would still be at the Board meeting and adding, 'Not that I imagine there will be so much to discuss, Anne. This scarcely seems the moment to invest a brass farthing in Angola.'

Understandably, Mother agreed. For myself I was reminded of the exact similarity between Father's intended investment and the amount of the ransom demand. I wondered how soon our message would reach him and whether he was able to keep any record of his experiences. A diary could be one way of retaining his mental balance under the stress he must be suffering, if his captors allowed it.

CHAPTER SIXTEEN

A light breeze sprang up in the late afternoon, as it did at dawn, rustling the tree under which the tent was pitched and scratching twigs against the canvas. Hartman shifted his bulk on the narrow safari bed they had allotted him, straightened his legs to stretch the muscles and caught an agonizing moment of cramp. He hated himself for sleeping in the afternoon, but there was nothing else to do and it took him through the hottest, least endurable, part of the day.

When he had rubbed the cramp away he checked the time. Four forty pm, Tuesday June 1st. He was thankful they'd allowed him to keep his watch. June 1st. Ten days since Edmundo had detained him. June 1st, the day that was to have been a triumph, when Consolidated's lease of Concession Twenty-Two expired and he acquired it. He swore, muttering 'verdammt' repeatedly with a kind of routine hopelessness, in the way a man who knows it will make no difference swears, to relieve his feelings. Why the hell did these bastards' long-range transmitter have to break down within minutes of his being ready to capitulate, when at last he'd drafted a message with the codewords? Had it even reached Anne? He had no means of telling.

The tent flap lifted and the black face of the guard appeared, shoulders and rifle silhouetted in the triangle of light.

'Haya! Make pi pi?' It was the same routine at dawn and now.

Hartman threw aside the army blanket, wondering again why today he was feeling unaccountably cold, swung his feet to the ground and levered himself uncomfortably upright, swaying unexpectedly as he did so. 'Jesus,' he thought, massaging the stiffness in his legs, 'and I'm privileged.' Of the whole group only Tina Humphries, the Russian colonel and he had beds. The rest slept on the bare earth. The East Germans were allowed groundsheets, the 'Cuban scum' nothing. The Cubans seemed

206

likely to be shot any day. He doubted if it would affect the Russian's morale and it certainly wasn't going to affect his own. The colonel and he were the prizes of the catch, the golden geese. He reckoned their survival was certain, albeit for very different reasons. He wrapped the blanket round him and walked across the clearing to the latrine among the trees on the other side. It was a pit with a rough screen of branches. The guard stood outside while he relieved himself, escorted him to the tent again, then went to fetch the transistor radio. It was now six minutes to five and the heat of the sun would soon decline.

At five, with the long chromium aerial of the radio extended, Hartman tuned his way through the static to pick up the familiar tune of 'Lillibullero' followed by the time signal's sharp bleeps.

'1500 hours, Greenwich Mean Time. BBC World Service. The news, read by . . .' a male announcer's voice, distorted by interference, faded and then gathered strength again. 'As British troops in the Falklands continue their advance towards the capital, Port Stanley, fighting has been reported only twelve miles from the town itself . . .'

The daily loan of the transistor was designed to undermine his spirit by reminding him of the outside world. He had recognized this risk and disregarded it, reckoning he would easily withstand such mild pressure. He had been correct, though diminishingly so as reports of his own disappearance persisted. With the BBC broadcast on Saturday that his crashed aircraft had been found, his resolve had begun to crack and he wrote out the message to Anne, laboriously, on a South African army signal pad provided by Captain Struben.

Normally – already this living in the bush had acquired its own unexpected normality – he listened to the end of the news bulletin and then shouted for the guard, who would return the radio to Struben. In the mornings the man would then bring hot water in a tin bowl for him to shave, and around seven forty-five he would join the others for their unvarying breakfast of pounded maize, mixed with water into a thin porridge. In the evenings they went for a similar meal.

This afternoon was different. When the soldier returned Struben was with him. Struben ran the Communications Centre. He was a stocky Afrikaner in his late twenties, who wore bush shorts and a shirt with the fancy stars of ALF rank on his shoulder straps, but made no secret of being on secondment from the Republic. He picked up the canvas stool and deposited himself outside the tent, Hartman took a minimum of notice, stripping himself to the waist and forcing himself to exercise his limbs.

'Well, man,' Struben spoke with the harsh, unmistakable accent of the Afrikaner. 'What an answer, eh?' He took a message pad from his shirt pocket, tore off the top sheet and held it out. 'Christ, you have stupid friends, man. I tell you that for free.'

Hartman stopped and read the message. He recognized immediately what it meant. The procedures he had agreed with Timmins's company had sprung from a specific threat three years ago. Then the basic assumption had been that he would not capitulate to extortion: he would resist and continue resisting until either the police located the kidnappers' hideout or they settled for a bearable sum. No one had envisaged circumstances where the demand might be less than the immediate financial loss resulting from his absence. Let alone a situation where his entire business empire was at stake and no rescue possible.

For an absurd few seconds he could not remember Alexandra's birthday. It had only been a few weeks ago. His brain struggled towards the date, confused with the days that mattered so much this month. Then it came. 'May,' he said. 'Give me the pad.' Balancing awkwardly, he wrote in capitals. 'ALEXANDRA MAY EIGHTH. MISS HUMPHRIES . . .' He left a space. 'SITUATION REMAINS FLUID STOP DUE DELAYS URGENT ARRANGE RETURN SOONEST STOP TINA HERE STOP LOVE JIM.' He handed the pad back. 'Since you refuse to let me speak to my secretary, you'll have to ask her yourself. Tell her it's not a joke.'

'Bloody right, man,' Struben remarked, reading the words aloud. 'Fluid. I tell you for free, we won't be here much longer. "Soonest" is bloody right.' He looked at Hartman's lined neck, the white skin of his chest and his belly. '"Soonest" is an army word, eh? You think you know about armies?'

'How old are you Struben?'

'What's that to . . .' The directness of the question disconcerted him. 'Since you are asking, I am twenty-nine.'

'When I was twenty-four,' Hartman said with deliberate contempt, 'I was a captain. I'd done four jumps and won a Military Medal.'

'Four jumps, eh? Blokes I know have done hundreds.'

'Operational jumps, for Christ's sake. Jumps into action. Tunisia, Sicily, Italy, Normandy.'

The names evoked sentiments Hartman could not have expected. As a teenager Struben had immersed himself in the campaigns of World War Two with a passion which led to his signing on as a regular soldier in the Defence Force instead of only doing the compulsory period of military service. An entire shelf in his bedroom at home was devoted to warbooks. Mostly these were about German units: Panzer Grenadiers, Waffen SS and the rest of them. He had found the German Wehrmacht more appealing than the British army, perhaps because South Africa too was a Fatherland. However the Airborne Forces were an exception.

'You were in the Airborne?' he asked, eyeing his elderly captive with respect. 'I have books about them.'

The way he spoke told the whole story, and Hartman recognized that he had stumbled on a potential ally.

'I joined up in 1942,' he said. 'I was a pathfinder sergeant and commissioned in the field. Given that I was born a German I was lucky.'

'Hartman?' Struben echoed the name, trying its sound for veracity. 'Can we talk about the war, when we have time?'

'I'm at your disposal,' Hartman replied drily. 'Now, how about getting off your backside and transmitting that message? I don't want to stay here longer than I have to.'

'The General's going to want you. You'd better dress. But I'll do this first.'

Struben did not actually salute, but he hurried away and Hartman smiled for the first time in a week. The Afrikaner must be an officer whom the South African Defence Force valued or he would not be seconded to the ALF. He was here as a political gesture, probably ordered to confine himself to maintaining a radio link with Pretoria and avoiding capture at all costs. But he had a weak spot, and weakness could always be exploited.

However the instant of amused euphoria was only an instant. His thoughts returned to the message. He hoped to God Anne would persuade Frank Stainton to respond this time. The codeword was his only fail-safe device for the unexpected. He thought about Captain Holz too, and the dead crew of his plane, as he had every day since he had heard of the disaster. Why the hell should the Gulfstream have crashed? It was not as though the defect he had ordered Holz to report after they left Nairobi had been real.

Mother opposed my returning to London after Stainton and Timmins had gone, divining my plans and intercepting them.

'Why don't you ask Camilla here for dinner, darling? She can stay the night if she likes.' She gave me one of the tight little smiles that had become the mark of this ordeal. 'I don't imagine she'll have unearthed anything unfit for me to hear.' She laughed edgily. 'I have been married to your father for quite a long time, you know!'

Accordingly I suppressed my apprehensions, persuaded Camilla over the telephone that she had no reason to feel embarrassed, and two hours later was standing by the ticket barrier at the local station. Watching the home-bound commuters jostle past, clutching their newspapers and briefcases, sweating from the crowded confinement of the train on a warm evening, I thought how sweet a satisfaction it must be for Frank Stainton to have escaped this drudgery. He lived in suburban Surrey and his career had been entirely in the City as an accountant, which was why Father's threats to post him abroad used to so unnerve him. Now, as a director, he possessed the sanctuary of a London flat. He had done well out of the Trust. The question was, having tasted honey, how much further did his ambitions run?

This reverie was broken by Camilla's arrival. She had dawdled on the platform to come through unhurried among the last. She was wearing a light summer dress and looked completely fresh in spite of the journey. The sun behind her momentarily turned her hair into a brown gold halo. I complimented her and she kissed me on the cheek.

'I'm charging you with a taxi to Victoria, I'm afraid.' She wrinkled her nose. 'The rush hour is not my favourite sport.'

'So,' I tried to sound relaxed as I guided her to the car, 'what's new at your end?'

'Since we spoke, this.' She handed me an evening paper, commenting that she hated the way the ink came off on her fingers.

At first I noticed nothing relevant. The front page blazed with news of the Falklands War and the aftermath of a battle at Goose Green. Then I noticed a sub-heading under 'Late News'.

HARTMAN EXPROPRIATION
Zaïre authorities today announced expropriation of all Hartman Trust assets. No reason given. Agencies.

'Any minute now,' Camilla said, 'the takeover of Consolidated is going to blow up in your father's face. Is he alive?'

'Yes.' I remembered Timmins's warnings. 'That's really all I know.'

We settled ourselves into the car and I was about to drive away when she stopped me.

'All this makes 1956 a bit passé, Bob. But perhaps you ought to glance at what I found before we get to Godstow.'

I stopped the engine and she produced her research folder, taking out another of those old newspaper cuttings from which any aspiring biographer, denied access to original material, would be forced to reconstruct Father's life.

'Those Italian scandal photographers were called *paparazzi*,' she said. 'This was taken in Rome in February 1957. You can see Sir James was caught napping.'

Staring in surprise were three people around a well-laden dinner table. Father's leonine features were unmistakable. He was raising

210

an open palm at the photographer, shielding himself. With him was another man, while a woman sat between them, an arm round each of their necks. I knew her too: Lotte Lohrey, blonde hair down on her shoulders, animated, looking stunning. She must have been exceptionally photogenic when she was younger because the flashlight cast no hard shadows on her face. From his beard I guessed the other man was Barba Nera, though I read the caption to make sure, and a bitchy piece of writing it proved to be:

Having the bailiffs in at home hasn't worried speculator James Hartman, snapped here in a Rome restaurant. When trouble hit his property empire last week he left his wife with their baby in Kensington and headed for Italian fun. His companions? Lovely German born Lotte Lohrey and Italian Communist MP Carlo Angelino. Yesterday loyal wife Anne, daughter of retired Major-General 'Freddy' Hewlett, would say only: 'My husband is abroad on business.' We say: 'Nice business if you can get it.'

'Gossip columnists may not have been so explicit then,' Camilla commented, 'but they still knew how to put the knife in. Your mother's family must have been wild. How could he have gone off like that?'

'God knows.' I looked at the date again. February 17th, 1957. It didn't connect with anything that I knew of, although something stirred in my memory. 'Was that all you found about the 1956 period?'

'Except that if your father was paid compensation for his Egyptian cotton estate so soon after Suez he was very lucky. The Foreign Office's arguments with the Egyptians dragged on for years.'

'He must have been paid.' The memory surfaced. 'What other funds would have been available to buy Rukanga only one month later? Patrick Van Rensburg told me he had a bank guarantee.'

'Well,' Camilla dismissed the inconsistency, 'it may have been the first time he did a back-door deal with an African government, but it certainly wasn't the last.' She tapped the folder. 'There's plenty more for you to look at later. Now, perhaps we ought to be on our way.'

During the short journey to Godstow, I asked how she had dug up another folder full of material in little more than a weekend.

'Newspaper libraries. And I tried some of the old-established magazines like *West Africa*. They all have files on your father and he's not exactly their idol. For a newspaper owner he seems to have the most extraordinary antagonism to the Press. Which is fully reciprocated. If they could be sure he was dead they'd launch into print in a big way.'

'For Ma's sake I pray they don't.'

'And I hope she doesn't feel I'm an intruder. She must hate anyone raking up the past.'

'The difference is that she knows you're on our side.'

In the event Mother was entirely composed and welcoming. She greeted Camilla as a family friend, while Hooson, standing in attendance in the hall, neatly capped the impression.

'Very nice to see you again, Miss, if I may say so. I trust you've been keeping well?'

Camilla assured him she had and Mother immediately dismissed me, on a pretext, so that the two of them could chat alone for a few minutes. When I rejoined them in the drawing room I caught the tail end of a conversation.

'I suppose I shall have to go to this meeting tomorrow. Robert can be so pushing sometimes, almost as bad as . . .' Mother looked round as I entered. 'What I have been telling Camilla, darling, is that I really don't care whether the Trust buys this mining concession or not. I want your father back and that is all.'

'Lady Hartman told me about the ransom, Bob. I'm so sorry.' Camilla checked herself. 'I mean, I'm very glad to know he's alive.'

'We still have to defend his interests here,' I said.

Two weeks ago I had been completely absorbed in academic life. My inheritance, when I thought about it, was a background of assured wealth and of a substantial shareholding in the Trust when Father died. How it would be utilized or disposed of was a matter for the future: a distant future. Now, suddenly, it was two weeks ago that seemed a world away and I was acutely concerned not only about my inheritance but about the Trust itself.

'If the Trust's assets in Zaïre have been expropriated then the shares will fall again and we'll be even more vulnerable,' I went on.

'I'm sure that's all very short-term,' Mother remarked with some asperity. 'What matters is to rescue your father.'

The conversation went no further throughout dinner and Mother's attention was only recaptured when Camilla mentioned that her research shed some possible light on Father's predicament.

'From what I've been reading,' she said, 'these ALF rebels belong to a tribe called the Lunda, which was split by the colonial frontiers and now is partly in Angola and partly in Zaïre. They're fighting the Angola government and they've been attacking the mine which Sir James wants to buy from the government. Another way of making trouble would be to persuade their relations in Zaïre to fabricate a case against him.'

212

She was probably right. Not content with holding Father prisoner, the ALF might well be acting against the Trust in other directions, particularly if they were egged on by the South Africans. It was the kind of situation that arose all the time in Middle Eastern politics. I said as much.

'It's still terribly confusing,' Mother observed. 'How could these rebels have captured him anyway?'

'Knowing him,' I commented rashly, 'he probably thought he could buy them off.'

There was a moment of awful silence. Camilla blushed and looked at the table. Mother flushed too, though with anger. 'That was quite unnecessary Robert,' she said, 'unnecessary and unhelpful,' then spoke to Camilla as if to an ally. 'Would you like to take coffee in the drawing room?'

The subsequent attempts at small talk failed. We all had the same subject on our minds and yet could no longer discuss it. As soon as she decently could Camilla asked to be driven to the station, refusing Mother's offer of a bed for the night.

Once we were in the car, she let fly. 'How could you say that to her, Bob? Have you no sensibility at all? She's tortured with worry and so would any woman be. Why make it worse? I could have hit you.'

'We all know how Father operates. Sooner or later she'll have to face the truth.'

'No Bob. She won't.' Camilla was unusually emphatic. 'You may be going to get to the bottom of this, but she just doesn't want to know.'

'Father's been playing the ends against the middle for years,' I insisted. 'The dirt's bound to come out.'

'Then it's your duty to try to stop it. She asked you to go to Africa and find him, not discredit him. You ought to be hiring lawyers, not arguing with Stainton.'

'I'm doing both,' I said shortly. As a result of Camilla's warnings I had already alerted the family solicitor.

'Oh.' She was caught wrong-footed. 'You didn't tell me. What else have you been up to?'

'In his letter Father asked me to mobilize the support of certain institutional shareholders. It might be a more effective way of hitting back at Consolidated then trying to stop the character assassination.' Her remarks had got under my skin and I quoted Mother's feelings straight back at her. 'One thing Mother has got right is that the only answer to gossip is to take no notice of it. Otherwise you bring yourself down to the same level. Anyway the publicity in court cases usually makes libel actions counterproductive.'

'I stand corrected,' Camilla said tartly, keeping her attention on the road even though she wasn't driving. 'Anyway my part in this is over, now you know where he is.'

'Would you rather quit?'

She waited until I had stopped outside the station to answer.

'Not if you still want help. I'm glad you're doing what you are.'

'You mean I'm not running away from my father any more?'

'I never said that.'

'You've always implied it.'

'Well, the School is an escape.'

'No.' I said, perfectly ready to lose my temper. 'It's a career and a well respected one. I shall be genuinely sorry if I have to give it up. Arab history may not mean a lot to most people, but it certainly illuminates what we're chasing now. The Arabs were the first invaders to plunder Africa while they developed it. They've had many imitators.' I cut myself short. This was neither the time nor the place, and before long the train would come. 'This isn't the same search we started with. It's become a campaign as well. Whether Mother likes it or not I'm going to hold the Trust together. It's my inheritance.'

'So you're declaring war?' she joked, defusing the emotion.

'And will you help me plan the tactics?'

She laughed. 'For once I shall approve of hocus-pocus.'

When we were on the platform she gave me an unexpected hug. 'Sorry if I went for you,' she said. 'I just felt for your mother, even though I don't know her very well. Please don't force a showdown that isn't necessary: for her sake.' She handed me her folder. 'I'm not sure this gets you much further,' she said. 'All it shows is that Sir James had been hand in glove with revolutionaries for years.'

Back at Godstow I found Mother had already gone upstairs. I knocked on her door and went in. She was sitting on the side of the bed in her dressing gown, quietly sobbing. I put my arms around her and tried to comfort her.

'Please, darling,' she said after a while, 'don't make things any more complicated than they are already.'

Eventually I went downstairs again, poured myself a whisky and settled down to read through Camilla's folder. Some of the photocopied cuttings in it dated back twenty years and there was hardly one that did not hint at corruption. They all had much the same flavour.

The Hon. Minister defended the contract awarded to Mr James Hartman's company. 'Its being announced before the official date for tenders is a technicality,' he told the National Assembly. 'This one is the best for us.' 15.8.1967.

Accepting Sir James Hartman's donation of land for the new co-operative project, the Minister praised his positive attitude and noted that a breakthrough in technical training would be achieved with the arrival of North Korean agricultural instructors. 22.2.1976.

Attached to this one was a cutting on thin blue paper from a confidential newsletter, which read:

Rhodesian sources allege the Hartman Trust's Tanzanian project is a thinly disguised base for training Marxist guerrillas of Mugabe's Patriotic Front.

Then there was a 1974 photograph of the Learjet Father had owned before the Gulfstream. Two uniformed Africans were disembarking in bright sunlight. The caption read 'COUP LEADER FOR TALKS. Capt. Kiassa, leader of the interim revolutionary government, arrived in the Guinean capital of Conakry last week.'

Snatches of Father's conversations came back to me. One in particular after his return from Dar es Salaam during the school holidays before I sat my 'O' Levels. He had met some African 'freedom fighters' there.

'The thing about revolutionary leaders, Bob, is that their aspirations are genuine enough. Militarily they're not so bad either. It's after they've gained power that everything falls apart.' He had grinned at me with knowing mischievousness. 'Couldn't organize a market stall, most of them, let alone a modern economy. That's the Third World's real problem.' He always enjoyed trying to open my eyes to the realities of life. 'I don't suppose it will help your "O" Levels but it's the truth of modern history.'

At the time his preaching failed to connect. Now, looking back, I understood. Father had brought those new rulers the business expertise they lacked. They'd given him contracts and he had built up local industries, making their policies acceptable to the Western aid donors and the International Monetary Fund. Through personal charisma he had weaned them to a limited approval of private enterprises: certainly so far as his own companies were concerned. The Hartman Trust proved that the West could do business anywhere in Africa. It was a conjuring trick that had made him inordinately rich. But without the conjuror could the trick be sustained?

On Wednesday morning I was roused before breakfast by Hooson saying that a Mr Timmins was on the telephone. Would I take the call? I hurried down.

'We've had a response, I'm glad to say. With the correct dates.' Timmins sounded cheerful and confident, as he was paid to sound.

215

'Better still, I'm now in direct touch with a representative in Switzerland.'

'What happens next?'

'We put forward an offer.'

So it had become straight commercial bargaining. 'How much?' I enquired.

'The underwriters propose one million dollars.'

'Only a million? You've been on to them today?' My surprise that they should be available so early in the morning was eclipsed by the figure. 'Why on earth should the ALF settle for so little?'

'We have to start somewhere.'

'We also have to be realistic,' I said angrily. 'Would you mind waiting while I speak to Lady Hartman?'

I buzzed Mother's bedroom extension. When she came on the line she reacted equally vehemently to Timmins's proposal.

'For heaven's sake, what is the point of offering a fraction when the other side holds all the cards?' Her attempt to be allusive faltered. 'You say my husband definitely is with these rebels. Why antagonize them by making such a stupid proposal?'

'The aim is to start a negotiation, Lady Hartman.'

'You seem to forget that my husband's being held a prisoner.'

'I assure you I do not, but I am an intermediary, not a principal.'

'Then please go back to your wretched underwriters and ask them to think again.'

'Mother,' I interrupted, 'why don't I meet Mr Timmins in London this morning? Before the Board meeting? It would only delay our reply a few hours.'

She agreed, hesitantly adding, 'If there's no normal way of rescuing my husband, Mr Timmins, I feel very strongly that we should pay.'

Half an hour later Hooson summoned me to the telephone again. This time it was Donaldson, the accident investigator, announcing that he was back from Zaïre and would appreciate a few moments of my time. He made it sound routine, but instinct told me otherwise. He must have gone straight to his office from the airport. The pressures were beginning to build up. Reading the morning papers, all carrying some mention of the expropriation and the continued mystery of Father's disappearance, I realized that the dramas of the Falklands war could not distract shareholders' attention from our misfortunes much longer. If I didn't contrive to take a grip on the Trust's affairs in Father's absence and make the headlines favourable, or more feasibly compel the Board to, outsiders would.

CHAPTER SEVENTEEN

The Accident Investigation Branch was housed in one of those featureless towers which have turned London's Victoria Street into a windy concrete chasm. When I arrived there late on Wednesday morning the uniformed doorkeeper asked me to sign a visitors' book, and then I was escorted to the fifth floor, where Donaldson himself was courteously waiting near the lift to guide me to his office. The uncarpeted corridors reminded me that most people, however responsible their jobs, did not work in such luxurious surroundings as Hartman House.

'Quite a small organization, ours,' he remarked, as he showed me into a Ministry furnished office. 'Only twenty-three of us Inspectors. Makes for teamwork, though.'

'How did you get on out there?'

'Pretty frustrating. Here, have a chair.' He pulled one out from its position by a large table. 'As you must have realized, my African opposite number was a nice enough character, but his masters had given him the answers in advance.'

'Which were?'

'Not implausible, given what you've told me about your father being held to ransom. Captain Holz had transmitted an amended time of arrival during the flight: amended by two hours. They insisted he had landed en route to pick up smuggled diamonds. I have only the local administrator's word for it that the packet was found on board at all. What does appear to have been on the plane is rather different.'

'You said there could have been a bomb,' I prompted.

'There was some species of animal.' He rose to his feet and went to a tall steel cabinet, painted green, from which he brought some drawings and diagrams. These he laid on the table.

'I found evidence of an explosion in the baggage hold. There were fragments of metal impacted into the rear bulkhead as well as discolouring caused by intense heat and pressure – what we call "gas wash". I was only allowed to remove a couple of samples and they're already down at our Farnborough laboratories. I also smuggled out these.'

He opened a white envelope and carefully withdrew several very thick black hairs.

'Did your father collect game trophies?'

'Not normally.' We used to have a lion's head at Godstow, sent as a gift after it had been shot at Rukanga, but Mother had eventually banished that to an attic. Although he had made me learn to shoot, Father had never been a hunter himself.

'Of course,' Donaldson said, almost carelessly, 'everything in the hold would have been affected by the detonation, just as everything of any size would have been sucked out. Even so, these hairs must have been very close to the bomb.' He went to his desk and brought a large magnifying glass. 'Take a look.'

I saw at once what he meant. The hairs were singed and frizzled as well as being naturally dark.

'Could you find out if anyone gave him a trophy in Nairobi?' he asked.

'Mr Van Rensburg should know. He saw my father off.'

'Perhaps you could telephone him. I don't want to jump to conclusions, but a bomb could only have been concealed in something acceptable to the crew.'

There was a fallacy in this argument somewhere.

'Surely, if they landed en route, as they clearly did, and they were late on schedule, then the timing's all wrong. I mean, so far as planting a bomb was concerned, it would have been set to go off within three hours of their leaving Nairobi, not after more than four.'

'Perhaps.' Donaldson seemed reluctant to admit the point. 'I would prefer to check the Nairobi end first, however.'

'Can we telephone from here?' I imagined there were severe restrictions on civil servants making overseas calls.

'Go ahead. I'll get you a line. Do you know the code?'

Half a minute later I was talking to Mrs Van Rensburg, feeling as though it was years ago I had been through the nightmare of the burglary, not merely last week.

'Patrick's amazingly better, I'm glad to say. Bandaged up and using a stick, but out of hospital. Let me fetch him.'

Van Rensburg himself sounded unchanged, if anything more gruffly monosyllabic than before.

'Sorry I can't make the Board meeting. How are things?'

'Father's alive. I can't explain on the phone. But that's not what I've rung about.' I wanted to keep off the subject of the ransom. 'I have a question.'

'Fire away.'

'When he left did Father's luggage include any kind of game trophy?'

There was both perplexity and alertness in the reply. 'Of course not. Hunting's been banned here for years.'

'Is he certain?' Donaldson's unemotional voice sounded in my ear. I passed on the query.

'One hundred per cent. A few rich Arabs have been allowed to shoot on the quiet, but Jim wasn't interested. Never had been.'

'No substantial gifts?' Again Donaldson prompted me. 'Nothing in a box?'

'I see what you're getting at,' Van Rensburg answered. 'No. All I saw was personal luggage.'

There was a great deal more I would have liked to discuss. In the circumstances I restricted myself.

'If you can't be here yourself,' I asked, 'can you give Mother a proxy for your vote today? And what about the Angolan concession?'

'The proxy will be waiting. On the concession I'd stall. Ask to obtain an option from the Angolans. Whether the mine's worth having outside the context of the takeover depends on a bunch of people your father probably failed to get in touch with.'

'You mean the ALF?'

'Hold on.' Van Rensburg was evidently shocked. 'Is Jim with them?'

'Allegedly.'

'Why the hell wasn't I told? I know Edmundo. Haven't seen him for years, admittedly.'

It was my turn to be thrown. 'You know the leader?'

'Correct. The bwana mkubwa. Listen, Bob, I'm not fully in the picture and maybe I wasn't meant to be. I won't be fit to travel for a few days either. But if you want to come here yourself, don't hesitate.'

'I need your advice.' Even if he had only known Father's captor a long time ago, there might still be some way of utilizing the connection. 'Would this Edmundo keep a bargain?'

'Depends whether he liked you. He's quite a man in his way, though it's his way and no one else's. I used to get on with him well enough.'

Donaldson coughed, reminding me of the time I had been talking.

'Would he give the kind of present we mentioned?' If so, this began to make sense. Poisoned or booby-trapped gifts were an oriental habit.

'A game trophy would be his style, yes.'

'I'll be in touch,' I said. 'If someone called Timmins rings you, please tell him all you can. I wish you could come to London.'

'There's not much I know that Frank Stainton doesn't.' With this double-edged assurance he rang off.

Donaldson looked at me. He had been making notes throughout. 'None of that will go beyond this office. I'm solely concerned with the direct causes of the crash. I gather no explosive device is likely to have been placed on the Gulfstream in Nairobi and Sir James might have been given an animal skin or head at some intermediate stop.' He stood up and shook my hand. 'Good of you to have come round so promptly, Mr Hartman. My final report may take several months, but we'll have an explosives analysis in a couple of days. I'll keep you informed.' As he opened the door for me he stopped. 'You ought to know that the Zaïre authorities asked me to sign a statement about the parcel of diamonds being in the wreckage. I refused. After that they became decidedly hostile.'

'They've just expropriated our assets.'

'Really? Doesn't surprise me. I'd advise you to treat any statements they make with considerable reserve.'

Following this altogether disturbing session I walked the short distance to the St Ermin's Hotel, where Timmins had suggested meeting, and tried to put my thoughts in order. There were far too many non sequiturs in what was happening. Why if Frank Stainton knew Father might have been with the ALF hadn't he said so? Could the ALF's leader have wished to destroy the Gulfstream when Father was not on board? Why the smuggling charge? Why was the ransom price the same as that for the concession? There were too many conundrums for common sense to accept. The only certainty seemed to be that they all centred on diamond mining: and as Van Rensburg had made me appreciate, diamonds involved sums that were huge by any standard short of space exploration.

I had never been to the St Ermin's Hotel before. Though tucked away near the St James's Park underground station, it was large, quiet and clearly favoured by businessmen. When I entered Timmins was seated in the lobby, wearing a dark suit and as well adjusted to his surroundings as a chameleon. Although he had appeared conspicuous yesterday by contrast to Frank Stainton, in reality he was the sort of averagely built, pleasant-faced man who would never attract attention or remain in one's memory. The same breed as Donaldson, the kind who kept order and sanity in a country's life. Whether he could cope with the turmoil Father created seemed another question.

He ordered a coffee and leant towards me as if he were a salesman concluding a deal. 'On my advice we have gone up to five million dollars. I'm hoping that will produce a positive response.'

I thanked him and asked if he would go out to Angola himself.
'I offered to. The powers that be decided against. Could find
myself being held as well.'

'One of our directors knows the rebel leader personally.'

He shot me one of those quizzical, twisted glances of his. 'That
is not necessarily an advantage.'

'If this is politically motivated it surely could be?' I repeated
what Van Rensburg had said about the rebel leader's character
and then confused the issue with the question of whether
Edmundo might have planted the bomb on the plane.

'They might have decided to kill someone of little importance
in order to stimulate your fears.'

'Then why don't they boast of having done so?'

'True.'

A waitress brought the coffee, interrupting us. When she had
gone Timmins sipped his, then put the cup firmly down again.
'Okay, it does not add up completely. Very few hostage situations
ever do. I still consider a conventional approach is likely to work
best. Getting them to respond is the essential precondition and
they are responding.'

'But this doesn't seem to be conventional,' I insisted. 'Don't
terrorist organizations like the Tupamaros or the PLO publicize
their threats?'

'Hijackers do. Political organizations want the world to hear
their case. The IRA normally claims responsibility after every
attack. On the other hand the money seemed to be the main thing
when two brothers were kidnapped in Argentina by the Mon-
toneros back in 1974. They were let go nine months later for a
ransom of $60 million. It can be a long haul. There's no rule
book, I'm afraid.'

Nine months was an unthinkably long time. Mother would age
as many years from the suspense. I should have to forget the
insurers and borrow the cash if there was that kind of delay.

'Have they mentioned Tina Humphries?' I asked. As yet she
hadn't entered into the equation, though Mother was in touch
with her parents. 'Are they demanding anything for her?'

'No, they're not.' He seemed puzzled by his own admission. 'In
fact, from speaking to the Swiss lawyer, she might be released.'

'Might?' I said quickly. 'Or will?'

He became uncharacteristically vague. 'Something about nervous collapse. On humanitarian grounds they might . . .'

Tina had lain awake all night, as she had for the last three, listening to the many strange sounds of the bush, as fearful of the
dawn as of the dark in case it brought the shots of another

summary execution. She knew that soon her nerves would break completely. When she did hear screams around seven she held her palms tight over her ears, shaking her head and begging them not to. The crack of the firing seemed to tear into her own flesh and she stumbled out of the tent to retch, doubled over in physical pain as she vomited. If she couldn't get out of here the tension of each new death would unhinge her mind. She had to leave. She had to save her sanity and tell the Trust they must pay because only they could stop the killing. There was a crazy inexorability about Edmundo's actions which she already regarded as unchallengeable.

At seven thirty she was brought coffee and coarse bread. She managed to swallow some coffee, but could not chew the bread, even though she had seen it being baked specially for her in an old biscuit tin over a charcoal fire. Then, unbelievably, Captain Struben came and told her to pack. She scrabbled her few belongings together into her dusty case, too relieved even to bother with making herself up properly.

'Where are you taking us?' she asked.

'To the Republic,' he said. 'But only you. Not Sir James.'

'He's not coming, you mean you're not letting him go?' She burst into tears.

'He has fever anyhow,' Struben said roughly. 'You can say goodbye to him now.' He took her arm. 'Come on, lady. The plane will be waiting.' He pulled out his own khaki handkerchief, let her dab at her eyes and led her across to the clearing where Hartman's tent was, carrying the case himself.

Even forewarned, she was not prepared for the alteration in Sir James's appearance since the awful ceremony of yesterday evening when the executions began. He lay on his back on the safari bed, the blanket drawn up to his chin and clutched in his fingers, his whole body shaking beneath the thin brown material, his face sallow under a day's growth of grey stubble. He looked haggard and old. When he became aware of her there, which was not immediately, he raised himself awkwardly on one elbow.

'You're going?' Only willpower enabled him to speak and his voice trembled. 'The letter. Take the letter. In my case.'

His leather briefcase lay on the ground beside a canvas chair over which he had laid his clothes before the fever fully gripped him. He stared at the case as though his gaze would snap the locks, and following his unspoken directions, she opened it and took out a single sheet of office paper lying on top of various others. The sheet of paper had been folded into three. She held it up for verification.

'My wife or my son.' He grated out the words. 'Tell them Edmundo knows too much, more than I . . .' His speech lapsed in

222

a fit of shivering, which lasted several minutes. 'Aspirin,' he managed to say. 'Have you aspirin?'

She put the letter in her bag, then opened her overnight case, found a packet of aspirin, took out two tablets and handed him a tin mug of cloudy water by the bed. But she had to help him take each one in turn. She felt as remorseful at deserting him as she was desperate to go.

'If you want, I'll stay.'

The drink helped his lucidity. 'No. Tell them what it's like. Tell them if they play straight, Edmundo will.' He lay back, staring up at the low roof of the tent. 'This'll pass. Must do.'

'Seven or eight days,' Struben commented, 'I gave him tablets. Come on, Miss. The pilot won't wait.'

'Goodbye, Sir James. I'll do everything I can.' Now she knew she was a traitor to leave him.

'If they do let her go, when would she be back in England?'

'One or two days. All depends.' Timmins continued to be imprecise, persuading me that his bargaining with the ALF's representatives in Switzerland was more complex than he would admit.

'So we can only wait?'

'I'm afraid so.' He made this more of an affirmation than an apology, as though events were entering some predetermined phase. 'Worry and tension are what kidnappers play on. We have to keep our cool.'

That was easier for him than for us, and I departed for the Board meeting little cheered.

Mother was already being looked after on the fourteenth floor of Hartman House when I arrived, and Stainton ushered us into the Boardroom with his newly established blend of ambassadorial authority and deference. The worse this crisis became the more he resembled a packaged product, the label replete with soft-selling assurances, the content less reliable. Precisely how un-trustworthy he had become was evident as we entered. Only two men were seated at one end of the long table: Lord Watson and Hugh Clarke. Beyond them the french windows were open and the fountain splashed into the small pool, its spray catching the sun, as if to say that this was not really a serious occasion.

'The overseas directors were unable to return so soon,' Stainton explained smoothly, as the two rose to greet us. 'However, we have the necessary quorum.' He drew back a chair for Mother, left me to choose a place for myself, and sat down. Significantly the agenda which Clarke handed round again bore only a single item: 'To consider the Angolan concession'. This time Stainton intended to get his way. He invited Watson to start the meeting and listened, gently rubbing his large and lobeless right ear between his thumb and forefinger, as if it helped him concentrate.

Watson indulged himself in various procedural formulae of the kind that so fascinate Parliamentarians, obtaining agreement that the minutes of the previous meeting constituted a true record and so forth. Then, almost farcically, he requested Stainton to report to the Board. Covertly I studied Stainton's angular face, the straggling hair carefully combed to conceal incipient baldness, the thin lips slightly twisted at the corners and the narrow, appraising eyes. If the ship sank he would have his own lifeboat and to hell with the rest of the crew.

'Hugh Clarke has prepared these.' He handed round copies of a financial and production analysis which ought to have been circulated beforehand. 'Concession Twenty-Two can only be operating at a loss, due to the Angolan political situation. Had Sir James received the assurances we hoped for from the government matters might be different. As they stand, and bearing in mind the adverse effects of yesterday's Zaïre announcement, I cannot recommend that we proceed.'

The conclusion had been predetermined. Nonetheless Watson gave the others a token opportunity. 'Does anyone else wish to speak?' he asked, his glance passing me by, as a reminder that I had no vote.

'I agree with Frank,' Hugh Clarke said languidly. 'The figures speak for themselves. Consolidated ought to be praying they do lose the lease. When you've dug yourself into a hole the first essential is to stop digging: in this instance literally.'

I held my tongue. Mother was the right person to contribute next. The last voice available, in fact. Arthur Watson turned to her. 'And your views Anne?'

'For myself, I really don't know enough.' She began, with Stainton smiling approval. 'But Patrick Van Rensburg is the mining expert, isn't he?' This was incontestable, and Stainton's smile faded. He could see what was coming. 'Patrick has telexed me a proxy and he thinks we should ask the Angolans for an option until Jim is back.'

There were exchanges of looks around the table. Watson glanced at Stainton for guidance.

'Do you want to talk about Jim, my dear?' Stainton said, all emollient concern. 'I had assumed not.'

'Well,' Mother was neatly caught, 'I suppose . . .'

'We know Jim's being held against his will,' Watson said. 'If that's what's troubling you Anne, you can speak freely with us.'

'Has everybody on the Board been told?' She was understandably alarmed.

'Not everybody,' Stainton assured her. 'The fewer the better. Carl Hoffman, for example, could contribute nothing from America. Nor Gupta in India. Nor, to be brutally frank, could Andrew Ferguson.'

'Well then,' Mother looked relieved, 'since you all know that he is alive and well and should be with us again soon, isn't there some sense in Patrick's idea?'

I listened carefully, watching the expressions of the others for reactions. It had not been easy persuading Mother that she ought to put Van Rensburg's suggestion rather than I, since she held the proxy. She had agreed, because the idea was essentially a compromise without any commitment.

'Shouldn't we try a delaying tactic?' She asked Watson, as Chairman.

'Is there any point, Frank?' He played the ball out of his court as fast as possible.

'Really very little. Even without the Zaïre expropriation the fall in our shares has made a bid for Consolidated out of the question, and the essence of Jim's plan was to use the concession as the pivot of the bid.' He allowed himself a twisted kind of laugh. 'In any case it takes two to make a deal and the Angolan government has not so much as acknowledged our last communication.'

This was more than I was prepared to take. I raised a hand to gain Watson's attention. 'May I say something?'

'Of course. If no·one objects.'

'The communication Mr Stainton refers to was not about the concession. It was about whether Father had arrived in Luanda or not. Since his trip was intended to be secret it is not surprising they failed to reply.'

Stainton flushed. 'I'm not sure it's your job to tell us our business, young man.'

'Have we telexed them about the concession since my father left?'

'As a matter of fact,' Clarke cut in, attempting a *coup de grâce*, 'in the circumstances our Acting Chief Executive outlined a moment ago there would be little point.'

'Let's have a show of hands.' Watson was anxious to end this confrontation. 'Excluding you, Robert. Is anyone in favour of continuing the negotiation?'

Mother had been visibly embarrassed by my intervention. She hesitated, then nodded. 'Patrick also wants to.'

'Against?' Watson enquired.

'I have proxies from Bertels, Cunningham and Hoffman,' Stainton said, raising his hand a few inches. Clarke followed suit.

'Then the "noes" have it.' Watson's relief at being spared the casting vote seemed despicable to me.

The haste with which this decision had been achieved obscured the victory behind it. In barely half an hour Frank Stainton had knocked out the keystone of the Trust's expansion, forestalling schemes greater than any Father had previously attempted. Arthur Watson, I was convinced, did not appreciate the scale of the retreat, nor that the moment an enterprise like the Trust was seen to falter the predators would be encouraged. But Stainton and Clarke did, because like Van Rensburg they were aware that the Consolidated takeover was a preliminary to establishing a selling consortium. Indeed they should have known it better than I, because my own knowledge of the consortium was so vague. Moreover Stainton had not finished.

'There is one other matter, Arthur. Our silence is having a bad effect on the market. The share price fell again sharply this morning after the Zaïre news. We ought to issue a statement putting all this in perspective as a temporary difficulty.'

'A Press release, you mean?' Mother asked mistrustfully. 'Saying Jim is safe but his return has been delayed?'

'Something of the sort. The precise wording would have to be agreed with the underwriters.' Since Watson appeared confused he added, 'The ransom insurance requires us to take their advice.'

'Ah.' Watson understood. 'Then I'm sure we can leave it to you to draft a suitable statement.' He glanced around quickly. 'Is there anything else?'

There was not, although I had an instinct that we ought to have agreed the text on the spot. What the shareholders read in their morning papers would have far more impact than anything they might receive in the post from the Chairman a week later. Publicity was a two-edged sword and we had handed the weapon, unsheathed, to Stainton.

'Well, Anne,' he took charge again, 'would you care for some lunch?'

Seizing the opportunity to excuse myself, I went along the corridor and snatched a few words with Christianne. The way things had changed was exemplified by my now regarding her as a confidante. Characteristically she was exploiting the warm weather with a sheer white blouse and a tight black skirt, slit to above the knee. A fortnight ago I would have worried about whose benefit this was for. Today I merely wondered if she was doing a number on Stainton, assumed she would pass on anything she had gleaned and asked quite directly if there was any news.

'In Zaïre they have arrested Mr Roeyen.' It was difficult to imagine the elegantly dressed self-confident lawyer in an African jail. 'The Industry Minister also. I am afraid it is the end for us there. In France we have a saying, "*Sauve qui peut.*" In Zaïre all those Sir James trusted will run to denounce him.'

Since she had paid their kickbacks I did not dispute her judgement, though I did wonder whether she would decide to position herself upwind of any scandal if those kickbacks became public. Christianne was not necessarily a friend, helpful as she had been at the last meeting. She was more of a barometer by which to judge the political weather.

'The silver machinegun hasn't turned up in Zaïre?' I asked. The gun must have relevance. Father's business presents always did, even on the bizarre occasion when he dispatched a single white lily to a company chairman whom he considered cowardly.

'We have not heard so.' She shrugged her shoulders delicately. 'I am sorry about the ransom, Robert. Truly. But as I told you, Sir James was taking a great risk. And do not ask me how he is with these rebels because I do not know.' She shifted the subject, passing an early edition of the evening paper to me. 'Have you seen this?'

The newspaper was open at the City page, and as I read it I realized how savagely the media could make us pay for Father having made himself rich and, one might almost say, notorious.

'HARTMAN TRUST BID SPECULATION.'

The gist of the speculation was simple. Consolidated's shares were rising, ours were falling. Stock Exchange rumour was that Consolidated was about to exploit Father's absence by making a bid.

'Hardly a new idea,' I commented. 'It's what we've been afraid might happen.'

'Some people more than others,' she remarked dispassionately, glanced down at her scarlet fingernails and then looked me in the face. 'Mr Stainton has been buying Consolidated shares. Two million pounds last week.'

I was astonished. Stainton wasn't a rich man. 'How do you know?'

'By a stupid mistake.' She was contemptuous. 'The clerk of a stockbroker telephoned to confirm his private address while he was out.'

I consulted the paper again to see when the present dealing period, called the 'account', ended. It was in nine days' time. If Stainton sold again before then he might make a profit without having to pay for the shares.

'Is he a gambler?' I asked.

'Absolutely no.' Christianne was emphatic. 'I never heard of him making bets. He is so careful it is a joke. I have seen him pick paperclips from the floor to save them.'

That left only one alternative. Someone must be funding him, and since he was not an investment banker or an arbitrageur there had to be more of a motive than merely helping push up Consolidated's price. I thanked Christianne warmly and hurried to rejoin the others.

The lunchtime conversation was stultified by everyone's fear of embarrassing Mother. Stainton had probably only arranged the meal in order to play host to us in Father's building. His mind worked like that. When I asked if he thought Consolidated's price was being artificially supported his reply was straightfacedly unconcerned.

'The buying could have been sparked by rumours of our own intended bid.'

'And are we under attack?'

'Again there are rumours. All I can tell you is that we have received no approach.'

'But you would fight a takeover bid.'

'The question is hypothetical,' he said tartly. 'And if I may say so, a matter for the Board.'

Possibly he thought that if his manner was sufficiently abrasive I would be forced to stop.

'For the shareholders, you mean,' I said. 'The company belongs to the shareholders.'

'If they have sense they normally accept the Board's recommendations.'

His expression told me I could vote my shares any way I pleased and the devil take me. The shares that mattered were those of Father's which my Mother was authorized to vote. And of the Fund Managers. Watson intervened tactfully and I let the question drop. In any case, I had my own plans.

After lunch, while Mother devoted the afternoon to having her hair done, I followed those plans through by going to see our family stockbroker at the Stock Exchange building near the Bank of England.

Philip Jardine was a long-standing family adviser and assiduously protective of my mother. Tall, rather pallid from having spent his working life in the City, grey-haired and dark-suited: a doyen of the Stock Exchange. He came down to greet me at the main Reception when I arrived, then led me to where he had a small office close to the entrance of the trading floor.

After I had explained what was happening, and showed him Father's message about approaching Fund Managers, I asked if he thought a takeover of the Trust was in the wind.

'The market's been pretty volatile. Let's see what movement there's been today.'

Reminding myself that stockbrokers live by the second, I watched him adjust the controls of a closed-circuit TV system which displayed market prices.

228

'As you'll remember,' he commented, 'your father's disappearance knocked the Trust's price straight down from 452 pence to 380. The finding of the Gulfstream precipitated a further slide, down to 322 at one point.'

In total, therefore, the stock market had valued Father at £130 million, which put quibbling over a $60-million-dollar ransom into perspective.

'HARTMAN TRUST 346' the screen announced in green, then in red '328'.

'Last night's close and this morning's opening,' Jardine explained. 'Marked down on account of this Zaïre news.'

To the right of the other figures, '34' in pale blue was followed as we watched by '37' and then '38'.

'Recovering fairly steadily,' he commented. 'Still a long way down on what they ought to be, though.'

The blue numerals recorded '341'.

'Someone's buying,' he remarked, with no great curiosity.

'If there were to be a bid for the Trust,' I asked, 'how would they time it?'

'One way's to buy heavily on a Friday. Then you don't have to inform the Stock Exchange authorities that you've acquired a substantial holding until after the weekend, Monday being the next working day.'

The technicalities of Stock Exchange rules, which Father would have cheerfully flouted if he could get away with it, concerned me less than what would happen over such a weekend.

'I can tell you exactly,' Jardine said. 'The bidder's brokers would go hell for leather after those Fund Managers who haven't already sold your stock. They'd phone them at home, buttonhole them at the golf course, follow them to the races. They wouldn't actually be able to buy shares but they'd extract promises to sell, conditional on their assembling enough to gain control of the Trust.'

The significance of Father's message was now apparent. He must have carried through similar manoeuvres himself many times.

'But as our family holds 18 per cent, surely no one else can obtain total control?'

'I'm afraid you need over 25 per cent to block any change in the company's Articles of Association: and that is what counts,' Jardine said. 'So far as I recall, there are eight or nine major institutions which hold over five per cent each of your shares: pension funds, insurance companies and unit trusts. Those are the people Sir James wanted you to approach. If they're unnerved for some reason and their brokers advise them to sell, a bidder could build up a holding very quickly indeed.'

'If we took them into confidence about the ransom, would they stay with us?'

'You're certain Sir James is alive?'

'Yes.'

'They'd ask a lot of questions, you know. Why hasn't your man Frank Stainton requested a suspension of dealing in the Trust's shares, for one. He'd be perfectly justified.'

'The argument is that any statement could prejudice the ransom negotiation. He may put out a Press release tomorrow, but it won't say much.' I thought of retailing Christianne's gossip, then decided against. Her remark about Stainton buying Consolidated shares was totally unsubstantiated. 'Could you bring the Fund Managers to breakfast with us at the Savoy tomorrow morning?' I asked.

Jardine laughed, not unkindly. 'Bit of a tall order. Why the rush?'

'I'd like to brief them before the weekend. They must eat breakfast somewhere. I'll have limousines sent to collect them from their homes if they want.'

'I'll do my best.' He eyed me with a mixture of paternalism and mistrust. 'Is there something you know that I do not?'

'I doubt it,' I said cheerfully. 'But if there is I'll tell you tomorrow.'

When I collected Mother from the hairdressers in Mayfair later, I did my best to boost her confidence, telling her she looked marvellous. 'That was worth coming to London for by itself.'

'Thank you darling. Compliments are always welcome. Now why don't we do something nice for a change, like going to tea at Brown's? We could walk there.'

So we did, and ordered thin cucumber sandwiches in the Edwardian country house atmosphere of the hotel. But even this magic, cherished since she used to take me there as a boy, failed to soothe her for long.

'I can't exactly say why,' she remarked, 'but I don't quite trust Frank over this. What will he put in a Press release?'

Whether intentionally or not, she had provided the opening I needed. 'It's nearly a week since the Gulfstream was found,' I said. 'We can't stay silent for ever. There's too much happening. Camilla feels the same and she has friends in Fleet Street.'

'That man Timmins said if your father was being held hostage in Europe the police would have asked the papers to keep quiet.' Mother drank a little tea. 'Does Camilla think they'll start raking up the past? Was that what she came down to tell you about?'

'I'd asked her to do some research on Africa.' I told a white lie. 'She discovered that reporters have been delving into Father's former activities.'

'I suppose they found that photograph of the Rome restaurant?' She sounded as though it was a ghost that would never be laid.

'And the court case before you were married.' I wanted her to be forewarned, but only earned an instant reprimand. Mother's femininity did not extend to being woolly-minded.

'I told you the other day, he was completely cleared. Even your grandfather agreed, and Grandpa had very strict ideas.' Her tone softened a little, though only a little. 'As for that vicious picture, that was what you would call "something else". It was the gutter Press at its worst.'

'You mean the photo was a fake?'

'No, but he hadn't been staying in Rome. He was on his way to Egypt and Carlo gave him lunch.' The memory clearly still annoyed her intensely after twenty-five years. 'It was also very stupid of your father not to tell me. That was what upset me more than anything: the way I heard about it. In fact it was all perfectly innocent, but I don't think I've been so hurt by anything before or since . . .'

When her friend Mary rang about the newspaper story with a nicely judged display of bitchy concern, Anne Hartman assumed there had been a simple case of mistaken identity. Newspapers often got names wrong and Jim had been in Cairo last week, not in Rome.

None the less Mary had undermined her morale, and her morale had been under strain for too long. First there had been the Suez landings last autumn, Britain's ignominious withdrawal and fears for Jim's cotton venture in Egypt. Nor was he able to go there. Then the expropriation happened. The bank that had lent money for the purchase demanded repayment. His only other investments were in property and the London property market was dead. He sold one conversion at a loss. The bank announced it would seek compulsory liquidation of his company. The bailiffs arrived unannounced at the flat.

Both Jim and she were exhausted, and she was preparing to take Robert temporarily to her parents when the miracle occurred. An Egyptian friend wrote to say that if Jim flew out at once he might receive a sympathetic hearing for his claim. He had gone and returned last weekend, triumphant, bringing a cheque drawn on a Swiss bank for the first instalment of compensation. Characteristically, he had taken her out for a celebration that night. But he had not said a word about staying in Rome en route to Cairo. Could it be true?

Leaving her toddler son with the cleaning woman, she went

round the corner to buy the paper in question, flipping through the pages before leaving the shop. She reached the gossip column page and swayed as if she was going to faint.

'You all right, dear?' another woman asked.

She nodded, unable to speak. The story must be true. She recognized Carlo, while Lotte Lohrey had a glamour which Jim had never mentioned. From his descriptions she had imagined a rather plain-faced, dull-haired student. But it was the caption underneath that caught her by the throat: '. . . left his wife with their baby in Kensington and headed for Italian fun . . . loyal wife Anne would say only: "My husband is abroad on business." We say: "Nice business if you can get it."' The whole story was unspeakable. The newspaper had never spoken to her. Then she realized that the unidentified man who had rung last Saturday asking for Jim must have been a reporter. Almost in tears, she dashed back home and telephoned the office.

'Sweetheart,' Jim's reaction was impatient, 'I am in a meeting. Yes, I met Carlo when I had to change planes. What of it?'

'Why didn't you tell me! I'm so embarrassed. When Mary Sykes told me I couldn't believe . . .' she cut herself short. She needed to have this out in person. 'Can you come home at lunchtime? Please.'

'My love, I am now with others. This moment is not good.' The Germanic inflection in his speech became pronounced, as it was liable to when he was under stress, at the same time as the words became more cold and measured. 'We have then a working lunch. There is nothing to worry about. I will see you as normal this evening, right?'

Worry she did, however, feeling more and more physically ill as the day passed. She forced herself through the routines of taking him to nursery school, fetching him again, and all the time rehearsing the way she would tackle Jim. She must be calm. She must keep her temper. She must say, quite straightforwardly, 'Will you please explain why you were in a Rome restaurant with Lotte Lohrey's arm around your neck when you told me you were in Cairo? I have every right to know.' She went through the same scene again and again. She would wait until he was in the sitting room and settled with a drink. Then she would ask him. 'I have a right to know, Jim. You owe me an explanation.' No outburst. No hysterics or tears. Just a perfectly calm request. 'It's not very pleasant for me, you know, reading about this in a gossip column.'

By the early evening, when it was time to bath Robert and put him to bed, she had a headache and her back hurt. She cut short his bedtime story. 'Mummy isn't feeling very well, darling. We'll read the rest tomorrow.' She took two aspirins and lay on the sofa, the questions still tormenting her. Even if Jim had an excuse for stopping in Rome, why had he been with Lotte? Was their old affair being rekindled? Suppose it had never died? She couldn't get Lotte's blonde good looks out of her mind. What if Jim was still in love with Lotte and had only married her because he needed a socially acceptable English wife?

When she heard the key grate in the front door she snatched the newspaper from where she had thrown it on the carpet, paused only a second to pat her hair into place in front of a mirror and went straight through into the narrow hall. Her head throbbed. As Jim entered she stood shaking, unable to say anything.

He greeted her with a kiss, as he always did, plunged his umbrella into the hall stand as if he were sheathing a sword, and made the remark he always made.

'Well, my darling, did you have a good day?'

'I . . .' The prepared phrases collapsed, running confusedly into each other. 'It hasn't been very nice for me, reading . . .' She thrust out the newspaper. 'Why did you lie to me? What were you doing in Rome? Why were you there at all?'

His reaction shocked her even more. He did not apologize, or embrace her. He did not move. 'I have told you. I changed planes. There was a long delay so Carlo took me for lunch.'

'But Lotte! She has her arm round you. Oh God.' She began to sob in spite of herself. 'If only I could believe you.' She broke down altogether and ran away from him up the stairs to fling herself in tears on their bed.

'Anne, my darling.' He was beside her, leaning over her. 'You have things all wrong. Lotte was with Carlo. You know him. He's an old wolf.'

'You're still in love with her.' Her face was half buried in the pillows and she didn't look up. 'Why don't you admit it? You always have been. This was all arranged.'

'No, my love.' He held her gently by the shoulders. 'Years ago I introduced her to Carlo. In Berlin. Until he fetched me from the airport I had no idea.'

'Why didn't you tell me you were going to Rome?' She was wailing now, realized she was, despised herself and struggled round to sit upright. 'Why didn't you tell me, Jim? I have the right to know.'

He looked straight back in her eyes. 'Because since Suez there have been no Cairo flights direct. If you don't believe me, ask the airline. Go to Piccadilly. The Egyptian Tourist Office is closed. I had to go through Rome and the flights do not make a good connection. So I told Carlo I was coming. Jesus Christ,' his anger swelled. 'You think I like this filth in the papers? I've told my lawyers to sue the bastards.'

'Why didn't you tell me?'

He became all tenderness again. '*Meine Liebe*, I do not want you to be hurt, that is all.' He caressed her cheek, wiping away the tears. 'I love you, Anne. We are having a crazy quarrel. Two hours in a restaurant with friends. What is it?'

'Oh, darling.' She reached out and hugged him. 'I'm sorry. There've just been too many things, that's all.' She kissed him again. 'I'm very stupid sometimes I'm afraid . . .'

'I was what, twenty-five, then?' Mother smiled, as if this painful reminiscence gave her a kind of pleasure. 'I just didn't know how to cope. I'd been brought up in a much more sheltered way than girls are nowadays. Newspapers haven't changed, though. They still twist everything out of recognition. The difference there is that now we do go straight to the lawyers.'

Father's reputation as a thrower of writs was undeniable. 'Didn't he take the newspaper to court?' I asked in some surprise.

'Not in the end. He decided the whole thing was best forgotten.'

'But he hadn't stayed in Rome as the story suggested? He had been in Cairo?' This seemed such a crucial point that I risked offending Mother again.

'What an odd question, darling.' She gave me a puzzled look, and I noticed that a couple having tea near us were taking an interest in our conversation. 'You might also keep your voice down. Well,' she went on quietly, 'if he hadn't gone to Egypt how could he have got the compensation? Anyway he told me about the trip so vividly that I felt eventually I'd been there myself. I remember a silly joke he made. He was staying at a hotel called the Semiramis and had dinner on the roof terrace overlooking the Nile one evening. He ordered Dover sole from the menu. When the fish came it was so huge it flopped over the edges of a very large plate. They said it came from the river so he christened it "Pharaoh's soul".' She laughed. 'Just the sort of stupid thing one does remember.'

'So the lunch that caused all the trouble really was irrelevant?'

'Yes and no.' Mother became serious. 'He was trying to build up more import export business with Italy and Carlo was helping him.'

'But in fact he went and bought the Rukanga mine?'

Mother blinked at me, as though astonished at my perspicacity. 'That's exactly what I pointed out. Kenya was in the middle of the Mau Mau Emergency. Your grandfather said he was mad. We had another terrible row a few weeks later. Grandpa insisted that if he was going to continue with these "foreign adventures" as he called them, then there had to be provision for you and me in case everything went wrong again.'

'Did Father agree?' I could imagine him being as obdurate as hell.

'To his credit he did. Your father does have a lot of good qualities, you know. We had the flat transferred into my name and a lump sum from the Egyptian compensation deposited in a bank. He promised we would never be left exposed again and we never have been. Then he went to Kenya and bought the mine.'

'Against your advice?'

She smiled again, rather sadly and introspectively. 'He provided the security Grandpa demanded. But from then on he stopped talking over the risks of what he was doing with me. It was like a curtain coming down over part of his life. I was so busy with you, I didn't mind at the time. I don't think I'd strike the same bargain again.'

While she was speaking the waiter had come with the bill, standing politely a yard off until she had finished. I paid him, helped Mother on with her light summer coat, and we left. She didn't say much during the drive home and I was preoccupied with various thoughts. When we reached Godstow there was a message from Jardine saying that American-style working breakfasts were not to the Fund Managers' tastes, but he had marshalled five of them to meet me for lunch.

After dinner Mother quite unexpectedly reverted to our tea-time discussion.

'Perhaps that's why I don't much mind what happens to the Trust,' she said reflectively. 'I want him back for himself. I can't bear to think of him being held out there in the bush by a lot of savages. What happens if he gets ill? They probably don't even have any medicines.'

I assured her that from all I had heard they might be rebels but they were fairly organized. I admired her devotion to Father enormously and tried to say so, however clumsily. We agreed that if Timmins made no progress tomorrow, we should try to force the insurers into offering a higher sum. By the end of the evening we felt closer to each other than we had for many years.

'It's an ill wind that blows nobody any good,' Mother said bravely, as she kissed me goodnight.

I was glad to have protected her temporarily from the one piece of news there had been, because it was so thoroughly disorienting.

When I had phoned Camilla before dinner to check on progress she had said one of the news agencies was carrying a report from Africa that Father's corpse had been found.

CHAPTER EIGHTEEN

Hooson's morning procedure with the papers was that he laid them out on a sidetable in the breakfast room before we came down. This morning, on my instructions, he broke the routine. At eight he tapped softly on my bedroom door and presented me with the whole lot.

'Forgive me, Mr Robert,' he said, circumspectly avoiding the actual subject of bad news, 'but I'm glad you are seeing these before Her Ladyship.'

He laid them down and retreated. At first all I took in were the now customary Falklands war headlines. This was Thursday, June 3rd, and President Reagan was producing a five-point plan for a ceasefire. Not that there seemed the slightest likelihood of Mrs Thatcher accepting it, what with the Marines and Paras advancing steadily towards Port Stanley. Then, lower down and relatively insignificant, I saw what Hooson had been referring to.

FINANCIER'S BODY FOUND

Kinshasa, June 2nd. The body of Sir James Hartman, 61, has been found approximately a mile from where his jet crashed eleven days ago. Zaïre authorities are quoted as saying extensive searches finally located the dead man this afternoon. He is presumed to have survived the crash and collapsed in the bush while trying to fetch help. Agencies.

As soon as I discovered that most of Thursday's newspapers carried the same report of Father's death, I phoned John Timmins. Mother was going to need immediate reassurance that the story was false and he had made it clear he would be available day or night.

'Caught me just as I was going out.' He sounded cheerful enough. 'I presume you're worried about the story. I can assure you I have no reason to believe it's true.'

'You're certain?'

'We've included a proof question in every communication with the ALF and every one has been answered correctly.'

'So we could issue a denial?' Although the motive behind this fabrication from Zaïre might be obscure, the likely result was not. The damage caused by the expropriation of our assets would be multiplied.

'I should prefer to say nothing for the moment.'

'Surely we could reveal that my father is in Angola and will return shortly?'

'That would be most unwise.' His reaction was immediate. 'The ALF have chosen to avoid publicity. The Angolan government would realize where he was and might attempt a rescue. The last thing we want is for Sir James to be at the centre of a battle.'

'Mr Timmins, the Trust's shares are going to be badly hit again.'

'With respect, Mr Hartman.' He echoed my formality. 'I think you are confusing two separate issues. Mr Stainton agrees with me that your father's safety is paramount. I spoke to him a few minutes ago.'

'This will be a bonanza for the gossip columnists,' I insisted. 'If they think he's dead they'll feel free to libel him. Do you realize how much damage the media can do?'

'I have some idea,' he remarked drily, 'and Mr Stainton tells me he is issuing a Press release to damp down speculation. If you'd care to meet me later I may have more positive reactions from the other side.'

Restraining the impulse to ask what he meant by this, I arranged to meet him in the afternoon at a coffee shop called Garners near Oxford Circus. The choice of rendezvous struck me as odd, since it was a long way from his office. He seemed to enjoy being conspiratorial. 'You're not likely to be recognized there,' he said, and it was true that my own photograph had also been in the newspapers.

As I finished dressing I asked myself whether he was right about not confusing Father's survival with our family retaining control of the Trust. Superficially, perhaps. But death is the key element of inheritance and I was in the process of coming to terms with both.

Then I went along to assure Mother that the reports she would soon be reading were unfounded. She was still taking her early morning tea, sitting up in bed and looking – though this is an uncomplimentary thing to say – a lot softer and more natural without her make-up.

'Robert, darling,' she said when she had heard me out, 'aren't you being a little like a bull in a china shop over the Trust? Your father's survived worse than this in business. He'll cope once he's back.' She put her teacup aside carefully, as if imbuing the action with great importance, and then turned to face me again. 'You can't step into his shoes, you know. Even if you might like to. No one can.' She smoothed the sheets across her. 'I'd much rather you concentrated on getting that man Timmins moving.'

'And what if Frank Stainton is encouraging him to be slow?'

'You think he is?' She looked at me enquiringly. 'No, you're suggesting more than that, aren't you?'

'He could have his own reasons for delaying Father's return. According to Christianne he's been buying heavily into Consolidated stock. He's suppressed the fact that Patrick Van Rensburg knows the rebel leader personally . . .'

She went very white. 'Patrick knows the man? Then why aren't we taking his advice?' She flung aside the covers and began to get out of bed. 'Why do you all have to make such complications? I'm going to tell Frank that I've had enough of this pussyfooting. I want something done. Now go away and let me dress.'

As I closed the door I heard her start to dial a number. She had come a long way since Father's problems could reduce her to tears, though how she would stand up to the kind of revelations I was expecting was another question. It only needed a leak from the Trust's staff for his African business methods to attract publicity in spite of the Falklands war being the daily background to all the news. Furthermore, there was a contradiction in Timmins's statement that the ALF did not want publicity. They were fighting for a cause, and he himself had said that publicity could be worth more than money in revolutionary politics.

Mother did not come down for breakfast and I left with only a brief goodbye, driving straight to the City, confident that Philip Jardine would guide me through a potentially tricky session with the Fund Managers. We had arranged to meet beforehand and when I arrived at the Savoy he was already sitting on one of the sofas near the swing doors at the entrance.

'I've booked a private room,' he said as he stood to shake hands, 'though whether they'll all turn up is another matter. They could have fifty free lunches a week if there were enough days. Shall we talk here or over a drink?'

I preferred to keep out of the bar and we moved to some armchairs further from the reception desk.

'Don't try persuading them the Trust's shares are undervalued,' he counselled. 'Let them be the judges of that. Concentrate on convincing them Sir James is alive.' He picked up the paper he'd been reading and waved it at me. 'This is wrong, I presume?'

'Yes.' I began to explain about the plots against Father in Zaïre until he cut me short.

238

'Don't tell me, tell them. Is there anything else peculiar going on?'

I hesitated, then decided that as our adviser he ought to be aware of Christianne's information.

'I'm told Frank Stainton has recently bought two million pounds' worth of Consolidated Diamond Concessions shares.'

'The devil he has!' Jardine exploded with gentlemanly indignation. 'You can't trust your own grandmother these days. We'll see if we can help him get his fingers burnt.' He continued with an exposition of the murky ways by which people with inside information could make a killing out of an impending takeover, and of methods by which companies supported the price of their own shares during one. 'It's illegal for a company to buy its own stock without the shareholders' consent. Doesn't stop them doing it though through banks or by lending friends like him the money. Used to be quite an ethical place, the City. By God, it isn't any longer.'

'Should I bring this up over lunch?'

'No.' He considered this reaction. 'No. Do not. The implications can only be that friend Stainton is buying Consolidated stock because he intends to recommend acceptance if – or when – they make an offer for the Trust. Immoral to say the least. But don't you touch on it. Steer clear, is my advice. What kind of a man is Frank Stainton?'

'Ambitious and devious.'

'Then be particularly wary of slandering him. In any case the people you're about to meet aren't fools. They'll put two and two together from the fact that you've invited them to lunch, not him.' He checked his watch. 'Shall we go through?'

My mental image of a Fund Manager was of a rather staid, prosperous, suburban nonentity in a blue pinstripe suit, who came up on the seven fifty train every morning and played golf on Sundays, while his wife organized bridge parties. As our guests arrived at the private dining room we had hired, named after one of the D'Oyly Carte operas, this preconception proved to be wrong. Two of the four who turned up roughly fitted the description, The third, named Friedman, was an overweight thirty-five-year-old who had transferred from merchant banking. Jardine whispered to me that he was a 'bit of a whizz-kid'. The fourth, and last to arrive, was a good-looking, well turned out woman of around forty, called Felicity Ames, who developed into an unexpected ally.

Initially, over sherry and small talk, I learnt that she had started her career as an ordinary secretary in a firm of stockbrokers. She evidently proved to have as much aptitude as her bosses because she had ended up a partner, only to be wooed away by the insurance company she now represented. When I enquired, tactfully, if she was married she said she had never found the time. 'Have you?'

'More a question of the right person.'

'Exactly. Why sacrifice oneself just to be conventional?'

Philip Jardine interrupted what was becoming an intriguing exchange, if unrelated to the business in hand, although mutual understanding never is, by asking us to come to table. He seated Felicity on my right and then made an introductory speech that was skilful, if slightly pompous.

'Robert Hartman has just returned from Africa, supervising the search for his father on behalf of the Hartman Trust. Contrary to Press reports, far from being dead, Sir James is alive and well. In the strictest confidence, we can tell you that he is being held to ransom and that negotiations for his release are in train. To many shareholders Sir James is the Trust. That sentimental view neglects the organization's very considerable assets. Nonetheless, I felt you should meet Robert himself, since Sir James's disappearance has seriously affected the shares and he has up-to-date information.'

Thus established as an expert, I had no problems with the conversations which followed. All that the Fund Managers wanted, as Jardine had predicted, was to be convinced that Father was still alive.

'Where exactly is he?' one of the two conventional types asked.

'With a rebel movement in Angola. I think he must have been captured when visiting a mine.'

'Taking one chance too many, eh?'

'That's what the newspapers imply,' Felicity Ames said. 'But are they justified?'

'No!' I surprised myself with my own vehemence. 'There's a campaign against him and I wish I knew who's orchestrating it.'

'I suspect Mr Hartman has a point.' She immediately took up my defence. 'There've been too many leaks affecting the share price. Too many, that is, to be coincidental.'

The tubby young Mr Friedman pushed aside his smoked salmon. 'Why, I'd like to know, hasn't an announcement been made to the Stock Exchange, Mr Hartman? You say you had a telephone call late Monday. It's now Thursday lunch and the shares have already taken a worse beating today than yesterday. Concealing facts material to the market, I'd call it.'

'Mr Friedman,' Jardine cut in urbanely, 'you should address that question to the Board. Robert Hartman is simply a shareholder.'

'Would an announcement affect the ransom situation?' Miss Ames asked sympathetically. 'Would it endanger Sir James's life?'

240

'It could do,' I said. 'That's the argument.'

'I still say the Trust's broker ought to make a statement,' Friedman insisted.

'I agree,' Jardine said. 'If it were my responsibility I'd try to find a way around the dilemma.'

The observation was neatly effective. He was only our family broker. The Trust employed a different firm, possibly because Father wanted to keep both on their toes, possibly to avoid conflicts of interest. He could safely criticize.

'May I make a slightly unconventional suggestion?' Felicity Ames took control of the conversation effortlessly, her voice light and almost humorous. 'If we believe what Mr Hartman has told us,' she gave me a quick glance of reassurance, 'as I do, then it is to our advantage for trading in the Trust's shares to be suspended.' The other three murmured assent, though in Friedman's case it was more of a grunt, since he was again absorbed with the smoked salmon. 'When Sir James returns and trading is resumed the price will be likely to rise.'

'Substantially,' Jardine said.

'And if he's not ransomed after all?' Friedman asked. 'What then? Or if it drags on? They can't suspend trading for ever.'

'Shall we just think about the announcement itself? Would the uncertainty over whether he's alive or dead be enough? Without mention of ransoms.'

'Should be,' one of the other two said. 'But if he doesn't come back the price'll fall.'

'And what about the bid in the offing?' Friedman demanded. 'We're in this on behalf of our policyholders and no one else.'

'There are rumours,' Jardine admitted. 'I doubt if a bid would do more for the price than Sir James's return.'

'Well gentlemen, it all hinges on what Mr Hartman has told us, doesn't it?' Felicity Ames said composedly. 'To save him embarrassment, perhaps the rest of us could stay on for a few minutes after lunch?'

There was immediate agreement. She certainly knew how to carry a meeting with her and when Jardine and I left after the meal she gave me the ghost of a wink.

'You seem to have made a hit there,' he commented, as we walked down a thickly carpeted corridor towards the hotel's Strand entrance. 'She'll win them round.'

'And then?' I asked, ignoring the innuendo.

'Between them, those four can vote a good twenty-one per cent of the shares. Your family holds eighteen. That's a formidable block. If Stainton doesn't yield then we could jointly go to the Stock Exchange Quotations Committee.'

I could visualize Stainton's twitching anger.

'If it's correct that he's bought two million worth of Consolidated,' Jardine read my thoughts, 'he'll have to unload them again. No bid would be possible for a while. Shall we take a taxi back and see what's going on?'

When we reached his office in the Stock Exchange there was a shock in store. The sharp fall in the Trust's price brought about this morning by the Press reports had been reversed.

'Up thirty points in a couple of hours! What's happening with Hartman Trust, Simon?' he asked a junior.

'Apparently Capel's are in the market, Sir.'

Jardine whistled. 'The devil they are. Wasting no time getting them cheap.' He looked at me apprehensively. 'They act for Consolidated.'

'The word is it's for nominees, Sir.'

'Could be the preliminary to a bid.' Jardine turned to me. 'The bidder, whoever he is, shelters behind bank nominees. If the price they're offering tempts enough sellers out of the woodwork they could pick up ten or fifteen million shares before the weekend.'

In our case fifteen million shares was fifteen per cent of the company. It sounded unbelievable; until I remembered that 'dawn raiding' used to be one of Father's favourite tactics.

'Nowadays fifteen per cent is the limit. Above that various procedures come into force. A buyer can be required to make a formal offer to the other shareholders. With luck this won't get as far as that. Our lunch meeting wasn't an hour too soon.'

'And if the Fund Managers don't line up behind us and there is a bid?'

'Then you call an Extraordinary General Meeting of all the shareholders to fight it. Quite simple. But let's see if we can have trading suspended first. Sufficient unto the day is the evil thereof.'

The quotation struck me as apt. If I did call an EGM I had no doubt there would be plenty of dirty tricks played. However I let that pass and arranged to phone Jardine later about the Fund Managers' decision.

'Don't count on anything,' he said. 'But you made a hit with the lady and she's not usually so impressionable.' He chuckled. 'Restoring a farmhouse down in the Dordogne, I've heard. Ought to angle yourself an invitation.'

'A certain friend might not appreciate that much,' I said, and later left myself wondering whether Camilla would care or not.

As I was leaving, I met Andrew Ferguson coming up the steps outside. He might just as well have run into Hamlet's ghost. He stuttered for a moment, then made a transparent attempt to turn coincidence to good account by saying he was thankful to have tracked me down.

'Where have you been, Robert? We couldn't get hold of you and equally we couldn't avoid making a statement any longer. I have it with me; would you please look it over?'

'Is the company broker asking for a suspension of trading?'

'Not so far as I'm aware.' He seemed taken aback. 'This is what we're issuing to the papers. These are copies for the Stock Exchange's announcements section.' He found a place on a stone wall to perch his briefcase and took out the top copy of a sheaf of papers. 'Our public relations agents claim they cannot much influence the situation. This is the best they could do.'

I studied the single sheet of the Press release, noticing it gave the phone number of the PR firm for enquiries, recognizing the style of Father's standard biographical sketch and being reminded of how he was forced to have that biography written originally. It was after a Sunday tabloid published a scurrilous account of his German origin, asking if a man with a Nazi past ought to be in control of a British public company. In retrospect his reactions were more illuminating than they had been at the time.

'Never trust a reporter, Bob.' Father had intoned this like a litany throughout my boyhood and he repeated it at the meeting with the PR Agency, which he had compelled me to attend 'for your education'. 'Bastards, the lot of them. Correct, Czernowski?'

The ex-journalist whose talents would transform this unpromising attitude into an acceptable Press release smiled. He was by birth a Polish prince and by profession one of the shrewdest operators in the indeterminate art of Public Relations. More important, perhaps, he had twigged that journalists made Father feel insecure. 'Power without responsibility' was a phrase Father often used and repeated now. It was a power he feared.

'There are bastards in every profession, Sir James.' Czernowski let the parallel speak for itself. A Slavonically handsome man, much the same age as Father and with similarly thick hair brushed back from a broad forehead, his confident smile told us clearly that if we didn't like his approach we could go elsewhere. 'On occasion it pays to be frank with the Press.'

'Damn few occasions. How dare they call me a "Hitler Youth activist"?'

'If you wish us to act for you, Sir James, I must have the background.' He raised a hand in anticipation of protest. 'I know that in the 1930s German teenagers had no choice. Unfortunately that is not a fact the present generation of leftwing media men care to acknowledge.'

'I was in the Hitler Youth,' Father conceded.

'We could make a virtue of your escape from Nazi Germany.'

To my surprise Father shook his head. 'I prefer to forget that period. I am now British.'

But Czernowski had a persistence that his elegantly Georgian Mayfair office did not suggest. 'The Nazi phenomenon will not go away, Sir James. Too many people have a vested interest in keeping it alive. Israel. The anti-apartheid movement. The militants.' He referred to the story which brought us to his firm. 'Is it correct that your parents were supporters of the Party?'

'The Party?' Father was as cautious as if he was actually talking to a reporter.

'The Nazi Party.'

'They had no choice. What connection has this with my fitness to run a public company?'

'The shareholders might feel it relevant.'

'Be persuaded to feel, you mean.' Father's annoyance showed itself. 'What shareholders normally get excited about is profit.'

'They also like to feel that business leaders are heroes of a kind,' Czernowski observed. He picked up a slim gold pencil, evidently preparing to take notes. 'Do you object to our releasing details of your wartime career?'

'You'll have to mention my internment, I suppose. After that . . .'

The account which followed kept closer to the truth, though when Czernowski prodded him into talking about the postwar period he omitted a great deal.

'We can produce a positive enough image, I think,' the prince concluded smoothly. 'As a fellow émigré I can sympathize. I'll deal with the Hitler Youth part in a separate note. We don't want it in a biography.'

'No point in denying it and no point in overstating it.'

'Have you never employed a PR consultant before?'

'We have a Press Officer. Doesn't pay to let him know too much. Would you like a year's contract?'

I listened fascinated. That was typical of Father. If he liked a man he hired him instantly. What I found less explicable was his not trying to sweep the whole Nazi bit under the carpet.

'Stress that I support no political party,' he said, after they shook hands on the deal. 'I'm simply a businessman.'

'Quite.' Czernowski was evidently willing to forget that knighthoods didn't grow on trees, except for civil servants.

As we walked out into Upper Brook Street Father remarked, in that ostensibly conversational tone which always meant I was under instruction, 'Success is the only thing that matters. If the bottom line's good, PR men can get you a good Press. If it isn't, they can't. If I get caught with my pants around my ankles the most Prince Czernowski will be able to do is hold up a screen while I pull them up again.'

None the less he subsequently agreed a fee which valued Prince Czernowski rather more highly. Its product was the seamless biography, which artfully made his progression through life appear so logical as to be almost predetermined, and could only have been written by someone who had seen through most of the pretences.

The Press release which Andrew Ferguson handed me outside the Stock Exchange possessed the same smoothly impenetrable style as the biography. There was only one difference. Father was no longer the hero.

On Saturday May 22nd the Hartman Trust's Grumman Gulfstream jet was reported missing on a flight from Nairobi to Kinshasa. On board were Sir James Hartman, Chief Executive of the Trust, his secretary Miss Christine Humphries and a crew of three. The following Tuesday, May 25th, the crashed aircraft was located in south eastern Zaïre. However, neither Sir James nor his secretary were in the wreckage and the assumption was made that both could have survived. News agency reports that Sir James's body has now been found are being investigated with the greatest urgency under the personal direction of the acting Chief Executive, Mr Frank Stainton, and with the full cooperation of the British Consul at Kinshasa. In the meantime Mr Stainton hopes that members of Sir James Hartman's family can be spared requests for interviews.

'Not be subjected to Press harassment is what we mean, of course,' Ferguson chipped in, with slight anxiety. 'Have you any objection to this going out? If you haven't I shall give copies to the Company Announcements section straightaway.'

I read it again, thinking that for quiet audacity it was a masterpiece. Stainton emerged as the hero, taking charge and soliciting consideration for my mother while the mystery was spiced by Tina having apparently vanished. Why had Czernowski consented to produce such a tendentious document?

'This is a load of nonsense,' I said. 'You can't send this out.'

'But . . .' Ferguson seemed genuinely distressed. 'A telex from Roeyen landed this morning. He has identified Sir James's remains.'

'Remains?' Even though this could not be true I was shocked.

'I am extremely sorry to be the bearer of this news, Robert.' Ferguson's Scots accent began to assert itself. 'Your father's body had been away out in the bush and Roeyen says the hyenas . . .' He left the rest unsaid and I began to realize that unless he was the most consummate actor, Stainton must have continued keeping him in ignorance of the ransom negotiation. '. . . however he recognized some pieces of clothing, a coat in particular.'

'Roeyen's in jail. Or he was yesterday.' If Stainton had encouraged Ferguson to believe the story that should demolish its credibility.

'Happily he secured his ain release.'

Visions of Roeyen came into my mind. Roeyen in his immaculate tropical suit, his beard neatly trimmed, cool and aristocratic, making some African minister feel honoured in spite of himself. Roeyen suggesting a bargain with elegance and tact. It would have had to be a damn good bargain too, something a lot more sophisticated than a wad of banknotes in an envelope.

'I presume that having identified the body, Mr Roeyen is being deported.'

'You're correct.' Ferguson appeared astonished. 'They'll be putting him on an aircraft this very night.'

'In other words, they're letting him free in return for identifying someone else's decomposed corpse as my father's?'

I wouldn't have put it past the Zaïrois to have murdered an unimportant European for the purpose. Someone out there stood to become vastly richer as a result of our assets being seized. The case against the Trust rested solely on Father's alleged diamond smuggling. Having him dead would make it unchallengeable locally. Even when he reappeared in Europe they would probably maintain he was deceased as far as their courts were concerned: and that was quite apart from the way the ALF's leadership might regard their captive.

The savagery of my thoughts must have emerged in my voice, because Ferguson wavered and stepped back as if I was threatening him.

'What on airth d'ye mean?' he asked weakly.

It was one of those moments that imprints itself timelessly on one's memory. Ferguson will be forever standing there, the windowless stone wall of the Bank of England rising blank beyond him, as much disbelief and horror on his lean face as if he had been physically assaulted. Far from seeking me out, he had probably been counselled to avoid me. We were about equally taken aback, though I recovered faster.

'There are a few things you ought to know, Andrew,' I said brutally, and told him about the ransom, dismissing the uneasy thought that if I went on taking people into confidence the bargaining would become common knowledge in the City. 'If you send this out,' I concluded, 'there'll be nothing to inhibit his captors from killing him if they feel like it. They won't even get themselves a bad image. You're incidentally also encouraging a takeover.'

Long before I had finished he was sweating far more than the

246

warmth of an early June day could justify.

'I give you my word,' he kept repeating, 'I had no idea of this, no idea at all.'

'Then go back and tell Mr Stainton the only acceptable statement is that the report of my father's death must be treated as rumour.'

'I'm sorry, Robert. It's too late. My job was to lodge this here for the record. The PR people will be delivering copies around Fleet Street already.'

I could have struck him then and almost did. But a weak ally was better than none and he hadn't engineered this situation. So I took the proverbial deep breath and asked him to tell Stainton that if the Trust did not ask for a suspension of dealings, others would. Then I left for my appointment with Timmins, only to find a message at the coffee house asking me to go immediately to a well-known Harley Street clinic.

Fearing that Timmins had somehow been injured, I told the taxi driver to hurry, then realized that this particular clinic's charges would be a long way beyond his price bracket. Father had gone there once for an operation, and I wondered, wildly and without reason, if the five million had been accepted and I would find him there now, recuperating from his experience, the *deus ex machina* to solve all the problems.

The clinic had tinted windows, massed flowers in the hall and several long-gowned Arabs sitting on one of the white leather sofas, toying with their worry beads. The receptionist was expecting me.

'The other gentleman is still with our patient,' she said, carefully naming no one. 'I will ask if you can go up.' She then phoned what sounded like a nurse on duty. 'Number 329. An attendant will show you the way.'

She pressed a buzzer and a broad-shouldered man in a white coat appeared, strong enough looking to have doubled as a bouncer. He escorted me to the lift, handing over to a starchily efficient nurse when we reached the third floor. Half a minute later we were entering a cool, pleasantly un-antiseptic private room and there, propped up in bed with Timmins seated on an upright chair beside her, was Tina Humphries. Her face was pale and no attempt had been made at making up her eyes to hide the dark rings of strain and exhaustion.

'How did you get here?' I held back the obvious next question, reckoning one thing at a time was enough.

'Miss Humphries was released early yesterday,' Timmins said. 'They flew her in a light plane to some place she doesn't know the name of, then drove her in a jeep to Windhoek in South West Africa.'

'We drove for about three hours,' Tina added. 'It was terribly hot and dusty. Then some Red Cross people gave me a meal and I was put on a flight to Johannesburg and here I am. Mr Timmins met me at Heathrow.'

'A little deception was necessary,' Timmins remarked. 'I was on my way to the airport when you rang.'

Things were starting to fall into place with a vengeance. Tina's return was being kept under wraps, and Stainton must have authorized the cost of her treatment in this clinic, which made the issue of the Press release even more monstrous.

'Have you seen anyone from the Trust yet?' I asked Tina.

'She hasn't,' Timmins answered for her. 'I can guess what you're thinking and you're probably wrong. The underwriters will be paying for this. The doctor has ordered Miss Humphries to have at least a week's complete rest. So far all we've done is assure her family that she is in safe hands. Apart from myself and the medics, you're the first person to see her.'

'Really, I'd much rather go home.' She sounded confused and worried.

'Miss Humphries was released as a gesture of good faith.'

'And my father?' There was no longer any need to keep off the subject that mattered.

'He has a fever. He got ill after the shootings began . . .' She shifted her eyes to Timmins. 'You must rescue him, I've told you.'

'For Robert's benefit,' he directed her, very gently, 'could you start at the beginning.'

She remembered the departure from Nairobi as having been as far removed from the hassles of holiday flight check-ins as a suite at the Ritz is from a youth hostel. Christianne had briefed her on precisely how Sir James liked things done, not without a trace of spite, because Christianne resented anyone else getting close to him and was additionally irked by his other secretary having the same name as her.

'If you wish to travel, *ma chère*,' she had remarked, 'you will do whatever Sir James asks. He says, "Pack, we are leaving", you pack his cases. You press his suit, if there is no valet. You shop for his wife.' Her eyebrows had arched delicately. 'Only one thing he will not ask and you do not offer. I hope that is clear?'

On the morning of Saturday May 22nd a company Mercedes was waiting punctually outside the Norfolk Hotel at 7.30 am. She watched the loading of the baggage and was not caught by surprise when Sir James preceded her into the limousine. The house manager waved them goodbye.

'Can we get away from this traffic?' Sir James demanded of the uniformed company driver when they were compelled to stop at a roundabout, where a queue of cars and trucks was forming on the main highway.

'No problems, bwana,' the man replied encouragingly, in demonstrable defiance of the facts, reminding Tina of a remark Sir James had made about Africans always giving the answer they believe is wanted.

On the other hand, she reflected, as fifteen minutes later they drew clear of the clogged entrance roads to the industrial area and the car gathered speed past the National Park, in his way the driver had been half right and they would only be slightly delayed. Perhaps Africans were more reliable than Sir James thought.

Certainly there were no problems at the entrance gates to the VIP building, with its forest of white flagpoles. They were expected and waved through by the guards. Porters carried the luggage straight to the plane, where the flight engineer supervised its loading, while Sir James devoted a quarter of an hour to chatting with the Minister of Mines over coffee in the lounge. The passports were unobtrusively dealt with and brought back to her. By 8.45 Captain Holz had the engines running and she was on board, watching through a cabin window as Sir James and the Minister strolled across the tarmac and shook hands at the foot of the aircraft steps. The police inspector standing by saluted, stiffly correct in his black uniform. At 8.50 they taxied out and took off a single minute late at 9.01 am. A Head of State might have envied the efficiency of the operation.

Thereafter everything changed.

CHAPTER NINETEEN

Shortly after the take-off, Hartman lifted the intercom phone by his armchair and asked the captain to come aft. When Holz appeared through the door from the flight deck, a neat, well-composed figure of a man in shirt-sleeves and tie, he spread out a large map of Angola.

'We have a change of plan, Captain. I should like to land en route. Here.' He pointed with his finger.

'Is that a usable airfield, Sir James?'

'The Portuguese air force used it until 1976.'

'Excuse me a moment, Sir.' Holz returned to the flight deck and came back with an open manual. 'It is listed as disused. Have you any information on the runway?'

'The Angolan government has made repairs, under East German guidance.' So far as Sir James was concerned the argument was over. 'This is an unscheduled stop, Holz. I need to have a discussion and continue to Kinshasa within the time frame of your flight plan.' He paused to let this demand sink in. 'I suggest you call Nairobi reporting some problem compelling you to reduce speed and giving a revised ETA. By my calculation a theoretical 300 knots would give us an additional two hours, enough for the diversion and my meeting.'

Watching the two men, her own apprehension growing, Tina saw something like rebellion flicker across Holz's stolid features, but he said nothing, apparently concentrating on the map.

'Are there any navigational aids?' he asked eventually.

'Not this time. There is a radio, but I want radio silence.'

'I advise strongly against this, Sir James.'

'And I accept responsibility. You are to file a revised flight plan as soon as we are clear of Nairobi's radar coverage.'

Fifteen minutes later Holz came back far from happy and said he had reported that a partial failure of the de-icing equipment was forcing him to descend, that he was reducing speed to conserve fuel and that their new estimate for Kinshasa was 1100 hours GMT.

'Any query?'

'They asked if we had an emergency. I told them my action was a precaution. I am maintaining normal speed and height. Sir James, I must insist we make a visual inspection of the runway before attempting a landing.'

Hartman grunted assent. 'Let's have some coffee then.'

While the flight engineer, who was doubling as a steward on this trip with moderate grace, came aft to the galley, Sir James called Tina to move to the seat opposite him.

'I'd like to deal with some correspondence. Nothing confidential, unless your shorthand's the kind no one else can decipher.'

He pulled a sheaf of documents from his briefcase, which he deposited on the table between them, then looked her in the eyes so intently that she felt forced to glance down at her notebook.

'We are going to make an unofficial visit to Angola, Miss Humphries. The man in question is called Edmundo. Like some film stars, he doesn't use a second name. We're interested in a diamond concession which can only be worked if his so-called army stops raiding it. His representative in Geneva says he's agreed, but I need confirmation and he very seldom leaves the bush. The snag,' his gaze never left her face, 'is that anyone visiting him is automatically persona non grata with the government. Whom we sign a deal with tomorrow. I hope I can rely on your discretion?'

'I'm not a chatterer, Sir James.'

'Good. Send a letter of thanks to Julius Mululu, who saw us off. Keep a copy for Christianne, she'll do the rest. He sings more sweetly when he's paid.'

For the better part of an hour Hartman dictated, while the Gulfstream flew on at its usual speed. Then he dismissed Tina and concentrated on other documents until the second pilot came through and announced that their descent was starting. Eventually, peering down through the wide oval window by her seat, she saw a swathe of cleared bush with a dull black strip of tarmac and trails of smoke rising from forlorn, corrugated iron roofed buildings. As Holz came in for a low pass overhead she realized to her consternation that the smoke came from burning military trucks, while the buildings themselves appeared abandoned. However, a group of African soldiers stood waving in front of them. One raised his arm and a green flare arched upwards.

Sir James, also staring out, reached for the intercom.

'How about it Holz?'

He smiled at her and gave a thumbs up sign, as though she ought to be thrilled. Evidently Holz had agreed.

The landing was frighteningly noisy. The wheels rumbled and juddered and the whole plane shook. She wondered how they would ever take off again. By the time they finally taxied in and stopped near the group of Africans she had begun to think this was an absurd risk. The engineer opened the door and the heat of day surged inside.

'You'd better come too,' Hartman said. 'You'll be roasted in here.'

She foraged quickly in the hanging cupboard for the overnight case which contained her make-up and followed him down the steps and towards the buildings, blinking in the sun at the ragtag of khaki-clad men facing them. Spent cartridge cases littered the cracked and weed-grown tarmac.

The leader of the Africans, dominant both by virtue of his physical stature and his smartness, was a tall, moon-faced man with a black beret clamped on his head. His belly bulged under a well pressed khaki shirt, gold stars decorated his collar, a revolver hung from his webbing belt and he carried a polished swagger stick. When he stepped forward two bodyguards automatically moved a pace closer as well.

'Glad to meet you, General.' Sir James grasped the leader's hand. 'This is my secretary, Miss Humphries.' Standing there in his dark suit, his thick hair ruffled by the wind, he might have been visiting a company headquarters in Britain, not a semi-derelict airfield in the bush with smoke blackening the sky above and every sign of recent fighting. 'Had a spot of bother?' he asked casually.

'Nothing to worry,' Edmundo said cheerfully. 'We celebrate that you come. We take a few prisoners. East Germans, Cubans. Now they are with the Russian from last week. You will see at my headquarters. Later you will see them.'

Watching the two men, Tina decided that this improbable general was decidedly cool and self-possessed, even if his men slouched like brigands. She also noticed a flicker of annoyance on Sir James's face at the mention of the headquarters.

'Is it far?' he asked.

'Twenty, thirty kilometres.' The African misinterpreted this question and gesticulated expansively. 'What I like to say is this, Sir Hartman. It is our country. We go where we want. Twenty kilometres, one hundred kilometres. Let them say.' He spoke slowly, in an inflected English which she did not entirely understand until she realized that he was leaving sentences incomplete.

'Frankly, General, our schedule is tight.' Sir James smiled blandly. 'Your Swiss representative told us the meeting would be here and we planned accordingly. I should be happy to visit your headquarters another time.'

252

'Our people expect you, Sir Hartman. They like you to know what we are. They will be sad, they will be unhappy. Too many of them are waiting to see Sir Hartman.' Edmundo's adverse reaction was not cloaked by his flow of words. 'Also,' he added, 'there is much to talk about, too many things.'

'Tina,' Sir James half whispered to her. 'We need the gifts now, tell Holz to bring them. Holz himself. Remind him to salute.'

As she walked to the plane, the heat buffeting her, she could hear Sir James apologizing. When she returned, preceded by Holz, bearing a gleaming brown leather case in both hands, the argument was still going on. She took the case while the captain saluted, then gave it back to him for the presentation. She could sense his distaste for these proceedings even from behind.

'General,' Sir James said as Holz stepped forward, 'a token of my appreciation.'

'Open it for us.' The African demanded, abruptly suspicious. Tina thought that odd, since if it had been a bomb, it would have killed everyone else as well.

Sir James stepped forward, flipped the catches, and lifted a satin-lined lid to reveal a silver sub-machinegun. The bodyguards peered at it, exclaiming in admiration.

A great smile spread across Edmundo's face. He accepted the weapon, unfolded the stock, twirled it round so that it gleamed in the sun, tried the trigger and bolt, and began practising taking aim, talking all the time.

'This gun will be famous. The gun to frighten shit out of Cubans. A gun legend is made from.' He stopped his monologue long enough to clasp Sir James's hand. 'I like your gun, Sir Hartman. I like to make an agreement with you. I think we can do business.' He suddenly began a pretence of firing from his hip, spraying imaginary bullets around the whole group of people, laughing uproariously. 'Maybe we can discuss here after all.'

To Tina, the presentation appeared bizarre and ominous. There was no question that the softening up process was working, but only slowly. Sir James might be shrewd; equally Edmundo was deliberately wasting time.

'General,' Sir James said, 'this gun was made specially for you. And to go with it,' he reached into his pocket and produced an envelope, 'an American Express gold card.'

'Okay.' Edmundo seemed to reach a decision. He pointed to the control tower. 'We can go there.'

The tower had seen better days. Its yellow paint was peeling and the lower windows were opaque with dust. However, the last upstairs room Edmundo escorted them to was in reasonable order. There were radios and microphones ranged above a long desk and maps on the walls. Tina guessed the East Germans had been using

253

it and there were signs of their having left in a hurry: a stubbed-out cigarette, a half-finished letter. The men sat themselves down around a large table, leaving her uncertain whether she was meant to stay.

'Do you mind if my secretary takes notes?' Sir James asked.

Edmundo shrugged his shoulders. 'If you want.'

The men talked for perhaps twenty minutes. The essence of the exchanges she took down concerned the Liberation Front receiving a royalty on future production from the Concession Twenty-Two mine. At first this discussion was amicable. However, a perceptible tenseness crept into it, until Edmundo stood up angrily.

'What I like to say is this. You should pay us, not that shit government in Luanda. This is our country, it is our mine.'

'Please sit down, General.' Sir James remained seated himself. 'We have to be realists. I agree you can stop Concession Twenty-Two from producing diamonds. One hundred per cent if you want. But you are getting one hundred per cent of nothing if you cannot sell the stones.'

'Through Zaïre.' Edmundo waved his hands angrily. 'We sell through Zaïre, Hartman, any time.'

'Only what you capture. You cannot run the mine because of the government. The government cannot run it because of you. Stalemate. No profit. If I run it things will be different.'

A look of satisfaction came into the African's expression, as if a point had been proven. 'Ah,' he said, sitting down heavily, 'you are so rich you pay both sides. You pay the shit government also.'

'To export I must have a legal concession.'

'My friends have told me you are so rich you can do this. I did not believe them.'

'Not me. The concession,' Hartman corrected him. 'You let us take out the diamonds and there's enough for everyone. I'll pay a five million dollar annual royalty.'

'You pay Luanda for the lease.' Edmundo picked up the silver gun and began playing with it, apparently in admiration. 'I know those men. You are paying them. You can pay us also. This is our country. Thirty million dollars. And the royalty.'

'Impossible.' Hartman made the word more matter-of-fact than dismissive. 'Five million down and five million a year.'

As if absent-mindedly, the African took a clip of bullets from the pocket of his shirt and began casually loading the gun. Then, as Tina watched with increasing fear, he drew back the bolt and cocked the mechanism with a loud click.

'Thirty million,' he said.

'I'm sorry, General. There are other mines in the world.'

'Thirty,' Edmundo repeated, took aim at the unlit and dusty

neon tube above them and fired. The noise was deafening in the confined space. Glass showered down and Tina ducked, clamping her hands over her head for protection. When she dared to look up, Sir James was calmly brushing the debris out of his hair with a handkerchief. He then flicked it around his area of the table.

'The gun works,' he said contemptuously. 'So do my contracts. You're better off with five million from me than promises from other people.'

Loud shouts came from outside and three rebel soldiers burst through the door, guns in hand. Tina was terrified that they would start shooting too. However Edmundo yelled at them as they retreated, casting suspicious looks at Hartman and Tina. He next spoke briefly to an aide, who left the room.

'General.' Hartman was impatient. 'Five million is my final offer. We have to leave. People in Kinshasa are expecting me.'

'Time! You white men are crazy about time. Let them in Kinshasa wait. Let them say. What is time, Hartman? I have fought here eleven years, against the colonialists, against the communists. What I like to ask is this: what does time matter, what is it?' He raised the gun again and fired a burst at the wall clock, which was working, although two hours slow. More glass cascaded to the floor. The hands ceased to move, the face was riddled. 'You see, the time has stopped: you can stay.'

'Unfortunately not. Why don't you come on my plane? We can talk in comfort. You'll be back in three hours.'

'Not possible.' Edmundo shifted his massive shoulders, his flesh rippling under the smooth fabric of the shirt, as if alert to some threat. 'Sorry for that.' He could make single phrases work for him when he wanted. His 'sorry' was completely dismissive, yet not without regret. He shouted some kind of order and another soldier appeared, who Tina decided must have been waiting close to the door. However it was not the soldier himself who caught their attention. It was his load. The African was staggering under the weight of a magnificent antelope head, with near black hair and huge scimitar-shaped horns, mounted on an appropriately vast though crudely finished wooden shield.

'Our finest animal.' Edmundo's volubility returned. 'The sable antelope. This animal is our symbol. It is for you. In Luanda they will not give such a thing. Those people do not know our country.' He continued with an explanation about the individuality of his area and how he would agree to take part in a government of Angola, but never submit or surrender to the existing one. Tina decided this was just another tactic. He talked to allow himself to think and throughout he was trying to read his visitor's expression: a futile endeavour, because even when he smiled, Sir James's blue eyes stayed cold. 'I like you to have this present all the same,' Edmundo concluded.

Hartman stood up and stroked the antelope's brow admiringly, then appeared to have a change of heart. 'Miss Humphries, would you mind returning to the plane. I want to talk to the General alone.'

As she left the other soldiers were hustled out and they all walked across the littered tarmac to the Gulfstream, its white paint shimmering in the heat. The engineer was on guard, keeping anyone from entering the plane, his shirt dark under the arms with sweat.

'Christ,' he exclaimed when he saw the head, 'what a beast,' and directed the soldier to load it in the rear hold.

Tina sat with him at the top of the steps, in shadow and free from the heat of the cabin, until five minutes before the departure time Captain Holz started an auxiliary turbine, partly so that the air-conditioning would begin to function, partly as an audible warning that they must leave. He had told her it used too much fuel to be kept running all the time.

However, when Sir James did emerge from the tower with Edmundo it was to announce that he had decided to remain.

'Listen, Holz,' she heard him instruct the captain inside the cabin, 'come back for me as near ten tomorrow as you can. Tell them I stayed in Nairobi. Make a new manifest. Coming back you'll have to cook up a flight plan for somewhere else. Zambia might be the best. You may tell Mr Roeyen, but no one else.' He turned to her. 'Find my overnight bag would you.'

She was bringing it through the cabin when Edmundo's bulk appeared in the narrow doorway. 'You are not leaving?' He sounded almost alarmed. 'You must not go.' A grin spread over his great face. 'We do not see so many pretty girls.' He shouted back to Hartman. 'Tell her she can stay. I like to have pretty guests.'

She made her way to the steps, with Edmundo squashing himself against the forward hanging cupboard to let her past, and looked at Sir James for guidance. She wasn't at all sure she could trust these people, whatever Edmundo might say.

'Stay if you like. Might be a help.' Hartman had more pressing matters on his mind. 'Holz.' He reverted to giving orders. 'When you get to Kinshasa phone Lady Hartman. Tell her everything's fine and I'll speak to her tomorrow.'

She grabbed her overnight case again and descended, to Edmundo's evident pleasure.

'You will be happy you have stayed,' he said.

The three of them stood and watched while the steps retracted into the Gulfstream's fuselage, the door closed and the plane taxied bumpily to the runway. Four minutes later it was disappearing in the clouds.

For all his supposed indifference to time, Edmundo didn't hang around the airfield. They clambered into a jeep and left immediately on a bumpy and dusty three-quarter-hour drive along tracks through the bush.

For Tina that afternoon and evening were unexpected magic. She was allocated a tent, and while Sir James argued with Edmundo, she was shown the life of the camp by a girl soldier. The guerrilla headquarters were spread around in the bush, some of the men living in simply constructed huts with their families. She saw women pounding millet and cassava, cooking on charcoal fires, living virtually with a baby in one arm and a gun in the other. It was informal to the point of chaos, yet she discerned a discipline of a kind. Her guide assured her that on raiding operations they all lived rough, and showed her with pride how useful supplies sent from South Africa had been: among them sanitary towels used as headbands and tampons for oiling rifles. She was told a woman had helped take the Russian colonel prisoner.

Next day Sir James failed to achieve agreement. When they left Edmundo did not accompany them to the airfield, where they waited all day, guarded sullenly by half a dozen guerrillas who dozed in the shade. The Gulfstream never came. Late in the afternoon they were ordered back into the truck, and it became apparent that they were prisoners.

Tina ceased her account, staring at Timmins and me as though she was struggling free from a nightmare.

'After the second day they kept me apart from Sir James most of the time,' she said, 'except at meals, when it was difficult to talk. There was the Russian and several East Germans and he felt they were listening. There was a South African too called Struben, who was quite young.' She grimaced 'On the third day he took me along to Edmundo's bunker.' She laughed, though with a disquieting shrillness. 'It was just a huge wooden hut with earth piled around the sides. Edmundo was very proud of it, though. Struben told me so, when he took me along, though I didn't understand why Edmundo wanted me. He was sitting outside under the trees, talking to Sir James, and took hardly any notice of me at all.'

'Hartman,' Edmundo said, glancing up to grin a welcome at Tina, then opening another beer for himself from a batch of bottles on the safari table, 'what I like to say is this. I keep promises. The

257

next plane from the south will take your girl out. No obligation, not commercial. But for you,' he swigged some beer with a gurgling noise then wiped his broad mouth with the back of his hand, 'for you Hartman, the flight out is sixty million dollars.'

'Yesterday it was thirty.' Hartman was not afraid of being caustic.

'Yesterday! How do you find yesterday? Bring yesterday to me Hartman and I will know. Today what I like is sixty million. We know that is your price.'

'Indeed.' The acidity was still there, because that was how he always reacted to threats, but it drained away because the figure had substance. Sixty million was the price agreed with the Angolan government for the Concession Twenty-Two lease, if the development investment was included. Edmundo had boasted of his friends in Luanda. He probably had spies in the ministry concerned. The question was whether he knew more than the simple figures.

'We know you, Hartman.' Edmundo's next remarks were lazily shrewd. 'You are a clever man, but we know you. You think we can be bought for peanuts and you think I will travel in your plane to have a conference.' He snapped his fingers in Hartman's face, leaning across the table so heavily that the beer bottles teetered. 'Wrong. We have been told your plan.'

'My plane is equipped for meetings. You would have been brought straight back.'

'Straight, Hartman? Or to Luanda? Or maybe to find a very hot time when we land?'

'No.' Hartman's tone had become completely matter-of-fact. 'It was a last-minute idea.'

'I do not believe you, Hartman. Lucky for you, you stay to talk.' He did not explain why. 'Now you can pay. You can pay soon. Send what message you like.' He jerked his thumb at the South African. 'Struben will send it. But the price may change, any time. When that Falkland war of yours is finished, then it will change. When the BBC tells us, everything will change. You can listen, every day.'

'You mean you want publicity?'

'For you.' Edmundo thumped the table so hard that the bottles danced and his own did fall. He caught it neatly and drank again before continuing. 'For what you try to do, Hartman. The truth about you can be more than money.'

'Only weak men demand ransoms. The outside world will reckon you couldn't hold the airfield, let alone the mine.'

The challenge angered the African. Although the government's army was ill-motivated and undisciplined, it could win an open battle. Edmundo's sole advantage was in this thick and all-concealing bush. He disliked being reminded of the reality.

'What I like to say is this,' he shouted, 'we can take what we want, any time. Ask the Russian. Ask the Germans. Ask those shit Cubans. We have driven away the Portuguese. Even we will drive those others out and we will kill the ones who trick us. We could have killed you, Hartman. But we are not savages. You think I am some leader in the bush. You are wrong. I have a degree from Lisbon.' He nodded to Struben as if seeking confirmation.

'That is true, man,' the South African said. 'He studied in Nigeria too and he trained with us. You can count on him. He won't start any hostage routine. Don't get the cat by its tail.'

Edmundo picked up the silver sub-machinegun, looked down at it and unexpectedly smiled. 'From this present you have gained much, my friend. Even you have saved your life. I like this gun. You say it was made for me?'

'For you personally.' Throughout the diatribe Hartman had remained completely unflinching.

'Thank you for that.' The African's tone changed abruptly again. 'You can hear your BBC and you can choose. Sixty million dollars or the world can know what you are doing with your mines and your contracts. What you are doing here, what you have done in Rhodesia. Things like that.'

'He'll have reporters flown in,' Struben said. 'He's done that before.'

'Send a message any time,' Edmundo repeated and strode off, swinging the gun in his hand like a talisman.

'Would they believe him?' Hartman asked, more for the sake of Tina's reaction than Struben's.

Taken aback and uncertain how to answer, she thought about this African graduate enchanted by a silver gun, his ragtag army with its Afrikaner radio expert, the girl rebels using tampons to oil their rifles. Was it all any more lunatic than the television reports she accepted as true at home?

'I think, well, it's what people expect Africa to be like.'

'She's right, man. You bitched yourself this time,' Struben said dispassionately, swigging his beer. 'You've bought your way around Africa for years. Okay, the others are just kaffirs. The General is different. He isn't going to be bought. Or betrayed. They could have told you in Pretoria.'

Hartman bit back an angry comment about the South Africans fancying themselves as power brokers. Edmundo's alliance with them was no less expedient than the Angolan government's with Moscow. What concerned him more immediately was why the Gulfstream had not returned. Holz had located the airfield the first time easily enough. Could he have been shot down?

'Have you any news of my jet?' he asked.

The South African shook his head. 'Couldn't land anyway.

The airfield's under fire again.' He drained his beer. 'Want to write out a message? Here.' He pulled a small pad from his bush shirt pocket. 'And sign please. I like things to be according to the book.'

Hartman took the pad. 'I'd like time to compose it,' he said.

'No panic. We have transmission problems anyway. I'm working on the set.'

Much later, after a silent meal with Tina and the Russian, who spoke some Portuguese but apparently no English, Hartman sat down to write a brief text. What exercised him most was the extent to which Edmundo might be bluffing. What proof could he have of Rhodesian sanctions-busting? Or of anything else? Journalists would want documentary evidence. He doubted if there was any. What disturbed him far more was being held prisoner at a critical moment for his underlying plans. The Angolan government would renege on the contract as soon as it became known he was with these rebels. Then it would be like dominoes falling. The takeover would collapse and the long-term scheme next. Sixty million dollars was a trifle compared with the totals at stake. He had to be back in London by June 4th. The ransom must be paid. Then, the full irony began to sink into his consciousness. On his orders, Stainton or whoever took responsibility would prolong negotiations while they investigated ways of rescuing him. He included the codeword he and Anne had agreed. 'Situation fluid'. She would know that meant 'pay'.

On the morning of May 28th he learnt from the BBC news that the Gulfstream's wreckage had been found in Zaïre and he himself was officially missing, though neither his nor Tina's bodies had yet been identified. The aircraft had been off course and mystery surrounded the circumstances. The Trust's shares had plunged on the stock market. With gestures and the smattering of pidgin Portuguese which he had begun to acquire he sent the guard for Struben.

'I told you,' the South African was irritated at being summoned, 'this damn transmitter's on the blink. You think I have spares here, man? No your message has not gone.'

'At least you must know something about my plane,' Hartman insisted.

Struben looked at him with the half-understanding contempt a young and active man might entertain for an ageing philanderer. 'Sooner or later you're for the lions, man. Just lion feed. What are you needing a jet for, eh?'

'Well, if you've any decency, don't tell the girl it's crashed.'

But when he joined her for the rough meal that passed as lunch Tina was distraught. He tried to console her, without effect. She felt as though her last link with the normal world had been severed.

For day after day no answer came. Edmundo was playing a game with him and Tina; letting them eat at the same table, yet always apart. In snatched sentences he told her not to worry, unintentionally increasing her fears.

Ten days after they had both been made prisoners, the reply arrived on June 1st, the very date when the Concession Twenty-Two lease expired and the Trust was due to buy it. By the end of this week his entire strategy could be defeated; yet Anne's reply indicated unmistakably that she was acting on the advice of a negotiatior.

'What an answer, eh?' Struben remarked as he handed over the message. 'Christ, you have stupid friends, man. I tell you that for free.'

There followed the aggravating necessity of transmitting Tina's birthday and Struben's extraordinary euphoria at discovering his wartime career. Struben, Hartman now realized, was created of the same mix that provides a proportion of every generation's soldiers: schoolboy adventurousness, idealism, energy and re-vulsion from the idea of being chained to a desk. After he had radioed Hartman's second messsage he returned to the tent, drawn back as if he had glimpsed an old recruiting poster, his attitude to the captive markedly more amiable.

'Would you talk more about the war, eh, before I take you to the General?'

Hartman was now dressed, and though feeling in poor physi-cal shape he was ready to make the most of this unexpected ally, whose friendliness might not last.

'First, have you heard any more about my plane? What went wrong?' Although he would never have admitted it here, the death of Holz and the others had greatly affected him.

'I am sorry to tell you this,' Struben said. 'There was a bomb on your plane.'

'Don't be absurd. My crew never left the Gulfstream.' Despite being so emphatic, Hartman felt a twinge of doubt.

'They took that antelope head on, didn't they?'

Hartman was silenced. He had ordered the trophy to be loaded himself.

'Why kill the crew, for God's sake?' he demanded at last.

'It was on before you changed your mind, eh?'

'That's mad.'

'We had a warning from Pretoria. You planned to kidnap him, right? So he had the bomb made.'

There was an African logic in the whole thing: a cunning re-prisal for attempted treachery, an unwillingness to lose face by asking for the removal of the trophy once it had been accepted.

'Let me tell you something, Captain Struben. Your damn

people in Pretoria got things wrong as usual. I was asked to abduct Edmundo and I refused. All I came for was the concession.'

'Is that so?' He was puzzled. 'I did not think it could be right. The General never goes from his army, except for the most important matters.'

Hartman could visualize the kind of muddled, under-analysed intelligence that had promoted Edmundo's reaction, though he had also begun to doubt the logic of his own recent planning. Earlier in his detention, with nothing to occupy his mind save worry, he had sought distraction by jotting down a rough diary of what was happening to him. He was alert enough to notice that his handwriting, normally regular and workmanlike, was betraying signs of stress, falling away from its accustomed precision. Furthermore he commented on the fact, even carrying self-criticism through to asking rhetorically why he had ever imagined that Edmundo could be bought off and recording that his incarceration was going to cost him the coup of his career. He deliberately left these writings in view in his tent. For him life was a continual poker game. Now he waited non-committally for Struben to react further to his assertions.

'I will tell him.' A note of caution came into Struben's words, as though he had seen through an apparently reasonable claim. 'But Pretoria was right about other things. It is a fact that they are right.'

Hartman was left to speculate on what those things might be and what other advantages Edmundo could expect to gain from the destruction of his jet. He shivered unaccountably and could not decide whether his sudden chill resulted from Struben's revelation or the onset of a fever. He began to appreciate that there was no requirement for Edmundo to maltreat him physically: the mental pressures were accumulating inexorably enough.

When Struben took him to the General the game took a crueller twist.

Shortly before last light the Cuban captives, all eighteen stripped to the waist, were marched to the centre of the clearing. The rebel guards lined them up, prodding them contemptuously with their rifles as though they were cattle until they were strung out a foot or so apart and all facing the audience. This, Tina had realized as she was escorted to join Sir James, had been carefully arranged.

The 'audience' consisted of some hundred ALF 'freedom fighters', grouped around the edge of the clearing. The guests of honour were Sir James and the Russian colonel, who she discovered was called Makarov. The two men occupied canvas chairs directly in front of the Cubans though shaded by a tall thorn tree. Seeing them together she was struck by how alike in appearance they were. She had thought Sir James had the head and profile of an emperor when she was first interviewed for the job. His every feature from the strong chin to the wrinkles around his eyes announced that he was accustomed to giving orders. Makarov's broad face gave the same impression, though he was at least fifteen years younger. Both sat there, impassive, exercising a presence without movement.

It was only after she had been seated immediately behind them for several minutes, while the guards jostled and laughed at their prisoners, that she realized why both Makarov and Sir James were maintaining an unyielding silence and what the nature of the ceremony was. The Cubans were about to die. Not only were they barefoot and stripped of all clothing except for trousers, they were unshaven. Their brown chests glistened with sweat and their faces were shadowed by uncertainty and fear as well as the growth of beard. They looked like convicts desperate for a reprieve. Only one, self-evidently the leader, was managing to hold his head high and stand erect. The others appeared completely cowed.

Edmundo himself walked forward, swinging the silver submachinegun in his right hand, and indulged in a charade of inspecting the men. He could have been declaring cattle fit for slaughter. Then he spun round – for a man of such paunchy bulk he was extraordinarily agile – and faced Makarov.

'Why do you not save them?' he demanded. 'You brought them here to kill our people. If we kill them, it is justice. You are responsible. Why don't you answer?'

The rhetoric was part of the show. Edmundo knew the Russian spoke no English. Nor for that matter did the guerrilla soldiers, who none the less cheered their general's obvious challenge.

Sir James spoke in German to Makarov, who inclined his head to listen and nodded agreement.

'These boys are teenagers,' Hartman said to Edmundo. 'Conscripts. They had no choice. Castro sent them here.'

'Mercenaries, Sir Hartman,' Edmundo shouted, adding a few words in the native language to instant applause from his followers. 'Mercenaries like both of you.'

'He's an engineer and builds bridges. I build businesses.' Sir James stood up, not very steadily. 'If you make an exchange, they must be included. All of them.' He swayed and was forced to sit down again, slumping into the chair and wiping the back of his hand across his forehead. 'God it's hot,' he murmured.

'Are you all right?' Tina asked in a whisper.

'It's nothing.' He waved her enquiry away, without turning round, his eyes still on Edmundo.

'You don't give me orders, Hartman. No one gives me orders. I exchange this one,' he pointed his silver gun at the colonel, 'and the Germans for the ones I want, for my men and five South African commandos. A straight deal. A straighter deal than the kind you do Hartman. But you're special. I know you. And these shit Cubans, they don't count.'

At the word 'Cuban' the leader reacted, stepped forward before the guard could prevent him and shouted at Edmundo in Spanish. The African swung round but did nothing to stop the outburst, letting him finish, then spoke to Sir James.

'He wants me to shoot him, not the others. He says he is the professional soldier. That is good. I like that. Today I will kill only him. The rest can wait.'

Edmundo gave an order and two of the guards began to frog-march the Cuban away, until he shouted at them and they allowed the man to walk naturally, and with dignity, out of the clearing. All three disappeared into the trees. Tina watched them go, unable to believe this was really happening. She hid her face in her hands and a minute later a fusillade of shots sounded from the bush. When she looked up again the remaining seventeen were being hustled off. The piece of theatre was over. To her amazement Edmundo sauntered back to join them, and stood facing Sir James, legs apart, swinging the silver gun self-confidently.

'What I like to say, Hartman, is this. One Cuban at dawn each day until you pay. Every day, one more dies. You can watch. Death concentrates the man's mind, people tell me that. In eighteen days either there is sixty million dollars or my friends will take the documents to London. When they are published, you can go. Anywhere you like. Go with him. Go when we exchange him.' He jabbed the gun towards the colonel, who disregarded the gesture as if taking no notice of an unruly child.

'And Miss Humphries?' Sir James spoke with control, though a moment later he passed the back of his hand across his forehead again to wipe away the sweat.

'Ah.' Edmundo grinned and nodded. 'You are afraid, Hartman. You try not to be but you are. I know you, Hartman. But you do not know me. When I make promises, Hartman, I keep those words. A plane is coming. Tomorrow early she will go south.' He spoke to Tina directly. 'You will be safe. You can tell Sir Hartman's family I keep my word. And you can say also, if they do not pay we shall tell the whole world what he does, because we know him very well, better than his own mother.'

The scene might have continued for hours, since Edmundo was getting into his verbal stride. However, he was interrupted by the South African with a message and ended the confrontation abruptly.

'Thank God, for that,' Sir James said, when he had gone. 'I don't feel too good. Must be the sun. I'm going to lie down again.'

264

Tina wanted to accompany him, but was forbidden to. She spent the rest of the day miserably praying that there would be no more killing. The switches from civility to barbarism in Edmundo's character had totally unnerved her. Although realizing that if she had not stayed she would have been killed in the Gulfstream's crash, she felt disoriented and horribly frightened. She didn't understand Africa and even less did she understand the nature of the threat against Sir James. She wondered if his nerve would crack, though even if it did there was nothing he could do to secure payment of the ransom.

By next morning, after lying awake all night waiting in terror for the shots and screams of another execution, Tina knew that her own nerve could not last any longer. Yet when she said goodbye to Sir James, taking with her a letter and some handwritten notes on looseleaf paper, she felt she was a traitor to desert him and was in tears intermittently throughout her long journey south.

Recounting this bizarre sequence of events Tina had become more and more agitated. When a nurse interrupted to check on the progress of our already lengthy visit we were immediately asked to go.

'We must hear more of Miss Humphries' experiences,' I pleaded. 'It's most important.'

'The doctor has ordered the patient to rest.' The nurse crossed to the bed and took Tina's wrist to feel her pulse. 'You'll have to wait until tomorrow.'

'Don't you even want the letter?' Tina tried to reach for her handbag with her free arm. 'Don't you even want to know what Sir James says?'

Timmins moved towards the bedside table where the handbag lay, but she wrenched herself away from the nurse to seize it first.

'Sir James meant it for his family, not anyone else. If you weren't so mean they'd never have started the executions and he wouldn't have malaria.' Her emotions overflowed. 'Can't you understand! Why didn't you do as he wanted?'

'Will you please leave. Both of you.' The nurse stepped authoritatively between us. 'How dare you upset her so. Now Miss Humphries, who is this letter for?'

Tina pointed to me and the nurse took it from the handbag and passed it across. 'Now off with you both.' Shooing us away with her hands she scolded us out of the room.

We stopped in the corridor, Timmins still flushed because he was a decent enough man trying to do a difficult job. Deliberately standing with my back to the wall so that he was unable to see over my shoulder, I opened the envelope. The handwriting on the message inside was shaky and trailed across the paper.

Dearest Anne and Robert. You must settle on their terms. Edmundo has somehow obtained documents that are highly compromising. Worse, he is now taking actions that must provoke Angolan retaliation. Far better to pay. My secretary will explain. Fondest love, Jim.

'May I read it?' Timmins asked.

Without being certain what documents Father was referring to, though it seemed probable they were the fruit of the burglary at the Van Rensburgs' house, I could only guess at why they were compromising. But I definitely did not want this known to Timmins, and so to Stainton.

'We'd better go downstairs,' I said, thrusting the paper back in its envelope, 'otherwise that dragon will be after us.'

In the lift he tried to persuade me to hand the letter over.

'Every aspect of Miss Humphries' experience is calculated to pressurize us,' he argued. 'What your father has written could be of great use in evaluating the situation.'

'What he's said is personal.' I kept my hand on the envelope as we stepped out into the reception area. 'He does say there are physical dangers. They may come under attack.' I paused, aware of the receptionist's curiosity. 'We ought to go and see Frank Stainton.'

'Agreed. I shall also have to talk to the underwriters.'

However, when I rang Christianne told me Stainton was with the Trust's brokers and completely tied up for the remainder of the afternoon. The earliest we could see him was tomorrow morning, Friday June 4th, the original cut-off date for launching Father's entire takeover plan.

'Tomorrow makes more sense,' Timmins remarked somewhat tartly. 'Given that you want us to hear the rest of Miss Humphries' story.'

I bit back a retort that if tomorrow did not see the ransom offer increased I would, as they say, reserve my position. I wanted to find out from Tina what the documents were. It also struck me as odd that he had disregarded one salient aspect of her account: namely that Father himself considered Edmundo a man who could only be dealt with face to face.

CHAPTER TWENTY

'Don't become a prisoner of ambition like he is, will you?' Camilla made the point softly, lighting a cigarette from the candle flame between us, her skin translucent as she leant towards it.

We were in her favourite restaurant – discussions with Camilla always seemed to involve eating – and I had just finished recounting the day's events. It had been a busy Thursday, culminating with one major decision which she was questioning: though not wholeheartedly.

'So the Fund Managers are on your side and now you're Sir Galahad, charging off on your sturdy chequebook to rescue your father in person!' She gazed at me with affectionate concern. 'I'm all for you becoming involved, but isn't this carrying it rather far?'

'No bid for the Trust is possible; at least for a few days.' I shrugged my shoulders at the risks. 'I think I can persuade the rebels to free him. How else d'you suggest I use the breathing space?'

She didn't question that I'd scored a minor victory against Frank Stainton, though the real confrontation was yet to come.

'Has it struck you,' she said, blowing smoke away from me because she knew I disliked it, 'that this entire business has been dominated by a series of deadlines? The Angolan concession. The ransom demand. The Trust becomes open to a bid and – bingo – a news agency immediately reports your father's death. Now Tina Humphries reappears, saying the ransom must be paid at once. But what is she actually telling the negotiators?'

Perplexed, I went over Tina's account in my mind. There had been no hidden message.

'She thinks she's told you that every day means another Cuban will be shot. But what she has really said is the crunch won't come for Sir James until the executions end.' Camilla drew on her cigarette as if it contained an elixir, let the smoke drift away and clinched the argument. 'There were sixteen Cubans left when Tina was flown out. That allows two working weeks for whatever else is being planned.'

It made sense. The threat did have a built-in delay which Timmins, and of course Stainton, would naturally be inclined to exploit. Perhaps Arab history had made me too aware of conspiratorial politics. But a lot could happen in two weeks, and there was a savage subtlety about this theory that carried immediate conviction. Furthermore, Father was involved in much more complex matters than the takeover of a rival mining group.

'Did you realize,' Camilla went on, with a casualness which warned me she was about to detonate some kind of revelation, 'that your father recently lost an associate who was always on hand at crucial moments before?'

'Van Rensburg?'

'Guess again.'

She reached down for her handbag and took out the notebook which was her inescapable companion. 'Signor Carlo Angelino, the wartime resistance hero and Member of the Italian National Assembly, died last week at his home in the Abruzzi.'

'When was that?'

'May 17th. He was sixty-seven.'

She had no need to remind me that Father had departed for Africa only three days later.

'I indulged in a little deception. I phoned his Rome office with a rigmarole about having missed him in Africa. They confirmed he was to have been in Kenya.'

The corollary was inescapable. I thought of the Rome restaurant photograph and Lotte Lohrey's arms around the two men's shoulders. 'When old friends meet they talk about the past.' I had doubted it at the time. 'I'll have to see Mrs Lohrey again,' I said, 'even if she does just stonewall.'

'Drag whatever she knows out of her.' Camilla abruptly became forthright. 'For crying out loud, she ought to be an ally. Unless she confirms what your father's objectives were, you can't negotiate. Though there are moments when I wonder why you should want him back.' She blew smoke in my face, as if to stifle any protest. 'He bought his title. He's destroyed umpteen men's careers. He's done everything illicit or immoral from owning brothels to insider dealing. The only institutions he's missed out on are Brixton jail and the House of Lords.'

When she got into her stride she could be as cutting as any columnist. I let her run on a little, then reined her in, as it were.

'We can't keep control of the Trust without him. I have to get him back,' I said, and threw in a calculated provocation.

268

'Felicity Ames made me realize that.'

'Felicity who?'

'The more attractive of the Fund Managers. She told me there were limits to what I could achieve.'

'Well, I don't agree.' As if she had said more than she intended, Camilla stubbed out her cigarette at last, remarking that since smoking helped her concentrate I ought to put up with it more gracefully. 'Now, we can order.'

She began scrutinizing the menu as if she hadn't eaten for a month, and only reverted to the main subject much later, after capturing an evening paper left behind by the couple at the next table.

'Listen to this. "CHELSEA GIRL MYSTERY. Tina Humphries, personal secretary of the millionaire financier Sir James Hartman, is still missing in Africa after the crash which killed Sir James ..." Hardly the result the Press release was intended to achieve! Or was it? A lot of dirt is going to appear in the Sunday papers this weekend.'

'Then a lot of editors are going to have writs on their hands.'

'Surely, Bob, you don't want to stop the papers now?' Camilla's arguments often had a sting in the tail. I waited for the end of this one. 'Suppose the story of Tina being in a clinic here in London leaked out? Even if reporters were denied access to her, they'd conclude that your father was alive. You wouldn't need any writs.' She gave me a mischievous smile. 'Just suppose it did leak?'

Playing the devil's advocate, I pointed out that the ransom negotiations could be damaged.

'I'm sure friend Stainton would say so. But would he be right? Especially if you're thinking of going it alone.'

The idea had merit. The City commentators would be alerted. It might provoke the Stock Exchange Council into suspending trading.

'Your father detesting the media needn't stop you exploiting it. Stainton has.'

'Better sleep on the idea.' Caution warned me to have matters out with him first. 'Tomorrow's only Friday. We have time.'

'Well, sweetheart, remember Sunday papers like to have their scandals organized in advance. They ought to be tipped off before tomorrow night.'

'For a well brought up girl you're incorrigible.'

'No comment,' she said, appropriately enough.

As things transpired the Friday morning visit to the clinic was less productive than the previous one, although Tina herself looked in better shape. There was some natural colour in her face, her eyes were less dark, her hair was fluffier.

'Now you don't dare upset her,' the nurse had warned Timmins, and when she began to talk we appreciated why. Mentally she remained locked in the events of her captivity, apparently unable to distance herself enough from the experience to be analytical about it.

'I should never have left Sir James when he was ill and there was no one to care for him.' She kept repeating things Father had said. '"There's no point trying to be clever. Tell them if they play straight, Edmundo will." I'm sure that's true!' She looked at us imploringly. 'I'm sure you can trust him. He promised I wouldn't be hurt and I wasn't. It is his country, isn't it?'

'What about the Cubans?' Timmins asked, and although he put the question quietly he should have known he would trigger an outburst.

'Oh God, I don't know.' She put her hands to her face and when she spoke again her words were made indistinct by sobs. 'Those screams, so . . . awful. I couldn't bear . . .'

I went and sat on the bed, putting my arm around her shoulders. 'Try to forget about the whole thing. It's over. You're safe again.' I could feel her body shaking through her flimsy dressing gown, and looked across at Timmins, leaning forward concernedly on a white-painted hospital chair. 'We must accept what she says.'

'You must,' she unexpectedly echoed me. 'Edmundo warned me you wouldn't.' Gradually she recovered herself a little and began articulating more clearly. 'He said so before I left.'

'What exactly did he say?' Timmins prompted.

'He used that silly phrase.' Paradoxically she sounded happier at the memory. '"What I like to say, Miss Tina, is this. We fight for our country where we live. Is this wrong? Men like to take it from us, when no one sees. But we know those men and we will fight them! Ask in London if this is wrong." Well,' she sat up, defiantly and I removed my arm quickly. 'Is it? Sir James was terribly brave. I don't expect I'll know anyone so brave again. But Sir James is the one who is wrong.' She made a half tearful gesture with both arms. 'All you have to do is pay and the shooting will stop and everything will be all right.'

Timmins made a show of believing her, but didn't wait for the nurse to come and chivvy us away. He thanked her, promised her parents would be along in the afternoon and ushered me out.

Once we were in the seclusion of the taxi he made his interpretation of the interview plain.

'She'd begun to identify with her captors in spite of being scared stiff. It's a common phenomenon in political kidnappings. Even when they're maltreated hostages become psychologically dependent on the group that's holding them.'

I remembered Tina's admiration for the women guerrillas. 'She

did seem torn between loyalty to my father and a kind of fascination with Edmundo,' I said.

'Precisely. My own view is that by releasing her he's signalling
a willingness to compromise. He wanted to save her from being
blown up with the plane for more reasons than her being a girl.'

'And the Cubans?' I threw his earlier question back at him.

'I question the whole performance. Africans don't hold executions out of sight. They go for a public spectacle, like the guillotine
during the French Revolution. In any case those Cubans could be
exchanged.'

I took the point. Edmundo wouldn't think twice about killing the
Cubans, but alive they could be traded, much as he despised them.

'So the whole ceremony was laid on for Tina?'

'I wouldn't be surprised. The aim is to give us a deadline.'

'Or a calculated breathing space during which to argue?'

'If they deal us cards we must play them.' He made it sound
entirely reasonable. 'They must have reasons.'

'That's what I'm worried about,' I said and dropped the subject
for the rest of the ride to Hartman House. I was right to handle
this in my own way.

When we arrived there was a definite sense of crisis. Executives
were hurrying around with worried expressions and at the fourteenth floor reception Christianne greeted us with an aloof formality that boded ill. If she was the bellwether I believed, then
Frank Stainton must be in the ascendant.

'He can spare fifteen minutes,' she said before ushering us
through, 'and only fifteen.'

Timmins, to his credit, gave a thumbnail sketch of developments in under half that time.

'So we have eighteen days in hand?' Stainton remarked, as if
this confirmed that the negotiation was far from pressing.

'Fifteen,' I corrected him. 'It's now three days since the first
Cuban was notionally executed. But I don't see how you can keep
Tina Humphries under wraps for two weeks, and as for your Press
release, that was indefensible. You should have asked for a suspension of dealings until Father's whereabouts are known.'

'We judged the statement expedient, given the essential secrecy
of the matter,' Stainton snapped. 'Our collective wisdom may
possibly be greater than your limited experience.'

'You were endangering both the Trust and his life. If he's
believed to be dead the rebels can do what they like with him.'

'Do the underwriters think so?' Stainton asked Timmins, disregarding me.

Caught in the crossfire, Timmins replied with all the prudence
of a mediator. 'On balance, Sir, we feel lack of publicity would
influence the rebels to settle for less.'

'So might the Trust being taken over,' I said, being in no mood for equivocation. 'So might destroying everything my father has created. They wouldn't be alone in that objective either. Then they could kill him out of hand. Share dealings should be suspended.'

Stainton had heavy-lidded, almost hooded, eyes and his right eyelid began to twitch. Apart from this tiny quivering he remained motionless and unyielding, his mouth set hard.

'That possibility is a question for the Board,' he said acidly. 'You are not a member of the Board. Sir James left specific instructions on how any kidnap attempt should be handled. He foresaw the pressures which might result and we are following those instructions. I understand you now decline to reveal the contents of the letter which Miss Humphries brought with her. There are times, young man, when it is not easy to keep patience with your demands.'

'You must make allowances, Sir,' Timmins intervened with as much tact as he could muster. 'Sir James's family are under considerable stress.'

'Thank you,' I said, dismissing him as an ally, 'but I have no need to be apologized for. The Press release was calculated to damage our family's interests. As it has done.' I turned on Stainton. 'You haven't got eighteen days' grace, or fifteen, or whatever you might find convenient. Evidently my father left more than one set of instructions. If you have not asked for a suspension of dealings by three this afternoon then I shall. And I will not be alone.'

With that I walked out, and if I cannot pretend Stainton was speechless, it certainly made an impact on Timmins, because he caught up with me in the passage.

'If Sir James left you instructions, for heaven's sake tell me what they were.'

'I'm sorry, they only concerned the future of the Trust.'

'In a kidnap all information is relevant. I shall be speaking to the ALF's Geneva representative later. I ought to know.'

'The most constructive move that you can make is to increase the ransom offer.'

He squinted at me in his appraising, interrogative way. 'You think so? It is essential to collaborate on this.'

'Of course. Let me know your decision.' I shook hands as though nothing had changed and went along to Christianne's office.

She was dressed demurely and I had a sudden absurd idea that perhaps she only dressed sexily for Father. Or was she, like a chameleon, changing colour to blend with a changing environment?

'Before I forget, Robert, I have given you wrong information.

272

This stockbroker's clerk I mentioned the other day was altogether stupid. What Mr Stainton had bought was two thousand shares of Consolidated Goldfields, not two million of Consolidated Concessions.'

'A different thing completely,' I remarked, not believing a word of it. 'Are Goldfields going up?'

'I suppose.' She immediately became dismissive. 'Why otherwise should he buy?'

Why indeed. Whether he was after Consolidated Goldfields or Consolidated Diamond Concessions Frank Stainton would only lay out money on winners. He'd have learnt about insider dealing from his earliest days as an accountant.

'So are Consolidated Concessions making a bid?' I asked. The question had become as constant as a child's complaint, but she delivered herself of a tolerably honest answer.

'I think it is possible, Robert. If Sir James comes back, he will come back too late.'

'*Sauve qui peut*,' I said acidly.

She flushed. 'For you, life is easy. For me, divorced, in a strange country, it is not so simple.'

I was slightly shocked. Father had never mentioned she had a failed marriage or that her circumstances were difficult. He presumed a lot on her loyalty.

'So you see Robert,' she smiled sincerely for the first time I could remember. 'I like to have a job on Monday.'

'I expect you will,' I said, feeling unexpectedly sorry for her. 'But don't assume Mr Stainton is going to have everything his own way.'

'May be.' She made a little twisting gesture with her wrist, a demonstration of 'this way, that way'.

'Thank you for the warning, anyhow.'

'Warning? I have said nothing to you, Robert. Nothing at all.'

She was convinced that Stainton had the whole business sewn up and I could see no point, tempting as it was, in dissuading her by mentioning where I was going next. Ultimately I might need the support of all the shareholders, and for that I required legal advice.

Mr Paul Crosthwaite-Eyre was one of those rubicund, rotund, Dickensian figures whom the British legal system continues to breed in defiance of the twentieth century. My mother had great faith in him, bolstered perhaps by his being so different from the TV image of a lawyer and by the gloomy Victorian chambers from which the partnership had operated ever since the building was new in the 1880s. He was pedantic, as ageing bachelors tend to be, and Father used to joke about where he hid the quill pens when we arrived.

The jokes concealed active antagonism. Crosthwaite-Eyre had always been the representative of Mother's family and the two men kept their distance, almost as though they were rivals for her affection. When he learnt that Father was speculating in property in the 1950s he had persuaded Grandpa to insist that the Phillimore Place house was transferred to Mother's name: a prudent move, but also an indication of mistrust. In fact, he had been both right and wrong. Father had always insured us handsomely against his death. At the same time, he would have pledged the plates we ate off if it would have clinched a deal.

'My dear boy,' Crosthwaite-Eyre remarked as he welcomed me, 'I'm extremely sorry to hear about this. Must be a grave strain on your dear mother. But if the Trust is handling the negotiation, how precisely can I help?'

I detailed my intentions, taking some comfort from the familiar room, one wall lined with old deed boxes on shelves and the family tree of the partnership framed on another, as I told him about Stainton.

'If there is no suspension of share dealing and Consolidated do announce a bid I may have to call an Extraordinary General Meeting of the company.'

'My dear boy.' He blinked at me over the half lenses of his gold-framed reading glasses. 'Let us initially discover how Philip Jardine has fared. The facts, dear boy. We must always have the facts.'

Fortunately Jardine was available and we learnt that his approaches to the Stock Exchange Council had met with limited success.

'As your family's broker,' Jardine explained, 'the Quotations Committee had to listen to me. But it ought to be the Trust's broker making the request. That damn Press release didn't help either. They've taken it to mean Sir James definitely is dead, in which case there's no longer uncertainty. Anyhow the market's read it that way. The price was badly down at one point. Until buyers came on the scene.' He paused. 'There are strong bid rumours again, I'm afraid.'

I told him there might be a rebuttal of Father's death in the Sunday papers and handed the instrument back to Crosthwaite-Eyre, who replaced it with the care of a museum attendant handling an ancient artefact, which in truth it was. I had never been surprised at Father's reluctance to employ him. However he was the only solicitor I had and this was no moment to hire another.

'Looks as though I shall have to call an EGM,' I said. 'Can you do it in my absence?'

'As a shareholder, I take it? By all means. I will draft a suitable letter. Under Section 132 of the Companies Act . . .' I did not hinder the flow of his good nature. '. . . it must propose a specific resolution . . . despite appearances we do have a certain experience in these matters.'

There and then he composed a request for an EGM to consider whether shareholders should accept or reject a bid from Consolidated. I signed two blank sheets of paper, so that his secretary could type it later, and undertook to inform him by telephone or telegram when to despatch it.

'By the way,' he remarked, as he bade me an effusive goodbye, 'that libel action idea you mentioned. You've abandoned it, I assume?'

'It might have been counter-productive.'

'Precisely, dear boy. Only the very rich can afford to sue the newspapers.'

'We are very rich.'

'Yes. Well,' he looked at me benevolently, as though forgiving an indiscretion on my part. 'Even so, the less contact one has with the ladies and gentlemen of the Press, the better.'

I agreed tactfully and after leaving him found a coin box and instructed Camilla to tip off the Press about Tina and the clinic. I hadn't wanted to use Crosthwaite-Eyre's phone for that. He would have felt it somewhat underhand, which it undeniably was.

Then I returned to my flat, looked up the name of the Swiss lawyers with whom Timmins was negotiating and rang them. I said I was coming to Geneva tomorrow, anticipating that they would take this as a sign of weakness and a divided front on our side. The man I spoke to certainly sounded as though he did and I made no attempt to disillusion him.

'I still think you're taking a big risk,' Camilla insisted that evening, deflecting her anxiety into a joke. 'If you must go trundling off into the bush again, please insure yourself. Preferably with me as beneficiary.'

'Who else?' I said and caught her so unawares that she blushed and hastily counter-attacked.

'What's more, if you're seeing the lovely Lotte Lohrey, don't let her soft-soap you again. Pin her down. She must know why your father wants the ransom paid.'

The logic was irrefutable, but I knew that by comparison Stainton was a walkover. Beneath her glamour Lotte Lohrey was as tough as old hide. If she hadn't been living in Switzerland, where women tend not to be welcome at the top, she would have been a tycoon years ago. Assuming, of course, that she had sought a role of leadership as opposed to the more nebulous one of promoting other people.

The next morning, Saturday, she was if anything more

composed and elegant than before, as if armoured for a potentially difficult encounter. She went through the complete routine of greeting me warmly at Geneva airport, taking me out to lunch before I went to the solicitors, pressing me to stay at her apartment overnight and generally acting like the sympathetic family friend. Yet when I challenged her about Father's activities she gave very little away.

We ate on a terrace overlooking the lake, sailboats bobbing on the water, the distant mountains hazy with summer heat, the whole setting out of key with the subject. Perhaps that was her intention, as if she wished to slide a diminishing lens between our conversation and the reality of Father lying on his canvas bed in the bush, alternately shivering and sweating as the fever ebbed and flowed. Perhaps she was simply favouring me with the most pleasant restaurant she knew. Either way, I had supposed the news of the ransom would shake her composure. It did not. She play-acted alarm and distress for a few moments, then became down-to-earth and direct.

'This negotiator of yours is correct, I think. To be under too much pressure can be dangerous.'

'Can we avoid it?' I watched her closely, because she ought to have known the answer.

'That will depend on you, Robert.'

'Father had a private code. He used it at first. Now he's completely open.' I showed her the last scrawled message.

'And this,' she pointed a pink-lacquered fingernail at 'compromising', having difficulty pronouncing the word. 'What is "highly compromising"?'

'Well,' I searched for the simplest explanation, 'the documents could be thought of by someone else – a lawyer for example – as very damaging to Father's reputation.'

'Could be criminal, *hein*?'

'Possibly. Not necessarily.' What papers might have been successfully stolen from Van Rensburg's house? 'You know more about Father's activities in Africa than I do.'

'I told you, Robert. He was visiting certain countries to make a consortium.'

'Yes,' I said sharply. 'He was trying to challenge De Beers' hold on the diamond market.'

'That is exact.' She remained unruffled. 'He was developing a larger concept.'

'With a political background?'

A flicker of disturbance crossed her face, which she masked instantly with a discreet shrug of her shoulders and a deprecatory remark.

'Without the right politics no scheme is possible in Africa. Do I have to tell you what is the biggest politic there, Robert? Surely not?'

276

'South Africa, of course.'

I spoke as dismissively as I could, not wishing to be out-manoeuvred and certain she would only reveal what I could have already deduced for myself.

'*Prima!*' she exclaimed, as though awarding marks. 'This is all that black leaders can agree about. How to attack South Africa; how to destroy apartheid.'

'So?' It was curiously easy to adopt her way of speaking without intending to, especially during this kind of verbal fencing. 'South Africa's trade depends on gold and diamonds more than anything else.' Camilla had researched the figures for me and I had them in my head. 'Fifty per cent of the Republic's export earnings come from gold. The diamond business is less concentrated there.'

'Exact. These little stones.' She slipped a ring off her finger and twisted it in front of me to catch the light, reminding me of the African manager's remark at Rukanga, 'pretty stones for pretty women'. 'These little stones do not all come from South Africa. They come from Angola, Botswana, Ghana, Liberia, Sierra Leone and Zaïre.' She slid the ring back on and raised her finger so that the diamonds glinted again. 'All black countries, all enemies of South Africa. Your father's scheme was intelligent, *hein*? He would take over a company owning diamond mines to create a new selling organization and the black leaders would join. They would strike a blow at apartheid, he would make a good business.'

'You might have told me that in Nairobi.'

'Would it make so much difference? He was already a prisoner.'

'We'd have been better prepared for the ransom demand.'

The political implications of the letter I found after the burglary hadn't struck me at the time. They did now. Whoever organized that raid could have been acting on behalf of the Angolan rebels, or the South Africans, or both. The South Africans could have paid handsomely in military matériel for the ALF to hold Father until the Consolidated deal collapsed and the consortium with it. However the explanation remained faulted and I believed I knew the reason.

'Why should Father have risked going to Angola?' I demanded. 'Why should meeting the rebels matter so much to him?'

She gave a tiny shrug. 'We can all make mistakes.'

'That was a fundamental one.'

'Only with the benefit of looking back. You forget he likes to gamble when he believes he can win, he always had done, ever since he escaped from Germany as a boy. It is his character.'

'Not because Carlo Angelino insisted he should?'

This time she could not disguise being taken aback. 'Carlo?'

'Yes,' I said firmly. 'Carlo. Barba Nera. The greatest single influence in my father's life: after you, perhaps.'

277

'My dear Robert.' She switched at once to sympathy. 'I would like to think I have sometimes helped. But Carlo! I suppose Patrick Van Rensburg has been telling you stories about the war. I can tell you, Patrick knows nothing. Since that time Carlo was, how shall I say.' She created a minor pantomime out of searching for the word. 'He was like an uncle, giving introductions. It was not like the war giving orders. How could he tell your father to take this chance? In any case, he was already dead.'

'But Carlo could bring the Russians into the consortium. Isn't that correct? And they don't only produce eleven or twelve per cent of the world's diamonds. They want South Africa destroyed. So when Carlo died you went to Nairobi in place of him.'

'What are you imagining?' Her English, always attractively incorrect, became more erratic than usual. 'Your father will be desolated for hearing this. I wanted myself to tell him about Carlo.'

'What matters is whether Edmundo knows,' I said curtly.

She looked at me keenly, the game of protests over. 'I think not.'

'Then it's worth my going out there to see him. He may be content with what he's achieved.'

'Let us first learn what the lawyers say, *hein*?' she temporized.

In fact, as I might have guessed, the ALF's representatives were circumspect to the point of obstruction when I called on them in the afternoon. The young, dark-suited, slightly flabby-faced Swiss facing me across a modern tubular steel glass-topped desk flinched when I mentioned the word ransom. I could have sworn the oil painting of the firm's founder hanging on the wall behind him quivered.

'Monsieur Hartman,' he interrupted, 'you have a regrettable misunderstanding. There is no ransom. The contribution to party funds will merely offset the cost of the military expedition required to bring Sir James to safety. Your Mr Timmins has suggested that this cost might be reduced. Unfortunately,' he allowed himself a smile, 'as all of us who have served in the army know, the costs of military exercises never go down. Always up.'

His own percentage too, I thought. However I persevered with my proposition, namely that with the Angolan concession lost to the Trust there never would be a mining deal. Edmundo had succeeded in killing that. Worse, Stainton and Timmins were going to make the negotiations drag on, and if Father became so ill with malaria that he died, then no money would be paid at all.

'The ALF should accept what's on offer,' I said bluntly. 'Five million dollars is better than nothing.' I added that I would go out myself if I could be guaranteed safe conduct. He agreed to relay the proposal, with half a dozen caveats over the precise terminology, and undertook to telephone me at Dr Lohrey's apartment, which he did while we were having dinner that evening.

'The condition proposed is acceptable.' He sounded surprised in spite of his reserve. 'They have named an airstrip for landing and ask you to bring certain supplies. If you come on Monday I will provide a list.'

'Does my father send a message?'

'They regret Sir James is too ill.'

I returned to the table and told Dr Lohrey those parts of the brief exchanges which she had not heard.

'So.' Her expression became concerned, as if she was encountering some private conflict of interest. 'Robert, I do not like to send you into danger. On the other side we have to get your father out and maybe you could succeed. From this answer they are prepared to talk. If Van Rensburg knows this man, can he go with you?'

'He was pretty badly injured. He can't have been out of hospital more than a few days.'

'If he can walk, ask him. Telephone him now.' She had made up her mind that the gamble was justified.

Van Rensburg, to his credit, did not hesitate. 'I'll charter a plane from here. But your mother's rung and asked me to be at Monday's Board meeting if I can.'

'Monday's?'

'You haven't heard? Consolidated made a formal bid this morning. Seems they acquired a significant percentage of the shares on Friday. Stainton's been on to all of us.'

I told him Jardine was trying to obtain a suspension of dealings, which would effectively freeze any bid, and he grunted something which might have been approval or might not. Then he promised that a driver would be at Nairobi airport to collect me on Tuesday morning, he would see me there, and that was that.

'You will stay with me until tomorrow, I hope,' Lotte Lohrey offered. 'Please do not feel because there is some delay you must leave. Beside you should go early to those lawyers.'

'I should like to stay. But I must speak to Mother at some point.'

'Prima!' She sounded genuinely delighted. 'Then tomorrow we take a small holiday from these worries, hein? If it is a fine day I show you a little more Geneva.'

Her tact made Sunday much more relaxed than it might have been. After a long discussion with Mother on the telephone agreeing what she should insist on at the Board meeting, and discussing how I might intervene, Lotte took me sightseeing among the old streets around the cathedral, then for a cruise on a lake steamer where we sat in the sun as the boat glided through the water and I became imbued with a self-indulgent content that was a million miles from what ought to have been on my mind. This, I thought, must be why international disputes can be resolved in Geneva when they seem totally intractable anywhere else.

'Here you can feel free,' she said, catching my mood exactly, then touching my hand to point out the hazily distant Alps. 'There also. In the mountains you feel free. A poem your father sent me said that. It is true.'

'And here you are a model citizen, so you can feel free?'

'Oh, là là.' She looked straight into my eyes, remonstrating, humorous, affectionate, all at once. 'You are a wicked man, Robert.'

'But you will be able to help with the "supplies", whatever they are?' I had no doubt there would be an element of illegality involved.'

'For you, I hope so.' She was still gazing at me, her head slightly on one side, her lips just parted, her eyes steady on mine. 'We should be on the same side, you and I, *meine Liebe*. We have the same objective.' She leant across and quickly kissed my cheek, her hair brushing my forehead. 'I am glad you have come.'

'So am I. Father should have warned me that I had a guardian angel.'

'Well,' she laughed, 'he likes to keep some things for himself.'

I laughed too, not forcedly either. We had each other's measure rather better now.

She was the right person to share the English Sunday papers with too, when we bought them later. The tabloids had gone to town on Tina Humphries. There were photographs of the clinic and strong suggestions that she was being held against her will. All the reports came to the same conclusion: if she was alive then Father probably was.

'This was your idea?' she enquired. 'I find it quite intelligent.'

'Alas, not mine,' I had to admit, and asked if I might phone Camilla to thank her.

She told me the leak had only just been in time. 'I've seen the story one paper killed on Saturday. It really let fly on Sir James's life and hard times: hard for his opponents, mainly. I suppose you've heard Consolidated made their bid official?'

'Van Rensburg told me. That must have been aimed at the Sunday papers too. With luck it'll have misfired.'

'And what have you been doing?' Camilla enquired. 'Has the lovely Dr Lohrey been looking after you?'

'I have to see the lawyers again tomorrow. We spent the day sightseeing.'

'So it isn't only your father who's an expert at reserving the hard times for other people,' she remarked acidly. 'Did you send a postcard, "Wish you were here" and so on?'

'I'll do that from Angola.' I brushed it off as lightly as I could and promised to phone when I reached Nairobi.

'This is your girlfriend?' Lotte asked.

'Not exactly. Was. She's also helping.'

'Well. I hope you do not tell her too many things. That would not be practic, *hein?*'

I could only agree. Lotte Lohrey's assistance was likely to be more valuable than Camilla's. But the thought gave me a distinct sense of *déjà vu*.

On Monday evening, with the lawyers having added Van Rensburg's name to the safe conduct, I left again for Africa. The supplies for Edmundo had been ordered. The medicines were simple: Switzerland is a country of pharmaceutical manufacturers. But how Lotte would obtain the other items was less clear. I wondered momentarily if the lawyers had included them in order to block the deal. 'There is nothing on this list that cannot be bought,' the young lawyer had commented. I had to hope he was right.

At Nairobi airport on Tuesday morning I found Mary Van Rensburg waiting with the company driver, Muthenge. She gave me an affectionate embrace – that burglary had counted as ten years' acquaintanceship – and told me that Patrick would not be back until the evening. He was taking a day flight.

'Poor man. Two nights in an airliner were the last thing he needed. But never mind, you can have a day off.'

'Has much happened?'

'You'll find a few changes,' she said noncommittally, and I was reminded of the historian Pliny's enduringly apposite phrase, 'Out of Africa always something new'.

The drive into Nairobi past the Game Park and out again to Karen stirred memories. Those violently eventful few nights of my first visit, only two weeks distant in time yet now indelibly etched into my past, made this seem like a homecoming. Some houses where I have stayed as a weekend guest have been forgotten almost within hours. The homestead at Karen, with its view across the forest towards the green knuckles of the Ngong Hills and the infinity of the African landscape, would be with me forever.

Over breakfast the good-natured, broad-smiling major domo Ambrose was noticeably absent and we were served by another of the staff.

'We had to sack Ambrose,' Mary said. 'He was in it up to the neck. You remember the African police inspector? That man was smart. Put the finger on Ambrose and two clerks from the office and arrested all three. Then suddenly, just as we might have been getting somewhere, everything went quiet. The cases were what they call "mentioned" in court on Friday and the men released on bail. Someone high up must have taken an interest. No normal thief gets bail.'

'Did you discover what was stolen?' I had a shrewd idea, but wanted confirmation.

'Documents.' Mary glanced round to check that the servants had left us. 'Patrick says he'll explain as soon as he's back. The important one was to do with breaking sanctions against Rhodesia.'

I blinked, the after-effects of the overnight flight competing with confusion at this news to disorient me. There had been absolutely nothing illegal about Father's diamond consortium; but trading with Rhodesia during the years of the settler government's Unilateral Declaration of Independence was a different matter.

'Was Father sanctions-busting?' I couldn't believe he would have laid himself open to criminal prosecution at home.

'I'm sorry, Robert. I don't know the technicalities. Patrick left you a note.' She passed me an unaddressed envelope from beside her plate. Inside was a short and laboriously written letter. 'He's only able to use his left hand,' she said. 'He's been extraordinarily brave about forcing himself to do things.'

The letter read: 'Dear Robert, Afraid this ruckus is partly my fault. Will go with you to Angola as promised. Regards P.V.R.' He had added a postscript. 'Ask Mary for anything you want.'

I showed her the note and she nodded sadly. 'I won't try to stop him. He's chartered a plane to fly down to Zambia tomorrow, if they can get the clearances. You'd be in Angola on Thursday.'

'Not before?' Far too much could happen in two days.

'One thing I do insist on.' Mary's habitual calm could not conceal her apprehension. 'Patrick must have a night's sleep before you get there. He had to go to this Board meeting. But he'll be whacked when he gets back. He's only just out of hospital.'

I could hardly press the point, since Mother would otherwise have been without an ally.

When I telephoned her after breakfast she related what had happened, and if it reads rather like a scene from a soap opera I can only say that most hostile takeovers do. Certainly Frank Stainton's ambitions took him beyond the frontiers of normal behaviour until he was thwarted.

CHAPTER TWENTY-ONE

'Anne, my dear,' Frank Stainton declared sententiously as he welcomed her on the fourteenth floor, with Christianne in attendance like a cat watching a goldfish, wary of the water. 'This bid for the Trust involves countless professional advisers. We didn't want to worry you with listening to their views. Martin Comins from our merchant bankers is the one who matters and he is here.'

'The man who matters,' she responded tartly, stung by his condescension, 'is my husband.' She had been infuriated enough to discover that a preliminary meeting with the accountants, lawyers and brokers had already taken place. Every director had been present and Frank's excuse that it had to be held before the stock markets opened hadn't been worth a puff at a bowl of porridge.

'Of course, Anne, of course. But in Jim's continued absence decisions have to be made.' This had become his ritual self-justification. 'The Board cannot simply stand aside from a bid. The shareholders expect leadership. So does the market.'

'If you need leadership you should concentrate on bringing Jim back.'

Stainton recoiled as if a snake had struck at him. Bob was right, she thought, Jim's ransom and the takeover bid are enmeshed with each other. He had also explained that although Jardine had encountered difficulties over a suspension on Friday, he might succeed today. 'Anyway, what is happening on the market?' she demanded.

Looking at his watch enabled Stainton to recover his poise. 'Nothing as yet,' he said. 'The Stock Exchange is only just opening. I imagine the Trust's price will be marked up in view of the bid.'

'Not as much as it would be if Jim were back.'

That was the line she and Bob had agreed on. But she needed allies. That was why she had beseeched Patrick to come from Nairobi, and why she had spoken to Lord Watson the night before with uncharacteristic sharpness. If he did not support her she would expose him. There was a dark side to Arthur's career and she knew most of the story, save one detail: how on earth Jim had been able to intervene successfully after Arthur confessed he was being blackmailed. By whatever means, Jim had retrieved the photographs taken through the ceiling of a hotel room in Moscow during trade talks, and the knighthood had followed, eased with a nominal £50,000 donation to Party funds. If Jim went down then she was determined that Arthur, ex-Cabinet Minister and Peer of the Realm, would go down too.

All this passed through her mind as Stainton stood by the Board-room door, still taut with anger at being admonished in front of Christianne.

'They're waiting for you,' he said shortly, and led the way in, introducing only the merchant banker, a well fed, sleek-haired man of about fifty with small, dark eyes, who had once or twice been a guest at Godstow anyway.

'A pleasure to meet you again, Lady Hartman.' Comins inclined his body in a slight bow instead of trying to shake hands across the table.

Van Rensburg rose to his feet awkwardly and indicated the vacant chair next to his. She noticed both his wrists were bandaged and he had been unable to fasten his shirt cuffs. He never looked comfortable in a City suit anyhow. As she sat down beside him he said underneath his breath:

'Never imagined you hadn't been asked to the first meeting. But don't worry . . .' He stopped speaking as the noise of the others sitting down subsided.

After calling the meeting to order formally, Arthur Watson began reading the minutes of the previous one, finally reaching the business of the day.

'We are here to consider an offer from Consolidated Diamond Concessions, and whether we should recommend the shareholders to accept or reject it.' He gave Anne a cautious nod. 'Perhaps for Lady Hartman's benefit Mr Comins would summarize the conclusions of our earlier meeting.'

The banker spoke for a quarter of an hour, principally about the relative values of the two companies' assets and profits.

As Anne listened she realized that, as she had feared, the entire exposition was centred not on the desirability of the takeover, merely whether the price being offered was adequate. Consolidated had acquired fifteen per cent of the stock during Friday's confused trading. They had been quick to exploit the news of

Jim's death and if they succeeded she had no doubt he would be cast out into the wilderness. How would that affect the ransom? She was terrified that the rebels might cease to care whether he lived or died.

'Consolidated's offer,' Comins was recapitulating, 'is one of their shares for each of the Trust's plus 100p in cash. They closed on Friday at 340 and 368 respectively. Superficially it is attractive. But it puts a substantially lower value on the Trust than before Sir James's unhappy disappearance.' He looked around the assembled group urbanely, his eyes finally resting on Anne. 'Nor does it take account of the major mining deals Sir James had in prospect. Both the accountants and the brokers feel that if those could be worked into our forecast they would justify holding out for a higher offer.'

'Could you complete those deals, Patrick?' Stainton asked. The question was doubly loaded, Anne realized. If Van Rensburg could not, then a higher offer was unjustifiable and they should yield to Consolidated. If he could, it was tantamount to saying the Trust could manage without Jim. Stainton had wasted no time laying it on the line. She stayed silent, wondering how Patrick would answer. He had his left forearm resting on the table and was mechanically exercising his fingers, slowly clenching and unclenching them, as if on a physiotherapist's orders. She imagined he was doing so as a distraction from his embarrassment.

'My political contacts aren't a patch on Jim's,' he said gruffly. 'Don't begin to compare. Let's face it, the whole diamond selling concept was more political than technical.'

'So who else could deliver?' Carl Hoffman demanded. The New York bank whose interests he represented had given him clear instructions. He had been straight with Anne when she rang him at his hotel last night. 'Sure, Lady Hartman. Frank Stainton met me personally at Heathrow. He has his objectives. We have ours.' She had only realized in the nick of time that he did not know about the ransom and presumed that Jim was dead. 'Jesus.' He was startled out of his composure, though insistent that he had to answer to his superiors. 'I guess they'd be sympathetic. Hell, who wouldn't be?' But she was left uncertain which way his vote would go.

'My husband could deliver,' she cut in. She was learning how to hold her own.

'Unfortunately,' Stainton remarked, 'our reaction to this bid has to be immediate.'

'Tell me, Mr Comins,' she demanded, 'what value would the markets put on my husband's return?'

The banker pursed his fat lips, making him look more than ever like a face painted on a balloon. He's cornered, she thought. This can't cost him his job like the others, but he'd still rather fudge the answer.

'Difficult to quantify, Lady Hartman. His safe return would unquestionably be reflected in the price. The sense of relief might well drive the shares above their original level of 452.'

Anne was busy with her pocket calculator. Jim could do this kind of thing in his head. She couldn't, but she knew the formula: the capitalization of the company was the number of shares issued multiplied by their stock market price. That price had dropped from 452 to 368.

'What you are telling us, Mr Comins,' she said, looking up from the silvery display of the calculator, 'is that my husband's market value is eighty-four million pounds.' She turned on Arthur Watson. 'Why have the underwriters so far offered only five million dollars?'

'Underwriters cannot be pressured,' Stainton snapped defensively, ignoring the Chairman. 'They pay the minimum and they pay in their own good time. Anyone who's claimed for a lost umbrella knows that.'

'Then I have a second question. Who is responsible for the false report of my husband's death?'

'We should possibly consider the two issues separately.' Watson tried to defuse the confrontation.

'On the contrary, Arthur.' Anne spoke with spirit. 'The report could hardly have been better timed to assist this bid.'

'So your son Robert had the kindness to inform me.' Stainton cut in caustically, his right eyelid beginning to be afflicted by its nervous tic. 'Before he tipped off the papers about Miss Humphries.'

'Well, he may be right.' Whether it was Robert or Camilla scarcely mattered. The point was that the lie about Jim's death had been laid. She glanced around the gathering. 'I might as well tell you all that I do not like what is going on.'

'That's a bit steep, Lady Hartman,' Hugh Clarke remarked in his plummy accent. 'Are you suggesting there's been some kind of conspiracy?'

'Perhaps you would like to prove that there hasn't? Who made the so-called identification of my husband's body?'

'Poor old Roeyen,' Stainton said, his sympathetic tone belied by the vibration of his eyelid, which appeared to be continually winking. 'We now learn he was beaten up and only released in exchange for identifying some unknown white man's corpse as Sir James's. He is recuperating in Belgium. I spoke to him on Sunday and he cannot be blamed.'

'That story stank,' Van Rensburg commented. 'Hyenas don't

disfigure a body, they tear it to pieces and scatter the bones.' He saw the horror on Anne's face. 'Sorry. It's a fact, though. If anyone had asked me I'd have told them.'

'But it exonerates you for the Press release, I suppose?' Anne remarked to Stainton. 'Not in my view. You should be concentrating on getting Jim back.'

'For better or worse,' Stainton's tone was a fraction higher pitched than normal too, 'the facts speak for themselves. Sir James agreed on a ransom procedure two years ago. It can hardly be considered conspiratorial to adopt the procedure now.'

'None the less,' Ramesh Gupta, the Asian director, made his first contribution to the debate, 'it is most adverse for the morale of other executives in the group if the Chief Executive can be held prisoner and not rescued.'

'Gentlemen,' Watson interrupted, 'can we address ourselves to the subject of the meeting? Given the hope of Sir James's return, do we recommend acceptance of a bid, or do we advise shareholders against and prepare a defence?'

'Against,' Van Rensburg snapped, not waiting for a vote. Anne blessed Patrick for keeping his word. Of the seven working directors only he and Gupta were prepared to risk their jobs by opposing Frank. The third man on her side, though only if it came to his casting vote, was Arthur Watson.

With her threat overshadowing his mind, Watson surveyed the other directors, sensitive as always to the mood of a meeting. Stainton was smiling benevolently at Ferguson, who was visibly nervous. Clarke was tapping his fingernails on a scratch pad; Hans Bertels, the German who ran the hotels, remained impassive; Jack Cunningham had voted against Stainton's aims last time, but being home based was vulnerable. At a quick reckoning Watson decided at least five of the ten present would be under pressure to follow Stainton's lead, which meant his own vote might not swing the balance, at least not if they followed the Board's normal procedure of a show of hands, where the nature of each director's vote was evident to all the others. He would have to employ a stratagem.

'In view of the extreme importance of this decision,' he said with the deliberate pomposity of his political days, 'and the need for each of you to express his true opinion without fear or favour, I propose a secret ballot. Would anyone objecting kindly raise their hands.'

No one did. If you put certain issues the right way, they were as impossible to counter as motions deploring prostitution.

However Stainton knew what a secret vote implied, and the beneficence faded from his expression as he looked round to rally support. Clarke, Cunningham, Ferguson and Gupta all gave tiny facial indications of agreement. Bertels, emerging from his cocoon-like stolidity, actually nodded. Anne, sitting tensely upright, looked at no one, as though afraid she had called the wrong card.

'Then it is to be a secret vote?' Watson enquired rhetorically. 'Excellent.' He took a sheet of white paper and carefully tore it into ten strips, taking one himself and pushing the rest to Clarke to pass on. 'You only have to indicate either "For" accepting the Consolidated bid or "Against" and then fold your slip.'

They all obeyed, Van Rensburg writing awkwardly with his left hand, Ferguson trying to shield his decision from Anne's sight, Bertels making firm capital letters with no attempt to conceal his 'For'.

Anne herself saw Patrick's 'Against' out of the corner of her eye, printed the same on her slip and creased it carefully down the middle before passing it across the polished table top. She was unable to stop her hand from trembling and was pleased to notice Stainton's eyelid still fluttering.

Watson solemnly gathered the folded votes together into a small heap. There were nine of them, excluding his own. He was less worried than Anne supposed. She had forgotten that on the last occasion Patrick Van Rensburg had been absent and so his own allegiance had been crucial. This time the most he could achieve was an impasse, if the voting was four to five, thereby forcing a second round. He had honoured his obligations by promoting the secret ballot.

'No spoiled papers on this occasion, I hope,' he joked and began sorting the crisp, thick slips into two lots. They made tiny scratching noises on the polished surface as he moved them.

The number of 'For' votes grew from two to three. A solitary pair were against. Four remained unscrutinized. Anne watched, unable to believe that the Board members would not have voted as the figures and their consciences must direct.

Slowly Watson unfolded another slip and placed it with those 'For'. On the next he recognized Anne's handwriting and it went 'Against'. Two remained. She needed both to win.

The tension was broken by a soft knock on the door. Watson ceased unfolding the next slip and they all looked around as Christianne entered.

'Excuse me,' she said to Stainton, 'the company broker is on the line. He says it is most urgent. Will you speak with him?'

Stainton stood up, controlling himself, and pointed at the extension on a table in the corner. 'Why didn't you put it straight through?'

'Normally I do not.'

Anne watched her face, uncertain what exactly she saw there. A kind of triumph? By her announcement Christianne had made it impossible for Frank to conceal what the broker said.

Stainton listened, and spoke in an undertone which they couldn't hear. Then he put the phone down, came back and stood behind his chair.

'Well, Anne,' he said, 'your son has succeeded in interfering with the company's business again. Gentlemen, the Quotations Committee at the Stock Exchange has suspended trading in the shares of Hartman Trust. Whether this precludes individual shareholders from dealing direct with Consolidated is another question.'

There was complete silence, during which Watson very deliberately gathered all the voting slips together into one pile, crumpled them into a ball and thrust them into his coat pocket.

'In the circumstances,' he said, 'the Board cannot give advice other than that shareholders wait for the resumption of normal trading.'

There was a general murmur of assent. Salving their consciences, she thought disgustedly.

'And now,' Watson suggested, 'does the Board wish to consider the question of Sir James's ransom?'

Again there was assent.

'Then I will take advice from the negotiator.' Stainton left the room without apology. Ten minutes later he returned. 'The underwriters have agreed to increase their offer to eight million,' he announced, as if expecting credit for the achievement. 'They would like to know,' he directed his gaze at Anne, unsmiling and coldly vengeful, 'if your son has been negotiating separately for Sir James's release. If that is the case, they may reconsider.' He paused, and added sourly, 'That kind of thing would be typical of him.'

'Unless you withdraw that remark, Frank, I shall leave.'

She had been about to pretend ignorance when that last attack stung her beyond endurance. She only knew the outline of Robert's scheme, but it was courageous if nothing else. Furthermore, Patrick had approved.

A murmur of embarrassment came from the others and Watson raised his hands in protest. During the silence that followed she wondered if she had gone too far. But secrecy was crucial. Bob had emphasized that. She caught Van Rensburg's eye across the table, saw the hard set of his mouth, and knew he was as furious with Frank as she was. If only they knew whether or not Bob's proposal had finally been accepted.

Edmundo brought the message himself, his bodyguards slouchingly alert behind him as he drew aside the flap of the tent.

Inside Hartman was lying on his narrow bed, a dirty towel clutched in his hand, the sweat gleaming on his skin. Earlier this morning he had felt better and had joined Makarov for their breakfast of maize meal porridge and tea. Tina's leaving without apparent result had made him dispirited; the sordid ritual of the execution parades had continued every evening, as if to mark another day of failure, though both Makarov and he had come to doubt if any Cubans were in fact being shot. He had grown to like Makarov, who could be monosyllabically humorous in German. They were both the same kind of man. After the meal they had been marched to their separate areas, a precaution against attempted rescues, so Struben said. Then towards mid-morning, with the persistence of an incoming tide, the fever began to return. But he was still in command of himself. He swung his legs slowly round and sat awkwardly upright on the side of the low bed.

'I have news, Sir Hartman. Good news.' Edmundo was ebullient, as though pleased for his prisoner's sake.

'Yes?'

'A man is coming to see me. One who is not afraid. One who will not lie to me.'

'You mean they are going to pay?' Hartman had no strength for the constant circumlocutions.

'Yes, Hartman. They will pay.' Edmundo heaved himself onto the only chair, a folding canvas affair, disregarding the clothes hung over it. The chair sagged under his weight. He leant forward, his fingers intertwined, his forearms resting on his thighs. As an attempt to bring himself down to the same level it was only partially successful. 'They will pay and also there are medicines I want. Things like that. If he brings those things safe they are worth more than money.'

'You mean I can go? I'm glad to hear it.' The words were incisive, but the edge had gone out of Hartman's voice. He would have been shocked to hear himself.

'Also, my friend, you will make an interview before you go, for the television.' He dismissed Hartman's expression of incredulity. 'They will come, they come when I say. We know you, Hartman, and we like the world to know also.'

'No one cares about Africa, General. No one cares what I do there. It's only business. What d'you expect me to say; that I'm interested in diamonds?' He wiped his forehead with the towel, and the movement made the bed sway beneath him.

'There is time.' Edmundo became vague. 'This man will not come for three days. You can think. About Rhodesia, about your consortium, about people you work with. When he comes we will decide.'

290

'And who is this negotiator?'

'This man?' Edmundo slapped his thigh, his great palm cracking against his trousers, as if enjoying a tremendous joke. 'You know him. You know him well. He is your son, Sir Hartman.' He raised himself to his feet, stooping a little to avoid brushing his head against the sloping roof of the tent. 'If he comes with those things I want, then you can go. We do not negotiate, my friend. We have agreed.'

'Not in my name. He has no . . .'

'How do you pay me, Hartman?' Edmundo laughed good-naturedly. 'You have dollars here? Under this bed? Shall I look now? Or you write a cheque? No, no. We have arranged these things. Let them say.'

When he had gone Hartman remained huddled on the side of the bed for some minutes, his chin sunk in his hands, feeling the drops of sweat trickle down over his fingers, and staring at the trampled earth on which the tent was pitched. Occasionally he muttered to himself. Then he shook his head, grunted and with an effort managed to stand up and move to the chair. His briefcase was on the folding camp table. He opened it and began to make notes.

'I must ask you to apologize, Frank.' Watson insisted. 'We've all been placed under strain by these events. I am sure Anne accepts that, even though she has been worst affected.'

'My apologies.' Stainton's brusque minimum spoke for itself. 'However, it is a fact that the underwriters stress we must maintain only one channel of communication.'

'I hope they're right.' She kept as calm and noncommittal as she could, while Frank glared at her. The trouble with him, she thought, is that at heart he is a jumped-up little dictator. He never did like being crossed, and now he's in charge he can't stand the idea. Behind the façade of that expensive suit and his every hair in place appearance, there's just an old-fashioned megalomaniac. Robert's right; he will destroy the Trust because everyone will grow to hate him.

'If there's no other business, Arthur, I suggest you close this meeting.' Stainton began collecting his papers.

'The chair will decide when this meeting concludes.'

'Then it can decide without me. Some of us have work to do.' He picked up the folders and walked to the door, turning to speak to Clarke. 'Come on, Hugh.'

Both Clarke and Ferguson shifted in their seats, making as if to follow.

'Sit down, for Christ's sake,' Van Rensburg said. 'Try to keep up a few appearances.'

Stainton waited a few seconds longer, then left the room, neither slamming the door nor closing it gently.

'Well,' Watson said. 'If there is no other business perhaps we can agree a date for the next meeting.' He was remarkably unruffled.

Afterwards Van Rensburg took her to tea at the Savoy. They sat on the deep sofas and talked quietly.

'Is Frank double-crossing us?' she asked. 'It sounds a ridiculous word, but I can't think of any other. Robert insists that he is. Apparently he bought two million pounds' worth of Consolidated shares last week, and he is not a millionaire.'

'I'm not one of your City slickers, Anne. I'm a geologist.' He talked about other things for a while, and then said, 'Men as shrewd as Frank only borrow that kind of money if they stand to make a profit fast. If we'd recommended acceptance of Consolidated's offer their shares would have risen and he would have cleaned up.' He stopped talking, as though regretful of the implications.

'Surely that's illegal?' She found most City manoeuvres confusing, but this one was clear enough, except for one aspect.

'I'm not sure if it's a criminal offence. Must be actionable in a civil court though, his failing to declare an interest, I mean.'

'Why should he take the risk? What would happen after the takeover?'

'Must have thought they'd keep him on as Chief Executive. An illusion, I'd say. Who'd trust him?' He checked himself. 'Completely unproven, all this, Anne. One word of it and he could be suing us.'

'At any rate, he's stalemated for the moment.' She shifted to the subject that was more intensely on her mind. 'Patrick, I'm worried about Bob going to Angola.'

'Don't be.' He grinned at her, flexing his fingers as though the remedial exercise was a promise. 'I'll see he doesn't get into trouble. Go with him myself.'

Van Rensburg gave me his account of the Board meeting on Wednesday, as the dusty yellow brown eternity of the Serengeti plains unrolled below us on our way towards Zambia.

'Miles and miles of bloody Africa.' He squinted down through the small plane's window. 'Wouldn't want to live or die anywhere else either.' He suddenly pointed. 'Hey, the migration's started.'

Ahead of us, spread across the country, were unending columns of what might have been black ants streaming westwards, but were in fact wildebeeste and zebra, miniaturized by our height above them, the occasional clouds casting puffy shadows across their path.

'Same route, every year, every century. A million and a half of them heading for the permanent water as the plains dry up. The biggest shareholders in Africa, going by instinct to the dependable dividend. Except that man is taking over the land and it's a miracle the dividend's still available. They'll drop foals on the way, drown in the rivers, lions'll take the stragglers. Still safer to move with the herd.' He ceased looking down and faced me across the narrow aisle of the cabin. 'Your father got rich by never following the rest. But he could smell where the water was and pitch up there first. Except that this time he overshot. D'you seriously believe you can talk Edmundo round?'

'He's given us a safe conduct. You said he was a friend?'

'Used to be one. Years ago when the liberation movements were based in Dar. Edmundo was one of the few who knew what he was doing. But he'll be on his own side, not anyone else's.'

'Mary thought he must be connected with your burglary. She told me Father had a Rhodesian involvement. Were there some documents?'

'It was a calculated risk.' Van Rensburg gazed out of the window, shading his eyes against the glare, as though searching the landscape, then turned back to me. 'Smith's settler government needed foreign exchange after its Unilateral Declaration of Independence. They gave us title to an emerald concession cheap. Whole thing was done through a Panamanian holding company. Officially the Trust only bought it when the UDI was over and the Africans came to power.'

The Rhodesian secession was fresh in my mind. Not its start, I was a schoolboy then, though Wilson's boast when he was prime minister that he would end it in 'weeks rather than months' stuck in everyone's memory. He had hated Smith and his government introduced the sanctions against trade with Rhodesia. None the less the UDI had lasted a decade and a half, only ending last year.

'I did still have the original prospector's report,' Van Rensburg went on. 'It's been missing since the burglary.'

I thought of the documents lying beneath his study curtain. By comparison with the scheme which they implied, a single emerald mine was a trinket. Would anyone care? On the other hand sanctions-breaking was a criminal offence. Was it possible that the raid in Van Rensburg's house had been staged to disguise what Moses the clerk had already taken? Or had he not stolen enough and been without an excuse for returning to the house legitimately?

'Sanctions-busting may have been criminal but the enthusiasm for prosecutions is bound to cool off. Are the Rhodesian reports worth sixty million dollars?'

'Could be. Your present government's been trying to nail the big oil companies. But they have too much muscle. The Trust would be about the right size, and Jim having been knighted while he was doing it would suit some people nicely. Honoured while breaking the law. A vindictive attorney could make a lot of play with that.'

Father was not the first, I reflected. Lord Kagan had been jailed for fraud and theft. Lord Brayley had died facing criminal charges of misappropriation. Father would be in distinguished company, if that was the word. None the less it was out of character for him to expose himself.

'I told you, Jim took a risk,' Van Rensburg said, adjusting his bulk in the small seat. 'He'd been planning a gem-selling consortium for years. Any production he could secure for the future, he bought. Consolidated was the eventual target, the lynchpin, whatever, you name it. With Consolidated under our belts, we had some chance of challenging De Beers, though that in itself would be like attacking Everest without oxygen. The margins were going to be bloody slim. You know what it's costing De Beers to keep the price steady in spite of the recession? Over a thousand million dollars in their stockpile and it's going up. All to restrict supply enough to maintain the price. Frankly, Robert, that's out of our league. Unless we had the thousand million output from Concession Twenty-Two and we stitched up our own selling consortium of African States. Then we could start to compete.'

I asked what made Concession Twenty-Two so special.

'Produces the high-quality crystals we call "close goods". Around 1910, people thought this area of Zaïre and Angola was going to be the world's largest source of diamonds. They reckoned the alluvial deposits spread among ancient river beds could cover 150,000 square miles. Probably does. Trouble is the stones are usually of poor colour, or awkwardly shaped; only good for industrial use. A lot has to be crushed into abrasive: Congo boart it's called. Concession Twenty-Two is the exception.'

'I wish I could see it.' The mine would probably be unspectacular, but it was still the prize that had cost Father his freedom.

'You will do,' he said. 'We're going there from Zambia. Can hardly flightplan to Edmundo's camp. We'll land at the Concession then push off again. Luckily I knew the manager years ago. He might just be civil, though God knows he has no reason to help your father out.'

So that was what we did, staying the night in the copper mining town of Ndola, at a local club which was trying hard to keep up appearances amid shortages.

'Can't get machinery spares here, let alone tomato sauce,' Van Rensburg commented over a somewhat Spartan meal in the club's ordered, old-fashioned and unashamedly colonial dining room. I felt as though I was eating on a period film set. In another twenty years this room would be a museum piece, if it survived.

At this moment, however, I was more concerned with our mission and raised the subject of the consortium, while our pilot, the same young captain who had been organizing the search for the Gulfstream, remained tactfully silent.

'Patrick,' I said, 'I have a proposition.'

'I'm listening.' He stopped talking about the copperbelt earning 98 per cent of Zambia's foreign exchange. 'What is it?'

'We've stopped Consolidated swallowing us up. If Father's in sufficiently good shape to appear in public the stock market will be reassured. Why don't we buy Concession Twenty-Two and launch this consortium?'

His eyes narrowed in surprise. 'Hell of a risk. Edmundo's boys have managed to stop a lot of the production getting out.'

'How much?'

'Consolidated admit to about half.'

'If Edmundo accepts one deal from me why shouldn't he accept another?'

'Reckon you can succeed where your father failed?'

'I think,' I said cautiously, 'that if you gave the technical direction and Father provided the figurehead for the shareholders we might pull it off.'

'Meaning you'd negotiate the contracts?' He was disbelieving. 'Fancy yourself as an Africanist, eh?'

'There are parallels with the Middle East in this situation. Don't misunderstand me, but both Father and you are an older generation than Edmundo.'

'If you'll excuse me,' the pilot cut in, seeming embarrassed, 'I've finished.' He got up to leave. Perhaps he had other things on his mind too. He had to get us safely into, and out of, an improvised camp airstrip which was not marked on any map. Edmundo had lost control of the airfield where Father had landed in the Gulfstream.

His departure disrupted the flow of ideas. 'Anyway,' I concluded, 'if I do hit it off with the rebels we can take it from there.'

'You still have Frank Stainton to outflank,' Van Rensburg remarked.

'Stainton will resign,' I said, not troubling to explain why. 'It's Father's health we have to worry about.'

'When we've rescued him. Let's not get too far ahead of the facts.'

Leaving Ndola the next morning, Thursday, we flew over an opencast copper mine, a huge, roughly terraced pit half a mile long, the adjacent high buildings of crushers and smelters incongruous among the scrub and trees, which otherwise stretched to a flat horizon.

'Fifteen hundred miles from any port,' Van Rensburg commented. 'Try that for size in Europe. You can't. Mining in Africa's a bloody miracle.'

Eventually, shortly before eleven, the pilot began a wide circling descent, and we saw Concession Twenty-Two diggings like mile-long paw marks scouring out an old riverbed around a central clearing, and away to one side the brown swathe of a landing strip. As we approached to touch down I saw a group of buildings to one side, single-storey bungalows and African huts.

'Bit like Rukanga,' I remarked, as the door was opened and the heat flooded in.

'Except for the product. The kimberlite here was located by a South African prospector in 1969 and never exploited because of the Independence war. Consolidated only started digging in 1977.'

Van Rensburg limped out down the step, I followed and when I straightened up, found myself looking into the muzzle of a rifle.

The soldiers, Africans in bush green uniforms, must have dashed up behind out of sight. Now they moved round into a half-circle, imprisoning us in the angle of the wing and fuselage. Van Rensburg very carefully lowered his briefcase to the dusty ground and raised both his hands. I did the same and a moment later the pilot joined us. For perhaps a minute there was silence, except for the engines ticking as they cooled. Then, cautiously, one of the men moved forward, ran his hands over our bodies in a search for weapons and went past me towards the open door. The next thing I knew he was jabbing my backside with his gun and shouting orders. The others fell aside to let us past and we were marched towards a truck parked at the end of the strip.

'Hope to Christ they leave the plane alone,' Van Rensburg muttered to the pilot, but I didn't catch the reply. The two of us had to help heave him into the back of the truck, while he tried to get leverage from his bandaged hands, unable to sustain his own considerable weight. Inside the truck we were forced to sit unceremoniously on the floor, while two of the soldiers balanced themselves upright against the tailgate and the driver careered away, bumping and juddering over ruts as though the devil was after him. Eventually we braked violently to a halt and heard an English voice shouting. A head appeared: a wrinkled, leather-dark old bushwhacker's face, a faded khaki bush hat shading its eyes.

'The name's Jackson,' the man said in a northern accent. 'Harry Jackson. Sorry about the roughnecking, I'll have you out in a moment. There's a bit of a scare on. Stupid bastards thought you were spies. The army's mounting some kind of sweep against the rebels and they're all as jumpy as cats.'

Next an African officer's head came into view, scrutinized us and gave the order to let us go. We climbed out, dirt now streaking our shirts and Van Rensburg's bandages filthy from trying to support himself against the truck's jolting.

'You got my radio message?' Van Rensburg asked.

'An hour ago. Lucky for you I did.' Jackson's eyes were mistrustful. 'You came to refuel?'

'To land and put in our own fuel,' the pilot, Andy, corrected him. 'We're carrying it in cans.'

'Just as well. We couldn't have sold you any. As I said, there's a big search operation. The rebels have captured some fellow and they want him back.'

'We work for the Hartman Trust,' Van Rensburg remarked, and I hoped that might stimulate Jackson to reveal if the captive was Father. 'In case you hadn't heard, your firm's trying to take us over.'

Jackson whistled crudely. 'One for the book, eh? Right bloody turn-up. So what are you here for?'

'En route to Luanda. Had to stop somewhere.'

'We heard Hartman copped it in an aircrash.'

Evidently the army activity was not on Father's behalf. It must be to rescue the Russian.

'That's what left us open,' Van Rensburg admitted, gently rubbing his wrists, which must have been painful. I noticed he did not specifically lie, merely concurred in Jackson's misapprehension.

'Well, I'll be damned.' Jackson seemed genuinely amazed and his attitude softened. His life out in this wilderness must have been pretty lonely at times. 'If you'd like a meal while you're here you'll be welcome.'

Van Rensburg looked at his watch, then at the pilot.

'Ought to be getting on,' he said.

'Have a quick look around, any road,' Jackson suggested. He clearly wanted a chance to talk. 'The sorting room's over there. Take a gander at how we're all making our fortunes!'

The sorting room was a shed, equipped with a few long trestle tables. A single African employee, an obvious veteran too, stood up when we entered. Jackson introduced us and the man pointed out various piles of stones, arranged in heaps on sheets of slightly grubby white paper. To me they seemed not only extremely small stones, but not like diamonds at all. Far from catching the light they were opaque, as though coated in a dull lacquer, and some had a definitely orange tinge.

'They usually do the preliminary sorting at the mine – saves trouble later on,' Van Rensburg began to explain; then stopped talking as he appreciated the paucity of the sight. 'This is a day's take, is it?' he asked.

'A day's!' Jackson laughed. 'This is last month's.'

'But . . .' for the first time I saw Van Rensburg seriously taken aback. He borrowed a black plastic-mounted eye lens from the sorter and began scrutinizing the heaps of stones, which were neatly divided according to either shape or quality, for myself I could not tell which. Finally he unscrewed the lens from his eye and faced Jackson. 'You haven't a decent diamond there,' he said accusingly. 'Where are the gemstones?'

'Seized in the last ALF raid. Filched by the workforce. In Zaïre most likely. Security is impossible. The men here are all Lunda and agin the government. We used to export quality stones three years ago. There were more then too. As we've dug deeper into the yellow ground, they've got fewer. Either that or the thieving's cleverer.'

Van Rensburg was staring at him as if he had just learnt that the Bible was a fraud. 'This is all you're getting out? Only industrials?'

'It's you should be laughing,' Jackson said. 'The geologists say the stones are there, but you try digging new areas under these conditions. If Consolidated's directors weren't afraid of the balance sheet they'd shut the mine. Your boys should be laughing all the way to the bank.' He shook his head mordantly. 'Bloody hopeless. None too healthy at this minute either. If I were you I would be getting on.' He jerked his thumb at a group of soldiers running past in the distance. 'They're all bloody hyped up. Next thing you know they'll seize your plane.'

CHAPTER TWENTY-TWO

When we were airborne again and heading towards the ALF's headquarters the implications of Jackson's remarks began to sink in.

'Reckon the army's going to clear Edmundo's lot out of here once and for all,' he had said.

If he was right we were flying into a battle zone and would have very little time to bring Father out.

We had hardly been going twenty minutes when the pilot, Andy, began to have trouble. He called Patrick forward into the co-pilot's seat and they began poring over maps. I moved up and crouched behind them in the plane's tiny aisle.

'The data on these charts is pretty sparse, Mr Hartman.' Andy twisted his head round momentarily, then pointed at the thick bush ahead. 'We could easily miss their strip. I'd like to call them on the radio.'

'We could tune in to their transmitter and use it like a navigational beacon,' Van Rensburg explained.

'We've been ordered not to use the radio,' I said. 'The Swiss lawyer was emphatic.' He must have known that an attack was imminent and added the crate of medical supplies we had in the back of the aircraft to the ransom list at the last moment.

'There's no option, Sir.' Andy reminded me that he was the captain. 'We're due overhead in another sixteen minutes. If there's no sign of the place I can afford fuel for half an hour's search. After that we have to return to Zambia.'

'Let's leave it as long as we can.' I didn't understand the technicalities and I had a gut feeling that we ought to stick to Edmundo's orders. There were going to be problems enough without antagonizing him.

The landscape slid slowly by beneath: endless trees, scrub and low rocky hills, empty of civilization's imprint except for occasional meandering dirt tracks, incoherent in their directions. This was a hell of an area to become involved with, even if to Edmundo it was sacred territory. I was wondering what he would be like and watching our slow progress over the bush when I realized that a series of little holes was appearing in the top of the wing, close to the trailing edge. Three sprouted from the white-painted metal with effortless rapidity. I was still puzzled by them when the first bullet to hit the cabin cracked up through the floor with a noise like a whip, tore a gash in the upholstery of the seat in front of me and expended itself with a splintering thud in the folded table, which fell open. In the same moment the plane tilted violently to the right, my briefcase slid into the aisle and as I clawed for support the engines roared and we began to climb as well as turn.

'Strap yourself in,' Van Rensburg shouted. 'Stay where you are.'

An eternity later – perhaps two minutes – Andy ceased his manoeuvres, levelled out and beckoned me forward.

'Ten thousand feet should be safe. I'm sorry, Mr Hartman, either we make radio contact, fly overhead the strip and then descend, or we return to the concession. I can't tell yet if a fuel tank's been hit. If one has we must land.'

'Who shot at us?'

'How the hell should I know?' He caught his breath. 'Sorry, Sir.'

'Could be either side,' Van Rensburg commented. 'Bloody bad luck. I'm going to call Edmundo's boys.' He clamped on a spare headset and I could hear him speak, repeating the same phrase over and over again until he had a reply. It must have been favourable. Andy immediately banked the plane to the left and fiddled with a dial, to line up a pointer. From the look of it we were considerably off course, too, because it was another ten minutes before a wide clearing came into view, though with no runway marked. The pointer on the dial suddenly swung right round.

'We're there,' he said and began a wide circle. Below us a puff of orange smoke erupted at one edge of the clearing, swelling into a thick, lazily drifting plume.

'Obliging of them,' Van Rensburg said. 'Let's get down.'

Andy throttled back, descended rapidly and came in over the trees to bump to a halt on the dry, patchy grass.

A man in a khaki bush shirt ran out, waving us to taxi towards him. The engines had hardly stopped before a crowd of African soldiers started pushing the plane into cover at the side of the clearing. We emerged into the now familiar heat to be greeted short-temperedly by the officer, who I guessed must be the one Tina had met.

'The name's Struben,' he said. 'I was on the radio. You want to give our position away?'

300

'No,' Van Rensburg said relaxedly, 'just find it.'

'Let's hope the Angolan air force doesn't. You all three coming?'

'I must check the plane.' Andy was eyeing the wing apprehensively, though no leakage of fuel was visible. 'We were shot at.'

'Where?' Struben was as tense as a spring.

'Roughly thirty miles north.'

'Not us.' He swore. 'We'd better go. I have a bakkie to take you to the General.' He spoke hurriedly to the Africans, then assured Andy he would have assistance. 'I'll come for you later.'

The 'bakkie' proved to be a pick-up in which we jolted over a rutted track, the three of us squeezed into the front seat, while Struben ejected occasional remarks that mostly required no answer.

'I give you some advice for free. The General knows what he's doing. He's reliable. Sir James had the cat by the tail with him. Couldn't have got him more wrong.'

'How is my father?' I demanded.

'The fever's bad.' He glanced sideways at me as he swung round a bend. 'Sir James is old and he's ill. I do not like to say this, man, but he is no better than an oxygen thief.'

'What do you mean?' I didn't like the sound of it.

'In the war he did great things, maybe. But today he is past it.' He enunciated his words with deliberation, although he was driving. 'He will have to do what the General wants.'

I did not reply. There was no point arguing with an underling and I was recalling Tina's story about Edmundo shooting out the clockface to stop the time. How reliable was 'reliable'?

When we reached the camp barely a mile away the South African took us straight to Edmundo's headquarters, a substantial single-storey building of mud, brick and thatch, more skilfully sited under the trees than I expected from Tina Humphries' description. At the entrance we were searched by two well armed guards, but Struben then unexpectedly ordered Van Rensburg to wait outside. He went ahead of me through the door to announce, saluting, 'Mr Hartman, Sir.'

The interior was one huge room in which a European camera crew were setting up equipment and lights. Seated behind a long trestle table covered with blankets in place of a cloth, and looking like a television personality anxious for his chat show to start, was a burly African in bush uniform who could only be Edmundo.

The silver sub-machinegun, glitteringly absurd, lay close to his hand, while the kind of ashtrays brewery companies give away were ranged along the rest of the otherwise bare blankets. The backdrop was a huge flag, on which a flaming red sun rose out of a green ground, outlining a sable antelope's tall curved horns.

Edmundo rose lazily to his feet and reached across the table to grasp my hand. 'So, my friend,' he declared in a cheerful voice, 'Daniel is come into the den. I like that. I like men who are not afraid.' He grinned and then suddenly bellowed at the camera crew. 'How much more do I wait? Two hours? Two days?'

'We'll have it fixed soon, Sir. We'll have it fixed real good.' The unit director, an American from his voice, sounded frightened. I didn't blame him.

'Media!' Edmundo made the one word stand for a fistful of invective. 'What I like to tell you, Hartman, is you people from the West are crazy. You believe this camera. But the men who work it know nothing, less even than an unborn child.' He roared with laughter. 'Okay, this time they may hear the truth with this thing. I make it easy for them. Too easy.' His explanation ceased as abruptly as it had begun. 'Sit down, take a chair.'

I fetched a canvas stool and faced him, the sub-machinegun like a talisman between us, while he began a near-monologue.

'Sir Hartman gave me this one.' He fingered the gun affectionately. 'Pity he is ill. He was to sit here.' He mimed welcoming someone beside him. 'You will speak for him.' He stared straight at me. 'You will tell America and Britain why you are here, you will say what is happening.'

'Like the bomb in the antelope's head?' Somehow the reaction was instinctive. I was at the end of my search and I wanted the lesser mysteries out of the way first.

'You know that thing?' A trace of respect tinged Edmundo's voice.

'Why kill the pilot?' I demanded, the disfigured bodies in the fly-blown mortuary vivid in my mind. 'What had he done?'

'He was marked to die.' Edmundo made a gesture of regret. 'In Africa we know those ones.'

The mysticism, the hint of witchcraft, carried a kind of conviction. However, I was determined to drag our negotiation on to a Western level of logic if I could. 'But you planned the bomb in advance?'

'For Sir Hartman. What I like to tell you is this, my friend. Your father came to trick me. He was making a deal with Luanda. He has planned to deliver me to my enemies.'

'Are you sure?' Father was capable of great duplicity, but betraying an African leader would hardly be good for future business.

'Our friends have told us.'

'So you made the bomb?'

'In your country what do they tell in newspapers every time? Crashes with planes!' He laughed uproariously. 'That is a thing they like too much. So I tell my friends, we will make this for them. Maybe they find the other things he is doing. Maybe they do not. When he is dead it is all the same.'

'But he stayed with you. He wasn't on board.'

'Okay,' Edmundo made an expansive gesture. 'When he said he would go, then I thought, "We will put that bomb, we will put it now."' He touched the silver gun. 'If your father did not give me this to scare shit out of Cubans, if your father did not stay to talk, then he was a dead man. He came to us. We did not kidnap him. Now we like the world to know him. So he must confess. And we want money, my friend, and we want also those comrades we have lost.' The rhetoric suddenly dropped out of his voice and he asked with anxious simplicity, 'Will they come?'

Edmundo's shopping list had not been simple. The rest of the 'supplies' were men of his who had been captured by the Angolan government and in exchange for whom he had been offering the Russian colonel, Makarov. The only acceptable intermediary in the exchange was the International Red Cross, who had their headquarters in Geneva. Perhaps he thought that while I was there I could talk them into hurrying the process up by pleading that my father's life was also at stake. The lawyer had been vague, probably because he had failed. At all events, I had handed over this delicate task to Lotte Lohrey. When I had phoned her from Zambia last night she had indicated that a Red Cross plane might come tomorrow, which was Friday. Exactly how she had achieved this I was praying Edmundo would not ask. The arrangement was laced with danger anyway, since it involved him being at his airstrip at a given time, and open to attack.

'Tomorrow, God willing,' I said.

'When? What hour?' For someone unconcerned with time he could be very precise.

'They will send a message. That's all I know.'

He nodded and smiled. 'I like you. I think you are an honest man.'

'Will you accept eight million dollars for my father? I can tell you, General, there is a possibility his company may be taken over, and if that happens the new owners won't even want him back.'

The argument had a lot of force: more than if I had attempted long explanations.

'The money and the confession, both those things.' The geniality dropped from Edmundo's manner and his eyes seemed to cloud. He wasn't bargaining; he was laying down terms. 'The money and the television. Today, now, you send the message for the money to be paid. Tomorrow, before the Red Cross bring our comrades you will tell these men,' he indicated the camera crew adjusting their lights, 'you will tell them everything. Then after they have gone you can take Sir Hartman. Take him anywhere. South Africa, Russia, Britain.'

Whether he wanted Father's indiscretions publicized at home in order to help Consolidated, and so the South Africans, or whether it was to spark the exposure of something more, I could not decide; and needed to know.

'What do you want me to say?'

'You will say why he has come to us, what he is doing all these years, who are his friends.'

'He's too ill to speak for himself. Isn't that enough?'

'No, my friend. It is not.' His left fist clenched on the stock of the gun, as though the feel of the silver gun gave him power. Any moment there would be an outburst of the kind Tina had witnessed. I gave way. My objective was not to save face. It was to get Father out.

'Then I'll say what you want. But we must talk about it beforehand.'

Edmundo relaxed as rapidly as he had previously become tense.

'I am glad,' he said. 'I am glad for that, because I like you, young man. Any African must respect a man who helps his father.'

In the next hour I learnt the answers to many questions. Edmundo had been behind the Nairobi burglary. He had followed the whole process of Father's Angolan deal through what I would have called spies in the Angolan government, though he insisted they were 'cousins'. He had not, however, discovered as much about Father's past as I feared. By the time we had finished there seemed some possibility of containing the damage except on the sanctions-busting issue. Even so, if Father himself would agree to my making the confession on his behalf its impact would be weakened though, oddly, Edmundo seemed not to have considered this. Eventually he shouted for Struben, who swiftly reappeared.

'What I like to know,' he said in his laborious favourite phrase, 'is how soon you will talk to Geneva.'

'When you do,' I added, 'can you get through to our representative in London?'

'Those Red Cross blokes will be on the air at four.' Struben eyed the chronometer on his hairy wrist. I guessed he had problems keeping Edmundo on schedule. 'Two hours, fifty-two minutes' time.' He looked at me. 'How do we know your man will be available?'

'Can you send a message in advance?' I held out my hand for the signal pad he was holding and carefully printed Timmins's full name and phone numbers. 'Say it's going to be Sir James speaking and we'll need the money tonight.'

Again Struben sought the African's guidance. I presumed he

was worried about interception, though he told me later this was a very long-range radio and different to the one we had homed in on.

'Have to hope they're listening out,' he agreed grudgingly.

'They should know this is an eight-million-dollar call,' Edmundo said, illogically, then led me out to find Van Rensburg, greeted him cordially, and personally conducted the pair of us through the trees to a small clearing beyond which was Father's tent. There was a lot of activity, with soldiers hurrying to and fro and others squatting on the ground eating out of bowls. They all cheered or scrambled to their feet when Edmundo passed. In response he displayed the silver gun, waving it triumphantly above his head and reminding me of the Bedouin leaders whom Lawrence described, encouraging their Arab irregulars to war.

We crossed the clearing, presumably the same one where Tina had watched the Cubans arraigned, and stopped outside a dark green tent, the flap of which was tied back. Edmundo gestured the guard aside and announced with a panache that seemed more pre-planned than instinctive, 'Sir Hartman, your son is here.'

Edmundo stuck his head through the tent flap. 'I like to tell you this, Sir Hartman. Your son is one to respect.' Then he walked away, and I wished he could have said almost anything else. I had to talk Father round, not antagonize him.

The silence lasted several seconds while I peered into the gloom inside, wondering if Father was too ill to reply. He was lying on a low and narrow bed, a red loincloth wrapped around his waist and legs, the grey hair curling on his chest wet with sweat, his face unusually pale. As I watched he raised his head and spoke, determination to overcome his weakness inflecting every syllable.

'About bloody time someone came. How are you Robert?'

As a young boy I used to kiss my father in greeting. School and the tensions of adolescence had subdued our shows of affection to a handclasp, or, on his part, a bearhug around my shoulders. The great birthday quarrel finished even that intimacy. This moment might have restored it, if those first words of his had not so crudely been intended to reassert his dominance. They were a masterpiece of barely restrained impatience. 'About bloody time someone came,' he repeated, and my emotions froze, killing any doubt about the deal I had struck on his behalf. 'Take the clothes off the chair,' he ordered, 'carefully.' Then he recognized my companion. 'Good God.' Real warmth illuminated his voice. 'You old bugger, I wasn't expecting a delegation. So you've found a way of getting me out.'

'Robert has. I thought Edmundo might be more amenable if I came too. Stupid. Made no difference. Mind if I sit down?'

'What happened?' Father asked, noticing Van Rensburg's

awkward movements and his bandages, then trying to shift himself to an upright position. I moved to help him, half lifting his body, feeling the clammy heat of his skin and realizing that he must be running a very high temperature. 'Thanks, Bob. Give me the towel.' He worked it feebly around his face and shoulders. 'Can't shake off this damn fever.' He looked at Van Rensburg again. 'Someone attacked you?'

'We were raided. The thieves stole the Rhodesian survey. I'm sorry, Jim. Edmundo knows about the sanctions-busting.'

'Knows a damn sight too much altogether.' Father wiped his forehead again. 'Jesus it's hot.'

He was swaying slightly and muttered that he had a headache. I sat down on the other end of the bed, which sagged under our combined weight, and asked if he had seen a doctor. He frowned in annoyance.

'There is no doctor. That South African's given me tablets.' He was quiet for a moment, then demanded again, 'What's been happening?'

I let that question pass to Van Rensburg. He had been at the Board meeting.

'Concession Twenty-Two has not been purchased. Nor has an option been kept on it. With the collapse in the share price no bid for Consolidated was possible.'

We both waited for Father's reaction. With it came a glow of his old, vituperative energy. '*Prima!*' he exclaimed sardonically. 'The moment I'm gone you all behave like chickens with your heads cut off.'

'Less simple, Jim. Consolidated just made an offer for us.'

'For the Trust?' He seemed disbelieving. Then he spoke more with hope than certainty. 'You defeated that? Threw it out?'

'Robert did.'

Again he was perplexed. 'How?'

'Organized a suspension of trading in the shares. They're frozen until you return.'

'Well,' he said to me, 'don't just sit there. Explain.'

'Bob has saved the company, Jim. Give him his due.'

'And I'd like to know how.' He might be weak, but he was unrepentant.

Under the pressure of questions which were, however, less perceptive than usual, Van Rensburg recapitulated the events of the past two weeks as he understood them. 'Mind you, I've been in hospital. Only had a day in London.' Meanwhile I was becoming increasingly worried about the passage of time. There were matters I could not raise in Van Rensburg's presence.

'Christianne gave you my letter?' Father interrupted, looking at me, and I knew he was about to claim the credit for what I had

306

done. 'It's my return the Fund Managers are relying on?'

'That's correct. As a backstop I'm calling an EGM in three weeks' time. Crosthwaite-Eyre should be sending the papers out today.'

'That old fool.'

'Listen.' I spoke more brusquely to him than ever before. 'We have the situation contained. But we have to get you home and well enough to appear at meetings, quite apart from Mother needing you. You may not like the deal I've done, but you're going to have to live with it.'

'What deal?' he asked, and his voice wavered. 'What bargain have you struck?' There was something uncharacteristically like fear in his eyes. His jaw muscles tightened, and the sweat poured off his face. I guessed he knew most of what Edmundo was after, though not the whole prescription. If I didn't force the medicine down his throat, he would never accept it.

'Eight million dollars paid by the insurers, various supplies which I've organized, and a recorded television interview admitting what you've been doing in Africa all these years.'

'In Rhodesia, you mean?' Van Rensburg intervened. 'Damn stupid to admit that. Might as well send the documents to the Director of Public Prosecutions in London yourself.'

'You think that muck would stick?'

'If Edmundo released the documents you could be jailed.'

I couldn't allow this to continue. Van Rensburg and I had come to agreement over everything except how to handle Father. Furthermore, he was wrong in thinking that sanctions-busting was the most dangerous issue.

. 'If you don't mind, Patrick,' I said, 'there are private things we have to talk about as well. Would you mind leaving us for half an hour?'

Van Rensburg looked at Father, who nodded wearily. 'Every dog has its day,' he said, and I could have hit him. 'Come back later.'

'Go on,' Father said, shifting his legs onto the bed again when I transferred myself to the chair. He lay on his back and stared upwards at the pinpricks of light where there were holes in the canvas. The atmosphere in the tent was stifling. I could feel drops of sweat running down inside my shirt. It was small wonder he looked so ill.

'Edmundo's idea is to show himself as a representative of Western values by releasing you, in spite of your trying to betray him to a Marxist government.'

'Go on,' he repeated flatly.

'He has documents about the diamond consortium you wanted to set up, as well as the Rhodesian ones. What he may not know is who was backing you.'

I was trying to make the conclusions that Camilla and I had reached sound less of a quantum leap than they had seemed a few days ago. We were certain that Father's backers were the Russians, and had been since the early 1950s. Yet, on reflection, was this anything to condemn? He had not been a spy. He had not, so far as we knew, betrayed his country of adoption. He had simply accepted communist support for ventures which, when all was said and done, created employment in Britain as well as in Africa. His approach had been completely pragmatic. He had traded with the rightwing Rhodesian government because he took a longer view of that colony's future than the Labour politicians who had imposed trade sanctions. Equally he took Russian money to create his own empire in Africa because of that same longer view.

'The Russians bankrolled you,' I said. 'Why deny it? What matters is whether Edmundo knows.'

'It would be better,' Father replied slowly, still gazing upwards, 'if you kept out of things that don't concern you.'

'They do,' I insisted. 'Because if we get you out of here with the media believing you're some kind of Russian agent, you'll be crucified.'

The false extremes of patriotism the newspapers were trumpeting over the Falklands war were an insult to the men fighting there. If they had cause to brand Father as a Russian agent of influence they would go similarly overboard. The argument that the only people he appeared to have betrayed were Edmundo and himself would carry no weight. Nor would the fact that he could only ever have exerted effective influence if his tactics were going with the grain of history, not against it. Both ideas were too subtle.

'You're talking nonsense,' he said flatly.

'I'm not attacking you,' I said – and it was true that I was not, because unpleasant as much of his past had proved to be, I had ended up understanding his vision. 'But why deny that Angelino underwrote your scheme for Concession Twenty-Two in spite of its appalling production record?'

'Don't be absurd.' Father raised his head for a moment. 'Patrick and I were on a winner.'

'Only if you either bought Edmundo off or he was captured.'

'Why isn't Patrick here to tell you?' He shook his head so far as the pillow permitted. 'I haven't the energy.'

'No,' I said firmly, aware that despite his condition Father would produce plausible reasons for claiming I had misunderstood the whole affair. 'You only took the risk of coming here because if you delivered Edmundo to the Angolan government the Russians would market their gemstones through your consortium. That was the end game. With their eleven or twelve million carats of stones added to Zaïre's, Angola's, Sierra Leone's, Ghana's and the other black Africans', you could break De Beers' grip on the market.'

'So?' He was lying back again, suddenly relaxed enough to sound reflective, and in the guttural, Germanic way he turned the word into a dismissive question, I caught an echo of Lotte Lohrey's earlier evasions. 'So? This was business, Bob. Russia trades with South Africa on the quiet, in gold as well as diamonds. With their twenty per cent of world production added to black Africa's we could break De Beers' domination. Our success was in convincing them that once we'd taken over Consolidated we'd be able to market as efficiently as the CSO. Ask Patrick, for God's sake. He'll tell you it was the coup of a lifetime. As for Carlo, he had the connections to bring the Russians in. I admit his death was a great loss. My mistake was the Rhodesian emerald mine. Worse than coming here. Never put yourself on the wrong side of the law, Bob, no matter what the pressures.'

This time his apparent frankness nearly did fool me. His self-control, despite the fever, was extraordinary. But I was not going to be led into regarding the sanctions-busting as his main offence. I had a fair idea of the pressures he had been subjected to, as well. They would have been close to blackmail. Carlo Angelino would have apologized while he insisted on the manoeuvre against Edmundo, and he would have no need to emphasize the size of the deals it could lead to. But the underlying fact was that Father had become too rich, and worse, too independent. His original bargain was being neglected. So his hand was forced and Lotte Lohrey was there to see him off, scribbling a note to wish him luck, of which she sincerely meant every word.

He wiped the sweat from his face with the towel again. The exposition had cost him much effort. 'As for trying to kidnap the General, that's imagination. You think I'm so stupid?'

I could only suppose that Van Rensburg would be as easily duped by this denial as he must have been by the explanation of Carlo Angelino's involvement, because the beauty of the overall scenario was its accuracy, just as its defect was what Father had omitted.

'Did you have an actual contract with Angelino?' I asked, guessing there must have been some commitment in writing for them to keep and threaten to produce, if only a receipt.

'What are you talking about?' Father was instantly wary.

'Attached as you were to him, I think there must have been one.'

'Carlo was a friend. Nothing more.'

'Much more,' I said firmly. 'Your parents were dead, and after that episode in the Abruzzi he virtually adopted you, a long-range godfather. He gave you ideas and direction. He promoted your first Egyptian investment and he saved you from bankruptcy after Suez.'

There was a great deal that was easier left unspoken. Father's desperate boyhood guilt at feeling himself responsible for his mother's death. His trust in the underground communist organization in prewar Germany that she had belonged to and which had helped to arrange his escape. He kept it all under wraps after the war, and the only clue was the paradox of his refusal to deny having belonged to the Hitler Youth, as any real Nazi sympathizer would have done. That was why he had been so cold-blooded over executing the partisans. 'Did Carlo order you to make a career in Britain and marry Mother? Or did Lotte?'

'You're as mad as Edmundo.' Father made the protest without conviction, however, and not because the fever had weakened him. Nor did he attempt to look at me.

'No British compensation demands were met during the winter of 1956 to 1957. Your cheque may have come through an Egyptian bank, but it was Russian money and you've been acting for them ever since, under Angelino's directions.'

'Damn nonsense,' he muttered.

I moved my chair closer to his bed, so that he could no longer avoid this unexpectedly low-key confrontation.

'It's time you were honest with me,' I said. 'I'm going to carry on this business one day, God help me. Your diamond consortium was instrumental to a long-term Russian objective in Africa: the destruction of South African economic power. You must know what Brezhnev said in Prague in 1973 – that it was the Soviet aim "to gain control of the two great treasure houses on which the West depends: the energy treasure house of the Persian Gulf and the mineral treasure house of central and southern Africa".' Father stared silently at the tent roof, as if unimpressed by Camilla's research, but I pressed on. 'The question that counts is whether Edmundo knows what you've been doing.'

Father shifted his head around sufficiently to bring me into his vision, and I could not decide whether the fever was as bad as his laborious movements suggested.

'He accuses me of spying for the Russians. It's baseless. You can't do a deal in Angola without meeting Russian advisers. You shouldn't believe all that nonsense.'

The way he said this made such assumptions about his ability to deceive that it took me several seconds to realize that he might in fact be inviting a complete moment of truth.

'Yes,' I agreed. 'You were too valuable. You've been in the game too long. They wouldn't take such a stupid risk. As a tycoon you could influence Third World leaders in ways no Russian diplomat could; and make Marxist regimes respectable to the West by trading with them.'

'Profitable.' Father spoke so quietly that I barely heard him. 'Why bother with labels? I'm a pragmatist. Carlo could have told you.'

I looked into these pale blue eyes, weary and dark-rimmed now, and they stared back at me as unyielding as ever. I think when his mother was killed by the Nazis his heart must have turned to ice, and the only people able to unfreeze it a little were Barba Nera and Lotte Lohrey, both fellow communists, both of whom had fought comparable battles in their youth.

'Deep down,' I went on, 'Africans still trust the former colonial powers more than America or Russia. Call it love-hate, call it anything. You could manipulate them and they had no political reservations about accepting your money.'

That was the true subtlety, and it was Van Rensburg's excellent relationships with Africans in Kenya which had provided the clue, again paradoxically, since Van Rensburg himself was straight. I could have continued, but there was no need for more of the re-construction Camilla and I had teased out of past history. Without a sign or an overt admission Father came to the ultimate point.

'What you're saying, boy, is that I can't come back.'

'What I'm saying is the reverse. If Edmundo hasn't sussed you out you can. He probably doesn't know what an agent of influence is. Just stop pretending with me. Except for the sanctions you might get away with it.'

A kind of hope came into his expression, as if a mental fever were abating.

'One of us has to give Edmundo his television interview,' I said. 'That's part of the price.'

'I told you all to pay the sixty million. Why the hell didn't you?' Already his tone was firmer.

'Amongst other things, Frank Stainton prevented us.'

He swore, and tried to get off the bed, faltering so that I had to help lift him off. He possessed a vast reserve of courage and de-termination.

'Would you like me to do the interview? Edmundo would agree, provided you're in the background.'

'No.' He steadied himself against the chair back, which swayed precariously. 'I'll handle this myself. Fetch Patrick.'

I went and found Van Rensburg. 'They're getting impatient,' he said. 'Had a job holding them off.'

We went back and assisted Father out of the tent, together with the guard, who then escorted the three of us back across the clearing. On the way Struben appeared and called me, so I missed whatever exchanges took place between Father and Van Rensburg.

They must have centred on the sanctions issue. At all events, a few minutes later I was perched on a stool in Struben's radio hut, talking on a faint but clear connection to London. To Timmins's credit he did not ask how I came to be here or what was planned next. He confined himself to one question of substance.

'Can you bring Sir James out safely?'

'Tomorrow. Provided the bank draft is with their lawyers.'

'Tell them this is once and for all. There won't be any second payment.'

'I will.' Perhaps naïvely I had trusted Edmundo's safe conduct, assuming I would not be held myself.

'Then I'll take the draft to Geneva.' Timmins allowed himself one lapse. 'I won't ask how you did this. Good luck.'

The response was generous. All that remained was to discover whether behind all Edmundo's loquacious boasts there lay knowledge or merely bluff.

CHAPTER TWENTY-THREE

My mother always used to describe certain occasions as being 'absurdly overplayed'. The phrase was completely appropriate to the filming of the interview with Father. When Struben brought Van Rensburg and me into the command bunker we found the personalities of the drama already in their places behind the long, blanket-covered table. Dazzling lights illuminated them, while facing them and behind the camera crew a selected audience of Edmundo's guerrillas were drawn up in several ranks, some women soldiers among them.

Edmundo himself was centre stage behind the table, his bush uniform beautifully pressed, the stars of rank on his epaulettes catching the light. The silver gun glittered on the cloth in front of him. On his right Father stared unsmiling at the camera, his only shirt freshly laundered. To his left sat a man whom I recognized at once from Tina's descriptions as Makarov, his arms folded, his broad rather handsome face completely impassive.

All this was a snapshot impression gained as Struben led me to my place at the end of the table, where I realized separate film clips could be taken of me and where I was too far removed from Father for any communication. Van Rensburg was made to stand apart behind me.

There was a sudden stir among the audience of soldiers, who laughed and jeered as the cameras began to whirr and a line of Cubans were marched in past me. I counted them as they were lined up along the side of the bunker, between the table and the audience. They numbered exactly eighteen. So Timmins had been correct and the 'executions' had been a carefully organized charade to frighten Tina Humphries.

Next four East Germans were paraded, all in clean guerrilla uniforms. The visual message was becoming plain: the ALF treated its captives well. To underline it Edmundo raised a hand

313

in salute as the Germans passed in front of him. The loudspeakers crackled briefly, had their volume diminished and a voice cut in.

'All these mercenaries of foreign powers were captured in battle. Angola is not their country. They are intruders. But they will now be released to the International Red Cross: proof that the Angolan Liberation Front under its famous leader General Edmundo honours its promises.' What those promises were was left unsaid. But I realized from the American accent of the commentary that it must come from the unit director, and indeed he was standing in the shadow behind the lights speaking into a small microphone. 'This ceremony is being witnessed by Colonel Viktor Mikhailovich Makarov of the Red Army and Sir James Hartman, the British financier, who are also being freed.' There was a slight pause while the listening Africans were cued in to applaud. 'General Edmundo, as founder and commander of the Liberation Front, what can you tell us about today's exchange of prisoners?'

Whether any Western television station would use such a contrived introduction seemed doubtful: except that Father was news whatever he was involved with. Certainly Edmundo did nothing to make the film more palatable by gravely addressing the camera with a long and philosophical dissertation about why Africa should be left alone to settle its own disputes. In fact, as I had already told him, I had every sympathy with his position. Russian advisers and Cuban troops were just the most recent foreigners to interfere in a continent whose backwardness had made it a prey to adventurers. From the African side of the looking glass Vasco da Gama was no more a hero than the slave traders. But would a TV audience weaned on pulp drama see Father and his multinational Trust in the same light when he was a captive?

Edmundo then invited Makarov to speak. The Russian shook his head. Now it was Father's turn and the semi-philosophical, enmity towards no one, approach was discarded.

'Sir Hartman,' Edmundo began, still maintaining near-Biblical turns of phrase, 'you are not in uniform like these others, but you are more dangerous. We have kept you because you came to betray us to our enemies. You came as a spy but we knew you.'

'I came to do business.'

'You came as a spy for the Russians to kidnap me.'

'Don't forget my secretary,' Father said sardonically. 'She came too.'

Edmundo's anger began to mount. 'Hartman,' he almost shouted, 'you tell the world what you are doing in Africa or you stay! You answer our questions or you stay!'

The minor tirade evoked clapping and cheers from the soldiers, but embarrassed the American, who stopped the camera, walked across to speak to Edmundo, then made a fresh start.

'Sir James, you have consented to this filming. Correct?' Father nodded. 'Tell us why you came to Angola.'

'To discuss mining.'

'With the Marxist regime in Luanda or with General Edmundo?'

'Both, if necessary.'

That single admission would cost us any option on the Concession Twenty-Two lease. I could only assume that Father was giving ground now in order to withhold it later. He mopped his forehead with a handkerchief and I noticed that as he did so he kept his left hand on the table for support. The heat inside the bunker room was mounting. Combined with his fever it must have been unbearable.

'But if the Luanda regime knew you were here they would cancel the concession.'

Father shrugged his shoulders.

'Unless you did them a favour. Like kidnapping General Edmundo.'

'How?' Even though his voice was becoming unsteady the contempt in it was unmistakable. 'I'm alone and he has an army. If you must know I came to buy him off.'

This was a definite point scored, and the accusation that he could be bought infuriated Edmundo. He leapt to his feet.

'You try to trap me with that mine,' he shouted, 'to trap me for the Russians who cannot defeat me.' He slammed his fist on to the table, only checking himself when he remembered the camera.

'It's okay, Sir,' the commentator hastened to reassure him. 'We can edit that out.'

None the less Edmundo was close to the truth. He had told me about his 'cousins' in Luanda warning him of a plot, and I was more inclined to believe his claims than Father's denials. But could he prove them?

'Admit this!' he demanded. 'Admit you work for the Russians!'

'Say what you like,' Father said dismissively. 'Do you admit blowing up my jet and killing the crew?' He sounded weary of the whole performance and suddenly uncaring as to how it might end.

'We have proof of the way you work,' the American cut in hastily. This was going to be a heavily edited recording. He produced a folder, displayed documents from it in front of the camera, then placed them on the table. 'Do you deny you broke Rhodesian sanctions?'

Father did not so much as pick up a single paper. He glanced at the top one, shrugged his shoulders in a mime of defeat, and answered evenly:

'We broke the sanctions for the ultimate good of Zimbabwe.'

'For its Marxist leaders, you mean?' The American must have been following instructions but he lacked the subtlety of mind to deal with Father, even when his vitality was weak.

'Is it likely that if I was a Marxist I would support a white settler regime? I'm in business, not politics. I broke sanctions because all they would do was destroy the country's economy. I had a long-term interest in that economy.'

I listened in fascination. The serpentine initiatives through which Father operated were beyond the American. He failed even to link the Rhodesian emerald mine with the gemstone consortium plan, which he must have known about. All he did was pursue Father's admission in the legalistic terms a jury might understand.

'You admit you broke the British law?'

'Maybe. I said, I'm in business, not politics.' Father wiped the sweat away again. His face was flushed and I saw his shoulders tremble, as if the cycle of the fever was returning to fits of shivering. He looked sideways at Edmundo. 'How much more?'

'Who do you work for, Sir Hartman? Tell us that. All over Africa you pay bribes, you tell lies. For the Russians?'

'For myself.' Father was making a final effort to shrug off the drift of the argument and if he did not do it brilliantly, at least he gave Edmundo a let-out. 'I admit I pay backhanders. I admit I broke sanctions. I also admit,' he let the sentence hang long enough to develop a little suspense, 'I thought I could bribe you, General, and I was wrong.'

The American was quick to applaud and the Africans took their cue, cheering wildly. If I could extract Father now, at least the interview wouldn't have to end on further denials. I rose to my feet and walked behind the table to Edmundo.

'He can't take much more, Sir,' I whispered, making a show of confidentiality. 'He's more ill than he seems.'

For a few moments Edmundo deliberated. Then he stood up, a smile wide across his face, and clasped my hand.

'Take him,' he said loudly. 'Take Sir Hartman. When I say a promise, I keep that word.'

Remembering how Africans like extended hand-shaking, I kept my hand in his and grinned at the camera until he released it, slapped me on the back and said, 'For you I say, come back any time.'

As I helped Father away it struck me that forty years before Barba Nera had said very much the same to him.

Throughout the filming Van Rensburg had been standing near the door. He now took Father's other arm, and together with Struben we walked him to his tent. Once out of the hot room he began to complain of being cold. It was nearly dark and the air buzzed with insects.

'One extreme to the other,' Van Rensburg commented. 'Ought to be in hospital. How's your urine, Jim? Okay?'

'Been very dark today. Don't know why.'

It was strange to hear him speak so uncertainly.

When we had laid him down and covered him with blankets Struben beckoned us out of the tent.

'Here,' he said, handing over some tablets. 'Give the old man these or he will be for the lions. Sounds like blackwater to me.'

'When can we take him out?' Van Rensburg demanded.

'Tomorrow you can go. After the Red Cross come. We had to film today because they will not come if there are cameras around.'

I suggested Van Rensburg should go and brief the pilot, while I saw to Father. Between us we had a hard decision to make. Could he return home? And if he did, could he expect to continue running the Trust with the prospect of a criminal conviction ahead of him?

Despite the histrionics and the makeshift interviewer's lack of personality, the film might well serve to destroy Father's business reputation. The setting had been genuinely dramatic: the honourable rebel, the Russian colonel, the missing multi-millionaire. I reckoned every TV station from Australia to Iceland would show parts of it. The result must be a lot of public questions from Father's many business enemies. I might have saved the Trust for the moment, but it was difficult to see either how Father could talk his way out of the questions or how an organization he headed could acquire Concession Twenty-Two and pursue his old objectives.

'God, my head,' he murmured. 'There's water somewhere. Give me the pills.'

He washed down four, one after the other, though not easily, then tried to take off his shirt. But he fumbled and was unable to, so I had to ease it off his shoulders, then put the blankets back around him. The shivering was becoming more frequent. He looked at me.

'Can I survive that film being shown?'

For the first time in my life Father was genuinely asking for advice. His seriousness wasn't only in his expression. He had shown apparent concern often enough when I was a teenager. 'What d'you think about this, Bob?' he would say: and then tell me what I ought to have thought. Now it was different. He knew that I held the key to where he went next.

'They'd have to cut the interview.'

'What about the sanctions part?'

'That's what they would use.' I had thought this out some of the way. 'Without the documents the government couldn't prosecute. But your own admission would do a lot of harm.' Even with the major distraction of the Falklands war, where the two landing ships had just been sunk at Bluff Cove with the loss of fifty or sixty lives, Father was too much of a household name for headlines not to be inevitable.

'The bastard wanted to hold me until the war was over. At least you outwitted him on that.' A flicker of the old paternal familiarity returned. 'I misjudged you, Bob.' He lay back, gazing blankly at the canvas of the tent, as he had this morning. 'Thanks old boy.'

'We'll get you to hospital. Mother won't know what to do with herself, she'll be so relieved.' I felt I had to cheer him up. 'She won't give a damn about the sanctions nonsense. She just wants you back.'

'She won't mind?'

It was as though despite the illness and the legal threats he suddenly divined some hope. I forgave him a great deal for that brief sign of faith and affection.

Then I outlined the basic structure of my plan for the Trust. As soon as he was fit enough we'd hold a Press conference. He and I would meet the Fund Managers. If Stainton refused to resign we would go ahead with the Extraordinary General Meeting at which the shareholders could vote directors off the Board. Finally, if Father was prosecuted and convicted, a process which might take a considerable time, I would resign my Lectureship and represent the family in his place, acting on his behind-the-scenes advice.

There was a long silence, disturbed only by his laboured breathing. 'I'm not dead yet, boy,' he said eventually, repeating the words with a half strangled intensity. 'I'm not dead yet. As for all this, I'll plead coercion. Fetch Patrick.'

Caught completely wrong-footed, I went and found Van Rensburg, noticing that the guard made no objection and thinking that the freedom of movement might prove useful.

'I tried the approach we agreed,' I told Van Rensburg with some bitterness. 'He wouldn't discuss it. He's too bloody used to putting the worst interpretation on other people's motives.'

'I'll talk to him,' Patrick said, though without much optimism. Half an hour later he was back. 'Won't give an inch. He's going to continue running the company.'

'From jail?' Despite the complicated political arguments about sanctions, breaking them had been illegal and I was certain Father would be made an example of. 'Anyway, will he be well enough?'

'Who knows? Blackwater's damn dangerous. He ought to go with the Red Cross tomorrow. Get immediate treatment.'

'No.' It was my turn to be inflexible. 'He must go with us.' For Father to be seen as part of a Russian, East German and Cuban contingent in an exchange of prisoners would arouse a host of suspicions on which I did not enlarge. If Patrick hadn't cottoned on to his linkages yet he could remain in ignorance. 'We have to present this as the end of a kidnapping and nothing more complicated. That's a situation the shareholders and the public know about and can identify with. A Press conference immediately on our return will take some of the sting out of the film.'

Patrick was persuaded. We returned to Father, bathed his forehead and tried to ease the torment of the fever. Around nine Struben came again.

'We had a message from Geneva,' he announced in his slow voice. 'The Red Cross are bringing those supplies. The General wants to see you. For myself I think that interview was shit, but he is happy.'

At the bunker Edmundo was surrounded by his commanders in a chaotic form of briefing. I waited patiently to be spoken to. Eventually he noticed I was there and beckoned me.

'When the supplies come, you are free.'

'Will you leave him alone after this?'

He looked me over, as if appraising an opponent in the ring. 'What those papers do, who may know? Would you trust such a man? We like the world to know what Sir Hartman is. If men do not listen now we will tell it again.'

A soldier came up, agitated and importunate, bad news in his whole bearing and expression. He spoke a few words and Edmundo turned to me.

'Now I am busy, too busy. Tomorrow Sir Hartman can go, when the rest have gone.'

I tried to argue that we should leave at first light, but Struben took my arm.

'You heard, man. The General's busy.'

Edmundo swung round. 'When I say a thing I keep those words.' He reverted to interrogating the messenger.

When Struben insisted Father was being nursed and I must go to the tent I shared with Van Rensburg, my unease increased. I had learnt that the African's utterances could usually be interpreted several ways. What did keeping 'those words' mean?

Nor was the confusion at his headquarters a good omen. Van Rensburg's first remark when I rejoined him confirmed the feeling.

'I've been listening to the *watu*. They're expecting an attack. We ought not to wait for the Red Cross.'

Our own guard had disappeared. We managed to join the pilot and plan an attempt to fly Father out at first light.

Next morning we needed no alarm. We were woken early by a distant thumping, as if some faraway giant was pounding the earth.

'Quiet.' Van Rensburg silenced my question. 'Either mortars or bombs. The bloody attack's begun.'

We threw on our clothes and went out. The sun was rising, sending shafts of light slanting through the trees, and we were alone. No guerrillas, men or women, were in sight. All I could hear were the distant guns and the waking noises of the bush's own life: bird cries and a dove cooing.

'Come on, Bob.' Van Rensburg began to half run, half hobble, the hundred yards through the trees to Father's tent.

I dashed ahead and for a moment thought I had taken a wrong direction. There was no tent. Then I recognized the trampled patch of grass and earth where it had been. Some shreds of foil wrapping from the malaria tablets lay there, but of Father, his bedding and his few belongings there was no sign.

'If they've pulled out we're in trouble,' Van Rensburg commented, although it was obvious. 'You are free,' Edmundo had said. I had been right to fear that his promise might have ambiguities. We were starting back to collect our own gear when the roar of an aircraft made us stop. An old Dakota transport plane lumbered overhead, its wings tilted in a turn, red crosses visible on its silvery fuselage. As we watched a jeep skidded to a halt beside us in a whirl of dust. The driver was Struben and the back was piled with radio equipment.

'Get in quick,' he ordered. 'Hadn't forgotten you.'

'Where's my father?' I demanded.

'The Red Cross will take him.'

'But we're going too.'

Struben's answer was to gun the engine and race through the trees to our tent, where he helped us load our two canvas grips, throwing loose oddments in on top. As he leapt back into the driving seat the Dakota passed overhead again, less noisily this time, and I guessed it was landing.

'Where's Sir James?' Van Rensburg insisted.

'At the airstrip.' Struben was hatless, his hair untidy in the wind, and he was concentrating on the rough track through the scrub as he spoke.

'Listen man, you two think you can fly around Africa with a lion like that. Are you crazy? Every jumped-up kaffir asking questions. He could die any time. Don't want you saying we killed him either. If he does the Red Cross can certify the reasons, right?'

There was a rough logic in the argument which I none the less mistrusted, though Struben didn't care whether we accepted it or not.

When we reached the airstrip the camera crew's small plane was taking off, carrying the film and the documents down to South Africa. Copies would be in London long before we were. Andy came up and said he been prevented from moving our own aircraft. It still stood parked in shadow under some trees, half a dozen men with rifles around it. The Dakota was taxying slowly along the side of the clearing, while more soldiers waited. The thump of gunfire sounded closer. All told there were at least two hundred ALF followers around, those who were not occupied holding their weapons ready as if the enemy would emerge from the bush at any second. The atmosphere was distinctly bad.

'Where is my father?' I asked again. I could see Edmundo on the far side, easily identifiable from his bulk and air of authority. But not him.

'That is our business,' Struben said curtly. 'You stay here, out of sight. No cameras. No unauthorized observers. Those are the conditions for the Red Cross coming.'

We watched the Dakota's door open and eighteen men file out, one by one, down improvised steps into the sunlight. Edmundo greeted each with a bearhug, the silver gun flashing like a talisman as he did so. He must have valued them highly, if only because their safe return would boost the morale of his troops. So he now had all his 'supplies', and I blessed Lotte Lohrey silently for their release. But where was Father? I could not believe that Edmundo would renege completely on his promises.

The captured East Germans and Cubans were marched out from their concealment and a European in dark trousers and a blue shirt emerged from the plane, holding a clipboard. He was given a sheet of paper and individually checked the captives aboard, first the Cubans then the Germans. Finally Makarov went up the steps. The Dakota must have been close to its capacity. From the way the European acted he was about to close the door when two Africans came out from the trees, carrying a stretcher, and I knew who the figure with a blanket over him was.

The Red Cross official made evident objections, raising his palm to stop Father's embarkation.

'Must be overloaded,' Struben commented.

'Then we'll take him.' I moved forward.

'No you don't.' He caught me by the arms and pinioned me. 'You are staying here, man. Right?'

Across the clearing the official relented. I watched, furious at being unable to intervene, now certain this was a planned manoeuvre. The stretcher was loaded. The Dakota's door closed. The plane's engines had never been stopped. As soon as Edmundo signalled to the pilot they were revved up and it began trundling towards the end of the clearing, where it swung round, headed down the strip and roared away. First the tail rose, then the main wheels lifted off the grass and it laboriously gained height, missing the trees at the end by what looked like only a few feet.

I twisted my head round to look at Struben. 'Satisfied?' I asked caustically and he let me free. I shook myself, tugged at my clothes and tried to catch a last glimpse of the Dakota, experiencing an unaccountable dead sense of loss. I ought to have been glad that Father was in good hands. Instead I felt defeated.

'They'll fly to Luanda in the Dak, then a jet to Moscow,' Struben remarked, answering my unspoken question.

I stared at him. He was the same age as me with half the intelligence, even if he was physically stronger. Yet he had fooled us. All that admiration for Father's war record had been contrived. Why should we have expected him to do other than play Edmundo's game? The two of them had carried through one of the oldest double acts, Mutt and Jeff, the unfriendly captor and the friendly one. Perhaps because he was ill Father had fallen for it. Timmins would not have done. For myself I had been stupid enough to suppose that Struben was some kind of ally, and because of that Father was on the way to Russia, labelled as part of an East-West exchange.

'You broke your word,' I said angrily. 'The pair of you.'

'Are you crazy man? The General said we would let him free and he has gone, eh? Let me tell you something. Last night we had a message from Pretoria, right? They asked us to hold the old man longer. Some business deal is not complete. They need more time. The General told me, "No. We must keep our word." "Can't we delay him?" I said. So he will spend a few days in Moscow, eh? You need not worry. They have good doctors there.'

The proposition was unanswerable, and I doubted if Struben knew that the incomplete business deal could only be Consolidated Diamond Concessions' takeover of the Trust and the final destruction of a plan acutely threatening to South African interests. Father wasn't the first adventurer to gamble for the wealth of this continent. He belonged to a long line of hard men; from the ancient Egyptians to the half-Arab slave trader, Tippu Tib; King Leopold of Belgium in the Congo; Cecil Rhodes, Alfred Beit and the developers of the Rand goldfields; most operating at a safe distance from European interference. If you threw the dice at those levels you only had to make a single mistake: and Father had made one, enabling Edmundo to exact a surprisingly sophisticated revenge for this still savage continent. Did even he appreciate its final twist?

'Your turn to go next,' Struben said. 'I would not hang around if I was you.'

As we were helping push our small plane out into the open Edmundo himself came across. He shook hands with Van Rensburg and clasped me on the shoulder.

'Any time, my friend. You like to talk about mining, come back any time. I like a son who is not afraid for himself.'

'Did you have to send my father with the rest?'

This was the last chance to discover how much the African really knew, and I looked keenly at him. Instantly his eyes became cloudy and opaque, mirroring a change of mood.

'I think for Sir Hartman Russia is a good place. In Russia they may know him.'

More explosions sounded in the distance, ominously recognizable for what they were.

'Go now,' he said abruptly. 'Before it is too late.' His concern appeared genuine and the animation returned to his expression. He took my hand quickly. 'I like to see you again one day.'

Further questions were impossible. I never was going to penetrate Edmundo's ambiguity. We boarded the plane. Van Rensburg, still resentful of Struben's interference, shouldered him aside and went forward into the co-pilot's place.

'Like to know what's going on for a change,' he muttered, as he clamped the earphones over his head.

We bumped across the grass, lifted over the trees and headed east, away from the fighting and towards the safety of Zambia. In the cabin I tried to relax, telling myself I had not done badly and in one way Struben had been right. Quite apart from the difficulty of tending an extremely sick man, we could have problems with the immigration when we landed. But would the Russian authorities cooperate either? In their eyes Father must have completely bungled his mission. Equally there must have been exceptional pressures and considerations for them to have insisted on it in the first place.

This far from either constructive or conclusive reverie was interrupted after a few minutes by Van Rensburg, who beckoned me to come forward.

'Bob.' His expression was a mixture of apprehension and hope. 'Listening to the transmissions I think the film crew's plane has been shot down. The Dakota's been relaying an emergency call with its position. Help me hold the map.'

I spread it open as best I could between him and Andy, while he plotted the reference, ending by marking a pencil cross in the same featureless area of bush where we had ourselves been fired at.

'Makes no sense,' he said. 'Why should they have flown north?'

'Their pilot told me,' Andy said. 'They wanted aerial shots of that mining concession where we landed. You want us to search?'

Van Rensburg hesitated, then glanced at me. Explanations were unnecessary. The pilot's code of honour required giving assistance, as it would at sea. We had a moral obligation.

323

'We have about thirty minutes' reserve of fuel,' Andy added.

I thought of the Gulfstream's flight deck crushed against the anthill and Captain Holz's corpse in the mortuary. There was no need to remind myself that the film interview and the documents might be destroyed if the wreck caught fire.

'No,' I said. 'Stay on route for Ndola.'

Andy was about to say something when Van Rensburg cut across him. 'If they weren't killed in the crash the army'll probably finish them off. They're dead men, or as good as.'

'If you insist, Sir,' Andy said with what he meant to be cutting formality.

'I do.' I wasn't going to plead that if we were short of fuel it would be risking our own lives. What I was thinking was that the camera crew had tried for one shot too many. Like Father, they could pay for their mistake. Then I thought a little further. 'Can you talk to the Red Cross Dakota?'

'If you want, Sir.' He was still being frigid. I didn't give a damn.

'Ask if they can tell Sir James the film crew have crashed. Ask them to say he must send his wife the name of the hospital he's taken to.'

After a certain amount of ritual chatter, which I listened to through a spare pair of headphones, I heard the answer. Mr Hartman was under sedation for the flight. They would give him the message later.

There was nothing more to be done. The next negotiation would be for his release from hospital. I was hoping Lotte Lohrey would handle that.

CHAPTER TWENTY-FOUR

Frank Stainton intended exercising the company's right to be heard first at the Extraordinary General Meeting. He was gambling everything on swinging the meeting his way in Father's continued absence.

The venue hired for the occasion was the ballroom of the Intercontinental Hotel, off Piccadilly. It was a huge, rather low-ceilinged room, laid out with many rows of chairs and well organized for the purpose. Shareholders were checked and searched at the separate street entrance, then climbed a semi-circular staircase to a series of doors, each signed with letters of the alphabet. Their names were politely checked a further time and they were given blue voting cards and pink outlines of the directors' places on the platform. Once seated they were kept entertained by video films of the Trust's overseas activities: newspaper presses rolling, the Rukanga mine today, hotels under construction. As soon as he'd seen the advantages of this meeting for himself, Frank Stainton had spared no effort to make it impressive. Everyone present had formal invitations to remain for a buffet luncheon afterwards.

When Camilla and I arrived the police were holding back a small crowd of anti-apartheid demonstrators, carrying placards and shouting slogans against Consolidated's takeover bid for the Trust. It had been a neat idea of hers to tip them off. Even though Consolidated's South African interests were small, a proportion of the shareholders might be influenced. As we joined the queue I tried to judge their mood.

The truth was that I had hoped to avoid this public confrontation, but had been outmanoeuvred after my return. With perfect propriety Stainton announced that Father was safe, though seriously ill and unable to return to work. So trading in our shares was resumed; but the price did not recover. What the market wanted was reassurance that Father was back in charge. Consolidated immediately re-launched their offer. I was caught. I dared not reveal that he was in Moscow, nor that his original fever had developed into tertiary malignant malaria. When Lotte Lohrey visited him the Russian doctors had said he could not be moved for at least two weeks. In a moment of lucidity he scrawled a message asking the Board to take no action until his return and to resist Consolidated. Stainton chose to ignore this, skilfully purloining my original argument that the shareholders owned the company and were the ultimate authority. That was his gamble: that they would vote to accept, after which there would be nothing much Father or I could do.

So now it was July 1st, nearly three weeks after Father's release and two weeks since the Falklands war had ended with the surrender of the Argentine forces. A month ago this EGM might have attracted only a few hundred shareholders. Today, newspaper editors were more alert for non-war stories, and with the Trust again under attack Father's whereabouts constituted a legitimate mystery. When we entered the ballroom – happily I had once given Camilla a few shares, so she could take part – virtually every row was full.

We had seats reserved in the front row, and sat down only a couple of minutes before the directors filed in to take their places at a long table facing the audience and slightly raised above us. Stainton himself was in the centre, with Plowright the Company Secretary on his left and next to him the Trust's solicitor. Only one director was absent, Patrick Van Rensburg, and as Stainton shifted his gaze around the assembly, thin-lipped and, I thought, a trifle nervous, he must have felt that an advantage. But if he hoped to manipulate the occasion into straightforward victory, he was optimistic. With luck, I would spring several surprises this morning.

As we watched him Stainton consulted his watch, saw that it was precisely 11.00 am and nodded to the Company Secretary, who rose to his feet.

'Ladies and gentlemen.' He waited for the chatter to die down. 'The directors of the Hartman Trust welcome you all to this Extraordinary General Meeting, which has been called by a shareholder to consider the resolution on the voting paper, namely, "That the offer from Consolidated Diamond Concessions should be rejected." In the absence of the Chairman, Sir James Hartman, who is unhappily too ill to attend, the acting Chief Executive, Mr Frank Stainton, will address you.'

Plowright sat down again. His statement had been carefully factual, taking no position, and when Stainton followed it he spoke with marked, if long-winded, self-control. He argued that the merger, as he called it, would be in the best interests of the Trust, and the figures showed that shareholders ought to accept the bid. It all sounded logical and reasonable.

Listening, I fingered the folder on my lap. One of my documents demonstrated exactly why he felt and spoke so convincingly. It had been passed to me by Christianne, as ever quick to sense when the wind might shift to a different quarter. She had approached me in Father's office – for several days I had reluctant permission to be there while clearing up the aftermath of the ransom payment – and handed me a photocopy.

'You may like to see this, Robert,' she had said, acting out an artless indifference, as much with her body as her words. 'Maybe it could be relevant for your meeting. Maybe not.'

She knew damn well it was, because what she handed across the desk was a letter from the Chairman of Consolidated to Stainton, indicating that if the takeover succeeded he would be rewarded with the Deputy Chairmanship of the combined company, and the shares he had purchased on their behalf would become his. It was more obliquely phrased than that, of course, but clear enough. I had thanked her with an assurance that her services would always be valued.

'I am glad to help, Robert,' she had remarked coolly, and left the room.

Having that letter in my possession gave me the consciousness of power an assassin must feel in the moments before he strikes. Stainton was now totally exposed through his acceptance recommendation. All I had to get right was the timing. This was complicated by the other bombshell I had prepared: one that ought to be utilized first.

'In Sir James Hartman's continued absence,' Stainton was winding up his plea, 'I urge you all to reject this resolution and take a more far-sighted view of the opportunities for expansion and growth which the merger would offer.' A few polite handclaps followed this oration. 'Does any shareholder wish to ask a question?'

A man who must have been the archetypal believer in Father's magic touch stood up: around sixty, carefully dressed in a business suit, yet with the fussy air of someone who knew he would end his days undistinguished. He would have watched his shares appreciate in value year by year, aware that for once he had backed a winner, and found it hard to comprehend the present humiliation. This was precisely the kind of ordinary shareholder I would be appealing to, whose votes might tip the scales. But his opening sentences were inaudible until one of the assistants hovering at the side of the room hurried to hand him a microphone.

'I would like to ask . . .' he began, stopped because the sound was poorly adjusted, and was instantly corrected by Stainton.

327

'Your name, please. Everyone who speaks must give his or her name.'

'Archie Franks,' he replied, not willing to be intimidated, 'and I seem to remember, though I may be wrong . . .' Oh God, I thought, he's one of those who can't ask a question without making a speech, '. . . that the founder of this Company, Sir James Hartman, would never miss a meeting of shareholders even if he had to come halfway round the world to be among us.'

'I am sure that is so,' Stainton interrupted testily. 'Have you a question?'

'The question I want to ask – and it's one I'm sure many here would like to ask themselves – is this. Why hasn't Sir James said anything about this offer, if he's alive? Where's he been since his plane was found and where is he now?'

This brought some applause, leaving the questioner still standing, wondering if he should say more.

'I would be prepared to answer if you would kindly sit down.'

Camilla whispered, 'What can he say without perjuring himself?'

Unexpectedly, Stainton took refuge in the truth. 'Sir James has sent a message from the private clinic where, as I understand it, he has been very seriously ill. He asked members of the Board to take no action until his return. Unhappily there is no date for that return, and meanwhile a response must be made to this offer.' His expression became sententiously grave. 'If Sir James were here and his normal self, things might be very different. As they stand, the Board feels that the Hartman Trust's strategy for expansion can best be achieved in collaboration with the strength of Consolidated Diamond Concessions.'

'You think he wants this then?' Franks had not relinquished his microphone.

'I think he may not.' Loud murmurs of surprise. 'But predominant as Sir James's role in creating the Trust has been, it is today a wide-ranging international conglomerate. The market has told us very clearly that the present uncertainties must be resolved. If we fail to resolve them we risk a further fall in the Company's standing, in its share price and its strength for the future.'

This undisguised appeal to the shareholders' pockets evoked sporadic clapping.

'May I remind you,' he went on, 'that so far the 1980s have seen the mining sectors of our business suffer the most severe conditions this century. The price of copper is at its lowest since the Napoleonic Wars. Your Board is dedicated to redressing . . .'

No other questioner brought Stainton so close to the crunch, yet he displayed considerable adroitness in suggesting that the shareholders' interests were being threatened by Father, not

328

secured. Then my own turn came. Camilla squeezed my hand and whispered 'Good luck', and I stepped up to the table. I had no intention of being confined to the floor. However, Stainton declined to yield his central place and I had to speak from a small lectern to one side. I made a pretence of adjusting the microphone, whilst focusing my eyes on the doors to the side of the ballroom. Van Rensburg should be here by now. Edmundo had taught me the value of a *coup de théâtre*. The question was whether I could pull this one off.

'Ladies and gentlemen.' I felt naked and isolated, but knew immediately that I had the shareholders' attention. 'You have all received the papers regarding this offer. I am asking you to reject it because my Father's absence has caused the Trust's assets to become seriously undervalued.' I shot a long and deliberate glance at Stainton. 'May I remind you of the fundamental strength of the company. If Sir James were here I am convinced few of you would for a moment consider accepting this bid.'

There were many shouts of 'Hear, hear.' I had been right to tackle this in the role of the loyal son, not pretending expertise I did not possess.

'I have only two points to add to those in my letter to you. The first is that I have reason to believe certain members of the Board have an interest in this bid succeeding . . .' At first this provoked only murmurs of puzzlement, then protests from alongside me. I swung round to half face the directors, and spoke in a voice I hoped the entire audience could hear. 'May I invite any of you who have an interest to declare it now?'

None replied. I looked at each in turn: Clarke, well dressed as usual, shaking his head; Ferguson embarrassed; Lord Watson, in a pinstripe suit with a gold watch-chain, looking incredulous; and Stainton, without expression.

'That is a ridiculous assertion,' Stainton said quietly. 'I insist it be withdrawn.'

'I shall substantiate it,' I said, and turned back to the audience, scanning the side and back of the ballroom. My accusation had been partly designed to gain time. A woman whose face was in shadow from a wide-brimmed hat had come inside. Close to her stood the tall, heavily built figure of Van Rensburg, with another instantly recognizable man between him and the woman. Van Rensburg raised his hand. I spoke into the microphone on the lectern.

'The other thing I want to tell you is that, despite his illness, Sir James Hartman is here today.'

As I spoke Van Rensburg began walking from the back of the hall, guiding Father by the elbow, with Mother at his other side. They progressed slowly, step by step down the long gangway between the wall and the rows of seats, with every man and woman in the room swivelling round and gaping.

'Good God!' I heard Clarke exclaim. 'It is Jim.'

If he had been privy to the organization behind the spectacle of this familiar grey-suited figure advancing slowly but erect towards the rostrum, he might have said a great deal more.

Father had been flown from Moscow in a private ambulance jet the day before yesterday, and taken by helicopter straight to the clinic, landing noisily but unseen on the roof. Yesterday our own doctors had advised that he should be strong enough to make a single public appearance for a maximum of an hour. They stressed that he would be unable to sustain himself throughout a meeting. He must be presented to the shareholders, speak immediately and leave as soon as possible. If challenged, we would not be able to deny that he was a sick man – indeed there was an ambulance parked close to the hotel, just in case. What Van Rensburg and I prayed was that his voice and manner would carry enough of his accustomed authority to convince people that he would soon be in control again, even if in practice we had to run the Trust.

As Father neared the platform people began to clap, and the clapping swelled into a great chorus of applause. I stood waiting to greet him, anxious in case he stumbled on the step up to the rostrum, yet not wanting him to be seen needing further help. I should have had more foresight. Stainton instantly stepped forward, grasped Father's hand and made a display of vacating his own chair and assisting Father into it, while Mother unobtrusively took my former place beside Camilla.

'Thanks, Bob,' Father said, as if Stainton were not there. He eased himself down and I moved the central microphone closer, then moved aside. His complexion was very pale and there were dark marks around his eyes. He coughed, looked up and raised his hand at the audience. Everyone obeyed his signal without question. The welcome died away, and the tense, appreciative silence which ensued was like that when a famous actor has come on stage and is about to speak his first lines.

'Thank you,' Father said, and I blessed the microphone because it gave his naturally deep voice additional resonance. 'I can tell you all that I am happy to be here. And lucky.' He paused, coughed and raised his eyes to the audience again. 'After the crash of my aircraft I was cared for by Africans in the bush. They saved my life. My son Robert brought me out.'

Quite apart from being gratifying to me, this revelation brought a collective gasp of astonishment and sympathy from his listeners. I glanced at my watch. Six minutes had passed already. So far, he was holding up.

'That is over, thank God,' he went on, and I was worried to

notice him shiver again, as though the memory triggered distress. 'I shall have to spend a few weeks resting. Then I shall be back.'

More clapping greeted this. There was no question that he had the meeting with him.

'Today I wish only to tell you that the Hartman Trust is strong. Its profits are not affected by recent events. Its assets are first-class. It is absurd that my own disappearance should have damaged the . . .' He had to break off. His old aggressive style was demanding too much of his voice. Happily, he only faltered after a statement that generated great applause. I noticed him clench his right hand, as though willing himself to continue, then convert this into a positive gesture, holding his fist aloft in response to the clapping, like a symbol of determination. He waited until he had regained his self-control. 'I ask you to support my son's resolution. I ask you to reject the bid.'

Afraid that he might overtax himself, I seized on this further acknowledgment as an excuse to lean across and take the microphone.

'Ladies and gentlemen, in the present quite exceptional circumstances I hope Sir James can be spared any questions.'

'Nonsense.' He waved me aside, and his angry growl was heard throughout the room. 'I'll take questions, but not speeches.'

There was a long, hesitant silence, as though no one wanted to add to a family quarrel. It was no surprise when the first man to rise was hostile.

'You seem to have an obsession with diamonds. As I understand it, you've tried to buy concessions in Angola . . .'

I pricked up my ears. Anyone who knew that must be a Consolidated plant.

'. . . where there is civil war. You've had diamond mines in Zaïre expropriated . . .' He continued with a catalogue of problem areas where the Trust operated, from Africa to Latin America.

'Thank you for pointing out some of the risks we run,' Father replied acidly. 'Unfortunately, if we are going to extract diamonds, we have to do so where diamonds are found. I agree it would be easier if we could mine them in Hyde Park.'

The laughter had barely subsided when hands and voting papers began fluttering all over the assembly. 'The lady near the pillar,' he ordered. 'Give her a microphone.'

To my astonishment the questioner was Felicity Ames, elegant in light grey with a wide velvet collar. She gave her name as a corporate representative, and went on to provide Father with a useful opening. 'In the long term, would you favour an association with Consolidated Diamond Concessions?'

'Thank you for being to the point. I don't think short-term considerations, such as my own recent illness, have much place in the development of this company. In the long term, yes, we might like an association with Consolidated' – he smiled for the first time – 'but it would not be on their terms. It would be on ours.'

Though gentle by his standards, the answer still had enough implicit pugnacity to draw appreciation. I took a quick sideways look at Frank Stainton. He had not been amused. He would be even less so when he learnt that I had been making private moves against Consolidated myself. The share price game set no limit to the number of players.

Father was casting around for other questioners to encourage. He always had a good eye for whom to select and deliberately let some of the perennial General Meeting opponents have their say. Indeed, he memorized their names beforehand, and greeted them. But he despised and hated hecklers. Suddenly a young man stood up.

'We want sanctions,' he shouted. 'What do you say about sanctions?'

Since the crash of the camera crew's plane no word had appeared in the Western Press about Father's sanctions-busting. But even though he knew this, he still glanced at me for reassurance, and when he answered it was with a diminished flash of his old fire.

'I'm opposed,' he said. 'They only hurt black workers. There are enough people trying to damage the industrial business of black Africa without putting blacks out of work in the south.'

The ingenious double argument was too sophisticated for the heckler.

'Vote against apartheid,' he yelled.

'That's what I am asking you to do, you idiot.' Father began to sound weary. 'If you don't like my strategy sell your shares. Now sit down, for God's sake.'

Someone had to intervene. He had already been in the chair for over twenty minutes, and was gripping the table with one hand, just as he had done during Edmundo's interview. I nudged Plowright, who obediently stood up and asked if the meeting could now vote on the Resolution.

'If everyone's ready.' Father was both reluctant and relieved.

Plowright then read the Resolution aloud and asked everyone present to hand in their voting cards. On a show of hands the response would have been overwhelming. But a far greater number of postal votes and proxies had been received and finally there were those crucially influential Fund Managers. If Felicity Ames and her colleagues had not been impressed by Father's performance, they might well vote against him. Worse, so might the thousands who had not come at all and had not heard him speak. If I'd been challenged on my stage management I would have claimed it was a calculated risk. But it was nothing of the sort. The outcome had not been calculable in advance.

The minutes while the voting slips were collected and collated with the votes received by post and proxies dragged on.

'How much longer?' Father muttered.

'Stick it another fifteen minutes, Jim.' Van Rensburg sat next to him, whispering encouragement.

The ordeal continued for ten, fifteen, twenty, twenty-five minutes. The hour allowed by the doctor was already past. Father had lapsed into silence and was shivering spasmodically. I couldn't understand why the counting was so slow; or had Stainton instructed Plowright not to hurry?

Then, at last, the Secretary did come back and announce the result.

'Ladies and gentlemen. Fourteen point four per cent of the stockholders did not vote. Nineteen point seven per cent voted against.' Murmuring began to anticipate his conclusion. 'Sixty-five point nine per cent . . .' The rest was lost in frantic clapping and stamping of feet. We had won.

Father rose unsteadily to his feet for the final effort in this proof of his charisma. He edged past Plowright and, while still touching the table for support, took the microphone with the other.

'Thank you,' he said, emotion fraying his voice as the applause swelled again. 'Thanks to you the Trust will remain independent.' He paused, summoning energy. 'And I assure you it remains committed to growth.' In plain print the words do not sound much, but Father spoke them with the intensity, almost the passion, of a haycart preacher quoting the Holy Book. Growth was his faith. 'Now please excuse me.'

He bowed to the audience, turned and placed his left hand on my shoulder, as if in parental affection, and thus supported let me lead him to the nearest of the doors, where Mother joined us.

'Didn't think I could do it, did you?' he said, grinding out the words as we helped him down the stairs to the entrance. 'Where there's life . . .' He lost the sentence in a paroxysm of shaking and the waiting nurse took charge.

Mother watched nervously as he was lifted into the ambulance outside, then embraced me.

'I'm going with him.' She forced a smile. 'I'm not letting him out of my sight.'

'We had to bring him here,' I said. 'He wanted it as much as I did.'

'That's as may be, darling. But he won't be going to any more meetings until he's completely well.'

'You'll have to tell him. He won't take it from anyone else.

Especially not from me.' I kissed her. No one understood the contrariness of his disposition better than she did. 'At least you've got him back in one piece.'

'And I intend to keep him.' She gave me another hug. 'Thank you, darling. Thank you for everything.'

When the ambulance had departed, I returned to the ballroom. The meeting had already broken up as shareholders queued for their promised lunch. They'd have plenty to talk about while they ate. As I looked around I was accosted by Stainton.

'You appreciate that any majority below seventy-five per cent imposes no mandatory decision on the Board, and I doubt if Sir James will be well enough to attend for some time?'

'Fifty-one per cent may not be mandatory,' I said, retrieving my folder from the chair I had imprudently left it on. 'Something else is.' I removed the photocopy that Christianne had thoughtfully provided. 'This and the record of your share dealings makes it mandatory. More than that. You can either resign today or see this in the papers tomorrow.'

To his credit, Stainton did not go white, nor try to seize the document and tear it up. He stared at me impassively, only the tic vibrating his eyelid giving him away, and said coldly:

'Only the shareholders can dismiss a director.'

'The Fraud Squad can help them along.'

He turned on his heel and I joined Van Rensburg, who was with Camilla in the far corner of the room.

'Congratulations.' She darted a kiss at my cheek. 'That was a triumph.'

'Took a bit of organizing,' I admitted.

'Touch and go,' Van Rensburg said. 'Jim's a bloody sight more ill than he seemed.'

'Will he get over this, what was it, malignant malaria?' she asked.

'Never completely. At his age you're permanently weakened. Can't stop it coming back at intervals, either. He's lucky to be alive.' He smiled, philosophically. 'Lucky Hartman. Always has been.'

'Well,' I said, not wishing to dwell on the subject. 'Next stop the Press conference. If we're going to tie this up, we might as well tie it up tight.'

'So you will speak to the Press on behalf of Sir James?'

After the meeting we had gone straight to Prince Czernowski's Mayfair office, in which he occupied a first-floor room with long Georgian windows overlooking the street. As he spoke he fondled a gold pen, made a swift note, then rested his arms on the leather top of his antique desk and continued quizzing Van Rensburg and me.

'You appreciate Sir James's reappearance will be the big story? Your EGM adds spice, of course. Financier returns to rescue company.' He shifted one hand to stroke his cheek. 'A good touch. Who organized that, by the way?'

'Bob here,' Van Rensburg said.

'Very neat. Not that the tabloids will be interested in the finance. They'll want to know how you found him, where he's been and the rest of it. I believe I told you once: the public likes to read about heroes. Heroes and villains.'

That startled me. 'Who do you see as the hero?' I asked cautiously.

'You are, old chap,' Van Rensburg said.

'No. We want all the emphasis on my father being safe and recovering.'

'It can pay to be frank with the Press,' Czernowski suggested.

I remembered his making that remark to Father and receiving an extremely robust reply.

'The objective of this is to boost the share price. Only Father can do that.' Whatever my past feelings about him, and they were mostly equivocal at the best, his charisma still worked. Whatever his faults, he had that God-given capacity for making people follow him. Even if I had wanted to, I could not provide a substitute for it while he was still alive. Van Rensburg, the other loyal directors and I myself might have to run the company if he failed to recuperate, but at all costs he had to remain the figurehead.

'In that case,' Czernowski temporized, 'tell me the story and we can decide what's fit for the Press. You can be frank with me.'

'I appreciate your helpfulness.' A degree of honesty would be necessary. No one could pretend that Father had walked away alive from the Gulfstream's crash. So I would have to mix a few facts with the fiction, and I reckoned that Czernowski was an excellent sounding board. If he believed what I was about to relate, then the media might. 'You're right that Father simplified the story for the shareholders. But only a little. When he told them he'd been cared for in a village, that was true.' I kept a close watch on Czernowski's expression. 'Except that it came later. At the beginning he was captured by rebels while he was visiting a diamond concession.' I allowed myself one of those laughing chuckles that people employ to underline the quirks of life. 'One which as a matter of fact the Angolans have now sold us, not that it would interest anyone much.'

'Are you sure?'

'Irrelevant,' I assured him. In fact the Angolan government had honoured our original option because its success against the

ALF was attributable to having been told the location of Edmundo's temporary airstrip. The International Red Cross would have refused to reveal where a secret exchange of prisoners was taking place. They felt their responsibility, in this case, was to the ALF. Fortunately Lotte Lohrey had no such inhibitions. To be exact, she had sold the information in exchange for my 'supplies' of rebel prisoners. *Sauve qui peut*, as Christianne would have said.

'Anyway,' I want on, 'the Gulfstream had crashed on its way back to fetch Father after his visit and I went to the area to negotiate for Father's release. While we were there the Angolan army attacked and in the confusion we escaped. That was when the villagers came into it.'

'When was all this?' Czernowski was making notes.

'Over three weeks ago. Father caught malaria. African bearers had to carry him on a stretcher.' I added a few details, aided by memories of how the explorer Livingstone was cared for on his travels in the 1860s. 'We daren't go west because of the rebels. We couldn't go north into Zaïre.' I reminded him of the expropriation there. 'We had to go east to Zambia.' I thought of the seven hundred endless miles of featureless bush over which we had flown. 'Occasionally we got a lift. But then the fever would come on again and we'd have to stop.' Who would know I had been in Switzerland at the time? 'It was a week before we got him to Ndola. We chartered a plane, and he's been in hospital ever since.'

'An astonishing tale.' Czernowski addressed himself to Van Rensburg. 'You were with them?'

'Part of the time.'

We had agreed earlier that anyone who did check up in Zambia would probably confuse him with Father. Since he had no desire for his own exploits to be rumoured around Africa, this suited him very well. 'Never defecate on your own doorstep,' he had remarked cheerfully. 'If you think the Press'll swallow all that guff it's fine by me.'

'How can they disprove it?' I had asked. 'What with Edmundo being dead.'

This was the point Czernowski picked up next. I think his credulity had been stretched, and he was a very sophisticated person in any case.

'These rebels,' he observed, 'why didn't they recapture you?'

'Their General was killed. Surely that was in the papers?' I knew damn well it had been, and forced myself to remember that at the time I had been trekking with ankles rubbing raw through the bush. 'I only heard much later.' I decided to let the PR man enjoy a piece of undiluted fact. 'He was quite a leader in his way.'

336

'Guerrilla commanders often are,' Czernowksi remarked, making me feel momentarily very foolish. His own ancestors and family must have known all about that in Europe, just as Father had. 'Did anyone who would have spoken to Sir James survive?'

'There was a South African adviser. I heard he was captured.'

Struben had been the first person, apart from Edmundo, to outwit Father in ten years or more. He had played the simpleton Boer extraordinarily well, letting Father believe he was impressed when he and Edmundo had been the old Mutt and Jeff act all along. I had been equally taken in. After the ALF's defeat Struben had been captured alive and was being held. The Angolans would ask a high price for him. Meanwhile he was out of circulation.

Czernowski had absorbed all this. 'Sir James is expected to recover?' he demanded.

'Definitely,' I wanted no speculation about that. 'And he remains Chief Executive of the Trust.'

'Can't afford to be without him,' Van Rensburg said. 'Personally I hope he'll ask Robert to join the Board.'

'It sounds as though he's earned it,'

'I do have a career of my own,' I said. 'You might put that in.' The further we could throw the Press off the scent the better.

'Well, gentlemen, if you'll give me an hour I'll have a statement ready. The Press conference itself will be here at four.'

In the event Czernowski handled the whole thing beautifully. He knew that what they called 'photo opportunities' were essential, and had persuaded Mother to attend. A lot of pictures were taken of us, and we handed out prints of Father addressing the shareholders in the morning. Not one reporter challenged the African saga, perhaps because Van Rensburg and I were able to recount such convincing detail of Edmundo's camp. Quite clearly the sanctions story had died forever with the camera crew. Nor had the Angolans let slip a word about the exchange of prisoners. Already those extraordinary events in the bush were sliding into the domain of forgotten history, with the new version replacing it. The sole awkwardness came over the hospital. On that we had to stonewall. Father was being treated for the after-effects of malaria and undisturbed rest was vital. The reporters objected, but Czernowski knew his job. They had a damn good story. They had pictures. They gave way.

'You'll need to let them meet Sir James,' he said afterwards. 'As soon as he's fit enough. I'd like to make a promise of that. Otherwise you'll never be left alone.'

Mother agreed. She was the official guardian, so to speak. Then when Camilla had arrived the four of us went to Claridge's for a mild celebration. It was only mild. Although the search was concluded, although Mother had back the husband around whom her life revolved, although the Trust was saved, we none of us felt jubilant. To varying degrees we all knew that too much of Father's past had been disinterred and that some of it might yet refuse to be re-buried.

Over dinner later, when we were alone, Camilla approached the subject with a directness impossible in front of Mother.

'You found him out, sweetheart, even if no one else has. Why are you going along with it? Why don't you at least force him to retire?'

I tried to laugh this off. 'As a tycoon? Or as an agent? I should imagine after all this, and with Angelino dead, they'll retire him anyway.'

'Please be serious.'

'We'll probably never know what took place at the Moscow hospital. What drugs they gave him. Truth drugs for de-briefing? Or a cure for malaria? Patrick says after three weeks he should have either died or be temporarily recovered.'

'You ought to have things out with him,' she insisted.

'How? He'd admit nothing. D'you want me to betray my own father?' I looked deep into her troubled eyes, challenging her to object. 'Wasn't betraying his own parents exactly what he was afraid he had done as a boy? It was the demon that's driven him ever since.'

'I'm sorry.' She reached out and felt for my hand. 'Perhaps I'm wrong. He is a very complicated person.'

'Very few people are what they seem.' I made a faint gesture of irritation. Father's example could have furnished an entire volume of truisms.

'You realize you'll be the hero tomorrow?' She tried a different angle. 'I overheard those reporters talking as they left.'

'Tomorrow maybe. In the long term it'll be Father.'

'No hocus-pocus?' She was disbelieving.

'He has the name and the reputation. Without him we can't raise the capital to take over Consolidated.'

'So you're not going back to the ivory tower as you told the journalists?'

'Temporarily. I owe Professor Muhsin a little loyalty too.'

'But only temporarily?' She wasn't letting me off the hook this time.

'I've been left with a feeling you don't like academic life.' She blushed attractively and squeezed my fingers. 'Besides I have other interests now.'

'Such as?'

'Didn't I tell you? I've bought a mine in Africa.'

338

CHAPTER TWENTY-FIVE

'In a sense it's a kind of exorcism.' The priest's words came back to me as we reached the church. 'What better way to dispose of grief than by invoking the love of God?'

The Reverend Christopher Fenton was elderly and gentle, white-haired, the spareness of his frame disguised by an ample black cassock, his voice mellifluous from long practice. 'You must think of the living rather than the dead,' he had reminded us, when we finalized the arrangements for Father's memorial service. The advice had given Mother little comfort. Despite the several years since his rescue the malaria had finally claimed him well short of actuarial averages, and she felt cheated of the retirement that should have been theirs together. Not, of course, that he would have ever willingly retired any more than either of us would have revealed the true background of his African intrigues to her. We had found common cause there, as well as in less predictable directions.

I had chosen St Michael's, Cornhill, in the City of London because it was at the very heart of the square mile, close to the Bank of England and the Stock Exchange, and that was where Father would most have liked to be commemorated. Back in that eventful summer of 1982, at a moment when it seemed he might well be dead, I had raised the subject of a service with Hugh Clarke, who if nothing else had a keen nose for what was socially appropriate. He had remarked condescendingly that since Father had been 'hardly a favourite of the Establishment and only nominally a Christian', we might not fill St Michael's. He was about to be proved conclusively wrong. Not that he was here to be impressed. He had gone down with Stainton.

The obituary notices had been long and sympathetic. Without exception they recited Father's war record, admired his spirit and commercial acumen and called him a major contributor to the cause of African development, even if his actions had been sometimes controversial. Our well publicized escape from South African-backed rebels had earned him the accolade which all Prinze Czernowski's efforts had previously failed to obtain. 'Lucky' Hartman had become a hero of the media. If the irony gave me amusement, I also smiled with satisfaction. The myth mattered to the shareholders and the shareholders had mattered to my plans. Without it we could never have pulled off the coups we had. I was only too happy for my own role in his adventures to be forgotten. The business world is short of heroes: about as short as it is long on self-interest. When a hero does emerge everybody else basks in the reflected warmth. 'Sir James,' a recent letter to *The Times* had declaimed, 'was confidently expected to receive a Peerage in the next Honours list. His untimely death is as great a loss to commerce as it is to the Commonwealth.'

Even so, late August was not a time when I expected many people to attend a service, except perhaps to express sympathy with Mother. London felt as stiflingly humid as Singapore and was largely given over to tourists, a few of whom stopped to gawp as we descended from the limousines by the narrow entrance to St Michael's, no more than an opening between office blocks. We must have looked odd too: the men in black frock-coats, clutching top-hats, the women extravagantly in mourning.

As family we arrived last. Mother, Camilla and I shared the Mercedes, to be greeted by Arthur Watson at the porch, where Patrick Van Rensburg and Mary joined us. Watson asked effusively though briefly after the baby: Camilla and I had been married three years now and had a son named James.

St Michael's was a handsome Wren church. Classical white columns supported the roof, the walls were set with old memorials and as we entered I noticed a great marble pelican on a pedestal at the back near the font. From the low noise of muffled conversations I guessed the church must be fairly crowded, and when the ushers escorted us to the nave I realized that every one of the elaborately carved pews was full. City dignitaries sat with their wives beside them, full of pomp, all graciously inclining their gaze towards us as we moved slowly past. These were people who would not have been deceived by the myth, and I could only guess at the paradoxical chemistry which persuaded them to honour Father's memory, whether or not they had loathed him in life and despite the holiday season's steamy heat. Perhaps it was just the principle of 'There but for the Grace of God go I.'

What interested me more acutely was to observe who was here from the Trust. Frank Stainton would not come. When he had demanded a golden handshake for resigning I lost patience and passed our evidence to the Fraud Squad. He was indicted on twenty-two charges – I was sure they formulated that number deliberately – and jailed for three years. Hugh Clarke escaped with a suspended sentence. But what of the rest? At first sight even Christianne was missing. I scanned the congregation as best I could both for her and for Lotte Lohrey.

Mother leant on Arthur Watson's arm as we progressed, Camilla and I behind them. The strain she was suffering seemed more apparent with every step; the determined way she kept her head up showed it. She was only just able to hold her emotions in check. I had given Father back to her, but neither she nor anyone else had been able to restrain his activity enough to protect his health. Although I had become an executive director, to take over responsibilities methodically had been impossible. The only initiative we agreed on was the diamond consortium, and even there his having to curtail his travelling infuriated him. So the malaria had won the struggle, giving Edmundo a kind of unplanned revenge in the end.

Then during our slow walk between the ranks of mourners I at last caught a glimpse of Christianne, her ash blonde hair shrouded by a hat and veil. But of Lotte Lohrey there was no sign. Yet I had been sure she would come, however unobtrusively, because the mesh of her life had been so woven into Father's. An usher guided us into an ornate oak pew, closing its narrow door behind us.

The gilded organ sounded its first notes and the choir sprang into life with the hymn 'Lead us Heavenly Father, Lead us'. The ritual of thanksgiving for a life of achievement had begun. I was seated between Camilla and Mother, and the hymn, which Mother so loved, brought tears into her eyes. I reached out and held her hand as Fenton intoned a bidding to the congregation, reminding us why we were assembled. We rose for a psalm, followed by a lesson from the Gospel according to St John, read by Andrew Ferguson, both tranquillizingly familiar and acutely emotional.

'In my Father's house there are many mansions: if it were not so I would have told you. I go to prepare a place for you . . .' In truth Father had earned a niche in several Pantheons.

At the back of the church, close to one of the white columns, there was movement. I sensed it before I turned and glimpsed a woman entering late, seeking a seat. Then the ensuing anthem claimed my attention and after that Arthur Watson left us to walk stoopingly forward, mount the steps to the pulpit and deliver the address.

'A certain kind of person offers to give eulogies,' Fenton had observed. He was not surprised when I told him that Lord Watson of Worksop, Privy Counsellor, Member of the Order of the British Empire, had offered to perform the duty. The priest could hardly have guessed Watson's relief at being able to despatch his own guilt to the grave along with Father.

'We are gathered here today,' Watson began, sweeping the congregation with his gaze, drawing us all into communion with his higher feelings, 'to honour the memory of a remarkable human being. Jim Hartman was a man – and I stress that word "man" – in the very best sense. He freed himself as a boy from Nazi tyranny to serve in the British army . . .'

Lord Watson had prudently spent the war as a civilian in a reserved occupation.

'. . . and throughout his career showed respect for the individual. Commerce with a conscience . . .'

It amused me to hear this old fraud, himself every inch as straight as an ancient vine, putting Father forward as a champion of honest dealing. But then the theory was crucial to him as well.

Camilla had worked her way through a mountain of research on Arthur Watson. Finding the clue to his association with Father became close to an obsession with her. She had indexed sly side references in speeches; mentions of overseas trips; the BBC Monitoring Service's records of Russian news commentaries. She could not have proved a thing in court. But she was ninety-nine per cent sure she had pin-pointed the period when Watson became an active collaborator of the Russians. His Party was in opposition and he was a consultant on East-West trade. Two years later he had become a director of the Rukanga Mining Company, the forerunner of the Hartman Trust.

'No man deserved his knighthood more than Jim: for his services to Britain, for his services to the less fortunate members of our brotherhood of nations.'

As the two men had climbed in their careers, Watson to full ministerial office and the Cabinet, Father to wealth and influence ostensibly outside politics, each had reinforced the other's prestige.

'I can honestly say,' Watson discreetly touched the corner of one owl-like eye with a white handkerchief, 'that when Jim offered me a seat on his Board it was as great a distinction as any in my career.'

Watson had been raised to the peerage shortly before the treason of Sir Anthony Blunt emerged. Most of their generation were dead now, which made it safe for books to be published about that effete circle of Cambridge communists called the Apostles. Father had been of a different younger, tougher breed, making no secret of despising Watson, whilst using him.

Historically men or women only work as foreign agents for two reasons: ideology or cash. A simplistic theory. Watson, I was certain, had worked either for money or under the threat of blackmail. By contrast Father's own motivation had been both more complex and more honourable. Angelino gave him a sense of direction, harnessing his regrets, his pride and his ruthless ambition to a higher purpose, while he would have become a millionaire whatever enterprise he had started. So he was doubly fulfilled.

Personally I had no great ideological convictions, though I could understand them in others. If I were to have taken Father's route it would have been for more prosaic reasons. In the twenty-first century the great African power play for the huge untapped wealth of that continent will for a time be in African hands and if history is any guide the African leaders will be fratricidally divided in everything except hatred of white South Africa. Therein will lie many opportunities.

'Sir James Hartman,' Watson was reaching the climax of his oration, 'was a man of action, enterprise and vision. Despite the illness of his last few years he had crowned his career with the formation of a worldwide diamond producers' consortium which has given African nations control over their own wealth at last.'

Camilla nudged me and winked: most improper behaviour on a solemn occasion. But then no one else present, least of all Watson, knew how Father's great dream had actually been made flesh. The pivot, as originally intended, had been Concession Twenty-Two. The Angolan government, grateful for information on where Edmundo could be attacked, had sold it to me for even less than Father had been offering. Thereafter everything had followed his plan. The Trust acquired the concession from me, we turned the tables on Consolidated and formed the consortium. Now the Russians were marketing a substantial proportion of their gemstones through us. Smiling quickly back at Camilla it gave me some pleasure that not even she had thought of asking where I had found the money to buy the mine. Not, of course, that raising cash had been a problem. The name 'Hartman' was a guarantee in many circles.

'. . . our world was the richer for Jim's inhabiting of it and is the poorer for his passing.' Watson stood silent for a moment before leaving the pulpit, pausing again to bow stiffly towards the altar before rejoining us in our pew. He had done his bit to carve Father's myth in letters of stone.

The priest proceeded to the Lord's Prayer and a final hymn. We knelt briefly for the blessing. The organist began to play. Mother pressed my arm gently and I noticed the tears in her eyes as I murmured that this had been all that Father would have wished for. She seemed reluctant to leave, as though this moment was a final parting. Then she quickly dabbed the tears away, picked up her bag and rose to her feet, holding her head high as we moved out of the pew and Watson again escorted her down the aisle, face to face with the congregation.

Now at last I could get an idea of who had come and could search for a sight of Lotte Lohrey; but she had vanished again. We passed Ramesh Gupta, bowing gravely, pressing his palms together in the Indian manner, his respect as supple as silk. Cunningham and Bertels were standing together and smiled as if to give us encouragement. Carl Hoffman was a row further along. These were all men on whom I could rely. The employees were mostly at the back of the church and gave us awkward, nervous smiles. Eventually we positioned ourselves between the stone font and the door to greet and thank the mourners as they left.

'There won't be another like him, m'Lady,' said one of the commissionaires, meaning every syllable of the well-worn phrase as he grasped Mother's hand, and she nodded her appreciation. He had indeed been a very different man to different people.

Then Christianne reached the head of the queue and stepped forward. Her wisp of black lace veil, more alluring than funereal, obscured only her eyes.

'Please allow me to admire your bravery, Lady Hartman,' I heard her say. 'We all so much miss Sir James.'

Mother's response was quiet and controlled. I don't think she was deceived. 'Thank you Christianne. It was very nice of you to come.' She held out her gloved hand and after a perfunctory touch of the fingers Christianne moved to face me, her eyes looking directly into mine through the fragile blur of lace. For a split second she flicked her gaze beyond me to Camilla. The veil would have prevented anyone else noticing the unspoken question it implied.

'My heart is with you, Robert. If there is anything I can do more . . .' She let her eyes complete the offer, her lips still slightly parted.

Even delicately phrased, Christianne's recent proposals had not been modest. In all respects I could continue where Father had left off. She would retain her second salary, which had been one of his best kept secrets, and also achieve a more influential official role. 'Now you are Chief Executive, Robert,' she had remarked a month ago, 'there are many things you will need to be aware about. To be your assistant would make good sense.' She was right. I was not so conceited as to think I could continue Father's autocracy. I should have to headhunt new directors, retire Watson and make other changes. I was going to need her inside knowledge, for a time.

'I'm sure there'll be a great deal you can help with,' I answered quickly, before the length of our conversation could become noticeable. 'At nine tomorrow?' So that was settled.

One of the ushers came up to me, a trainee executive with the firm, whose name I ought to have remembered but could not.

344

'Excuse me, Mr Hartman,' he whispered, 'a lady was asking for you. She said she would be in the church garden. I can show you the way.'

Pleading necessity, I left Camilla with Mother to say goodbye to the remaining people and turned out of the church into a short alleyway which led round to a small paved garden, made even smaller by the high buildings enclosing it. Seated on a bench was Lotte Lohrey, her face shaded by a wide black hat. She patted the wooden slats. 'Sit down for one moment, I know you have little time.' She opened her handbag. 'This is for your mother. You should read the letter I think.' She passed me a heavy envelope. 'It is open.'

Inside was a diary of Father's, dust-stained still, the black leather scratched, his gold initials in the corner dulled. Attached was a letter in his writing, weak and wandering, dated in June 1982. It is in front of me now as I write.

> Darling Anne,
> This may be my last chance to write. Look after yourself and Robert. Things resolve themselves in the end.
> Your adoring husband, Jim.

I re-read this most uncharacteristic message, expressing finality, love and doubt, and looked up at Lotte.

'He wrote this before you brought him back from Moscow?'

'For some days he was afraid he would die there.'

I sat silent, thinking. Edmundo had certainly intended that if Father succumbed to the malaria, he should do so in Russian hands. What the Russians themselves had thought of that I had never been able to discover: any more than whether they had initially refused to release him from hospital because he was too ill or because they were questioning him.

'Your mother should now have it,' Lotte said firmly,

'Why not before?'

'It was his wish. "After I am dead," he told me.' She gazed at me affectionately. 'You are so like him. I am glad we work together. We have done much, have we not? Almost a tradition, *hein*?'

'Excuse me, Sir.' The usher caught us by surprise. 'Lady Hartman is asking for you, Sir.'

'Would you like to see her?' I asked Lotte.

'If she can come, definitely.'

'Then you give her it.' I handed back the diary and hurried along with the usher, past young City men and girls drifting into the alley with drinks from a neighbouring wine house, and found Mother, Camilla, Watson and the Van Rensburgs alone save the other ushers and the priest. They all looked annoyed and perplexed. The church seemed cavernously quiet and my footsteps unduly loud on the stone floor.

'Where have you been, darling?' Mother sounded as if my sudden disappearance had been the final ingredient of her exhaustion.

'Please.' I glanced at the others. 'Could you wait? Would you mind, darling?' Although Camilla seemed dubious I guided Mother, protesting, out to the garden and then watched as she recognized who was there.

The scene remains with me, printed on my memory, as though in slow motion. The two women broke into a spontaneous embrace, Mother's shoulders shaking as she burst into tears. They talked for a few minutes, Mother occasionally nodding her head, until Lotte embraced her again and brought her back to me.

'You will help her.' It was as much an order as a suggestion. 'She needs you.' She kissed me formally on each cheek in turn, murmuring, 'Next Tuesday then, the lunchtime flight,' and walked quickly away, before anyone else could come.